Goody Wing,
An American Foremother

Goody Wing,
An American Foremother

Beverly Smith Vorpahl

Authors Choice Press
San Jose New York Lincoln Shanghai

Goody Wing, an American Foremother

Authors Choice Press
an imprint of iUniverse.com, Inc.

For information address:
iUniverse.com, Inc.
5220 S 16th, Ste. 200
Lincoln, NE 68512
www.iuniverse.com

This is a historical novel,
a work of fiction based on the author's ancestors

ISBN: 0-595-20102-4

Printed in the United States of America

*This book is dedicated to my beautiful grandchildren: Michelle,
Axton, Alexandra and Payton; Katie, Scott and Megan; and
Carylee—and other descendants yet to be come.
If we know our ancestors, we care.*

"May the Good Lord cause his eyes to shine upon you."

The Reverend Stephen Bachiler
1561-1656

Acknowledgements

The first to be recognized must be my husband, Dr. David P. Vorpahl, who, for 40-plus years, has been my champion in all things. Also thanks to Dr. Donald Goodwin, a now-retired English professor at Eastern Washington University, who tirelessly helped me bridge the gap between journalism and prose, and to Gloria Kempton, a Seattle writing coach and instructor, for her polishing. Also kudos to my daughter Illa, good friend Erdene, and Dave for proofreading—and to all those who listened and listened while "Goody Wing…" took shape.

Introduction

Deborah Bachiler Wing, my eighth great-grandmother, assumed a personality as I researched life in 17th century England and New England to learn about the circumstances of women, Puritans and others who sought religious freedom by daring to cross the Atlantic Ocean to a little-known continent. The right to worship as they believed God directed them was the driving force of the earliest Europeans, who, with their noble quest and perseverance, established the basis of our nation's character. Much has been written of our forefathers, but of equal importance were the wives and daughters of those men—women we know little about. As I read and wrote, Deborah—from her world of four centuries ago—developed from a name on my family group sheets to a wide-eyed young lady into a heroic woman. I hope she would approve of this narrative.

Chapter 1

(Prequel)
*Aboard the **William and Francis***
1632
Deborah

The ocean spray stung Deborah's face like a tail full of porcupine quills as she clutched Matthew at the ship's railing so he could be rid of what ailed him. A few moments later she eased her six-year-old back onto the deck and, kneeling beside him, blotted his face with the hem of her petticoat.

"Feel better, Darling?" Deborah asked. She could have wept at the sight of him. His face was so thin, ashen. Seventy days of fighting the Atlantic's roiling seas was exacting its toll on the passengers, especially on the very young and the very old—with the exception of her own father, of course. The Reverend Stephen Bachiler was never easily daunted, and sea storms were no exception.

Most of the sixty passengers aboard the William and Francis were or had been sick. *Oh, dear God,* she thought as she measured the angry clouds gathering on the horizon. *How can we survive another storm? We should have landed in New England a fortnight ago. Will we ever get there?*

When the William and Francis began its voyage of freedom for this latest band of Puritans on March 9, 1632, Captain Thomas had told them to expect a crossing of about sixty days. It was now mid-May, ten days past that date. The passengers had long ago given up conjecturing as to when they might dock in Boston. One storm leap-frogged another, tossing about the ship and its one-hundred-eighty tons of cargo as though it were a toy being roughhoused by a lad at the seashore.

"Look at them glib-gabbety puke stockins losin' their breakfast," the mean-spirited Mister Gimp sniggered to Luke, a young lad with three crossings already under his belt. He was tall, lanky; all arms and legs. Deborah thought a boy Luke's age ought to be at home coddled by his dear mother, not crewing across the ocean.

Mister Gimp's crackling voice caused Deborah to turn and look at him.

"Heh, heh, heh," Mister Gimp chortled as Deborah hurriedly picked up Matthew. "Ya wanna make them fish sick, do ye, Sonny?"

Deborah picked up Matthew, who immediately locked a stranglehold around her neck. Mister Gimp appeared startled to see Deborah's eyes snap as she glared at the malevolent old tar.

"Mister Gimp, you began this journey as a miserable coot, and you haven't improved a whit," Deborah snapped. Matthew looked at his mother. He had never heard her be so cross. "From the first day, you have taken delight in the passengers' ailments. You actually snicker when anyone slips and falls because they're too old and too weak to keep their feet under them when the ship lurches. But for you to jibe a child is beyond the pale."

Deborah was astounded at her ire and the words that spilled from her mouth. *How unlike me.* She felt her face redden—and her spirits bolster. What an amazing sensation! A deep breath cleared her head and fed the surge of wrath and self-righteous anger. If she could stand up to Mister Gimp, she could cope with a gale of any size. Like a she lion protecting her cub, Deborah snapped: "I have never, in all my years, taken anyone to task like this, but, God forgive me, 'tis time someone spoke up to you. Most don't have the strength, weak as they are because there's not enough healthy food."

It was true. The disheveled passengers on the William and Francis had paled to a prison-pallor from too many days below deck

Mister Gimp shifted his weight from his withered leg to his sturdy one so he no longer stood at a list. His eyes narrowed.

"You through?" he hissed. "Don't reckon no one's sassed me like that since I was a young cock a-crowin'." He whistled a spit of tobacco past Deborah's face and over the ship's railing.

His lips parted into a sneer. Tobacco juice oozed from the corner of his mouth, dripping on to what might have once been a white beard its color now forever dyed tobacco-stain brown. Still, that scraggly beard was more palatable than his chipped, broken teeth discolored to a rotting brown.

Deborah heard Luke apologize for his elder sailor: "Pardon him, Ma'am. He don't mean anything. He'd whup any man who'd ever dare talk to his ma like he jest talked to you."

Mister Gimp glared through slitted eyes at Luke and snarled as he hobbled off, "Don't need no pukin' weedy-looking sailor 'pologizin' for me. Jest ye mind yer own bizness, Mate."

Once the sea-weathered old salt had stomped out of earshot, Luke doffed his cap and repeated to Deborah: "Sorry, Ma'am. He don't mean no harm. Sometimes he gets mean when his leg gets ta ailin' 'im."

"Thank you, Luke," Deborah said. "Most days I pay him no mind, but I couldn't seem to stop myself today. Tell me, what is his Christian name?"

"Ain't never heerd him called nothin' but Mister Gimp. 'Tis told he got ta drinkin' too much one night and passed out cold on the wharf. Seems his leg got caught in a coil of rope that pulled him into the water and near drowned him when the boat that rope was 'tatched to put out to sea."

Deborah frowned at the image.

"St. Elmo musta been with him though," Luke said, "'cuz he didn't drown. But he ain't never walked right since. He's walked with a gimp, ever after."

Just then, that man fated to spend the rest of his days known by his gait, hollered, "Luke, get ta work." Luke nodded to Deborah and walked off to make her way back to the ship's hold.

Chapter 2

Banbury, Oxfordshire
1603
John

"Are ye standing straight, son?" John Wing could hear the exasperation in his father's words. He was kneeling, hemming his son's coat. "'Twill not hang properly lest ye stand erect."

John, standing straight and still on the low stool, couldn't resist dropping his eyes to examine the ever-expanding circle atop his father's head. *At this rate*, he thought, *Father's pate will be shining bald in less than half a score of years.* He smiled. *I suppose that's how I'll look one day.*

In another month, John, the sixth of Matthew and Mary Wing's ten children—their third son—would graduate from Queens College at Oxford. The long black coat, as heavy and stiff as the profession John had chosen—that of a minister of God—was to be his graduation gift.

"Father, I'd like to discuss something of great importance with you," John said with as little trepidation sounding in his voice as possible. "Did you read the John Knox books I gave you?"

"Turn a bit," his father said gruffly, gripping pins between his teeth. "To your right. Too far. Turn back."

A silence fell on the room that was as chilling and as deep and wide as an iceberg's chasm. John was prepared for a negative response, and wisely waited for his father to speak.

After a long moment, John heard his father say warily, "Yes, I've read them." Another silence. "What about this John Knox," Matthew asked, muttering around the pins again clamped with clenched teeth. "Dead, isn't he?"

"Yes, Father," John replied, "he's dead. But his teachings aren't. They're more popular now than when he was alive."

There was no reply from the floor. The tall, mahogany case clock, standing against the far wall, noisily ticked off another full moment of silence. The only sounds John could hear were the works of the clock and the over-loud breathing coming from his own flared nostrils. The clock chimed the half-hour. John took a deep breath.

"John, mind how you stand!"

Carefully choosing his words so not to sound impertinent, John continued, his heart rate increasing: "Father, John Knox was opposed to Catholicism, as I am."

His father looked up at him, sighed and raised heavily to a standing position, one hand pushing against a knee until he was upright. He said, "You best mind your tongue, John, lest it lead to more trouble than ye can handle. You know the Anglican Church is no longer Catholic." He sighed. "Leave me have the coat."

John stepped from the stool and carefully removed his coat so not to be pricked by errant pins. Sounding much like the student he still was, John resumed the conversation where his father left off:

"True, the Anglican Church is no longer Catholic, Father, but 'tis very much flavored by its Catholic past. The more I learn about the structure and doctrine of the Church of England, the more I question those foundations."

When John saw his father's left eyebrow raised, he knew there was more dissension to come. Coat in hand, John watched as his father moved to sit by the window where the white winter light was better. He often sat there in late afternoons so he wouldn't have to light a candle just yet. Like everyone in the family, John knew his mother would fuss if a precious candle were lit before it was absolutely necessary

At last his father asked, "What do your professors say about these 'foundations'?"

"Most glower at those who dare broach the topic," John said. "But some talk to students who seem genuinely interested—usually after class so 'tis not a part of their official instruction. Professor Bayly suggested I read the writings of John Knox."

"Why would an English professor have a student read something written by a Scotsman?" his father asked with a sniff.

"Mr. Knox thought highly of Puritanism," John said quietly, mentally cowering against the clap of thunder he expected in reply. "He preferred its manner of worship."

John could almost feel his father's look that was as sharply pointed as the needle he sewed with. Then a tired sadness blanketed his father's face.

John took a deep breath and continued in a rush: "The more I read and the more I learn, the more I feel called to leave the Mother Church and"—could he say it?—"and embrace the Puritan philosophy."

There. It was said.

Tick-tock. Tick-tock. John feared the clock's metronome click, mixed with the room's heightened friction, might cause an explosion.

His father's gaze dropped from John's face and fell upon the gift he was fashioning for John.

Likewise, John looked away. *At any rate,* he thought, *Father now knows.* John could hear his own breathing and feel his heart racing. But, his soul soared.

His father put down his sewing, rose heavily and walked to the fireplace. He picked up the billows and whooshed new life into the dying embers. John knew his father was disappointed that he would not ply the needle and thread of his own profession. Be a tailor, my boy, like me, John had been counseled a thousand times—and just as many times, his father's advice went unheeded.

"Father," John said, "the Anglican Church is all but Roman Catholic with its rules and doctrines. There are simply too many. God's rules are the only ones that count and they ought to be followed the way Jesus, the son of God, taught them—simply. There is beauty in purity, Father, and there is purity in simplicity. We must first reform ourselves, as Christians, then reform the church—and then tackle the rest of the world."

"Son," his father said, returning to his post by the window, "'twill be nothing but trouble ahead if ye buck the Mother Church. You know that. John Knox was a troublemaker of the first order. 'Tis my prayer you not make mischief in any order."

John felt as though his father's needles had jabbed him. Still, he had to continue: "Reverend Knox was not a troublemaker, Father," John challenged. "He was a reformer, and in order for things to be better, there must be change. And someone must make that change."

"Change is not the safe way to live," his father snapped, causing John to jump and his eyes to blink. Then he spoke slowly and quietly. "'Tis dangerous, son. Change is dangerous."

Chapter 3

Banbury
1603
Matthew

Matthew resumed hemming. It was rare for him to be alone in his busy tailor shop in Banbury's town center. But he knew John wanted to talk, and this was the best place—on his own turf. He had sent his workers home and placed a "Closed" sign in the window.

But would his words of warning make an impression on this headstrong son of his? Matthew's needle worked itself in and out, in and out.

While Matthew sewed silently, John rose and idly counted the scores of fabric bolts piled high on the shelves of his father's shop.

The clock's ticking filled the room. That damnable clock!

At last Matthew spoke: "John, I have never repeated this story to any of my children, but the time has come for you to know."

He laid John's coat on his knees.

John warily returned to his stool and sat down, looking at his father. Matthew realized John was frightened by what he saw.

"When I was a lad, scores of people—women and children included—were burned at the stake in the town square for refusing to recognize the 'real presence' in the holy communion," Matthew said. "They would rather die a horrendous death than surrender their beliefs. 'Twas a public execution, John." He looked briefly at his son, then out the window as though the cruelty was being repeated right now, in front of his shop. "I was there. In the town square. I saw it happen. I stood between my parents, a mere lad, and watched."

Matthew first looked at his son, stunned into silence, then at the end of his right numb thumb. He rubbed his fingers over it as though to determine if, by chance, feeling might have returned. It numbed years ago. Decades of stitching.

"I can still hear their screams," he said, speaking to his thumb. "They haunt me, those terrible screams." His voice became a rough whisper. He was a youngster again, clinging to his father's pant leg, his only hold on Earth. "Those screams made my skin crawl as a child." He lifted his head to look John in the eye. "And it still does." He bared his arm and placed its prickly flesh before John's eyes.

John stared and swallowed. "Father, I had no idea. You never spoke of such things."

Matthew didn't hear. "Even now, those screams wake me at night. And I remember again, as though 'twere yesterday, how the fires licked at those poor folk, 'til they were burnt to cinders. The pain they felt. I can't imagine. But worse than the screams, was the smell. Sometimes, when I'm remembering and can't forget, I'll blow my nose. I blow and blow, trying to blow away the memory of that stench."

Matthew saw that he had become a frightened stranger to his son, reliving a ghastly horror. He blinked, picked up the coat and expertly knotted the short tag of thread with a single motion, snipped it clean and set about threading the needle's slender eye. "But the smell doesn't go away. There's nothing more vile than the smell of human flesh burning—especially when it's burning right in front of you." He laid the coat down. "The fires," he spoke to no one in particular. Matthew touched each fingertip with his thumb, callused from years of working needles through countless miles of fabric. "The fires grew bigger and brighter as they consumed those people. They burned even after the screams stopped, 'til there was nothing left to burn."

Matthew was aware that John sat, his folded hands dropped between his legs, staring at the plank floor. Then he saw his son cast his sight to the ceiling's silver-gray beams of old, weathered oak. He knew John was surprised and affected by his words.

He cleared the cobwebs of his mind and brought himself back to the present, his shop, the heart-to-heart, soul-to-soul discussion.

Matthew sensed a sneer crossing his face. And when he spoke, hatred sounded as he spit out the words. "The executioners told those poor, condemned wretches that 'twas better to burn a short while on Earth than to burn an eternity in hell."

Matthew looked squarely at John. "It is foolish to go against the Monarch's wishes, Son. Worship publicly however they require, and pray privately however you want."

Matthew returned to the fireplace, leaned against the mantle and stared at the sparks as they flew up the chimney.

"A few generations back, our Pagan ancestors worshipped Thor," he said. "'Twas the religion of their day. For years, I worshiped as a Catholic because Christianity had come about and that's how we were told to worship. When the King or Queen changes his or her mind on how to glorify God, then you glorify in that same manner and none other."

As he looked long at his son, Matthew recalled how he and Mary made the sign of the cross during John's christening on Jan. 21, 1584, at the Saxon baptismal font at St. Mary's Church in Banbury. The church was Anglican then, but earlier, the same building, led by the same pastors, had been Catholic. "What difference can it possibly make, the way you worship? 'Tis best not to bring attention to yourself by challenging the way things are, John. Don't tell me that things are different now. I know they are.

"I'm but a simple tailor, still I've made a good life here in Banbury for you and your mother and your brothers and sisters. And that's because I've kept me private thoughts private—and stayed out of trouble. That's the best advice I can give you, Son. Pay me no heed, and you will find yourself locked away in the Tower. There will be no courtesy of its fine quarters for the likes of you. No, a man of your stature will be thrown in to rot with the worst of the thieves and butchers. And, that's if you're fortunate.

"John, in the year of your birth, Queen Elizabeth, 'Good Queen Bess,' delivered England's religious life into the hands of forty-four commissioners, empowering them to do what was necessary to reform all heresies and schisms. These men, in the holy name of God and Queen, took delight in punishing 'rebels' whose religion differed from her highness. A man could be thrown into prison for simply praying with another man in the privacy of his own home. But prison, grim as it was, was still far less painful than being tied to the rack and physically stretched into proper belief and behavior."

Neighbors once eavesdropped on one another and reported what they overheard to the commissioners for the reward of a few coins. Before the modernization of chimneys, conversation spoken in the sanctity of one's own home filtered through the gap between the top of the wall and the roof's eaves—smoke outlets for fires used to warm the house and cook the food. It's called eavesdropping.

"It would break my heart to have my son sent to prison—or worse." Matthew closed his eyes.

"Father, I don't want to hurt you or be disrespectful," John said. "But, I cannot be a puppet, preaching what is handed to me. You know most sermons are homilies prepared by prelates for vicars to read. All they do is extol the Queen's goodness and exhort the congregation to obey her. I believe God wants me to be a minister to save sinners from eternal damnation, not to make the Queen's life easier. I want to help people earn God's grace so they have a chance to spend eternity with Him in heaven."

Matthew shook his head. "I should have known sending you to Oxford was a mistake. You were at a vulnerable age and yet we placed you in the midst of miscreants."

"Father," John began, his voice sounding of exasperation, but Matthew waved the objection off, and John spoke no more.

Oxford, twenty-three miles north and west of Banbury, was the hub of a literary expansion crisscrossing the island. William Shakespeare, who lived in nearby Avon, was touted for his poetry and plays; Spencer's "Faery Queene" had been published only a few years earlier—and then, there were those abysmal books of John Knox. Things were changing, all right, and Matthew didn't like it.

But, in spite of himself, he liked what propelled John's belief: Beauty in purity and purity in simplicity.

Chapter 4

Wherwell, Hampshire
1605
Ann

"It promises to be a beautiful day, Stephen," Ann Bachiler said as she drew back the window coverings. The night's darkness was beginning to scatter with the softness of first light penetrating the morning fog and warm the air's chill. "Just listen to Wherwell waking up," Ann said, unlatching the windows and pushing them open. Wagon wheels noisily clattered over rough cobblestone streets slippery with dew; caged chickens squawked, roosters crowed, pigs snuffed and oinked, and geese honked as they waddled along the street past where the vicar's two-storied manse stood. Farmers were herding and hurrying their stock and goods from miles around, shouting to one another over the din, each vying for the most advantageous niche to hawk their wares.

"Market days are my favorite days," Ann said as Stephen Bachiler finally sat up and watched her dress. If it was market day in Wherwell, it was Thursday. A day for farmers to sell and villagers to buy fresh produce, eggs and meat; for neighbors to visit—*and gossip,* Ann thought with a sudden shudder.

After the breakfast dishes had been cleaned and returned to the cupboard, Ann got her five children ready for market. Once dressed and inspection passed for clean hands and faces, the boys sprang out the door in their rush to get to the town-square. Ann peered into the looking glass as she fashioned a bow from her whitest bonnet and tied it under the first of her double chins. She frowned at her image, and it scowled back. What happened to the cheeriness she'd felt earlier? A chilling premonition worried its unformed being into her thoughts; her own personal dark cloud was trying to obliterate the day's sunshine. A sense of dread shivered her shoulders. There was no particular reason for the sensation, but it was an annoyance that would make her be alert.

Ignoring the omens, Ann started for market, basket on her arm, her three daughters in tow. "Are we going to meet Aunt Prudence at market?" asked Deborah, the Bachiler's eldest daughter at five and ten. "Can I take Theodate and Ann and run on ahead?"

Ann nodded her answer and said, "Watch for your father and Aunt Prudence."

At the first straw-filled cart she came upon, Ann picked a mess of turnips and, holding them by their leafy green-and-purple tops, praised the farmer: "These turnips look especially nice today. I'll surprise Mister Bachiler with them for dinner tonight. 'Tis his favorite vegetable, though the children favor it less."

She pocketed her change as a cloud in the sky appeared from seemingly nowhere. She drew her shawl closer, but it was more than a physical chill that set upon her. She had been forewarned. She should have known enough to stay home. *Why do I continually ignore the premonitions the good Lord sends me?*

Where is Prudence? Instead of seeing her sister, however, Ann saw, out of the corner of her eye, the town's two most vacuous tittle-tattlers. She looked for an escape, but before she could flee, the hiss of their coarse whispers filled her ears—as intended:

"Did you see the Vicar," the first woman clucked, "the way he set his eyes upon the Jennings girl, as though she were clothed in scarlet!" It was uttered as a statement, not a question.

"'Tis a bloody shame, that's what 'tis, him being the minister and all," the second added. "Why, she's young enough to be his daughter."

Ann felt her soft, round pink cheeks flush, her forehead dampen. Soon, she knew, her head would be as wet as if she were standing in a downpour; rivulets would trickle down her spine to puddle in the small indentation of her lower back, where they would be blotted by her clothing. It was such an annoyance when her body betrayed her. She took in a sharp breath and forged on.

"Something should be done," the first one said. "I couldn't agree more," the second one said. "Why he gets away with such things is beyond me," the first one said. "He'll have to answer in a higher court than the one on Earth," the second one said. "In the meantime…"

Ann felt her sister's presence beside her and smiled just as she always did whenever Prudence came into her life.

The two were close in age—a little more than a year apart—but they were opposite in build and demeanor. Where Ann was short and plump, Prudence was tall and lean. Ann was a worrier; Prudence approached life matter-of-factly

"My dear little sister, whatever is the matter?" Prudence said. Ann saw the loving concern on her sister's face and heard the alarm in her voice. "You look as distressed as a mother hen, feathers all ruffled, about to attack the wolf at her chicken-coop door. It's so unlike you."

"I am so grateful you're here," Ann said, nodding her bonneted head in the direction of the Stephen-haters. "Those two over there are having themselves quite an enjoyable time at my expense." Ann looked up at her tall, elder sister who always seemed to make things better. "They're spewing the latest, hurtful rumors about Stephen." Ann's brow wrinkled. "The nerve of those giddy-headed women, spreading false rumors that are as putrid as warmed-over cabbage." She spit the words out.

"Just ignore the biddies," Prudence said calmly

Inconspicuously, Ann hoped, she retrieved her nose cloth from the wrist of her dress and patted her forehead. The Bate sisters moved on to examine tomatoes at the next vendor. "Not a whit of pleasure will they receive from any reaction of mine," Ann whispered to her sister.

Prudence smiled. Ann knew her frustration was only too readable.

"I just pray they will not notice my damp discomfort," she said, blotting beads of perspiration on her upper lip. "'Twas the same thing last Sunday, with the women from church." Ann absentmindedly picked up a tomato and toyed with it. "Women I have long counted as friends, members of Stephen's congregation—and them, so hateful, supposedly striving to be jewels in their husbands' crown. They chopped their words the second they saw me coming towards them, and scattered, each going her own way." Her throat was full as she said, "I felt abandoned, standing alone and seeing only the backsides of those women."

"'Tis no doubt their best side," fumed Prudence.

"Lady, ye want that tomato?" The churlish-sounding words made Ann look up to see the farmer-merchant glaring at her. "They ain't to be squeezed, ye know—they're tender victuals. Buy it and ye can squeeze it to yer heart's content."

"I am so sorry," Ann apologized. She bought the tomato, as bright red as her face, and six more. She'd fry the bruised one for Stephen's breakfast tomorrow. Prudence made her own selection.

"How dare they criticize Stephen so." Ann said. "He's vicar of The Church of the Holy Cross and St. Peter, for goodness sakes. He's a man of God. Those scratch-abouts should respect him."

Prudence guided Ann towards vendors in the opposite direction of where the two tattlers huddled together, anxious for another go at clucking their way through a fresh bag of chicken feed.

"Scratch-abouts?" Prudence said, a little louder than normal, knowing her alto voice carried well. "That's quite the illustrious word, Ann. Just make it up?"

Ann smiled appreciatively at her sister as she saw the two hens spin away in a huff. "You would think I'd learn to ignore such insulting chatter by now," Ann said. As a vicar's wife, she knew about gossip achieving a life of its own—complete with wings—as it travels from here to there. She dabbed her eyes with the nose cloth as though a foreign something had flown into them. In another ploy to stave tears, Ann turned her face toward the sky—now a gray slate, a barometer of her mood. "A shower's in the offing," she said. "I shouldn't wonder the day turned sour."

Ann wished she could spot Stephen. She looked in every direction, but those who towered over her—which was nearly everyone—hampered her view. She wanted to stand beside her husband this very moment and tuck her arm into the crook of his, not only to gain comfort from him, but also to show her support of him. Not, bless his heart, that he had the foggiest notion he needed it.

*   *   *

Ann realized that if the good reverend had a failing, it was his attraction to women and the attention he paid them. Truth be told, he wasn't entirely to blame. Many women clamored to be the focus of his attention, if only for a brief moment. Ann knew the scenario usually went:

"Oh, my dear Reverend," Goodwife Cartwright would whine time and again, "I've had such horrid rheumatick attacks of late. The rain, ye know. Percase you would say a special prayer for me?" Stephen would look sympathetically into the sorrowful eyes of the aged woman, gently pat her hand, and say, as he had been saying for years, "Indeed, I will remember you in my prayers today, Sister Cartwright. But," he would gently chide, "you must help God by taking better care of yourself. When it rains, stay inside your cozy cottage, brew a pot of tea and warm yourself in front of your fire. Avoid getting a chill." "Yes, Pastor, that's what I should do all right, and I will be certain to do it with the next rainfall." Pastor and parishioner would part: the pastor to remind God of the pains suffered by his parishioners, and the parishioner to report to her clique about the good Vicar being an absolute godsend. She was blissfully unaware that the women would turn the minister's act of kindness into something vile. The bibble-babblers would cluck, cluck away:

'Tis not right for a minister to have physical contact with any woman. At all. Ever. You can't tell me he's an innocent. He knows full well what he's doing. Verily, he knows he is breaking the "lusting" commandment. I tell you, the man is lusting!

Cluck, cluck, cluck, cluck...

Yes, Ann was fully aware of Stephen's attraction to women—and theirs to him.

Chapter 5

Wherwell
1605
Stephen

The Reverends Little and Bachiler sat side by side on a bottom-weary hard, straight-backed oak pew in the frigid sanctuary. That morning Stephen had lit the fire in his church library, which was now toasty. But he did not care to entertain this particular visitor in the warmth of his private sanctuary.

The sound of Mr. Little's carriage scrunching over the street's gravel at half past the nooning hour had caused Stephen to look up from the notes he was preparing for Sunday's sermon. As he watched Little tie his horse to the post just outside his office, he felt a knot form in his stomach. He had not expected anyone, let alone a superior from Canterbury.

Now seated in the church, Stephen frowned as he listened to the prelate.

"It would be in your best interest, Reverend Bachiler," intoned Reverend Little, "if you spent more time in silent solitude, listening to God, instead of you doing all the talking. 'Tis beyond me why you think God speaks to you about these foolish notions of Anglicans reforming themselves and then reforming the church—and then the world! What audacity!"

Clouds of breath puffed from Little's mouth whenever he spoke, punctuating his every word. Stephen wasn't cold; he loosened his coat. Fact was, Stephen was hot—especially under his clerical collar.

"Who do you think you are, Stephen?" ranted Little. "Why doesn't God speak to me? Why not the Archbishop?"

Stephen's frown deepened.

"Pride, Stephen Bachiler," Little said, wagging a finger in the parish pastor's face. "Pride will be your downfall."

At that, Stephen's bushy brows coursed themselves on a collision. He sat a little taller, cornered his back in the pew, folded his arms over his chest and turned to look Timothy Little directly in the eye. And said nothing.

Reverend Little, whose name aptly described his stature, began to squirm amid the silence that put him on the defensive. Stephen watched with satisfaction as Little fidgeted with the muffler his mother probably knit for him. He wound it tighter around his neck, then tugged at it to loosen it so he wouldn't choke. He brushed an invisible something from his tall black-felt hat. He worried the ring on his finger.

Stephen made no attempt to relieve the man's dis-ease. It was Little's mission to make Stephen uneasy and Stephen delighted at turning the tables.

Stephen continued to look at Little, saying not a word. Just looking. Right at Reverend Little. Right into the narrow slits that housed the man's beady, watery, pale blue eyes. As Stephen studied Little's face, he wondered why God had forgotten to give this man a chin.

"I realize you don't like me, but that matters not," Little said to break the stifling silence that Stephen created. "This is not about our liking one another." When he received no response, Little harrumphed and said, "I will get to the point straight-away."

Stephen nodded.

"I'm here to tell you," Little sputtered, "you must follow the dictates of the Anglican Church—or pay the consequences. You are hereby officially ordered to immediately stop fomenting public disturbances from behind the pulpit. You must stop provoking your parishioners with statements like 'the Catholic Pope is the Antichrist,' 'God spurns the Church of England's finery' and he disapproves of our worship's elaborate nature."

You little pip-squeak, Stephen thought, *you don't even know what you're talking about.* When Stephen made no audible comment, Mister Little stood to move from his position in the pew. He awkwardly squeezed past Stephen who sat next to the aisle and moved not an iota to facilitate Little's escape. Once freed, Little grasped the end of the pew in front of Stephen.

"You are hereby instructed to immediately stop agitating the citizenry of Wherwell into thinking it is sinful to partake communion from a golden chalice. If the manner in which we worship is good enough for our Sovereign King, then by God's breath, 'tis good enough for you! Do…You…Hear…Me?"

Is this little, Little man going to stamp his feet like a child throwing a tantrum? Stephen wondered. He continued to stare from his seat in the pew and narrowed his eyes the least little bit.

"Think what you will about me," Little yelled, wagging his finger again, "but know this: the Church will remain intact in spite of you and your misguided mates who insist on trying to change our doctrine to suit yourselves.

"That kind of action is going to stop. YOU are going to stop!"

Reverend Little's speech was racing. Ranting.

"And don't think we haven't heard stories about your flirtatious ways with the women-folk, because we have. We know all about that."

Stephen rose and stood toe-to-toe with Little, towering over him so the short man had to crane his neck. Stephen lowered his head just the least bit to make room for his prickling nape hairs.

"All of this will be the end of you, Reverend Bachiler," the Anglican official screamed, backing away from Stephen, tripping over his own feet. "The very end. You know what happens to those who are excommunicated as well as I do." Little's little voice was now big. And high. "You will lose your right to vote, you risk deportation from your motherland, you could be thrown in prison for the rest of your life. Is that what you want?"

Stephen glowered.

"Well, is it?"

Silence.

"All right. Don't speak to me, but you better watch what you speak of from behind the pulpit, Reverend Bachiler. We have our eye on you. The King has said he will harry the likes of you out of the kingdom, and Mister Bachiler, I will personally see to it that you are among the first to go. Such will be my great pleasure."

Little slammed his hat atop his head and stormed from the church. Stephen rose and followed him to holler from the church steps: "May the good Lord cause his eyes to shine upon you."

But the benediction, spoken less than reverently, went unheeded. Surely God would understand if Stephen didn't love this particular enemy on this particular day.

Like other Puritans, Stephen detested Roman Catholic trappings left over from previous reigns that had been incorporated into the Anglican worship. This new Puritan movement sweeping the country preferred its religion simple, lean, uncluttered by ceremonial rituals originated in Rome. Like his "misguided mates," Stephen feared the "Bishop of Rome" would worm his way back into their religion and their country.

In short, Stephen found Catholicism repugnant.

As he watched Little's carriage disappear down the lane, Stephen thought, *I will not allow that little weasel of a man to vary my course. He has a worm in his brain.*

Neither Stephen's stomach, nor his nape hair relaxed as he returned to the church to pray for forgiveness and deliverance from the likes of Little.

Chapter 6

Wherwell
1605
Ann

"Yoo-hoo. Anyone home?"

"Oh, Prudence," Ann said, answering the door. "I cannot tell you how happy I am to see you."

"Ann, what is it? You've been crying. What has caused you such anguish? Are the children safe? Is Stephen all right?"

A grimace answered the last question.

Ann took a long breath and when she blew it out, she was able to recover her senses and emotions.

"You remember those rumormongers at the market last week?" Ann said, dabbing at her eyes with a handkerchief. "Well, they must have passed their gossip on to Canterbury, somehow, because Stephen was called onto the carpet again by his Anglican superiors. Prudence, it was terrible," Ann said, tears leaking from her eyes again. "Stephen was all worked up. I feared he might split something inside of him, he was so red in the face.

"The problem is," Ann said as she led Prudence into the room just off the great room. Prudence gasped at the heap of silver: silver chalices, silver cups, silver trays, silver teapots that littered the table, which resembled a silver-maker's table during a sale.

"Forever more, Sister, where did you dig up all these silver pieces? Surely, you are not planning to clean these all by yourself?"

"Oh, no, Prudence, look! Here's a polishing cloth with your name on it," Ann said with a smile. Then, frowning again, she said, "I'm all worked up inside and thought it might be good to put all that excess energy to good use. I just went around the manse and picked up piece after piece. Some of it's ours, and some belongs to the church—but I'll shine up anything."

"I'll brew a pot of tea for you," offered Deborah, "and then go mind the girls."

"What a love," Prudence said, picking up a candlestick and lightly began polishing. Ann returned to the communion plate she had been working on, and continued her ferocious buffing.

"Ann, Dear, if your don't relax, you will wear that plate inside out," Prudence said.

Once Deborah brought over the teapot with its cozy atop, and two cups, she excused herself and left.

"What a remarkable niece I have," Prudence said. "She knows exactly what to do.—and then does it."

"The problem is," Ann said, "Stephen is an elegant man to behold." Prudence blinked. She was still thinking of Deborah. "You do agree that he's exceptionally fine looking, would you not?" Ann asked, not expecting an answer. "But, being such a fine specimen to behold is not a trait that always serves him well."

Prudence poured them each a cup of tea and sweetened both with a spot of honey.

"Everyone looks up to him," Ann continued, " and not just because he's so tall. She smiled at her little joke. Her sense of humor was returning.

"There's not a door in Wherwell, save the church, where he can enter without ducking, lest he bang his head."

Ann smacked her forehead with the palm of her hand to imitate the contact of her husband's head with a doorjamb. The vision of Stephen forgetting to stoop made the sisters laugh. The tension that had ricocheted around the room the past while began to ease. "I always say when he does that, 'Tis a blessing God gave you such a hard head.' Aye, since the day we wed, this husband of mine has created so much joy for me—along with more than enough consternation."

Ann envisioned her husband: "Stephen's coarse black hair had always been a problem," she said as Prudence placed a cup of tea in front of her. She wiped her hands, black with silver polish, on a clean cloth. "Stephen's mother used to tell me that when he was a lad, his hair was as thick as the wool on an unshorn sheep. A black sheep." The irony made her smile at Prudence. "As he's gotten older, his hair is still nearly as thick, but wily strands of gray hair are beginning to replace the black ones."

She stirred another spoonful of honey in her cup, unaware that Prudence had already sweetened it. "Mmmm, this is good tea," Ann said. "I'll have to remember that brand."

Prudence resumed the physical description of her brother-in-law, who was not her favorite person, but if Ann loved him, that was enough for her. "That Bachiler nose is his only distraction from an otherwise comely face," Prudence said. "I've heard some people make polite reference that his nose is 'prominent.' Oh, and, those eyebrows of his. They all but meet in the middle of his face."

Ann looked at her sister, the only person in the world she would allow to critically describe her husband.

"Oh, Prudence, life would be much more pleasant if he would stop providing fodder for those small-minded biddies," Ann said, her voice catching. "Why can't he keep his hat on his head where it belongs and speak only to men?"

She looked at the teapot she was polishing and blushed at how it shone. She looked at her sister and raised her eyebrows. "'Tis said some good comes from all things. Even if it's polishing silver while fighting the Devil in one's mind." She picked up a tray. "I don't doubt the love of my dear Stephen. He's a good man, Prudence, and I am blessed to be his helpmeet." Her elbow grease removed all sign of tarnish. "Our parents made a good match when they paired us," she mused, forgetting she wasn't alone.

Her eyes lifted and to see a look of concern on her sister's face. "Prudence, I am sorry for troubling you with my woes. I should bear this cross by myself. Besides, 'tis sinful to speak against your husband. I constantly pray that the good Lord in heaven grant me the strength and courage to forbear…"

"Once again," Prudence finished the sentence, once again.

Ann was spent, physically and emotionally. She looked at her sister. "I have been favored by the Almighty to have you as a confidante, a trusted sister—and friend."

"And for me, as well," Prudence said.

"You know that Stephen's a good husband and father," Ann said, resuming her polishing and conversation. "I don't question his love for me and the children."

"Yes, he is a loving father and mate," Prudence said, giving Ann the expected response, "but I know full well that you have nagging doubts. Any woman would. You are not the one in the wrong, dear Sister."

"It's Satan that places doubts into my head," Ann said. "I want my mind clear to think only praiseful things and to give God all the glory."

"Ann…" Prudence began.

"Do you know what Stephen says?" Ann interrupted, not hearing Prudence. "He says, 'God made Eve for Adam to enjoy.' And he winks at me when he says it."

"The audacity," Prudence began. Then the two women looked at one another and burst out laughing. "Stephen is Stephen."

Deepening her voice to mimic her husband, Ann said, "God did right by creating such a wonderful helpmeet for us helpless men." And the women laughed some more.

"How could I ever doubt the love of a man who thinks I'm so wonderful?" Ann asked. "I just wish others could understand Stephen better." She studied her upside-down reflection in the spoon's bowl and adjusted her cap. "When people first meet Stephen, they assume him to be gruff, judging by his looks when he's not smiling—those eyebrows, don't you know—and by the way he pounds the pulpit on Sundays. Aye, he can be stern, but not in all ways.

"Did I tell you what happened a fortnight ago, when Stephen and I went walking the pathway along River Test? We came upon the Smythe boy, just outside of town. He was leaning against a tree, fishing. Stephen asked if he'd caught anything. 'Yes sir,' young Paul replied, immediately standing up. Such fine manners. He held out a good-sized trout for Stephen's admiration. 'Mother said if I caught anything, she'd cook it on the morrow.' And Stephen, who had kneeled down close to the boy by that time, said, 'Appears to me that you'll have a mighty fine meal.'

"Prudence, you should have seen the boy stare at the Reverend. Stephen looked behind him as if to see what the boy was looking at. He asked, 'What is it?' and—you won't believe this, Prudence—but Paul actually said, 'Mother told me your eyebrows are so bushy that a bird could build its nest in them. Is that true?'"

Ann and Prudence rocked with laughter.

"I couldn't help but laugh, even then, but poor mystified Stephen didn't understand," Ann said. "He puzzled his brows together like he does, and turned to me and asked, 'What'd this young scalawag say?' When at last he reasoned the question, Stephen tilted his head back and roared." Ann relished Stephen's laughter. It begins in his belly and gurgles upward through the throat until it bursts, free at last, ringing through space. "Finally," Ann said, "Stephen asked the very red-faced boy to look closely at his brows. Stephen's reaction had taken the lad off guard, and he knew he had spoken out of turn. But Stephen said to him, 'See, Son? Nary a bird.'"

"What did Paul do then?" Prudence asked.

"He was shaking in his boots, but he was so cute. He said, 'Yessirnosirsorrysir.'"

Ann and Prudence reached for the same serving spoon to polish, and they touched hands. Ann didn't challenge her sister. Instead she leaned back to rest her back against her chair.

"I'm proud that Stephen laughs with children and shakes hands with the chimney sweeps just as he does the most noble of men. He realizes that that casualness riles those who say he should be ashamed of stooping below his station. But Stephen truly believes that everyone deserves the same attention. 'We're all God's children,' he says rightfully, 'and that's all that matters.' But 'tis that same free spirit that causes so much grief." Ann looked at her sister. "Whether he's behind the pulpit or walking down the street, it's his gumption that causes him problems. And his woes are my woes."

"Stephen truly is a puzzle," Prudence said, rising to pour more tea. "People line up on either side of what he says and does. Some admire him for the very same things that others condemn him for."

"Those who admire him are mostly those who fear the Pope will get a foothold into England's religion again," Ann said. "But, unfortunately, there are more who say there's no need for him to carry on so about reform." Ann whispered her next words, her chin quivering: "Church officials say he's an embarrassment."

"I know that Stephen is widely respected among some of his peers for his scholarly achievements," Prudence said, "and for his outstanding ability as a minister—even the gentle side of his pastoring. It seems Stephen is unconditionally loved or hated."

"Isn't that just so?" Ann said. "Stephen has such a talent for sizing up a situation, reckoning God's will about it, and then acting upon it. He deliberates his decisions a good while then makes a pronouncement—and stands by it. Have I ever told you how Stephen determines if he's right with God? When the hackles stand up on the back of his neck, he knows he's right."

The two women laughed at the imagined site of Stephen's nape hair standing at attention.

"When those fine, minute hairs stand up, he becomes all the more determined," Ann said. "It's as though God is saying 'Do not be deterred, Stephen.'

"When it happens," Ann said, "and I know full well when it happens, I keep still. My voice is no match for God's."

The women polished a while in silence. Then, "I worry about his pride," Ann said. "He strives to be humble, like the Bible says, that our hearts are not to be proud."

"He is rather prideful," Prudence said.

"Every time he writes his signature, pride oozes through the quill and ink as he draws all those curly-cues beneath his name," Ann said. "Those large, flourishing letters betray any denial of pride. I worry that the Anglican officials will dismiss him and take away his license to preach, based on his signature alone. 'Twoud kill him, were that to happen."

"What is it that Stephen does that provokes the church hierarchy so?" Prudence asked.

"They don't think Stephen—or others like him—should talk openly about reformation of the Anglican Church. Especially not from an Anglican pulpit," Ann said. "But that's exactly what he feels God has bid him to do. First off, he wants to eliminate hierarchy, so it's no wonder the Anglican leaders want to be rid of him—as well as all the rest who think like he does. Stephen says the powers that be look upon him and his radical ideas as though he were a blotchy, angry, irritating rash that has spread, itched and annoyed—and will not go away. What scares me though, is that he's been warned time and again to keep his non-traditional thoughts to himself. I fear the consequences even if Stephen does not. Last week, Reverend Timothy Little, Stephen's superior, specifically traveled all the way from Canterbury to Wherwell to chastise Stephen and warn him of the consequences if he didn't curtail his tongue and keep his hat on his head."

Chapter 7

Wherwell
1605
Stephen

August 9, 1605, was a miserable day in Wherwell. The Earth vibrated with thunder and flashes of lightning zigzagged through the dark sky.

Stephen looked up as a stranger reigned in his horse in front of the church. Man and horse alike were drenching wet. The vicar left his office to meet the young man in the vestibule. The lad handed Stephen the papers sealed with the identifying mark of the Archbishop of Canterbury's ring. "Come in out of the rain," Stephen said absentmindedly as he opened the special delivery. His face wrinkled into a frown.

Malachi, the messenger from Cambridge, stood first on one foot and then the other. Water dripped from his cloak to form a puddle on the slate floor. His body shook, causing the drops to form wobbly rings in the ever-enlarging puddle that rained down from him. Stephen noted the young man's discomfort, but knew it wasn't cold enough to make Malachi shake. The summer rain was wet, but not cold. *His teeth chatter because he knows my reputation,* Stephen thought as he made his way to the office. *What is it they call me in England's Rome? Oh, yes, I'm a bear of a man. Unlucky lad probably drew the short straw to make the delivery and face the bear's wrath.* Malachi was left standing alone, silent and forlorn, knees knocking, chin quivering, watching his puddle grow bigger, drop by drop. Plop, plop, plop.

Alone in his study, the walls lined with myriad books, Stephen broke the seal to read the contents of his letter. The room began to close in on him; he grew hot and knew his face was flushed. His eyes burned and blurred as he read and reread the most damning paragraph:

"You are to immediately remove yourself from Wherwell. Your services are no longer required in the Church of the Holy Cross and St. Peter, or in any other Church of England establishment. On Sunday next, upon your ejection, John Bate, A.M., clergyman, will assume the position of Vicar of Wherwell."

John Bate! Ann's brother! Of all people.

Stephen sensed another being in his presence and looked up. "Pardon, Sir, is there to be a reply?" Malachi asked from the office door.

"God's teeth," Stephen spurted, angry at the intrusion, but immediately sorry. He fought for control. He would give the courier no cause to report to his superiors that the Reverend Stephen Bachiler was in the least daunted. Unaware his bushy eyebrows met in the middle of his crimson-colored, slightly contorted face, he said, "No, there is no reply," he barked. "Be gone."

Once Malachi was atop his horse and clopping out of sight, Stephen stomped across the soggy lawn to the parsonage next door to tell his family the news. Opening the door, he thundered, "By God, I have been de-churched."

Ann covered her mouth with both hands to stifle the cry that screamed in her throat.

"Oh, Reverend Bachiler, now what?" she breathed after a moment. "What's to become of us?"

"Never you mind, my good wife." Stephen sounded harsher than intended. "This is not God's will. This is the work of those hypocritical, mealy-mouth…" He took a deep breath and said softly: "God will provide. Expulsion from the pulpit is not what he intends for this humble servant of his. I may no longer preach from behind a Church of England pulpit, but I will not be stilled from spreading God's word wherever I can.

His face reddened. His voice rose. His brows furrowed.

His nape hair prickled.

Chapter 8

Newton Stacy, Hampshire
1606
Stephen

"Goodwife Bachiler," Stephen said in a rush as he pushed the door open and entered their new parsonage in Newton Stacy, Hants, a neighboring village of Wherwell, "I want you to prepare an especially fine dinner for after services Sunday."

*   *   *

It was less than a fortnight before Stephen resumed preaching. Reports of his ostracism from the Church of England spread like manure over a farmland and word quickly cropped up all over the county. It was all anyone talked about.

Wherever he went, Stephen confronted former friends and parishioners who lowered their eyes or looked away as he approached, or crossed the street when the shadow of his impressive size cast its image. Mothers nudged their youngsters along, allowing not a word with the banished priest who had been their friend since the day he baptized them. But

Foster, the chimney sweep, shook Stephen's hand and cheerily greeted him with "G'day Vicar."

There were, however, those who sought Stephen out as a man of courage—compatriots who shared similar thoughts and were also troubled by the ever-increasing stifling "religious laws" imposed upon them.

*   *   *

Ann and Deborah, sitting side by side on the settee, jumped in unison at Stephen's abrupt entrance. Ann was teaching Deborah the finer points of embroidery, and with the clamorous arrival of her father, Deborah's needle pricked her finger instead of the sampler and she stuck her finger into her mouth to stem the bleeding.

Little Ann and Theodate played with their dolls nearby.

It was Friday. Stephen had been away most of the week, at Oxford, addressing the graduating class. He had been invited to his alma mater months before that final brouhaha with the prelates. With his expulsion, however, some deans clamored his appearance be canceled. But the Reverend Stephen Bachiler would have none of it. He had been asked to speak, and speak he would.

"I've invited a young minister to worship on Sunday," Stephen said, hand on hips, legs wide apart—his natural stance—"and I know he'd appreciate a good meal afterwards. He'll be staying with us 'til he can travel again on Monday."

Stephen looked at his wife. "That is all right, isn't it? It won't cause a problem, will it?"

Ann smiled. "Of course 'tis all right," she said, adding softly so Stephen could barely hear, "Isn't it always all right, dear Husband?"

"Eh?" Stephen asked.

"Nothing," Ann said.

And as if no words had disrupted his thought pattern, Stephen continued: "This John Wing graduated Oxford last year. He's an assistant pastor up at Newbury. He heard I was to lecture and made it a point to attend the exercises. After the ceremony, as I was returning to the inn, he caught up with me and asked if we might have a few words."

Stephen strode to the fireplace, picked up the stoker and jabbed at the logs. The chill of the spring air penetrated the parsonage walls.

"Turns out the young pastor is struggling. His enlightened mind and conscience can find no solace with the dictates of the established church—not to mention his father's wishes for him to accept the status quo. The lad is asea with jumbled thoughts plaguing him. He is verily wrestling with the Devil himself."

"Sounds as if he and you would get along nicely," Ann said.

"'Tis my very thought," Stephen replied boisterously. "I know I can help the lad sort things out, see the way of how it should be."

Stephen turned to Deborah, now four and ten and soon eligible for marriage.

"This John Wing might be pleasing to you, Daughter," he said, giving her a broad wink and even broader smile. Deborah felt her face flush. Embarrassed, she lowered her eyes. "Oh, Father."

"Men with Mister Wing's potential don't come around often," Stephen continued, "so, my darling Deborah, I want you to help your mother with all the preparations. 'Twouldn't hurt for him to know dinner was readied by both mother and daughter."

Stephen crossed to the window with its triangular panes of thick, wavy glass held fast with wrought iron. The glass creatively distorted God's handiwork outside, and Stephen focused on nothing in particular as he looked out.

"I'll preach a phenomenal sermon," he said, turning to face his women-folk, "to be topped by your phenomenal meal."

He took a deep breath and puffed out his chest.

"How does that sound? We Bachilers will present such a fine example of the ministry—from behind the pulpit and around the table—that this Wing fellow will want to forever be a part of us."

"Company on Sunday, Father?" asked Nathaniel, entering the room late in the conversation. He was Deborah's senior by two years.

"We won't be breaking the Sabbath by entertaining John Wing that day," Stephen assured his keen son. "In fact, he will help us keep the day holy with our devotions. If he's to be the outstanding minister I think he will be," Stephen continued as he restlessly ambled around the room, "he will need an outstanding woman, such as you, Deborah, to be his wife and stand by him. Just as your mother has done for me."

He stood in front of Ann just now, knelt to her level on the settee, and gently took her face into his hands and searched her bluer-than-blue eyes: "You know I couldn't have accomplished all I have without thee, my good-wife."

Stephen adored looking into Ann's iris-blue eyes. They held such purity, and they sparkled whenever he stared into them before Ann would become embarrassed and blush.

"You are my most blessed helpmeet, my lovely Ann."

"I'll just see to supper," she said, and with a pert smile she rose and said, "Stephen, you make me blush. Shame on you."

Chapter 9

Newton Stacy
1609
Deborah

Deborah's nose was tight; her facial muscles simply would not relax. Stealing a glance towards John, she saw he was also in distress; he kept wiping the palms of his hands on his pants. *What's wrong? Why are we both so fidgety?*

Deborah and John walked down the lane away from her overly enthusiastic father, her ailing mother, her teasing brothers and giggling sisters.

Neither spoke a word. Only the sweet songs of birds returning from their winter hiatus broke the silence. The ground's spring dampness seeped through the soles of Deborah's shoes. *Oh, I do hope they won't squish.*

It had been three years since the phenomenal sermon and dinner had been delivered and served to Mister Wing, now Stephen's protégé.

Many nights, long after the Wing family wished the two Puritans a good night, Stephen and John huddled over a flickering candle to discuss philosophy, religion, John Knox, Presbyterians, Puritans, the Church of

England…They would talk until the candle snuffed itself out, leaving them in the dark.

The Bachilers had not expected John on this particular day, but everyone welcomed him. He was the family's favorite guest. Deborah couldn't help but wonder what was afoot. Why had he come unannounced and uninvited?

After the noon meal, John said, his voice sounding so formal, "Mistress Bachiler, it appears that the rain has stopped and the sun is shining again. Might I interest you in a walk?"

As Deborah excused herself from the table, she noticed the queer grin covering her father's face and gave him a quizzical look. *What's he thinking?*

This walk was the first time Deborah and John had been alone together. That's why her nose was tight. When she was nervous, her nose muscles knotted as tight as the tiny French knots in her stitchery. And, at this moment she was grievously nervous.

Deborah was certain something was in the air besides trilling birds. She wondered if John felt it. The longer they walked and the longer each waited for the other to speak, the tighter her nose became and the harder her heart thumped. She feared it might burst.

"What was that?" she asked. "'Twas a most peculiar sound."

"It's nothing," John said, looking around. Then, "'Twas me, trying to catch my breath."

John walked on one side of the rutted path that meandered beside the River Test; Deborah on the other, arms straight down, eyes straight ahead. Her bonnet, with its brim framing her face, acted as blinders and restricted her view to the path before her.

"Mistress Bachiler," John said at last, breaking the silence.

"Yes?" Deborah answered. *Can he hear my heart? It's so loud.*

"I've been called by a congregation in Rochester and I intend to take my leave at the end of this month." He darted a look across the road. Their eyes met as Deborah snapped her head to look at him.

She dropped her eyes and studied a persistent blade of coarse grass determined to push its way through the path's trodden ground. Her eyes stung and her vision blurred. John was going away. She wanted to break into a run and leave him far behind. Rochester was in Kent County, forever away from Hampshire County. They would never see one another again. Ever. Her eyes blinked rapidly.

John turned and walked back towards her since she had become rooted in the road. A lace glove covered her mouth.

"I would be most happy, Mistress Bachiler," John said, wanting to take her hand but staying on his side of the road, "if you would allow me to speak to your father about asking for your hand in marriage."

John's words—and voice—sounded stiff. As stiff as his backbone. Once his proposal was out, he took a deep breath. He frowned as he looked closely at her. She caught her breath. *What,* she thought. *What did he say?* She turned fully towards him so her bonnet would not obstruct her view. "What," she said. "What did you say?"

"I said I want to marry you. To have you be my wife. My helpmeet. The mother of my children. To remove to Rochester with me—and wherever else God directs me."

Deborah stood dumfounded. Staring.

John cleared his throat and continued: "I also asked if you would object were I to speak to your father. I realize that at six and twenty, I'm nine years your senior, but I feel we would make a good union, Deborah. I will do anything humanly possible to make you happy."

John crossed the road and took Deborah's hands into his. "Deborah. Dear Deborah," he began. "My heart beats so, I'm afraid 'twill never calm itself." Deborah watched his Adams-apple bob as he swallowed a few times in succession. "I do believe God would lovingly sanction this union."

Deborah timorously smiled; she bashfully dropped her head, but looked up with eyes wide, and whispered, "I'd be honored to be thy wife, Reverend Wing."

John gently untied Deborah's bonnet and removed it; her shining dark hair freely fell about her shoulders. He gently kissed her lips.

Deborah felt a stirring inside her that was completely foreign. She didn't know what it was, but it was pleasant and she didn't want it to stop.

"Deborah, I bought a book of William Shakespeare's sonnets a while back and committed a favorite to memory just for this occasion."

Quietly, he began, looking into her eyes:

Shall I compare thee to a summer's day?
Thou art more lovely and more temperate:
Rough winds do shake the darling buds of May,
And summer's lease hath all too short a date:
Sometimes too hot the eye of heaven shines,
And often is his gold complexion dimmed,
And every fair from fair sometimes declines,
By chance or nature's changing course untrimmed;
But thy eternal summer shall not fade
Nor lose possession of that fair thou owest,
Nor shall Death brag thou wandr'est in his shade,
When in eternal lines to time thou growest:
So long as men can breathe or eyes can see,
So long lives this, and this gives life to thee.

*　　　　*　　　　*

Home again from the walk, Deborah fell into her mother's welcoming arms as her father pumped John's arm as though it were the handle of a well. "God bless ye, son," her father said. "I told the wife that no doubt you were going to propose to our daughter." Her father's expression curled his face.

Normally, Stephen and John's father Matthew would have made marriage arrangements for the young couple, but John was now a man and on his own, allowing him to enter into his own contract.

Ann gathered a corner of her apron to dab at her tears of happiness. "These are happy tears, Deborah," her mother said. "Happy tears."

"'Tis a match made in heaven, I'll say that," her father said. "Yes, indeed."

*　　　　*　　　　*

A fortnight later, Deborah was hesitant about leaving home for the unknown of Rochester. She had never been away without family for even a day in her entire life. The only homes she knew were those in Wherwell and now Newton Stacy. She would miss her family and familiar surroundings.

She took Ann Junior and Theodate to the garden in back of the ivy-covered cottage with its tightly woven "straw hat" of a thatched roof. She wanted to spend a few precious moments with her sisters before she and John wed the next morning.

Ann, eight, and Theodate, six, sat on the stone bench amid a patch of lilies of the valley. The air was sweetened by the scent of the tiny white flowers, their miniature bells peeking from the folds of strong, waxy, protective green leaves. Deborah, sitting on the squatty, three-legged stool she brought from the house, faced her sisters.

She took one little hand of each sister into hers.

"Are you really going to move away?" Theodate asked with a pout on her face. "I don't want you to go."

"I know, Theodate," Deborah replied. "And, I will miss you, too. But we will see each other every now and again. Nothing is forever. But, before I go, I want to talk about Mother. You must do what you can to be on your best behavior and not tax her."

"What's the matter with your voice?" Ann asked. "It sounds funny. Are you crying?"

Without an acknowledgement, Deborah continued: "Nathaniel, Stephen and Samuel are older than you girls, but, because they are boys, they won't be of much help to Mother. So, it's up to you two. You can be big girls, can't you?"

She was chagrined about telling these little girls that they must do more to help than their older brothers simply because they were girls.

Part of Deborah's soul urged her to stay home and care for her mother and the girls. But her father insisted. This marriage, it seemed, was as important to him as it was to her. Maybe even more.

Chapter 10

Rochester, Kent
1609
Deborah

With every revolution of the coach's wheels, John and Deborah bounced, jarred and jostled over rough, dusty roads from Hampshire County, across Surry County and on towards the north of Kent County.

Hugh cracked his driver's whip over the four horses, already lathered with sweat, urging them nonstop through small villages that materialized every three or four miles on either side of the larger market towns. At market towns, Hugh stopped long enough to allow departing passengers to unload and new ones to load, and time for those who continued their trip to exercise their "sea legs" while he watered the horses or, at near-breakneck speed, changed a spent team for a fresh one.

With each stop, Deborah billowed her new green traveling dress, now camouflaged to a lighter hue with the road's dust. *I'll whisk it clean again, once we're settled,* she thought.

There was no escaping the dust and grit that worked its way into the coach. Just as there was no way to escape the bone-jarring ride.

"We have ta make time," Deborah heard Hugh say to a complaining customer. "That's why I prod the horses to beat the devil. That and ta have a runnin' chance of escapin' the devil's highway bandits. Them terrible pirates, they hide 'n wait for coaches, then they ambush 'em and rob me passengers of every farthing they're carrying. But if we're a travelin' ta beat hell, why then, we have a fightin' chance."

Deborah jumped as she heard her husband's voice confront the driver. "Here fellow," John said as he took hold of Deborah's shoulders and turned her away from the rascal's sight. "There's no call to use such language in the presence of these women whose very ears you offend." She had never heard such anger coming from him.

Deborah gasped at the grimace that distorted her husband's face and the tone of his voice. She'd never heard him display such temper. She looked askance at him, swallowing the lump in her throat.

Oh, my goodness, she thought, *I must be weary. John, what is wrong? Oh, mother, how I'd love to talk this over with you.*

"'Tis a cruel day when me riders complain about their ladies' delicate ears," Hugh grumbled as he turned to tend his beloved horses that never censured his language. "'Tis me backside that deserves to complain, 'tis. Turned me into a right miserable contrary fella, I s'pect. But who the devil cares."

✳   ✳   ✳

That night, after a supper of veal chops, bread, cheese and beer—and entertainment from a tinker playing a Banbury kettledrum—Deborah sat on a plush chair, grateful for its softness, in front of the inn's fire. With closed eyes, the scene between John and Hugh replayed in her mind, again and again. And with each telling, John's attitude grew more belligerent. *I've never seen this side of him* she thought.

"Are you sleeping, Deborah?" John asked but continued even before she could open her eyes and shake her head. "What's troubling you?" They had exchanged few words that evening.

"Nothing," Deborah replied.

Just then, Hugh came over and proffered his hand to John. Deborah shrank back into the chair.

"Me apologies, Sir," Hugh said. "Guess we're all a bit travel weary. Still, there's no excuse for usin' such language in front of a lady," he said, nodding in Deborah's direction. "But, after the fine meal we just et and a good night's sleep ahead of us, we'll all travel better on the morrow."

"Yes," John said coolly. "Your apology is accepted." Deborah couldn't help but smile to see Hugh's hangdog expression. Then John added, in a more gracious tone, "I imagine 'tis a hard day's work, driving a stage and wrangling a team of horses."

"Oh, yessir," Hugh said, cozying up to the sympathetic ear. "These here roads are a hazard, they are. I don't know what the guvner's thinkin' lettin' 'em go untended like they is. Means we can't cover but six, seven miles in an hour's time."

The roads were remnants of those laid by conquering Romans centuries earlier, and were to be, according to law, fifty feet wide. More often, however, they were but twelve feet wide, nowhere broad enough for two wheeled conveyances to easily pass one another.

John and Hugh left to join the other men gathered around the trestle table to smoke their pipes and continuously empty their mugs of ale. Deborah heeded her father's parting words to read and read again biblical passages of a wife cleaving to her husband, obeying him, being subject to him and unquestionably following him wherever he goes.

About an excellent wife being her husband's crown.

Seems the burden of a good marriage is the wife's responsibility, Deborah thought, then blushed at her impertinence.

Her time of study done, she absently thumbed through her Bible, the page edges darkened by daily use. She stopped at the seventh chapter of

First Corinthians, her eyes drawn to the third verse: "Let the husband render unto the wife due benevolence; and likewise also the wife unto the husband."

Deborah smiled. *Teamwork,* she thought, *now, that's better.*

She rose and cast a shy smile towards her husband who mumbled apologies about calling it a night, and the newlyweds retired to their room.

*   *   *

Deborah saw John smile. "What makes you smile so?"

"Nothing," he replied. "I enjoy watching the wonderment on my bride's face as the miles revolve beneath the coach's wheels."

Deborah's curiosity about the continuously changing scenery kept her spirits buoyed. Uncertain as she sometimes felt, Deborah had to admit this new phase of her life, as the wife of the Reverend John Wing, was intriguing.

"Every time we come to the rise of a hill, or round a curve, there's something new and wonderful to behold," she told John. "These perfectly beautiful green hills that look as though they roll off into tomorrow, and the miles and miles of stone fences, and the fluffy white clouds in the sky…" Deborah found every sight fascinating: cows lazily munching in the meadows, ever-present herds of bleating sheep…

And every day there were new people to meet, passengers who traveled with them from one post to another and the ever-changing inn owners who welcomed them with a decent meal and a bed made up with fresh linens, England's hallmarks to seventeenth-century travelers.

Finally, five days after their journey began in Newton Stacy, John and Deborah arrived in Rochester, situated at the mouth of River Medway, and close by to Stroud, John's parish.

The big-city sights dazed Deborah as the horses clopped through Rochester.

The castle in the ancient walled city built by Romans had been keeping fortress over its inhabitants since before 1085, when William the Conqueror took a head count of England's subjects in order to tally their value, their worth to him. The castle's Gundulph Tower had been a presence along the Medway River ever since the Normans captured England.

A passel of barking, yapping dogs suddenly appeared alongside and behind the coach—a noisy escort. Some dogs dared now and again to venture a nip at the great horses' hooves. Hugh answered the clamorous dogs with well-placed snaps of his whip's long tongue.

"Just look at the size of this city," a wide-eyed Deborah said. "It certainly makes home seem small. There are people everywhere!" And they all seemed in a rush, scurrying down one street, turning a corner to scurry down that street. She had never seen anything to rival Rochester's double-storied, half-timbered houses that shared common walls, making for very close neighbors. "'Tis so big. I'll never find my way about—all the people, all the buildings."

Moments upon entering the city's gates, armored soldiers at the guard, Deborah rudely learned the city wasn't as sweet smelling as its sights were intriguing. Taken aback by the odorous air, she pressed a gloved hand to her nose as a filter. Culverts in the streets collected garbage of all description, all of it adding to the air's stench.

Deborah leaned with the coach's listing as Hugh maneuvered the narrow cobble-stoned streets. As it lumbered past one house, a woman leaning from a second-floor window threw out her master's leavings collected overnight in a crock beside his bed.

Restraining a gag and turning to look in another direction, Deborah's attention was drawn to a more civil scene: "John, just look at that magnificent cathedral," she said, pointing to a looming gray-stoned building that all but swallowed up the small neighboring church in its shadow. No sooner had the words escaped her mouth than she could have bit her tongue.

"That's St. Nichols," replied her chagrined husband in a too-even tone. "Are you disappointed we're not to minister in such a formidable cathedral?"

Deborah ducked her head. She hadn't meant to infer anything. She didn't care John's congregation would meet in a small chapel, but she did think he deserved better. John was destined to become a great preacher—or at least that's what her father said, and he was rarely wrong.

"No, of course I don't care," Deborah stammered quietly. "I just thought…"

"The physical presence of a church is not the sum-part of a church," John lectured. "A church can be as simple as a group of people who gather together under a tree to worship our Lord. It matters not where they worship, Deborah. A so-called building is nothing more than bricks or stones stuck together with dung and straw."

Deborah turned her face away from John and rapidly blinked her eyes and struggled for composure. She would be glad not to travel anymore. She truly was exhausted. *But,* she thought, *John needn't have preached to me. Not in that tone. But I'm sure he, too, is weary beyond belief.*

John patted Deborah's hand to get her attention. His stern look was replaced with a gentle smile when he said, "Deborah, my dear, forgive the quickness of my tongue. But be not swayed by the outer beauty of anything. 'Tis only inner beauty that counts."

Deborah smiled the tenuous smile of a child rebuked and said nothing. She didn't want to displease John. She wanted to learn from him, to make him proud of her. But it wasn't easy to curtail her natural, childlike enthusiasm to mimic his serious demeanor.

Chapter 11

Rochester
1611
Deborah

"So, are thee with child, Daughter? Are you in travail?"

Deborah felt her face redden. She dropped her eyes to evade those of Goodwife Emma Hilliard, whose smiles were as warm as bread straight from the oven. The older woman clasped her hands and patiently waited for her to look up.

"Are you in travail?" she gently asked again.

"Yes," Deborah whispered. "I knew I couldn't hide it much longer. My middle grows at such an amazing rate. At first, I didn't know what was wrong, why I was so sick each morning."

Goodwife Hilliard smiled. "Deborah, dear, don't be embarrassed. Every woman who's been a mother knows only too well the changes that occur during pregnancy. Your breasts swell; your back begs for relief; you run an embarrassing number of times to the necessary. Your newly acquired bulge defies any attempt at keeping a secret; and the unborn babe, whose movements at first feel like the flutter of a butterfly, grows in strength to punch and kick as it grows and stretches inside its cozy womb.

"Yes, Deborah, every mother knows these truths of travail."

"'Tis so embarrassing for everyone to see my apron jump," Deborah said.

"No one but you notices," Emma said.

"Do you have children?" Deborah asked.

"Oh, my, yes," was the reply. "Of my six children who lived to adulthood, there's not a 'she-chick' among them—only little roosters. And since those boys have grown to start 'nests' of their own, not a one has presented me with a 'she chick.' Lots of grandsons, but not a baby girl amongst them. And every mother wants a daughter, don't you know. I did have two, but they didn't have the strength to survive. On their birth dates, I pick flowers from my garden and go visit with them for a bit."

Deborah had seen Goody Hilliard sitting between two small markers in the churchyard cemetery, pulling weeds from the small headstones. Deborah didn't mean to intrude, but she couldn't help but watch. After a while, Deborah saw Goodwife Emma kiss her fingertips and touch each stone.

"Ever since I met you, when you and the Reverend arrived here," Emma said, "I feel as though God has given me a chance to cradle the daughter I was denied. I may be past my years of childbearing, but I still have a lot of mothering left. I have much more love to share."

Deborah looked shyly at Emma, then reached over and kissed her cheek. "You can mother me," she said quietly. "I and my God-given mother, who is so far away, would love for you to be my 'adopted' mother."

After the hug that followed, Emma asked, "How are you feeling?"

Deborah blushed as she told of the three months of vomiting every morning, about dreading to cook because the smell of food nauseated her, about not having enough energy to properly do her chores. About shedding tears at the least thing.

"I saw a mother duck get caught beneath the wheels of a cart the other day," Deborah said. "Her chicks were frantic, cheeping and running every which way. I sobbed and sobbed. I couldn't stop. After a while, John got cross with me and told me to save my tears for something really important."

"So that's how you come to have those ducklings running around your yard."

"I couldn't just leave them. Their mother had been killed. They would have died lest someone adopt them."

"Of course you couldn't leave them," Emma commiserated. "But don't you be upset with Mister Wing. Men just don't understand these things. Now, then, when is the child to be born?"

Deborah looked at Emma with astonishment. How ever was she to know that? Emma questioned further. The women talked on, both ignoring Deborah's face, which in her entire life had never been redder or hotter, and together they arrived at a tentative date when her travail would end.

*   *   *

The long-anticipated day came and went. Be patient was all anyone could tell Deborah. Babies come in their time and God's time. Deborah and Emma had arranged everything well in advance of the expected day. Patience Goodspeed, a midwife who had delivered dozens and dozens of babies in Rochester and beyond, would tend Deborah's birthing. Five church ladies were ready to assist whenever Deborah needed them. As if she were preparing for a party, Deborah baked the traditional "groaning cake" for her attendants to enjoy during the birthing time. She gathered special herbs to help ease the pangs she had so often been warned about, and she knew Mistress Goodspeed would bring more.

One woman nursing her own child would also suckle the Wing baby the first few days after birth, until Deborah's milk came in pure, replacing the first that soured from all the commotion of delivery. Even a neighbor's litter of puppies was on stand-by should Deborah became engorged. She wouldn't even consider that disgusting prospect. She could never ever nurse a puppy.

For the coming event, Deborah and Goodwife Hilliard made and stored extra butter for Mistress Goodspeed to apply during the delivery to help Deborah stretch and ward off ripping.

And, after the birth, Mistress Goodspeed would apply a healing dressing made of a heated egg mixture.

*   *   *

Deborah's back ached more than usual this day and her stomach was harder than it had ever been. It took a supreme effort to stand at the fireplace, hand on one hip, stirring their evening meal, bubbling in the pot. Suddenly, out of nowhere, a ferocious cramp grabbed her insides and wrenched. She let out a cry.

"What is it?" John asked, alarmed.

"I think 'tis time to go for Mistress Goodspeed," Deborah said once she could talk again.

*   *   *

The women walked the room with Deborah, around and around, hour after hour, mile after mile, holding her up when each pain increasingly begged her to double over. She wanted to lie down, curl up, cry out, but remembering her station in life—she was the minister's wife, after all—she closed her eyes, grit her teeth, bit her lip, held her breath and tightened her grip on those pacing with her. Besides, Deborah had been warned that Mistress Goodspeed did not suffer simpering women. She who had never borne a child.

"This childbearing pain is all Eve's fault," chided Esther, one of John's parishioners, as she walked with Deborah, recalling her own walks in her house, usually once every two years.

"If Eve had not disobeyed God and tempted Adam," Esther said, "children would have come into this world in a different manner." The other women echoed her sentiment.

These distaff philosophers, who discussed the subject anew with every delivery, had no idea how an alternate birthing process might occur, but they agreed it certainly wasn't fair that all women for all time must suffer because of Eve's one-time lapse from grace.

Deborah interrupted the philosophizing.

"I need to lie down," she panted after a particularly strong spasm.

She couldn't be brave much longer. She wanted to scream and didn't care who heard.

"I had no idea 'twas possible to bear this much pain, or that it took this long to birth a baby," she said miserably. "Is there no relief? Herbs, Mistress Goodspeed. I need more herbs."

"Nonsense," Mistress Goodspeed replied, buttering her hands. "Lie on the bed and let's have a look," after which she proclaimed it was time for the birthing stool.

Deborah's assistants guided her to the midwife's stool with its gaping hole. Deborah eased into a squat, sat and clenched the stool's edges worn smooth by countless other women who had gripped the very same spot. Her women friends continued to hold her upright, encouraging her in this rite of passage each first-time mother must endure.

"Push," Mistress Goodspeed ordered from her position on the floor, ready to catch the baby. "Push. Again. Again."

From deep inside of her, a primal scream that would not quit escaped from her throat.

*   *   *

Goody Hilliard, the woman privileged to cut the baby's umbilical cord, was careful not to leave too much lest the infant grow into an immodest adult. Gently she washed the infant, swaddled her and presented the minister with his infant daughter.

"Just look, Mister Wing," she cooed, "a chickadee. Isn't she the sweetest thing ye ever saw? Feel how soft her skin is."

John was speechless. The last twelve hours were the longest he had ever experienced. He winced whenever he heard his wife moan or cry out. It was agonizing not being able to help her, comfort her.

Besides, it smarted, being banned from his own home by a group of women. They were certainly in charge and he knew better than to question them.

Now he looked at this tiny babe in his arms, the cause of the entire hullabaloo, sleeping peacefully. Her tiny rosebud lips sucked at nothing. John's eyes filled.

"'Tis truly a miracle, isn't it, Mistress Hilliard? This baby is truly a miracle from God."

He went in to Deborah and knelt by her bedside.

"My Dear," he whispered so the others, pretending not to listen, could not hear. "You have blessed me with a beautiful daughter. Thank you. Bless you." With a whisper, he said, "I want to name her Deborah, after you, my dear wife. After you."

Chapter 12

Rochester
1613
Deborah

Even though her back was to John, Deborah knew he was watching her as she sliced a loaf of bread still warm from the oven. She knew his eyes were closed when she heard him breathe in deeply, savoring the aroma that can only come from fresh-baked bread. It was a regular ritual between them. "Was there ever a more delicious scent?" he would ask. "I don't think so. My mouth waters in anticipation."

The Wing family was about to have tea with bread and jam. Deborah Junior sat on the bench along side the table, eagerly waiting for her cup to be half filled with rich cream, topped with tea and sweetened with honey. John Junior snoozed in his cradle near by.

"Deborah, you bake the finest loaf of bread I've ever eaten," John told her once again. "You're too young to realize how lucky you are to have such a baker for a mother," John spoke to his daughter. "Why, I do believe her bread is even better than my mother used to bake, and 'twas your grandmother's reputation of being the best in all of Banbury."

"John," Deborah chided, even as she smiled sweetly, "all the flattery in the world is not going to gain you an extra slice. You can have your precious heel and one more, but that's all."

He buttered his treat and topped both slices with heaping spoonfuls of blackberry jam.

"When we go to heaven, my dear wife, I will ask St. Peter to allow you to bake me a daily loaf of bread. You'd be willing to do that, wouldn't you?"

"Of course I'll bake you bread in eternity," she said wryly. "Nothing would give me greater pleasure."

John winked at Deborah.

She smiled in return.

Deborah wiped away the traces of jam from her daughter's face and scooped her up to sit in her lap, when there was a rap on the door and Stephen opened it and stuck his head in.

"Father," Deborah cried. "John, Father's here."

Deborah, still holding Deborah, fondly embraced her father and broke only to give him a kiss on the cheek. "I'm so happy to see you," she said, and stepped aside so the two men could greet one another.

"Come," Deborah said. "We've just had tea. Let me pour you a cup."

The three sat at the table, idly chatting: Mother's fine; she misses you, too; the little girls are growing like little weeds; the boys are at last becoming gentlemen. No, you cannot hold baby John, he's still napping.

When a lull presented itself, John said, "Stephen, I'm sure this is not just a social call. What brings you to Rochester?"

Deborah swallowed hard. Instinct told her the news was not good. She watched as her father rubbed his thumb around the rim of his cup.

At last, he asked, "Have you heard of the disgraceful punishment of William Pyrnne?"

"No," Deborah said, involuntarily shivering with a chill that coursed through her being. "The pamphleteer you and John think so much of?"

"I've heard," John said quietly.

"Why didn't you say something, John?" Deborah said rather than asked. "Why didn't you tell me?"

John stirred a teaspoon full of honey into his tea and watched it slowly dissolve.

"It would have done no good for you to know," he said.

"I'm sorry," her father said. "I didn't mean to cause disharmony."

"'Tis all right, Father. But now I want to know all. He's an outspoken Puritan, the same as the two of you," she said, looking first at her husband, then her father. "I want to know the full extent of his punishment. I worry so about the two of you these days, and what plight might befall either of you. Please, I need to know."

Reluctantly, her father said, "William Pyrnne had his ears cut off while imprisoned in Westminster pillory. And his cheeks were branded with the letters 'S' and 'L' for seditiousness and libeler."

"That was his sentence for his latest broadside, which was judged libelous," John continued. "And the man who printed the pamphlet, likewise had his ears lopped."

What the men didn't tell Deborah is that the hangman, whose duty it was to brand another human being as though he were an animal, botched the job. He pressed the red-hot iron's letter "L" upside down, subjecting William Prynne to yet another branding so the letter would be legible to all that looked upon him.

Deborah felt herself pale; she blinked and stared at the dainty pink flowers painted on her teacup.

"Despite his pain," John said, "I'm told that the martyred Puritan said to those who witnessed his sentence: 'The more I am beat down, the more I am lifted up.'"

"'Tis so," her father said. "Heard it with me own ears. And, when they took him down from the pillory, he summoned enough strength to say, 'Now blessed be to God, I have conquered and triumphed over the prelates' malice and feel myself so strong that I could encounter them all together at this very present.'"

"The man is a saint," Deborah whispered. "How awful it would be to have something like that befall either you or Father. I can't stand the thoughts of it. I fear for you, especially you, Father. You are forever trying the patience of Anglican officials. I can't help but worry."

John shook his head. "True, this is not the time to try the patience of judges and prelates," he said. "But would you have us go against our beliefs?"

"Aye, Daughter," her father said, "we cannot be still just to save our own ears."

"They say Goodman Prynne is so shamed by his disfigurement that he's taken to wearing his hair long to hide his ears," John said. "He, who has long spoken out against worldlings who wear their hair long and flowing."

"Poor Mister Prynne," Deborah said. "How his heart must ache. But long hair or no, no one will ever accuse him of being a worldling."

The three sat at the table, their cups of tea turning stone cold, each lost in their own thoughts and fears of what could be.

Chapter 13

Rochester
1614
Deborah

"A letter from home," John said as he handed Deborah a letter from her father. There was no mistaking Stephen's writing, bold and cursive.

Deborah held the letter to her face, as if to breathe in her father's scent. She was relieved to hear from him, but she wasn't at all sure she wanted to know the letter's contents.

For weeks now, the Wings had heard snips of gossip surrounding her father Stephen and her brother Stephen. Even here in Rochester, the young couple were subjected to gossip's barbs that blew across the green hills of England like parachutes of a noxious weed whirling about, searching, searching until they swept down, vicious venomous stingers at the ready.

Now, looking at the letter, Deborah felt the blood in her veins go cold, chilling her entire body. She shuddered from her toes to her head.

"John," Deborah said with a deep sigh as she placed the letter on the table. "I don't know that I can open it. The news is most apt to be bad."

She set her jaw.

"And what if it is not?" her husband answered. "What if the news is good? What if it holds a rational explanation to the irrational gossip we've been hearing? Procrastination does no one any good, Deborah. Once we truly know what demon we are fighting, we will be able to defend it so much the better. What we need, my dear, is something with which to defend your father, and if you do not read his letter, we may never receive it."

Responding to John's comments, Deborah raised her head and look at him. Mister Prynne filled her senses, and she could not release the image.

She watched as John moved to stand by the open window, which he leaned against as he looked out. When he spoke again, it was in a softer tone: "Your father has done nothing against God. You know that. And no matter what others say, you will love him as you always have, and I will continue to admire his keen mind as I always have, and we will both respect his love of God, even as we know God does."

John would never abide gossip in any form. Not about anyone, and certainly not about family.

Deborah felt her eyes well with tears, but she didn't know it was because of potential shame of her father or of immense love for her husband who was trying to make her feel better.

"With his mouth, the godless destroys his neighbors," John quoted from Proverbs. "We will not listen to gossip and will believe the event as told to us in your father's letter. Stephen Bachiler is a man of God, not a liar. If he says something is so, then 'tis so."

That's what Deborah wanted to hear—John's assurance. Not only was she scared for her father's safety, she was angry. And hurt. She no longer trusted her own mind and heart. John didn't allow his mind to become cocooned in the fluff of emotions like she did. Try as she might, her heart still led at least as often as her head. She rose from where she sat and moved toward John and his strength. She absorbed some of his assurance as she closed herself into his strong, open arms that encircled her tense shoulders.

She and John sat at the table in the center of the room to read the letter. Sunshine streaked in through the open windows creating the sense of warmth, while a breeze, fragrant with spring, fluttered the thin white curtains.

Deborah needed warmth—physical and spiritual. She shuddered again with a chill that came from nowhere.

Once more, trying to prepare herself, Deborah took a deep breath, broke the wax seal to read what her father had to say.

It seemed her father, and the son he named after himself, had not quite extricated themselves from trouble with the law, the church and Stephen Junior's school. They were fined and expelled, but they had not been jailed. They had, however, become the topic of conversation—with one conversation spoken in hushed tones at best, or worse, through clenched jaws, or worse yet, with hearty, taunting laughter.

She knew John first heard the rumor when he tried to join a clutch of men laughing heartily, only to be shut out cold the moment the revelers recognized him.

Deborah had overheard snippets of whispers buzzing around a circle of women friends. "Nothing speaks louder than a whisper," her mother had once told her. "And nothing smarts so cruelly as the sting of gossip."

Stephen and Stephen, so the story went, were said to have composed a poem of scandalous, libelous verses and then, with audacity, sung the verses to the Reverend Josiah Underwood, a neighboring clergyman who turned a deaf ear to their liberal persuasion. The Church of England, as it was run, suited him just fine and Stephen and Stephen would do well to mind their P's and Q's and leave him alone.

'Twas true. Her father and brother had indeed written the poem, and yes, they had been hauled into court for same, according to Stephen's letter.

"But my dear daughter and son-in-law, our parody was written in humor," her father wrote. "We did not think the verses libelous or scandalous—only uproariously clever. We simply wanted this rigid man to flex his attitude just the least little bit."

However, instead of taking them lightheartedly, Mister Josiah Underwood took them to court.

Their behavior, her father allowed, upon being forced to examine the situation in the sober light of a judge's perspective, could only be construed as crude, he supposed.

"Daughter, truly, our only 'sin' was to perform to Mister Underwood outside his window as he prepared his Sunday sermon," He had written in a hurried scribble. "We distracted him. We interrupted his concentration. Is that a sin? Moses did not speak of such things as sinful, and neither did our Lord.

"'Twas no more than a lark to vent our frustrations. The man simply would not listen when we tried to engage him in a civil conversation. So we wrote the poem, thinking to at least gain his attention."

"They gained it all right," John said, interrupting his reading.

Deborah flashed a look at John and frowned. Why had he said that? Surely, he would stand behind Father. Surely, John, of all people, would understand Father's point of view.

She raised an eyebrow at her husband.

"Please go on," Deborah urged. "Read what he says next."

John read aloud: "We were only having a bit of fun. And, regardless of what Brother Underwood or the Court says, some of the verses are funny. So funny, my daughter, that it took all our effort for Stephen and me not to double over in laughter as we staged our orations.

"And 'twasn't only us who thought the poem worth a laugh. The crowd that gathered 'round us as we serenaded the good reverend also thought it a lark. The more they laughed, the bigger the crowd grew. We were asked to repeat the poem again and again so all latecomers to the gathering could hear it."

Deborah groaned.

So, they had repeated their poem not only to Reverend Underwood, but to what began as a small group of passersby that grew into a crowd—like a handful of bread dough plopped into a pan, covered with a cloth and placed on a window sill to warm and rise until ready to pop into a hot oven and baked until its crust is golden brown. What had been a handful of listeners to the Bachilers' libelous verses had grown into a full-blown audience. With that crowd, the two Stephens had popped themselves into the coals of the fire—there to be baked until done. Their "crust" nearly charred.

To make matters ever worse, Stephen and Stephen printed copies of the poem and thrust them into out-stretched hands. He included a copy of the poem with the letter.

"Their broadside broadsided them—right into court," John said.

"Father and Stephen compounded their 'error of ways' with everyone who heard their poem and with all who read the copies they distributed," Deborah said. "How could they have been so fool-hearty?" She didn't expect an answer.

"I do hope you will not think ill of us, Deborah dear," John read her father's plea set forth in the letter, "and I hope you will at least smile at a little of what has occurred.

"Your Loving Father."

Deborah sighed and turned to the poem:

A Simple Poem Written
To Convince Reverend Josiah Underwood and
Others Like Him of the Wrongness of Their Beliefs
And to Show Them the Purity of Puritanism
By
Reverend Stephen Bachiler
and
Stephen Bachiler, Esquire

Blinded, he trod
on towards hell,
Yet he signed the
cross so well.

"A man of God,
I," he said,
And knew not his
soul was dead.

This minister
Preach'd God's word
though he be sour
as sour curd

We say:

Know thyself 'fore
ye know God,
so ye can show
us where to trod.

He who would not,
could not, see
A deaf ear turn'd
to who'd be:
His Guide to eternal life.

Tree top with leaves
of gold'n hue
Open eyes, ears
Hear me, do

Let go rituals,
false piety.
Embrace our God
in purity.

Bend your knee, sir,
under wood.
Bare your soul, sir,
as thee should.

Prithee, have no
bishop, pope.
Direct from God
comes your hope.

Seek God's holy,
perfect will.
Let His light shine,
seek its thrill.

Our dear Lord Christ,
who work'd with wood,
led the plain life,
said we should
Live like fishers of men.

As Deborah re-read the poem and her father's account of their "terrible deed," she smiled in spite of herself. She could see the humor, but then, she knew her father and brother better than the Reverend Underwood could be expected to know them.

The rub came because the good minister was not amused.

The court did not present Mister Underwood with the hide of the two Bachilers as he'd wished, but their antic was expensive, nonetheless. It cost Stephen Senior a dear sum in fines, and resulted in the expulsion of Stephen Junior from his religious studies at Oxford's Magdalene College. And, Stephen Senior received yet another reprimand from church officials growing increasingly exasperated with the good reverend and his capers.

Deborah and John sat still, neither saying a word. Finally, Deborah looked at John.

"Your father did not show the greatest sense by engaging in this folly," John ventured. "I don't want to hurt you further, Deborah, but I can't help but be irritated with Stephen, if for no other reason, than the pain he caused you. Like I said before, when we talked about Mister Prynne's punishment: this is not the time to make the prelates angry."

Deborah didn't say anything. She was not happy with her father, either, but she would not say a word against him.

"Father is exceedingly fortunate he was able to pay with money and not his ears," she said at last.

"Yes," John replied. "I was thinking those very thoughts."

Chapter 14

Sandwich, Kent
1617
John

A fortnight ago John had received his walking papers from the Crown's Anglican officials. And, like Stephen Bachiler, was told to immediately cease preaching in any Church of England.

"God will not disappoint those who believe in him," he told Deborah as the family ate their breakfast of steaming gruel dished into wooden troughs. He wanted to allay her fears. "If we but have faith, we will be delivered." Neither of them said any more, and the meal was finished in silence.

John rose and shut himself in his study, a small room lined floor to ceiling with books along three walls. On the fourth wall, his desk was centered under the window with panes of thick, wavy glass. Rain pelted against it.

John sat at the desk, holding his head in his hands. His stomach muscles ached from worry about how he would provide a roof over his family's heads and food on their table. He had never felt so alone.

"Love thy enemies," he said aloud as he thrust himself from his chair, turned and knelt in front of it, his eyes squeezed tight and fingers knotted together. "Dear God in heaven," he prayed, squelching a sob, "it's not easy to love those who have placed my beloved family in physical jeopardy. They have done no wrong."

John knew that to not love thy enemies would place his spiritual soul in jeopardy of hell's fiery flames for all eternity.

Englishmen across the land were experiencing financial difficulties, but that didn't make his worries any less. In fact, he felt even more vulnerable.

The textile industry was plunging toward a depression, casting bleakness throughout England. Everyone was affected, not just cloth workers. When one group suffered such a loss, the entire country would feel its effects: textile employees hadn't the money to buy produce to stave off their hunger, which caused farmers to be hard-pressed to raise their lease money to pay their landlords. It was not a time to lose one's job, not even that of a clergyman—especially when Anglican rulers barred their church doors to reformation-minded Puritans. John was concerned. How would he provide for his family?

Heavenly Father, please take this cup from me, he prayed. *Guide me in the way you would have me go.*

He rose from his kneeling position to see a figure cross in front of the window.

Mister Edward Ford knocked on the Wing door that bleakest of mornings. And altered the course of the family.

John hung the sopped coat of the visitor, and first-meeting amenities exchanged, the two men removed to the study. John's unexpected guest was Edward Ford, a well-known, well-to-do London businessman much the same age as John. He spoke right to the point:

"Mister Wing, I am a member of the Merchant Adventurers. I don't know how much you know of us, but we feel as called to our service as you to yours. Our mission is to provide our fellow Englishmen with bargains from around the world. Today's English citizens are no longer satisfied with only goods manufactured at home, and we Merchants provide diverse and sundry items we find on our travels."

Dear God, John thought, surprised at the lecture he was hearing. *I pray there is a rationale behind this man's visit.* John's weariness was becoming acute. He stifled a yawn. *Please, Father; do not let me nod off. He felt his eyes lose their focus. He blinked. Keep me awake, Father. And alert.*

"Everyone benefits, Mister Wing," Ford continued. "We Merchants make a living abroad, providing England's shoemakers with bristles to ply their craft. Wives in every hamlet in every county use our pots and brushes to keep house. Princes buy our imported cloth to be made into the finest clothing available. Every year, we Merchants ship home thousands of bolts of white cloth, colored cloth, and the finest kersey for garments of twilled wool, or for hose and trousers."

John's guest sat in front of the study's window. Where there had been clouds, now sunbeams now streamed in through the window and high-lighted the shoulders of Mister Ford's splendid suit of clothes. John wondered who the man's tailor might be. *Father would have been impressed with his bearing. Father.* John automatically straightened at the thought of Matthew.

John wished he knew Mister Ford's purpose in calling. Every English citizen knew of the Merchant Adventurers, their power, their money. He needed no history lesson, and he could not endure much more. The weight of other things—personal, vital things—bore down on him. Things like, *What on Earth am I going to do now?*

Edward Ford continued on, innocent of the knowledge that John feared he and his family were headed pell-mell to the ragged edge of catas-trophe. In his dreams, John would hear the clank of booted footsteps as soldiers arrived to cart him off to debtor's prison. He would jerk upright in bed, drenched in the sweat of his miserable dream, panting for breath.

John now breathed deeply. He squirmed. His patience was spent. He could no longer listen. Abandoning any gentlemanly code of ethics, John interrupted: "That's very nice, Mister Ford. I don't dispute..."

"Just a moment longer, please, Sir," Edward said. "I am coming to my point."

John reneged and Mister Ford continued. "However many miles and oceans away from our homeland we roam, we are first and foremost Englishmen. It just happens that we must, by necessity, live abroad. We are and always will be true and loyal to England's Crown. Not only do we swear our allegiance and revere our native land, but no matter where we are, Mister Wing, we worship our Almighty God in the same manner as we worship him at home."

These words piqued John's interest. He leaned forward in anticipation, elbows on knees, frown lines in his forehead replaced by a quizzical look.

"In fact, we spare no cost to hear God's word delivered in our native tongue," Ford said. "It is important enough for us—we lowly merchants and followers of our Savior and our Sovereign—to tax ourselves to enjoy that privilege."

John was now keenly interested in what this man had to say, this well-dressed stranger who might, indeed, hold the promise of salvation from his dilemma.

"Merchant Adventurers have long entertained godly and learned preachers with liberal stipends and other benefits to ensure we worship abroad in the same manner as at home."

John nodded. *Yes. Indeed.*

"Which, Mister Wing, brings me to the reason for my visit. We would like to extend an invitation for you to minister to our group of Merchant Adventurers in Hamburg."

John's mouth went dry. Dry as the sand on the Sinai Desert. He tried to swallow. Nothing happened.

"We have heard positive reports of your ministry, Reverend Wing, and we are well aware of your—forgive me—your predicament with Anglican officials. That matters not to us. We feel you and your message will suit our liberal group of Protestant men in the best of manner."

John smiled cautiously. When the conversation that would change the course of his life had begun just a short while earlier, John's lips had been drawn tightly over his teeth. Now, he dared to smile.

When Mister Ford (*an angel without wings?* John wondered) excused himself to attend to other business in town, John folded the Merchant Adventurers' contract and placed it in the breast pocket of his coat. He patted the pocket and rested his hand where it was, above where his heart beat, and thought, *I am going to like you, Mister Edward Ford. I imagine we will one day be fast friends. I believe 'tis foreordained.*

"This is surely God's doing," John said to Deborah, closing the door behind the departing guest. "Indeed, 'twill be perfect; 'tis truly an answer to prayer."

*   *   *

Deborah

That night, John and Deborah sat before the fireplace in silence. The room was lit only by the light of the fire.

"Deborah, why so quiet, my dear?" John asked, taking her hand into his. "Can you not see this is truly a gift from God?"

"John," Deborah said, measuring her words, "I do not for a moment doubt God's bounty or your appreciation of it. It's just, of a sudden, everything is happening so fast. What do we really know about this Mister Ford? How do we know that what he says is really so? What if we move to Germany and hate it? Or, what happens if the Merchant Adventurers pull up stakes? Then, where will we be?" Deborah took a breath and calmed herself. She lowered her voice an octave and spoke quietly: "John, I know 'twill all work out for the best, but I cannot help but be a bit apprehensive."

"Deborah," John said, his voice rising with excitement, "the Merchant Adventurers are the very men to understand the message your father and I, and others like us, are trying to get across. These countrymen of ours, engaged in world trade, are direct in their dealings with other business-men. They have no time for intermediaries. They have no 'bishops' in their business lives, just as we Puritans want no bishops in our religious lives. They deal directly with the man at the top in their operations, just as we advocate doing with God."

Deborah turned to watch her husband as he continued. It had been months since she'd heard such animation in his voice.

"Yes, these Merchant Adventurers are our kind of people, Deborah. They will support our doctrine. They acknowledge the purity of Protestantism and are well aware of the dangers of the Pope and that we must guard against allowing popery into our churches and our country."

The fire cracked and sparks flew up the chimney. John watched them. "I am truly sorry, my loving wife, that we must leave England. I know 'twill be difficult."

Deborah blinked. *Heavenly Father,* she prayed in her heart, *be with me. Guide me. Guide my thoughts, my words.* She sat silently a moment longer and then quietly said, "John, we will be just fine." She desperately did not want her voice to betray her inner-self. If ever she wanted to be strong, it was now. "You have been called by God to witness to the uttermost parts of the Earth and we—the children and I—are privileged to go with you." She feared her heart would trip itself up, it was beating that fast. *Dear God,* she prayed where she sat, *I truly mean those words, but I ask for the power to carry them through. I pray for strength that I might be a stronghold for my husband.*

*   *   *

John

"I'm coming," John scolded as he stepped over and around the wooden crates to answer the insistent knock at the door.

How is it possible, he thought, *for a family of five to need so many crates to hold its goods?* Irritated, he opened the door.

"Yes?"

"Beggin' yer pardon for the intrusion, Guv'ner," said a short, aging sailor with more teeth missing than not. "We've come for your goods, my mate and me."

"Yes, yes," John said. "We've been expecting you. They're just here, ready to go."

In a few hours, the Wings would cross the English Channel in their move to a new world.

Chapter 15

Crossing the Channel
1617
John

Reverend Little, Stephen Bachiler's nemesis, was at the Sandwich Port to see John Wing and his family depart. He and his companion, the Reverend Chitburn, presented a comical sight. It would have made Stephen Bachiler guffaw right out loud. Little was a mere shadow to Chitburn's towering frame. Little tried—but failed miserably—to add height to his slightness. He paid the bootmaker to add extra leather on the heels; he wore the tallest of hats and was constantly shifting his shoulders backwards and upwards, urging them to grow taller. He puffed out his chest.

But his most pathetic try for stature was stretching his neck, lifting his slight, quivering chin, pointing it towards heaven.

The dock at Sandwich in Kent County teemed with people, traffic, and noise, including the high-pitched, plaintive cries of sea gulls screaming at one another over a stolen bite of fish. The pungent smell of fish was as overwhelmingly present as the non-stop squall of the birds.

"Here comes the Lord Mayor," Deborah said, nudging John in the ribs, which wasn't easy as three-year-old John Junior clung to the folds of her dress on one side, with Deborah standing as close as possible on the other side, all the while cuddling baby Daniel in her arms.

Mayor Peke tipped his hat to Deborah before speaking to John. "We are so very sorry to see you leave, Reverend, " Peke said as he shook John's right hand and clasped his arm. "'Tis a sorry day for all of us, John. I pray you won't forget us and will return as quickly as you can."

"Thank you, Mayor," John said. "You will never know what you being here

means to me. I appreciate your support."

"Are you certain that leaving is the best thing for you and your family? That it's what God wants for you?" the mayor asked. "I know you have thought this out every which way, but England is losing so many of its finest men with this flood of ministers crossing the channel.

Deborah excused herself to visit with other well wishers surrounding them.

"There's not much else we Puritan ministers can do," John said to the mayor. "Until we have a new monarch, there are few other choices."

As the mayor took his leave, Deborah rejoined her husband. "John, look," Deborah said. "There's Goody Hilliard." Deborah and John left their children in the care of a woman parishioner and hurried to the Deborah's surrogate mother that taught Deborah about childbearing and presented John with his first child.

"Oh, my beloved daughter in Christ," Emma told Deborah as she wrapped her arms around the young woman. "I just had to come and tell you goodbye and Godspeed." She hugged Deborah so long and so close to her ample bosom that John feared Deborah might suffocate.

John patted the elder woman's shoulder, encouraging her to release her hold on his wife. "'Tis exceedingly good of you to come all the way from Rochester to see us off," he said.

"Here, Deborah," Goody Hilliard said, pressing a cloth bag with the pungent smell of mixed herbs. "Here are starts of herbs for you to plant in your new home. The sweetest of them all is for the bond between thee and me. Rosemary, the herb of remembrance."

John and Deborah both choked back tears. *Is this right?* John wondered. *How can I ask Deborah and the children to wander around Europe with me? Ought I find another craft and stay here?*

Emma's voice brought him out of his momentary dilemma. "Deborah, take good care of yourself and those darling chicks of yours, and," she said with a wink to John, "that lovely husband. Ye are a fine young woman, Deborah Wing, and I know God will be with you. We will pray for you always." Tears spilled over her fat, rosy cheeks.

"You will always be special to me, Goody Hilliard," Deborah whispered in her friend's ear. "You have been a second mother to me. God bless thee."

"Come Deborah, we must go," John said urgently, and the two turned to walk towards the gangplank, which would take them from solid ground across a gap of water, on to the ship—and a new life.

"John," she said quietly, but with a hiss, "don't look now, but there's Reverend Little with another man. What are they doing here?" John heard the bitterness in her voice.

Of course John turned to see. "You're right," he said. "He's with Milton Chitburn, another Puritan-hater. They're here, don't you know, to see this pestilent preacher and his family walk the plank and board the ship that will take us out of our country—and their hair." His hoarse whisper spewed undisguised rancor.

"What drives these men that they would so detest you and father," she asked, expecting no answer. "How can these two hate-filled men claim to be God's Christ-filled emissaries, attending to God's business? Their being here is nothing short of menacing."

They did hover like buzzards, circling, circling, circling, never letting their prey out of sight. They salivate until the moment is ready for the picking.

"Don't let them see you looking at them, Deborah," John said. "Don't give them the satisfaction of seeing any inner turmoil."

Just as they were boarding, Deborah cried out, "I heard Father, John. I'm sure of it." They searched the sea of faces until at last they spotted him, his height towering above all others, hurrying towards them, waving his hat and bellowing from the depths of his rich bass vocal chords.

The little family turned and made their way back to shore, despite complaints from those anxious to shove off.

"'Tis only by God's grace I made·it before you sailed," her father said, panting.

"Where's Mother?" asked Deborah, her eyes filled, as she swallowed a sob.

"She couldn't make the hurried trip," was the reply. "I only just heard you were indeed departing this day. She's well, Daughter, and bids you Godspeed. John, son, I couldn't let you leave the country without wishing you well…" Deborah had never heard him speak so fast, but time was limited and he had lots to say. "I know this expulsion is difficult for both of you, but it must be God's will. Remember that we are not to seek our will, but the will of our Father who is in heaven. I will pray daily for all of you, my children. And John, I will do my part, here at home, to make our cause known howsoever I might." He folded Deborah into the great warmth of his enormous arms and kissed the top of her bonneted head. "God love thee, Daughter." His voice choked.

"Oh, Father, I am so grateful you came," Deborah said, even as John was pulling her away. "I couldn't bear the thought of leaving England without a proper goodbye to you. Please tell my mother that I will think of her every day."

Then, at last, John, Deborah and their three tykes boarded.

Standing at the ship's railing, John and Deborah saw Stephen broadly wave his hat, and heard him cry out his blessing: "May the good Lord cause his eyes to shine upon you."

With the next blink of an eye, a scene appeared that made both John and Deborah laugh through their tears. They watched Reverend Bachiler back up, sending Little into a sprawl, his hat sailing. Stephen retrieved the hat and started to ask forgiveness of the unfortunate soul he had bumped into, unaware of just whom his victim was.

Bachiler and Little righted themselves and stared at one another. Neither moved nor spoke. Finally, Little snatched his hat out of Stephen's hands, backed up a step, swiveled on the ball of his foot and stomped off, stumbling from the awkward elevation of his shoes.

"Chitburn must be puzzled at this absurd puppet-show," John said to Deborah, as he saw the man looking first at his departing associate and then at the scowling Stephen. He shrugged his shoulders and followed his mishap of a colleague.

The final scene of the drama faded from the couple's sight, the forward movement of the ship closing the curtain.

*   *   *

"You've heard of wandering minstrels?" John asked Deborah. The two had been silent ever since they left England's shores. They stood, mesmerized by the choppy water as the ferry plowed through the waves across the English Channel to the Continent. "Well, my dear, I'm now a wandering minister. 'Tis not exactly the same, but there are similarities: Through their antics and singing, misguided minstrels seek to entertain and enrich the lives of their audience. However, ministers, through prayers and preaching, bring the Gospel to enrich the lives—and souls—of their congregation and others."

John tried to check his bitterness, but there was no disputing his anger. Love thy enemy. Turn the other cheek. Do unto others… It seemed every appropriate Scripture flooded his thoughts unsought, as though his subconscious was determined not to allow his soul to slip into bleakness. Despair is, after all, a sin.

John felt betrayed, hurt. Discouraged. But he remained stoic. His stance as rigid as always, his face as stern.

Deborah placed her hand atop his. "I wish I could make you feel better," she said. "I do love you, John Wing." She hugged his arm.

"Actually," John continued as though she had not spoken, "this could very well be the adventure of a lifetime."

He stilled himself and patted her hand. His mouth opened and more words were said of their will, not his: "It won't last forever. We will one day be welcomed home again. And our time in Europe will, of course, be exactly what we make of it. 'God helps those who help…'"

John's voice dropped before he ended the cliched homily. The words, written centuries ago by an anonymous God-inspired man, held good advice all right, but he wearied of the running commentary designed to make him feel good. He'd feel better in the morning. He'd see to it. But at this moment he wasn't ready to ease the sting inflicted because his theology differed from royalty.

His: plain, independent, down-to-earth with no bishops as intermediaries.

Royalty's: regal, full of idolatry, pomp and circumstance with a hierarchy headed by the Crown.

"'Tis like gnawing at a sore tooth," John rationalized to Deborah. "You desperately want relief from the pain, but still you bite down on that tooth and chew at it, knowing full well you are only aggravating it."

John's ego was assuaged knowing other ministers had also been banished from England. Non-conforming ministers by the score were being driven from the country, like St. Patrick drove the snakes into the ocean. At least John had been hired by the Merchant Adventures and had a church to welcome him. He had a position. A destination. Others weren't so fortunate. They truly would wander.

"John," Deborah said quietly, "you know that I will be beside you, wherever you go. I will be thy helpmeet Looking on the bright side, my dear husband, 'twill be exciting to visit the countries and cities we know about only from textbooks. What an education our children will have, to learn these things first-hand. I'm grateful Father insisted that his daughters receive the same early book learning as our brothers. Too many of my friends were taught only how to cook, sew and keep house—how to be proper ladies and dutiful wives. But Father insisted we learn how to read, think a problem through or tot a column of figures."

"You will be well able to teach our youngsters should English-speaking schools or tutors not be available," said John.

Puritans insisted their children learn to read, so they could pore over the Bible's inspired pages for themselves and personally learn about God's covenant and how to apply it in their day-to-day lives. The Bible, after all, was the infallible guidebook on how to establish God's kingdom on Earth. Written between that book's covers was all any man or woman needed to know about how to obtain salvation and how to live so the good Lord would shine his eye upon him and his.

Every man, woman and child had a calling and it was up to that man (or woman) to continually strive for improvement for God's glory.

Clearing his fog-clouded mind, John said, "You know, Goodwife Wing, 'tis both a blessing and a curse to have my abilities considered such a thorn in King James' crown that they think me a threat. Yet, at the same time, it's those very same talents that attracted the attention of the Merchant Adventurers." He thought a moment. Then: "Why do you suppose the Crown and his men are afraid of us—me, your father and other Puritans? I don't understand." He shook his head. "I truly do not understand. If they believe themselves to be right and are truly acting under God's instructions, then a preacher as insignificant as I could surely do them no harm. 'Tis not the Puritans' intent to harm the King. And, we do not want to separate ourselves from the Crown or the Church as the Separatists have done." John sighed. "We only want compromise. Why can't the Anglican governors see that?" Again, he said, "I don't understand."

They watched the sea part as their ship sailed toward the coast of France.

"Deborah," John said, sounding a bit melancholy, "I thank God that you have come to be a partner in our relationship. Not 'just' a wife. I have come to appreciate your keen mind. You are indeed your father's daughter: intelligent, witty, full of perseverance—and not a little stubborn. I see now that, without formal thought, I have made you my confidant."

"Thank you, John," Deborah said quietly. She tucked her arm into the crook of his, and laid her head against his shoulder. Regaining her composure, Deborah said, "John, I don't know how many times I have heard you say 'natural man cannot understand the nature of the Spirit.' Well, it seems to me that King James and the yes-men around him do not understand that Spirit, and they are afraid of you and others like you because you fill people with the Spirit of God.

"That is what makes them afraid, John," Deborah said. "You have found the Spirit of God and are helping others to find it."

John digested what she said. "My dear wife, you are quite wonderful. You do realize that don't you?"

The voyage across the channel was a time for reflection. The Wings left one life at home on the eastern shore of the waters and were about to begin another life on its opposite coast.

"If my congregations hadn't grown so rapidly and if my sermons had stayed within the Anglican confines, we might not be in this situation today," he said, staring at the white-capped water. "Still, it was my intent—my calling—that my message be heard by others."

Deborah, with tremors in her voice, said, "John, this truly must be God's will. God, in his infinite wisdom, is working through you and others like you."

Warming to their building enthusiasm, John jumped in to finish Deborah's line of thought: "This way, our message will be heard by more than just those in England," he said. "That is the reason for our deportation. You are right, Deborah. We will be fine. We will make new friends in Christ, we will sow new seeds for God in new lands. Yes, God has blessed us with these events. That is how we must look at it. We were preordained to follow this curve in our lives."

"I can't help but wonder where the next curve of our God-ordained road will be, and what it will unfold for us," Deborah said.

I wonder too, Deborah, John thought. *I wonder, too.*

Chapter 16

Holland
1620
Deborah

"For you, my good wife," John said expansively as bright red and yellow tulips tumbled from his arms onto the table. "A Welcome-to-Holland gift from the garden of Mistress Van Blarcom. She picked them for me to give to you as a 'welcome to your new home' gift."

The top half of Deborah was lost in the bottom reaches of a packing crate as she stretched her small frame to retrieve the last of the wooden trenchers.

Strewn around the Wing's new great room were opened and unopened crates which had toted their goods from England to Germany and now to Holland. On any of the room's flat surfaces—table, benches, windowsills—were ceramic mugs, pewter steins, iron kettles and sundry buffers of linens and clothing. So it was an aggravated Deborah who hauled herself to a standing position and brushed aside the strands of dark brown hair escaped from the confines of her cap.

"I wonder if I will ever recover from this latest move," Deborah said before really looking at John. "Of all the moves we've made, I'd say this one from Hamburg in Germany to Flushing, here in Zealand, is the most arduous of all." She was still regaining physical and emotional strength following a stillbirth a few months earlier. And now all this unpacking.

Finally looking at her husband, Deborah gasped as she saw the flowers. "John, their beauty takes my breath away." She drew a brilliant yellow long-stemmed flower up close to breathe in its beauty. A quizzical look crossed her face: "They are most admirable, John, but I wish they smelled as beautiful as they look. Such splendid colors."

"They are regal, aren't they?" John asked.

"They are indeed," Deborah agreed. "What are they called?"

"Tulips," he answered. "They're a relatively new flower, grown only in this country."

Deborah started a search amid the chaos of unsorted dishes to find a vase for the exquisite bouquet.

"Mistress Van Blarcom is a parishioner I met just now at the church," John said. "I think you will take to her."

He paused. Deborah looked at him, questioning the silent moment. Then he smiled, saying, "Wait until your eyes feast upon the church, Mistress Wing. 'Tis built of some of the finest sticks and bricks God ever had made."

Deborah dropped her eyes and tried to repress the little-girl smile that crept onto her face whenever she was embarrassed. She bit the inside of her cheeks to check a giggle and erase her silly grin. She blushed and sank into a straight-back chair next to the table and rested an elbow to prop up her heavy head.

"True, it is in need of some repair," John was saying, "but 'tis a building befitting the deepest wishes of a pastor's wife."

Deborah had never forgotten their newlywed dispute of a decade ago about church versus church buildings, but her face reddened to realize John also remembered, even though neither had ever broached the subject again. Shyly, she raised her head the least bit to look at her husband and was relieved to return his warm smile beaming down on her. True, John is a stern man. Puritanical to the core, but sometimes the warmest smiles she ever saw crossed his face. *'Tis a shame,* she thought, *that your smiles are mostly reserved for the children and me.*

She set about unwrapping crockery as she sat at the table, warming to the conversation with her usually reticent husband who rarely bared much of his soul.

"Tell me what you've discovered on your first go-round of the town," Deborah said, glad to sit and rest a bit. "What do you think about it? Is it what you expected?"

"The congregation," John said, "as we already knew, is largely Englishmen and their families living abroad. For all practical purposes, this church, although it's Dutch Reformed, is Presbyterian in character."

As if speaking to himself, he said, "We have preached God's word to a variety of denominations, haven't we? In Germany, like in Rochester and Sandwich, it was Congregationalists. I suppose it doesn't matter much if the pulpit faces a church filled with Presbyterian, Congregationalists or Puritans. They're similar enough in doctrine. 'Tis a marvelous thing, " he said, smiling at her with false modesty, "that one of my God-given strengths is versatility. All that truly matters is that I—and your father and others like us—be allowed to help build God's kingdom here on Earth. The actual denomination, within reason of course, is not the most important thing."

*   *   *

Travels had widened the Wings' perspective: In England, John ministered to small congregations in small villages, some even without benefit of four walls and a roof. Here, across the Channel, they had lived in some of Europe's largest and most sophisticated cosmopolitan cities where John preached to worldly men of intellect.

From his first years in the ministry, John's popularity as a speaker had grown. Word spread in a broad sweep—including across the Channel it seemed—about the manner in which this son of a Banbury tailor interpreted God's word. His listeners understood his insistence that to do God's will they, must first be filled with the knowledge of that will. Only then, after Christians reformed themselves, could they expect to recreate the church and then assume the ominous task of renewing the rest of the world. Only then could God's will be truly done. But, first things first—and the first step was to look inward.

*   *   *

"You say it doesn't matter where your pulpit is," Deborah said, "but I know you would dearly love to be called to a church with Puritan doctrine, in a place where we could settle into a permanent home."

"Ah, yes," John said. "But, 'tis an elite group I belong to. There are now more than a hundred of us non-conformist ministers who have been exiled—'harried'—from our motherland. These men are well educated and articulate. Without a doubt, they undeniably rank among the most intelligent in all of England."

Deborah found a vase, which she filled with water from the fireplace kettle, not yet heated. She brought the bouquet back to the table where she would unwrap more crockery and listen to her usually reticent husband.

"While none of us like banishment," he continued, "we know that one day we will be rewarded, if not now, here on Earth, then when we meet St. Peter. And, if we must wait until 'kingdom come' for our reward, that's all right because we know our mission is pleasing in God's sight."

"Still," John said, removing a deep-red tulip and inquisitively touched the firm petals, "I do admit to a longing for contemporaries who shared my ideas of Puritan reform. I keenly missed my conversations with your father," he said, looking at her, "when we talked the night away those many years ago in Wherwell." Despite his bravado, John was influenced from the misery of loneliness more than he would admit. Deborah recalled the Sunday when he uncharacteristically revealed his vulnerability in a sermon: "I may fall in judgment," he had said, "and soon slip in some unsound passage while being here alone, in this foreign land, and if I fall, having no one to help me up."

Deborah gently took the flower from John and returned it to the vase.

He smiled at her as he said, "I know that our banishment makes your heart ache as well, Deborah." He looked at her. "You have soldiered your role well as wife of a wandering minister."

Then in a more spirited voice and changing the subject, he said, "The countryside here will remind you of home."

Zealand was a series of flat islands constantly in danger of being reclaimed by the North Sea. They began as a wide, shallow lagoon, which over time filled with river deposits until the area was overgrown, resulting in an enormous swamp. Fragile as it was, there was land enough for the industrious Dutch to expand their cramped living space: They ingenuously installed dikes and canals and developed windmill power to dry out the land.

*　　　*　　　*

Shortly after their arrival in Holland, the Wing family strolled down a lane that turned into a bridge crossing a canal. In England, God's beauty was displayed by a countryside of rolling, lush green hills. Here, in Zealand, they absorbed God's glory through flat green meadows dotted with grazing black-and-white cows chewing their cud on rich grass. The red brick farm buildings with steep tiled roofs were foreign to the simple but intricately thatched roofs of home.

"God's world is beautiful, no matter where you see it," Deborah said.

They watched the sun, hanging heavy in the west, as it disappeared to become a sunrise elsewhere.

"There it goes," John said to the children as the last of the brilliant red ball sank out of sight.

"All gone," said Daniel. "Where'd it go?"

"To the other side of the world," John Junior said. "And tomorrow, it will come up over there," he said, pointing as he turned around.

"Very good, John," said a proud father. "You're learning your lessons well."

To Deborah, John Senior said, "I heard a most remarkable story today. It seems that some people are so astonished when they first see Holland, with its great system of land, water and dikes, that they say, 'God created the water, but the Dutch created the land.'"

Husband and wife smiled at the arrogance of some people.

*   *   *

Many foreigners now lived in this country that gave new meaning to the term "low lands." Holland had become a home away home for thousands of displaced persons from around the world. The Dutch government and its people openly welcomed all those set adrift from their homelands.

Like England, Holland suffered its own Spanish Inquisition, during which tens of thousands of its people fled, scattering to other countries in search of safety and freedom. Philip II of Spain finally admitted defeat to these hard-driving Dutchmen. Enough was enough. He had sacrificed more than three hundred thousand of his own soldiers in the attempt to conquer Holland—"the country nearest to hell," as he sullenly described it.

For eighty years, Hollanders fought for liberty of conscience as well as civil liberty. The war, which some feared would never end, had made this nation wiser, worldlier and more tolerant than their European counterparts. Travels abroad turned them into learned merchants, who, between them all, knew the laws of every European country. The Dutch came to realize it was advantageous for them to open their dikes and their doors to merchants and those who had been religiously persecuted. Race and religion mattered not a whit.

It was incomprehensible to the rest of the world how Lutherans, Calvinists, Anabaptists, Puritans, Jews and Catholics could all live and worship peacefully side by side as they did in Holland, the little patch of Earth some described as a bog rescued from the waters.

Hollanders were honest, to be sure, but they were also skillful. Savvy. They knew religious toleration and open markets would be beneficial, that it would swell the country's population, which in turn, would swell the country's coffers and eventually help make Holland—this little bog of a country closest to hell—the world's richest country.

The Wings found Holland to be a country that offered them a lifeline. Temporarily, that is. A group of Separatists sailing to the New World across the Atlantic was the topic of conversation all over the country.

Chapter 17

Holland
1620
Deborah

"Are the children dressed?"

It was John's urgent voice Deborah heard calling from the next room. She knew that tone well: it was the one he used in his most fervent sermons. John was becoming impatient, but she had one last ringlet to form on her daughter's head. She wound the hair around her finger and brushed the curl smoothly into place.

"Is Father angry?" Deborah Junior asked.

"No, dear, he is simply anxious. This is a very important day for him. Why will this ringlet not stay in a curl?" Deborah fretted as she wrapped it around her finger again, and again tried to brush it into place. Your father is to be ordained as minister of the two churches by the Reverend Mister. John Paget, who is coming all the way from Amsterdam, and by two other clergymen from the city. Deborah, do sit still. The more you wiggle, the more difficult this is."

Once more, she curled the reluctant ringlet around her finger. "Today," she said, her vision filled with only the stubborn curl on her daughter's head, "today, the church will be filled with important people like the burgomaster and other magistrates."

Deborah sat back to admire her work, satisfied at last. "There, now, let me see your curls. Aren't they beautiful?"

The night before, she had tightly wrapped her daughter's hair in strips of rags—so tight, in fact, they pulled Deborah Junior's hair away from her scalp.

"Mother, I think my eyes are going to bulge out," little Deborah had complained.

But this morning, the resulting ringlets were splendid. They bounced when little Deborah skipped around just so they would do that very thing.

John called again.

"Coming, my dear husband. The children are dressed and ready," she said as they joined him. John stood in the middle of the room, brushing lint visible only to him from the shoulders of his black coat before he once again ran the sleeve of his coat across the brim of his tall black hat. It was the coat his father had made all those years ago.

"Goodman Wing, you look most handsome. I am so very proud of you," Deborah said.

"Enough," John tersely responded. "We must be on our way. It would never do to be late today."

My dear, Deborah said silently, *you are nervous. How unlike you.*

"Come, children," she said aloud, "we mustn't keep your father waiting." They wouldn't have; John was already out the door.

As they neared the church, John's long strides put distance between him and his family. Before he could gain any more yardage, Deborah quickened her step, caught up to him and whispered into his ear: "John, as Father would say, 'May the good Lord cause his eyes to shine upon you today.'"

John stopped, turned to his wife and smiled.

It was June 19, 1620, and on this very day, in a matter of a few precious moments, he would be officially ordained as the only English minister in Holland.

"Come, children," he called back to his youngsters.

"Father, do you like my curls?" his daughter asked, bobbing her head. "They are especially bouncy today, don't you think?"

"They are beautiful," John said. He looked at his wife. "You are all beautiful—and not just in God's sight!"

Chapter 18

Holland
1622
Deborah

"The Lord bless thee and keep thee and cause his face to shine upon thee and bring thee peace," the Reverend Wing prayed in benediction with hands raised as he closed the four-hour Sunday service two years after their arrival in Holland. "Amen."

And, with the age-old blessing, John picked up his worn, well-thumbed, leather-bound King James Version of the Holy Bible and descended the elaborately carved, curved stairs from the elevated dais. Although the ornate ornamental carving on the lectern was far too intricate to suit him, it was, after all, a pulpit from which he could praise the Almighty until the day came when he had a church built to reflect the Puritan preference of simplicity.

The gold of the sun was transformed into a kaleidoscope of colors as it streamed through stained-glass windows, each a work of art. John walked down the center aisle, past rows of box pews, whose occupants sat with bowed heads, until he reached the church entry where a parishioner opened the heavy, ornately carved doors onto the afternoon. There he stood to greet his flock as they filed out to finish the day in quiet reflection at home.

The Bible said to keep the Sabbath holy, and working or indulging in pleasure was not a proper way to keep it holy. Like all Puritan women, Deborah prepared simple Sabbath meals on Saturday so their holy thoughts need not be diverted by the task of cooking. More than once John fretted to Deborah that Church of England officials were far too lax in keeping the holy-Sabbath rule. Some Anglican Church members were so brazen as to take buggy rides on a Sunday afternoon. And, even with hefty fines issued against those with the audacity to plow a field on a Sunday, there always seemed to be another laggard who insisted on breaking the rule of solitude and contemplation.

That, according to John and his Puritan compatriots, was more than a sin—it was a slap in the face to God. Relaxing a primary law like keeping the Sabbath holy was just another indication of the need to reform the Church of England.

The young, idealistic minister withdrew his hand from one parishioner to reach for the next.

"Reverend John Wing, my friend, your sermons have only improved during our years apart. 'Twas an honor to be in your congregation today."

"For Heaven's sakes," John said, clasping Edward Ford's hand with both of his. "What are you doing here? Have you moved to Middleberg? It is such a pleasure to see you. I have missed you sorely. Deborah," John said, looking at his wife as she greeted parishioners along side her husband, "look who is here. Tomorrow, sir, I hope to see you and enjoy a long visit."

"Tomorrow," Edward said.

And on to the next hand.

"That was a formidable sermon, Pastor," Hans Van Blarcom said in parting.

"Deborah, please come to tea tomorrow," Catharina Van Blarcom said. "Say, four o'clock?"

The women were fast friends. They reveled in a closeness that began the day Deborah called at Catharina's home to thank her for the welcoming flowers. The tulips had brightened the topsy-turvy room, lifted Deborah's weary spirits and seeded a friendship that grew to full blossom.

*   *   *

Deborah and Catharina sat in the Van Blarcom's garden with its great expanse of lush, green grass growing to where a canal edged their property. The women watched as punters poled boats up and down one of Holland's many water highways. A breeze lazily rotated the slats of a nearby windmill, causing it to groan as it completed one turn after another. Deborah's three children and Catharina's four played while the women visited—the girls dressing and undressing their soft, cloth dolls with painted china faces, and the boys romping around them, astride hobby horses. The ability to roughhouse was restricted by the children's clothes. Dressed nearly identical to their parents, they looked liked miniature adults.

The women had talked their way through the weather, child-rearing, shopping, managing a household…Now they sat silent, soaking in the warmth of the sun and the beauty of the scene spread before them.

Quietly, Deborah said, "God truly blessed us—me—when he called John to Holland, and me to you."

"No more than he has blessed me, bringing you here," Catharina replied, looking closely at her friend.

"Catharina, I am learning so much from you," Deborah said in a rush. She paused. Seventeenth-century women didn't often share more than surface emotions with one another and Deborah was a bit uncomfortable. Openness was not characteristic for her. Her mother—and most of her mother's friends, female servants of God whose Earthly purpose was to fulfill the wishes of the Almighty, and their husbands—suffered in silence. To do otherwise was to risk being a shrew, and Deborah measured her actions according to her mother's pristine example. Yet, today Deborah could no longer be still. Her soul was nagging at her to discuss questions she once relegated to the unthinkable.

"You Dutch women are all so strong," Deborah said. "I know I am a much more capable woman now than I ever was in England, but still," she paused, searching for an example to express her feelings. "I am a fragile white lily compared to you hearty tulips who grow so tall and stand so straight and do it with such glorious color."

"Whatever are you talking about?" her friend asked, abashed.

"Women in this country have so much more…" Deborah faltered. "I don't know…so much more strength and freedom than we English women have. I envy you. Oh, I shouldn't have said that. 'Tis a sin to even think such things, let alone speak them aloud. Christ, the Son of God, tells us to envy not."

Catharina reached over and took Deborah's hand. "Have no fear, Deborah, I will not repeat anything you say to me. Tell me the differences you see."

Deborah thought. She wanted her words to be correct and certainly not sinful. She wanted the Devil to stay out of her mind and out of this conversation.

"For instance," Deborah said, jumping right to the heart of the matter, "in your country, all girls, regardless of their social standing, are educated, right along with the boys. It's true I received schooling, but my learning was not as complete as my brothers. Still, some of the town girls teased me because I could read and write and they could not. It sounds so silly now, but they would taunt me, saying I would never marry because men do not like women to be as smart as they. Of course, they were wrong, but their jeers made me feel different, not a part of them. Here, there is no stigma at being educated."

There was no stopping Deborah now. Her mind was racing so fast that her tongue was hard put to keep up. She would not be stilled.

"The women in this country have as much say about how their households are run as their husbands. In fact, more than one woman in our church, here, is actually the sole manager of the family estate."

"That surprises you?" Catharina asked, herself surprised.

"Of course it does," Deborah answered. "And, the other day I was introduced to a woman poet, of all things. Now, that's truly astonishing. The way this woman poet expressed herself was exquisite; her talent is obviously a gift from God. And then, John was telling me of a woman who lives on the outskirts of town who took over managing the farm when her husband died. She became a farmer!" Deborah shook her head in disbelief of what she had just said. "That certainly would never happen in England.

"Catharina, I hope you won't think this as too personal, but it seems as though you are equal to your husband."

"Oh, I don't know if I'd go as far as that," Catharina interrupted.

Deborah smiled and continued: "Goodman Van Blarcom truly does not mind when you voice your opinion, does he?"

"Oh, dear me, I should hope not," Catharina said with a laugh. Catharina was a tall, sturdy, big-boned blond woman whose braids crossed one another atop her head. "Hans and I would both have trouble if he did object. What you say is true. We Dutch women are strong women with strong opinions, and I must be able to express mine. To not have my say would build up inside me like so much water behind a dike. I'm sure I would burst."

Deborah felt as though she were about to burst with the questions that infiltrated her mind.

"Here," she asked her friend, "women are taught the intricacies of their husbands' businesses, is that not right? Catharina, ever since I have known you, you have spent much time with Hans in his place of business. You must know as much about making and exporting the china he fires in his kilns as he does. So, heavens forbid, if he were to die, you would be perfectly qualified to run his business—and it would all be legal. Am I correct?"

"Yes, you are correct. We Dutch believe God gave brains to both men and women and that it behooves everyone to use the gifts God bestows upon them. If something should happen to my dear Hans, I would be perfectly capable of assuming his position in the business. I would be able to manage the business and our finances and continue to support myself and our children."

*   *   *

That night, Deborah tucked her children into their beds and stoked the logs in the fireplace so embers would still glow in the morning to re-kindle into fire. She entered the dark of their bedroom where John had only recently retired.

"Husband, are you asleep?" she ventured quietly.

"No," he replied.

She snuffed the candle she carried, took off her day clothes and changed into her nightclothes, pulled back the covers and slipped into bed.

"Catharina and I had a long talk today. About Dutch women and how independent they are." John was quiet. "I admire that strength, John, and I wish I were more like that."

"Deborah," John said, gently pulling her to him so her head rested on his shoulder. She snuggled close. "You are much wiser now than when I married you. I am certainly pleased, because it is an answer to a prayer I have uttered daily on your behalf. You seldom shed those abominable tears these days, and I haven't seen many stray ducklings in our yard of recent years."

"John." Deborah sighed. "That's not what I'm talking about!" Exasperation sharpened her tone, and her eyes snapped in the darkness.

"Yes, I realize that," John replied, sounding properly chastened. "I apologize for being flippant."

"Here, when a man dies," Deborah continued, "his wife can legally conduct family matters and business matters. A man's property is inherited equally among his children, not just by the eldest, like in England.

"It seems to me, John, women are more important here than anywhere else we have lived. They are more than chattel…"

"Chattel!" John exploded. "You think you are…"

"…like so many English women are treated," Deborah finished her sentence. "I'm not saying you treat me in that manner, John—but still, women are more respected in this country." Her voice quieted. Her mother would not have approved of how boldly she was speaking to her husband.

John and Deborah silently mulled the differences between the two countries they called home.

Finally, John broke the silence that was becoming strained.

"Deborah, I, too, admire the capability of our new women friends and parishioners. And I know how hard Goodwife Van Blarcom has worked to learn Goodman Van Blarcom's affairs. There is no doubt a practicality to this business of women assuming men's responsibilities. And, I suppose, if anything should happen to Hans, Catharine would be ready and capable of holding their family intact without having to marry again simply to have someone support her and the children."

He said nothing for a while and Deborah did not interrupt. She liked the path his thoughts were taking and didn't want her words to make him stray.

"Holland has certainly been good to us," John finally said. "My salary is much dearer than I ever dreamed it would be. We live in one of the world's finest cities, I minister in one of the city's finest churches, and our home is in one of its finest houses." John smiled to himself in the dark. "I think my father would be pleased even though he was deeply wounded when I was unceremoniously booted out of England. If he could see our church, our house, our children…He would be pleased, God rest his soul. You see, Deborah," John said, renewed, "there is good in everything that our heavenly father gives us. Even in being separated from our family and home, there has been good. Our stay in the Netherlands has truly been a blessing from God."

Deborah was disappointed that John was wandering from the heart of their discussion. Still, a seed had been planted. She felt at peace with herself regarding her frankness and would be unafraid to bring the subject up at another time. She closed her eyes and slept soundly.

*   *   *

More than a week later—after dinner, after the children were abed—John and Deborah sat in front of the dying fire soaking up the last of its heat and comfort before retiring.

John said: "Remember our conversation of a while back? When we talked about Dutch women? I've given it quite a lot of thought. Without divulging our specific talk, I brought up the subject with Edward and Hans and a few others. I have more keenly observed the women and how they go about their daily business. And, certainly, I've prayed about it."

Deborah waited, expectantly, giving no influence.

John leaned forward and rested his elbows on his knees and locked his hands together. He stared at the last flames feebly flickering while he organized his thoughts to continue the conversation he now wished he hadn't started. Conversation such as this was foreign to John Wing, minister of God, pastor to more than a hundred in his fold. He was master of his household. He was a man in control, called by God to help all souls get right with their maker. But now his enthusiasm for the discussion was waning just like the flames extinguishing themselves to smolder as embers.

"A woman's role in this country is certainly not biblical. But…on one hand it does seem to make sense."

When John began talking, Deborah had looked at him. Now, she avoided any direct eye contact for fear he would stop. She felt as excited as the day he asked her to marry him. Her nose was tightening in anticipation.

"Edward had a point when he said we must take a bit of what we learn from each country where we have lived in Europe and add it to our private lives. And I agree, we must learn from our experiences. Indeed, I feel we must be open to other points of view in some subjects. Still, women were created by God to be man's helper. That is one of the Word's very first lessons."

Silence. Then, "But, on the other hand."

Again, John said nothing. The fire was nearly cold. Deborah saw her husband's face cloud as though he were wrestling with the Devil himself. *What is he thinking*, she wondered. *John, think out loud as you sometimes do.*

She knew it was best to sit silent and wait. After all, she was the woman.

At long last, John solemnly said: "Deborah, if anything should happen to me, I want you to remain in Holland, manage the inheritance and raise our children here."

"John, what are you talking about?" Deborah's reaction was swift. "Are you ill? Don't speak of such things. I want us to grow old together. Please do not ever leave me. Let's talk no more of this. I was wrong to have brought up the subject in the first place."

"Deborah, be still and listen to me," John said evenly. "You would be much better off in this country than in England. The Dutch people are honest, noble people and the leaders of this republic are wise. England could learn much from them."

Disgusted with herself, she wiped away a tear. Why, in heaven's name, could not those tears stay in her head instead of spilling so freely down her face?

"Deborah," John chided quietly. "I have told you time and again to save your tears for something real, something important. There is nothing wrong with me, dear wife. You have jumped to a wrong conclusion. But we never know when God will call us to serve him in heaven. Besides, I do believe," he continued, "that if something were to happen, you are now as strong and able as any of our neighbor women. You could very well carry on without me, not only with raising our youngsters, but also with spreading God's word in your own manner. Goodwife Wing, you are no longer the sweet, innocent young girl I married. While you are still and always will be a female child of God, you have matured into a beautiful woman." He looked at her and smiled. That special smile; the one Deborah so loved—warm and loving.

John poked the fire, took Deborah's hand and led her into the bedroom. Slowly, he undid Deborah's dress, removed it from her shoulders and arms until it fell down around her feet; he watched as she stepped out of her layers of underclothing. He removed the white cap that kept her beautiful thick hair hidden from the world, but not from him. He ran his fingers through her hair, cut short now that she was a woman; he led her to their bed and laid her down. The two slipped beneath the quilt. John leaned over and gently kissed her forehead, her eyes, her cheeks. Her lips. He reached beneath the blanket and ran his hand, uncalloused as a man unused to physical work, over her smooth body that resiliently retained its shape even after all her pregnancies. Deborah turned fully towards him and together they lovingly made love.

Chapter 19

Holland
1624
Deborah

"'Twill be good to see Father again," Deborah said to John as she packed a small trunk of clothing for her, Deborah Junior and three-year-old Stephen for a visit to London and Newton Stacey, where her father had lived ever since his expulsion from the Church of England. "I've been concerned about him ever since Mother's passing," she said, folding a pair of pants for Stephen Junior to romp around in at her father's house. "I know he still wrestles with his grief, bless his heart. Father is unpredictable enough when he's in his 'right mind,' what might he do in a mind that's wrong with sorrow?"

She sighed and stopped mid-fold. "If only he could be comforted by the assurance that Mother gained immediate access through heaven's gates. Surely, John, God would grant his gift of grace to Mother, so saintly and precious, so she wouldn't burn in the ovens of hell."

"Mmmm," John replied.

Deborah continued: "That's one drawback I have with the Puritan faith, saying 'tis more difficult to enter heaven by grace than by good

106

works. No one can ever be assured of an eternal home in heaven unless explicitly chosen by God. You can never be sure. John?"

"Mmmm," John said, so involved he was readying a package for Deborah to deliver in London.

Deborah, too, had been grief-stricken at her mother's death, but it was her father who nearly broke her heart; the image of his shoulders convulsively shaking continued to haunt her. It was frightening to see this giant of a man—her father, her warrior—bought to his knees by her mother's death. Because Stephen struggled so with his loss, it sometimes seemed he was not right in his head—which made Deborah afraid he would muddle his way into another folly.

Deborah returned to packing.

"I'll be pleased to renew the acquaintance of Father's new wife," Deborah said. "It's already a year since Father married the Widow Weare. I think it's a step in the right direction, don't you?"

When John didn't answer—again—she looked up to see him reading the sermon he was suppose to be wrapping.

"John?" Deborah said. "Whatever are you doing? You have read and re-read that sermon time and again. You will wear it out just by looking at it. I thought you were wrapping it."

"Sorry," John said, looking up. "Did you say something?"

"I have been saying something for several minutes," she answered. "Have you not heard a word?" Hearing no comment, she sighed and said, "I was saying what Father needs might well be a woman, a wife, in his life. That might be just what he needs."

"Yes," John answered, back into his project. Deborah knew he wasn't listening, and thought, *Goodness, John*, a *man as smart as you ought to be able to wrap a simple package and talk at the same time.*

Their life—hers and John and their children—was about as perfect as it could possibly be, and she prayed nothing would disrupt it. Life in Middleberg and Zealand had been like moving from night into daylight. Night first blackened their sight as they crossed the English Channel seven years ago. By the time they debarked in France, it was metaphorically so dark they could not see their hands before their faces. Dawn, with its promise of light, rose in Germany, and now their life in Holland was like the great burst of noon's warm sunshine in spring.

Everything is as it should be, thank God. Our little family is growing and thriving. I have a special friend in Catharina. John had good friends in Hans and Edward. Our four youngsters are well and happy. She smiled. *The good Lord's eye is indeed shining upon us.*

When they arrived in Holland, John worked diligently to learn the native language and won a special place in the hearts of the entire city with his translation of the catechism into Dutch. Each Sunday, his congregation swelled as word of his preaching passed from one household to another. Just how that information spread from the commoners' house to royalty's palace, Deborah didn't quite understand, but Queen Elizabeth was often in attendance. Queen Elizabeth, wife of Frederick V, King of Bohemia, now exiled in Holland, was also Princess Elizabeth, daughter of John's foe, King James I of England.

It was an irony not lost on John that the daughter of the man who exiled him was a faithful patron of his church.

City lords and church officials took note of who was in attendance and the building in which she worshipped. In no time, a hundred pounds was raised to repair and beautify the chapel. If royalty was to worship there, then by all means, the building must be worthy of her regal presence.

Likewise, church officials raised John's annual salary from three hundred to five hundred pounds, to "afford him the means of living in affluence," read the document he received with the increased pay.

And now, John's sermons were being printed into books. He was an author! His spoken words were so highly regarded they were being preserved on paper. While it was not unusual for a minister's sermons to be published, that laurel was reserved for the very best.

John dedicated his first printed sermon, "The Crown Conjugal," published by John Hellenius of Middleburg, to the Mayor of Sandwich.

"He was the first government official ever to boost my morale," John told Deborah after he penned the dedication. "He was a friend in deed."

The dedication page for "Crown Conjugal" read:

"To the Right Worshipful Master Matthew Peke Esquire, Mayor of the Town and Port of Sandwich, and to the Worshipful, the Jurates his brethren, the Common Counsel and the whole Corporation of the same John Wing, doth with Grace and Peace and all good from the living God through the love of our Lord Jesus Christ, by the work of the Holy Ghost.

"Your former favors and the abundant fruits of your love (Right Worshipful and well-beloved in the Lord), which I have from time to time experienced, ever since it pleased the Lord to cast affliction upon mine external state, do daily provoke and deeply challenge from me, the manifestation of a thankful heart unto you all, to whose kindness I stand a debtor much engaged to this day."

That first publication was followed by "Jacob's Staff," his farewell sermon to the Merchant Adventurers in Hamburg; and "The Best Merchandise," published and sold by parishioner and friend Martin Abraham vanderNolck of Flushing.

And now Deborah was "commissioned" to serve as John's courier and deliver "The Saints Advantage" to John Dawson who asked to publish and sell it at his London shop—at the sign of the Three Golden Lions.

*   *   *

John handed Deborah his precious package now protected to his satisfaction.

"Here you are," he said. "Now don't forget, John Dawson's shop is right near London's Royal Exchange. You should have no trouble finding it."

"Of course not," Deborah replied. "A sign with three golden lions can't easily be mistaken."

"I will enjoy seeing Father and Ann and Theodate, and finally meeting Christopher Hussey, the young man Theodate's to wed." Her little sisters had grown up without her. "But I will miss you," she said to John. "How will I stand to be away from my little boys while I'm in England? I'm so grateful Catharina will help look after them."

"'Tis only a short while," John said. "We will do just fine. And so will you."

"Truth be told, John, I'll be anxious to return home. I so enjoy our life now."

Yes, life truly is wonderful, Deborah thought. *Yes, the sun is shining.*

John placed a kiss on her forehead.

"And, I, too, will miss you, Deborah." He held her close to him for a moment. "Be sure to ask your father what he has heard about the Dutch settling New Amsterdam in that country across the Atlantic, and tell him I hope we will meet soon to discuss it together."

*　　　*　　　*

Stephen straddled his mother's hip and wiggled against her arm that held him fast.

"I want down," the three-year-old complained.

"Absolutely not," Deborah said as she admonished her daughter, three and ten, "mind where you walk."

"Mother, London is putrid," Deborah Junior said, covering her nose with her gloved hand. "No place in Holland smells like this. I've never seen or smelled anything so putrid."

Putrid, Deborah thought. *That's a new word. I wonder how she came upon it.*

Last night, after docking at Tower Pier on the Thames, Deborah and her children were safely escorted to a close-by hotel on Gracechurch Street. Now they were afoot, searching for John Dawson's shop with its sign of three lions near the Royal Exchange said to be close by.

Besides wrestling with young Stephen, Deborah clutched her husband's manuscript, not wanting either to escape from her care. It was consternation, being in the huge, noisy, smelly—no putrid—city of London; a woman alone with two children, to say nothing of transporting the invaluable paper cargo.

The innkeeper had them walk to the corner, turn left on Lombard Street, which would, in no time at all, have them at the traffic circle where Lombard, Cheapside, Cornhill, Princes and Threadneedle streets intersected.

All right, Deborah told herself, *all I need keep in mind is Threadneedle, which the innkeeper said would be on our right.* It was daunting to envision so many streets converging at one junction. Once on Threadneedle, the next intersection would be Old Broad Street, she'd been told, but they would see Dawson's shop before they reached that corner. His place of business was next to Drapers Hall and across the street from the Royal Exchange. They couldn't miss it.

I certainly hope not, Deborah thought, not feeling at all assured. She wished now they had hired a carriage. The distance was much further than she anticipated.

Walking along cobblestoned Lombard, they peered down side streets and marveled at buildings on either side, whose second-story windows jutted so far out they nearly met in the middle, making for streets perpetually shaded.

"All one would have to do to shake hands with their neighbor is lean out the second-story window," Deborah Junior said.

If the sights were quaint and pleasant, the stench was not. As Deborah remembered from Rochester, the streets here, too, were open sewers. Shopkeepers and homeowners tossed whatever waste they accumulated directly onto the street.

"Owwww Lady, I nearly got ye and yer chillens," one shopkeeper's wife cried as she tossed out remnants of breakfast for stray dogs to scrap over. "Keep yer eyes open, is me advice."

Deborah, Deborah Junior and little Stephen did keep their eyes open—about as wide as they would open.

At last they reached the traffic circle.

"Let's stop a minute and get our bearings." Deborah eased her lively load down and readjusted her package, the wrapping now wrinkled from her damp hands. "Stephen, you stay right next to me. Don't you dare move."

Stephen could hardly hear his mother for the din of horse-drawn carts, wagons and carriages coming from every which way, clipping along much too fast and much too close to the street's edge to suit Deborah. There seemed to be no right way or wrong way, and the traffic traveled howsoever it wanted.

"Look, Mother," said Deborah Junior, pointing, "across the street. Threadneedle. That big building must be the Royal Exchange."

"When our friend Edward Ford is in London, that's where he conducts his business," Deborah Senior said. "There and at the Drapers Hall. How on Earth are we going to get across?" Deborah wondered aloud. She hoisted Stephen back up on her hip, firmly tucked the manuscript under her armpit and took Deborah Junior's hand.

"Mother, I'm not a child. I don't need to hold your hand."

"You may not need to hold my hand, but I need to hold yours—just until we get across."

Finally, the wild wagoneering parted and they darted into the street, hurrying before some oncoming carriages and nervously stopping to wait for others to pass. She stood straight and tall as if to make herself as slender as a quill to avoid the traffic coming too close. Once they safely navigated to the far side, Deborah uttered a silent prayer of grateful thanks.

Sure enough, across from the Royal Exchange, London's busiest building in the world's biggest city, and next to Drapers Hall was the sign she sought, the one bearing three golden lions. It was a handsome sign.

"Goodwife Wing?" Printer Dawson asked as he opened the door to greet Deborah. "I've been keeping an eye out for you."

John Dawson ushered them inside the door, its bells tinkling all the while. The wide-planked wood floor creaked as they entered; dust particles speckled in the sunshine streaking through the front windows, the room's only light. Once their eyes adjusted to the dimness, they saw books everywhere: shelved behind the counter and around the room, lying on low tables, high stools, stacked on the floor.

"Surely you did not walk here," said the man whose shoulders severely hunched beneath his black coat. Looking at the old man, Stephen, high on his mother's hip, cupped his fat little hands around his mother's ear and whispered: "He looks like old bent-over Widow Dunlop."

"Stephen, be still," Deborah hissed, looking apologetically at the shop owner. Stephen took in a sharp breath, which let Deborah know he spied wiry gray hairs springing from a black mole on top of the man's ear. Deborah pinched her son's leg to forestall another comment.

"Never seen anything like that, eh, Sonny?" Dawson growled, tapping his slouched shoulders with the cane he was never without. He'd been the object of staring children before and was used to it, but he still didn't like it. "'Tis from years of setting type and putting it into trays. Don't you be a-feared of it. 'Tisn't going to hurt you."

John Dawson said nothing about his remarkable ear as though he were unaware there was anything unusual about it.

Bug-eyed Stephen continued to stare.

"Now, then, Goodwife Wing," Dawson said, ignoring the boy's probing eyes, "you have something for me, I believe."

Deborah lowered Stephen—who immediately glommed onto her skirt, never blinking, ever staring—and handed John's package to the printer.

"My husband asked me to tell you what an honor it is to have you print and sell this sermon. We have heard many good things about you and the work you do."

"Yes, yes," was the short reply. "I only hope 'tis not too radical like so many thoughts of today's Puritans."

"Oh, I'm sure not," Deborah began, her defenses immediately on guard. "My husband would never…"

But before she could continue, Dawson interrupted: "I've heard a good deal of praise about your husband, Madam. I'm in the business to print and sell books, as you know, and I am assured that both your husband and I should reap great benefits from this manuscript."

Deborah unclenched her jaw and relaxed. John didn't need her protection after all.

The transaction completed, Goodman Dawson fetched a carriage for Deborah and the children. "'Twill not do to have you walk the streets, Madam, not a woman of your stature and certainly not with these children," he said as he helped her into the cab. "Good day to you."

*   *   *

Some days later, a hired carriage reined to a stop in front of her father's home in Newton Stacy. She saw Stephen burst through the door, knowing he must have flung it open at the first sound of horse hoofs. Before they came to a complete stop, Deborah heard her name being called: "Deborah, daughter, 'Tis so good to see you."

A coachman helped Deborah Junior from the carriage. She curtsied to her grandfather, whom she hardly knew.

"My precious granddaughter, how like your mother you look," Stephen said, hugging her. "You bring back fond memories of your mother as a young girl."

After young Stephen scrambled out of the carriage, Deborah accepted her father's hand as she stepped down and into his outstretched arms.

"Daughter, how I have missed you," her father said in a voice swollen with tears.

"And I you," she said. "Are you well?" she asked as she pulled away from her father's embrace.

"Of course I am," he said, wiping his face unabashedly.

"He is just so grateful to see you," a voice next to Stephen said.

"Here she is," Stephen said. "Say 'Hello' to Widow Weare, Deborah. Your new

stepmother."

"Widow Weare?" was Christian's incredulous question. "Stephen, I am now Goodwife Bachiler." To Deborah, she said, "Don't fret about me being your stepmother. We'll just be friends. She extended her hands to Deborah who took them and clasped them in her own.

"My dear, I am sorry," her father said, looking sheepish at his wife and daughter. "I must say I'm beside myself."

When they went to bed that night, Deborah sank onto the feather mattress atop the brace of ropes laced above and under one another from one rail to the other. The ropes must have been made taut for this homecoming occasion.

She snuggled beneath the feather quilt and felt like a child again. Her bed, her mattress, her quilt from her childhood days. Everything around about her was familiar: the warm smell of down and the prickles she felt as feathers tried to work their way out of the casing. She looked at the shadows the moonlight played on her bedroom wall. And, in the morning, she knew she would awake to streams of light coming in through the window. That is, if there were no clouds and rain.

It felt especially good to be in the country after their eye-opening (and nose-plugging) experience in London, followed by the days-long stage ride, which brought her and her children to Hampshire County.

It was reverse of the route she and John took when they were first married. This time she was the protector and not the protected. That felt good.

Yes, she thought, stretching full out, *it's wonderful to be home, but it's strange not to have Mother tuck me in and kneel and say prayers with me as we did for so many years.*

It was even stranger to visualize the Widow Weare, Christian Weare, Christian Weare Bachiler, actually, sharing her father's bed. Her mother's bed!

Even though his children were grown and no longer in need of a mother's attention, Stephen had married again. And Deborah was pleased. She knew he could not fend for himself, not after a lifetime of doing by first his mother and then his wife.

Theodate, her youngest sister, was now twenty and would undoubtedly marry Christopher Hussey, a man with Puritan sympathies who had been courting her and waiting for Father's blessing.

*   *   *

The night before Deborah and her children were to leave, the entire Bachiler family came home for an evening meal conversation. Having eaten to excess, they gathered in Stephen's book-lined library and huddled around the fireplace to warm their bones chilled from the soggy day, and to warm their blood with the brandy-wine Deborah brought from Holland.

Five of Stephen's six children and their children were present, complete with four young Stephens. There was Nathaniel and Hester and their children, Stephen, Anna and Francis; Deborah with Deborah Junior and Stephen; Samuel, the Bachiler family's second minister, and his wife, Honor, and their son Stephen; and Ann and husband John Sanborn, with their three children, John, William and Stephen.

And Theodate was there with Christopher Hussey, who, Deborah was told, often attended family gatherings.

Stephen Bachiler Junior, whose ruckus with his father resulted in his expulsion from Oxford, was now a London businessman and still a bachelor.

Deborah saw her father's eyes grow misty as he looked at the faces of his children and realized anew that these people around his table were a product of him. *We are his creations,* Deborah thought. *And mother's, too, of course. God rest her soul.* Deborah couldn't help but smile at the pride written on his face.

"I can't tell you children how wonderful it is to see such an assembly of Bachilers—and to be blessed with so many Stephens in my humble home. My, my. You realize, don't you, Theodate, that you must name a child of yours Stephen, as well?"

"Father, please," Theodate said, lowering her eyes.

Stephen beamed. "Yes, indeed. And when Stephen Junior marries, he no doubt will name his first son Stephen, and that will make it unanimous. Each child of mine will have a child named Stephen. What an honor and what a blessing."

Father is overwhelming himself, Deborah thought.

He wiped at his eyes with a nose cloth ornately embroidered by Christian.

Christian was even now embroidering as she sat on the settee. *That's where Mother and I sat when she taught me stitchery.* Deborah was smiling at the memory when Christian looked up and met her eyes. Deborah smiled at her and Christian smiled back.

She's a nice woman, Deborah thought. *She's good for Father. I'm sure Mother would approve. I just pray his wandering eyes have been stilled.*

She saw—and heard—her father honk his nose, regain his composure, and say, "'Tis especially pleasurable to have all of you around, now that you are grown and can carry on a decent conversation."

He cleared his throat.

"So, Deborah, tell us what John has to say about Hollanders settling New Amsterdam," Stephen continued. "I am very interested. Yes. Yes, indeed. We all are."

"John asked me to ask you what you have heard," Deborah said, and then told about Protestants from Holland who had established a colony on the banks of the Hudson River and along the shores of Manhattan Island in the country Christopher Columbus bumped into nearly two-hundred years earlier.

Dutch colonists had been unhappy with their settlement in the Roman Catholic territory of Brazil. America would be better, they reasoned, because they wouldn't have to put up with tropical soil, tropical climate—or Catholics.

"They say the soil in America is much like Holland's," Deborah said. "But, more important, John says, is that people can live, work and worship however God leads them."

"I've heard," said Christopher Hussey, "that the climate is very much to the liking of the Dutch—and, therefore, should be very much to the liking of the English."

"Yes, "Deborah agreed. "Our Dutch friends fully expect New Amsterdam to succeed. In fact, Hollanders by the hundreds are sailing for America with every ship that leaves their shores. Or at least, that's what's being said. Entire families are moving—men, women and children—which is a good sign of permanent settlement."

"Children," Stephen said excitedly, "what do you say about our starting a new life in this new England? I think it sounds like something God would lead us to do. If we can't spread the true word here, well then, over there to all those who cross the water."

No one answered him. "Well, let's think it over, shall we?" Again no one answered. "We'll pray about it."

Later that night, after the entire house was asleep, Deborah heard a noise downstairs and went to have a look. There was her father, still in the study, staring into the fire. He poked it, added another log, poured himself another brandy. *His mind must be galloping faster than any horse in Hampshire County could possibly travel,* she thought. *I'm not sure I like the direction I think his mind is taking.* She looked at her father and realized just how much he had aged since her mother died. On her retreat to the bedroom, Deborah prayed, *Heavenly Father, please tell me that immigration is not the only way.*

Chapter 20

London
1630
John

John stood in front of St. Paul's Cathedral and watched as workers razed the houses and shops that had been build smack against the cathedral. Noise and dust filled the air as the shanties were knocked down, some board by board, their wooden pegs hammered out in a time-consuming effort. Others, more vulnerable buildings, came crashing down in a thunder of confusion, pulled apart by a straining team of horses.

"Mind your heads," a warning yell would sound as a building began to collapse in a heap of rubble. "She's a topplin'." With each dismantling, a roar of approval rose from the "Gentlemen's Gallery," where men gathered to supervise. On some days, even the noble John Donne, dean of St. Paul's could be seen in the crowd, watching as his beloved cathedral assumed a new shape.

*   *   *

Two years' hence, upon the death of Donne, one of England's most beloved poets and priests, a full-length effigy would be built in his honor. The Arms of the Dean and Chapter would be combined with Donne's Arms to adorn the top of the monument. It would be St. Paul's only memorial to survive London's Great Fire of 1666.

*   *   *

John Wing watched one cold spring morning in 1629 as steam snorted from the horses' nostrils and from the mouths of cheering spectators. He was fascinated with the unorganized chaos unfolding before him. Had there been some organization, perhaps a bigger profit could have been realized from the demolition. Among the paid crew were thieves, used to working in the dark of the night who now risked life and limb in broad daylight to swipe a board or two, or as many as they could possibly carry off in a dead run. The lengths of wood would bring a good coin from the right customer, or, if nothing else, would build a right cheerful fire in a man's home.

St. Paul's had fallen into a disgraceful disrepair since the Reformation during the reign of King Henry VIII. Now merchants brazenly hawked their wares on the cathedral steps and horses were disrespectfully led through the church of God, down the long nave known as "Paul's Walk," their hooves slipping on marble floors, filthy with the animals' waste. Services were confined to the old choir loft.

But last year, King James named Inigo Jones, England's noted architect, as the King's Surveyor, and the cathedral was once again undergoing restoration. The first order: tear down the eyesore shanties that clung to the church walls like barnacles on a ship's belly.

It was the architect's intention to remove the medieval tracery with its lacy openwork and encase the same with square stone blocks of ashlar masonry and windows of the classical style.

He also planned to alter the west front by removing the Norman entrances and erecting a splendid portico in the elegantly ornate Corinthian style.

And there was much patchwork to do, much strengthening to do. The cost would total at least the colossal amount of one-hundred-thousand pounds.

How many churches have been built on this very spot, John wondered as he looked at the immense edifice only a few blocks from his new London home. A church had sat atop Ludgate Hill since the time of the Saxons in 604. Through the centuries many succumbed to fire, and conquering warriors destroyed others. But the ashes of one charred church were barely cooled before construction was begun on another.

Acknowledging the cathedral's staying power, Ingio Jones ordered the word "Resurgam" carved into store: "I shall rise again."

As a Puritan who had literally given his all to the establishment of worshipful simplicity, John could only shake his head at the bedeviled act of reconstruction played out in front of him.

"What folly to spend so much money on such ornateness," he muttered to no one in particular. He leaned on his study walnut walking stick, a going-away gift from his Zealand congregation. Both his white-gloved hands, one on top of the other, covered the stick's silver-plated crown.

"Don't these fools know the sin of idolatry? Do they not know golden domes are no better than Aaron's golden calf?"

"John? John Wing? Is that you?"

John turned and there stood his old friend Edward Ford. The two men embraced and clapped on another on the back.

"By my leave. However have you been?" Edward asked, and without waiting for an answer, continued, "I'd heard you were moving to London, but I had no idea you were already here. When did you arrive, and are Deborah and the children with you? Let's see, how many children do you have now?"

The men edged their way out of the crowd and its din.

John laughed. "We have five children, my friend, and they're all enjoying good health, God be praised. Matthew, our youngest, is three. And Deborah, our eldest you remember, was only recently wed to a fine young man, Adam Millsap, a Londoner who was a member of my congregation in Flushing. They will live here, now that he's been transferred back home.

"You are only recently returned to London, yourself, isn't that right?" asked John.

"Yes, indeed. I've been out of the country for such a long spell, and I can tell you, 'tis wonderful to be back home."

Edward stopped and looked solemnly at his dear friend. "I guess I don't have to tell you how wonderful that is, do I, John? Come, let me buy you a cup of coffee."

The two friends made their way to the nearby coffeehouse, The White Horse, crowded with others of the same mind. Coffeehouses were quite the thing in seventeenth-century England. Wits and writers gathered regularly to exchange puns and pleasantries. Business transactions were conducted in coffeehouses, the places to see and be seen.

At last John and Edward found a table, removed their tall hats and placed them on adjoining chairs; they removed their gloves finger by finger and laid them atop their hats and placed their order.

"So, bring me up to date," Edward said. "What are you doing? How did you happen to return to England and what are your plans?"

John laughed. "So many questions." His laughter brought on a coughing spell.

"Are you not well?" Edward asked.

"'Tis but a cough, remnants of a bad cold I caught a fortnight ago," John replied. "I've not been out much since then. Deborah has kept me close to home. But, finally, I said I had to go for a walk. I needed to stretch my legs. And I am so glad I did," he said, beaming at Edward. "It is truly a blessing to see you, my friend. How long has it been since we last saw one another, since you left Holland?"

"A little more than three years. Before Matthew was born. So, John, are you going to join the emigrants sailing to America? Is that what your being in London is all about? Or, has the King rescinded your banishment?"

John was silent. Then, "Yes, Edward, we are going to America, and yes, I was granted permission to return home to make those plans." John's face had clouded with the word "banishment." "Deciding to go—to sail across the Atlantic to a foreign land, an unsettle land, so far from England—was a difficult decision," John said. "Probably the hardest I have ever made. But Deborah's father is bound to go. He's formed a company—the Plough Company—and they have a land grant up north, in Maine.

"Reverend Bachiler is no longer a young man, you know. He's eight and sixty this year."

Again John was silent. He took a deep breath that caused another bout of coughing.

"I owe him so much, Edward," John said after he returned his nose cloth to its inside pocket, trying to hide the bloodstains. "Stephen taught me much. He was my mentor. And, he is the father of my dear wife, the man who allowed me to wed his beautiful daughter. Actually," John said with a laugh, "I think 'twas as much his idea as mine that we marry. Stephen Bachiler is as dear to me as my own departed father.

"Edward, he's been so abused by the Anglicans," John said, shaking his head. "I cannot tell you how badly. He has not had a proper pulpit to call his own for years, yet he has a faithful congregation of followers. And they're going to sail to America with him.

"All the man wants to do is save souls," John said. "So, I guess if he wants to save souls in America, the least Deborah and I can do is go with him and support him. I'm certain there will be enough souls for me to even save a few" He coughed again. A wrenching cough.

"Do you want me to walk you home?" Edward asked, concerned.

"No, no. I'm fine."

"I heard that Reverend Bachiler has married again," Edward said tentatively.

John smiled wryly. "'Tis true, but don't say anything about it in front of Deborah. She's not very keen about the new Goodwife Bachiler. The third Goodwife Bachiler."

"Why's that?"

"You mean your source didn't fill you in on all the particulars?" John asked. Edward shook his head. Of course, he had heard, but, gentleman that he was, he didn't want to own up to it.

John continued: "Stephen's second wife died after they'd been married but three years. She'd only passed over a year when Stephen took a new wife, the widow Helena Mason. She's six and thirty, which makes her junior to Stephen by three and thirty! Two years younger than Deborah."

Edward tried to hide a smile behind his coffee cup. He swallowed and wished he hadn't. Now it was his turn to cough.

"We've met her," John said, ignoring Edward's embarrassment, "and she seems a nice-enough woman. It's just that she's so young."

John looked at his friend whose face was slightly contorted with a crooked smile.

John grinned at his friend. "'Tis perfectly all right to smile, Edward. It really can't be helped. But not in front of Deborah. She sees no humor in the situation at all."

John coughed again.

"Come," Edward said. "I want to walk you home and say hello to Deborah and meet the newest little Wing."

Chapter 21

*London
1630
Deborah*

"Goodwife Wing," Doctor Millstone said gently, "Come and sit down."

They had just left John's darkened sick room and stood now in the kitchen, flooded in bright summer sunshine.

Deborah blinked, readjusting her eyes from the light-less room where her husband lay so still. She blinked again. Her eyebrows knitted in a frown, as if to say, how can the sun possibly shine? It ought to be a somber, rainy day. A day when a solid slate sky continuously weeps a penetrating mist.

"There, now, Goodwife Wing," Doctor Millstone was saying. His voice was so quiet. Deborah looked at him and thought, *why doesn't he speak louder? I can hardly hear him. What is he saying?*

"I am sorry to tell you, madam, but your husband is dying. He has improved not an iota since I saw him yesterday."

"Really?" Deborah said, surprised she could actually speak. Ignoring the first part of the doctor's remark, she said, "I thought he was some better."

"In fact," the apothecary said, "he is worse. I regret having to say this, but he will not recover from this terrible cough."

"Oh, I'm certain he's not worse," Deborah replied testily. She was appalled that this Doctor Millstone thought John was worse. *Of course he was better. A little better. What is this man saying? He is saying horrible things. Why is he saying these things?*

Her frown deepened. She rubbed the temples of her head.

The doctor spoke again, gravely: "'Tis only a matter of days, or maybe even hours, until he passes over."

Deborah focused her eyes anew at the man. His words would not register in her mind. It had been so long since she had slept even as long as a cat naps. Her brain refused to function. She looked squarely into the gray eyes of the person sitting so near to her. They were kind eyes. But they seemed a bit clouded. *They are old eyes. Doctor Millstone is old. I wonder how old? What was he saying? What did he tell me?*

Oh. Yes.

She stopped looking at him and bowed her head. What she saw in his eyes affirmed what she feared she had heard from his mouth. She repeated to herself the most terrible words she had ever heard: *He said my beloved John is going to die.* Her sagging spirit rallied a bit. *He's wrong,* she thought. *Doctor Millstone is wrong.* She lifted her eyebrows. *'Tis impossible. John cannot die. He is still a young man. He is only seven and thirty. It cannot be. We have a family to raise. We are going to America. He cannot die. God will not let him die.*

She looked at the doctor again. Her own eyes were red. Red and dry. They smarted. The doctor was staring at her. She looked away from this messenger of sorrow and at the vase of flowers in the middle of the fine, oak table. They were wilting. She pulled the vase towards her and began to pick tiny brown blossoms from the stalks of what had been white lilacs. If she removed the dying blossoms from the living blossoms and gave them a drink of water, they would perk up. Once the problem blossoms—those brown and dying—were removed, the stems could deliver more energy to the living ones. That's the way flowers work in the ground, and it might be the way they work inside, in a vase. But there were so many flawed flowers in Deborah's vase. The more she fussed at them, the more imperfect ones she found. She would never be able to snip off all the dying parts. She began to feel panic rising in her. Anger.

Deborah heard Doctor Millstone's voice. He was talking. Again.

"You must take care of yourself as well as your husband," he was saying. "You look as though you have not slept for many nights. That will not do, Goodwife Wing. You have your children to consider. For their sake, you cannot let your health go. Is there not someone who can spell you for a while?"

Deborah's attention was still focused on the flowers.

What did this man say? He's waiting for me to answer.

Deborah cleared her mind and found her voice again. "I don't want anyone to nurse John but me," she said defiantly. "Friends are caring for the children and I am all right." Any further thoughts of self-care were dismissed. "What can I do to make John comfortable?"

She looked at Doctor Millstone, squinted her eyes a bit and thought, *You are old! You have forgotten how to doctor a sick man back to health. I will call in another doctor, a younger doctor. Yes. Someone who knows modern medicine.* She felt her face flush in anger.

"You are doing all you can," the physician said. "Keep his head and chest propped upright on pillows so he does not choke on the phlegm. Keep him warm and continue to give him the potions I left. They will help ease his pain a little."

What? she shouted inwardly. *Herbs? Herbs! My husband is dying and you want him to take herbs?* She wanted to scream—like her anguished screams in childbirth when the herbs she was given were insufficient. Watching John slip away from her day by day filled her with pain. Not the same pain as childbirth, but it hurt ever bit as much.

She wanted to yell at the doctor, to tell him how ineffective she thought him. She wanted to grab the lapels on his gray, pinstriped coat and shake him. Shake him, like she was a shrew and he a naughty child. She wanted to tell him he was about to be replaced. That his services would no longer be needed.

But generations of proper training held Deborah's tongue. It would not do to question the authority of a man, let alone a doctor. Deborah feared she was about to choke on those generations of silence.

"I'll be back on the morrow to check on him," the physician said as he left. "There's nothing else I can do. You have my sympathy, dear lady."

Deborah shut the door behind him, backed up against it, bracing either it or herself. She told herself as soon as Edward came, she would have him send for another apothecary. A bright, young man who had been trained in the finest school. Edward would know just the right man, he would know what to do for John. She had to act fast, though. The new doctor would have to act fast. But together, she and the new physician would nurse John back to health. Of course they would. Why hadn't she thought of bringing in someone else sooner? But it wasn't too late. Thank God, it wasn't too late.

Having a new plan of action was comforting. She felt renewed vigor.

Deborah quietly opened the bedroom door to take her place next to John, in the chair by his head. A small candle stand was nearby. The fluted round table, its pine wood painted black, was just big enough for a candle in its pewter holder, a small clock which had long ago run down, and a china teapot snug beneath a cozy to keep the tea hot, and a cup to serve it in.

The black chair, its rush seat formed into an X by tightly woven, cord-like strands, had come with them from Holland. For the past five days and nights, this chair had been her seat, her table, her bed. Ever since John collapsed in church during prayer and a makeshift litter was concocted to carry him home.

Every time Deborah closed her eyes, the scene of John's collapse would play itself out again. It seemed as if the entire catastrophe was etched on the inside of her eyelids, just waiting for them to close so they could replay the event over and over. That's why her eyes were red. She didn't want to sleep. If she shut her eyes she had to relive the worst moment in her life.

She had been so hopeful on Sunday. *John looked a little pinker*, she thought. *Not so pasty white.* The pastor at St. Mary Aldermary's had asked him to participate in the worship service by offering the prayer. John said the nicest prayers. He talked to God as though God were a friend. People felt comforted when John prayed.

I wish I could remember the prayer, Deborah thought as she sat next to her husband's bed. *I would say it for him, now.* Instead, she could only remember hearing John struggle to suppress a cough during his invocation. At first, she paid no mind and uttered a silent prayer that the cough would pass quickly so he could continue. I'll fix him a cup of tea with honey when we get home, she had said to herself. That will help.

Then from her front-row pew she heard John gasp.

Her head jerked up as though someone had yanked a handful of hair from behind, snapping her head backward.

She heard an unearthly scream of "John, John."

The cries of terror—"John, John"—echoed off first one stone wall and then another until the sanctuary reverberated with the distraught sounds. "John, John."

It wasn't until later that Deborah realized it was she who cried out his name.

Immediately men sprinted to John's side and women scurried to Deborah. Bedlam. Chaos.

Edward and three others carried John's limp body home on a crudely-made stretcher, while women friends walked with Deborah, cooing to her, clucking to her, trying to assure her that everything would be all right.

Deborah didn't hear a word they said.

Ever since the men dressed John in his nightshirt and put him to bed, he woke only when Deborah tried to coax him to swallow a bit of broth she fed to him with a spoon, or sip the slightest bit of herbal tea. He awoke then, and when coughs racked his chest that sent him into spasms. Mostly, he slept.

"Deborah?" John whispered. "Is that you, my dear?"

"Yes."

"Deborah, bring me my coat. Please."

"What? Your coat? Why do you want your coat? You need to rest."

"Deborah, please. Bring me my coat."

She did as he wished, and as she laid the coat next to him, he asked that the curtains be opened.

"'Tis daytime, isn't it? Let's have some light," he said. "And, Deborah, open the windows please. This room has been closed so long that there's not a breath of new air in it."

Deborah pulled back the dark, heavy brocaded drapes and the sun shone in. Reluctantly, she unlatched and opened the window the least little bit. She did not want John to catch a further chill. Still, the crack to the outside ushered in a welcomed whiff of fresh air to clear out some of the sickroom stuffiness.

When she returned to John's side, she was sorry the drapes were opened. In the daylight, John looked a hundred, no a thousand, times worse. The unforgiving sunlight harshly exposed his pallid complexion. It screamed his gauntness. It lit up his whiskers, unshaved since the day he took to his bed. John looked unkempt, unhealthy. Never before had he ever looked unkempt or unhealthy.

She used her fingers to comb John's hair. She pushed his black hair, sprinkled here and there with strands of gray, back from his brow. She caressed his cheeks as if to color them. She resisted the urge to pinch them as she sometimes pinched hers for color.

John nudged his coat toward her. She took it and returned it to a wooden peg on the wall, next to the large, double-door pine cupboard that held much of their wardrobe. *What is he doing?* she thought. *First he wants his coat, then he doesn't. I don't understand. It must be the fever.* She had not seen him remove a package from a pocket.

By John's side again, she fluffed his pillows, pulled the blanket up under his chin. "Please, Deborah, sit."

She sat.

"Deborah, my cherished wife. I now realize that the dreams we dreamed together are not going to be fulfilled. I can hear our Savior calling my name. When I close my eyes, I see his great light. It's bright and it's warm. It's welcoming. I know I am to be in his blessed presence sooner than I ever imagined." He paused to gather more strength. "And that, my dear," he said as emphatically as his condition would allow, "is a blessing. Not the blessing we might have hoped for. But a blessing nevertheless."

"John, hush. Don't speak of such things. You need rest. You will be well again. I pray to God for the return of your health with every breath I take. I am going to hire a younger doctor who will know just what to do for you. Everything is going to be just fine, darling. God has answered our prayers before and He will answer these prayers."

"Deborah, I have known for a long time, weeks now, nay, a month or more, that God is going to answer this prayer of ours in a way other than we requested."

As usual, John was matter-of-fact. Deborah never became used to that annoying trait of his. If things were wrong, then why not get stirred up a bit? She did. She was like her father that way. If an injustice made her angry, she would say so, or at least she would *want* to say so and would struggle with herself to keep her tongue still. But John, who could have said anything he pleased without rebuke, was ever so practical. Don't waste your emotions on something you can do nothing about, he would tell her. 'Twill do no good and you will be the only one harmed.

Even now, about his impending death, John is practical. How like him, she lovingly thought while she stayed irrationally cross. *How very like him.*

"I have a gift I had made for you, once I knew we would soon be parted.

"But first," he said, "we have practical matters to discuss." Talking taxed John, but he continued. "There will be enough money for you and the children to live comfortably for many years. There is enough for their education. And, if the money runs out, sell our property in Strood. When I bought that land after we were first married, I thought we might spend our last days there together." He tired and was silent. His mind returned to their earliest days as man and wife when they lived in Strood, next to Rochester in Kent County. His first church: St. Nicholas, it was. "I guess not," he finally said. "It wasn't meant to be." It was as though he were talking in his sleep.

Becoming more coherent, he said, "Deborah, I hope thee will accompany your father to America just as we had planned. But, if his plans for emigration do not materialize, then take the children back to Holland and live there. It will be better for all of you. Like we discussed earlier. Years ago. Our good friends, the Van Blarcoms, will help look after you and the children. And I know all the other blessed parishioners from the church will also be a source of strength for you."

Tears streamed down Deborah's face of their own will. She wiped them away and blew her nose. It irritated her that her nose would always give her away whenever she cried. A person might hide tears, but it was impossible to hide a dripping nose.

"Maybe Daughter Deborah and her husband will return to Holland with you. I'll talk with them."

Exhausted, John stopped talking and slept.

Deborah didn't move from his side. She sipped the tea she brewed for him. It was cold, but the honey in it was the first nourishment she had taken in hours. She sat and waited. She didn't even take John's hand for fear of rousing him. She looked at him as he slept. His cheeks were sunken and his lower jaw sagged, parting his lips. His thin face, thinner than ever, appeared emaciated.

This is what death looks like, she thought.

Deborah closed her eyes. *There,* she said to herself. *This is what John really looks like.* In her mind, she saw John and herself as they walked down the country lane the day he asked for her hand.

That's strange, she thought. *I can see us like I'm another person looking on. He's on one side of the road, and there I am, on the other.* Her vision was delicious. Deborah relaxed. *John was so sweet that day. He was so nervous. To think of it now makes me smile. And that beautiful sonnet he recited. By the bard, Shakespeare, wasn't it? Yes. I think I remember hearing that he died a few years ago.* She thought. *It doesn't matter.*

Blissfully lost in the sweet scent of that spring day, her diversionary meditation was abruptly halted. Startled, she opened her eyes and saw John looking at her, his eyes flooded with love. A small smile played at the corners of his mouth.

"What were you thinking?" he asked. "Your face looked like it did when we were young."

Deborah smiled. "I was remembering the day you asked me for permission to speak to Father. To be your wife. Do you remember that day?"

"I could never forget it." John smiled. Feebly, but a smile.

They were silent. They held hands. John's was so bony. And cold. His blue veins so prominent on the back of his hand. They stood up so high. His hand looked like that of an old man.

"Deborah, a fortnight ago I had a jeweler make this for you," he said reaching for the small package he had placed by his side, away from Deborah. "'Tis a gift I had hoped not to give you. But now, I want you to have it."

She took it and slowly untied the string and removed the wrapping. It was a ring. She knew it would be. A funeral ring. She held the circle of gold that had no beginning and no end. Her finger traced the ring's swirls, so simply and beautifully engraved.

She couldn't say a word. She looked quickly at John and back at the ring. She loved it. She hated it. She wanted to cry. She wanted to scream. She heard a rushing inside her head. But the room was deathly quiet.

"'Tis the last gift I can give you, my sweet heart," John whispered. "Read what it says inside."

Through the blur of her eyelashes, wet and clumped with tears, she saw the words "Until We Meet Again." When she breathed in, she sobbed a desperate-sounding gasp. She could not say the words aloud.

"Oh, John," Deborah finally whispered. "John." She slid this final recognition of their love on the ring finger of her left hand. "I will wear it always. Always."

Chapter 22

London
1630
John Junior

John Junior stood in front of the closed door that would open into his father's sick room. He rubbed his sweaty palms on the front of his pants.

"Go on, John," his mother said quietly, standing next to him, her hand on his shoulder. "He asked for you. He wants to talk to you."

The heart in young John's body beat as though it were a drum rhythmically pounding out a frantic message. He had been summoned from outside where he and Daniel and Stephen solemnly sat on the ground in the shade of an ancient oak tree, trying to reason out what was happening as people continually filed in and out of their house.

"He may be sleeping," his mother said. "If he is, just sit next to him and wait for him to wake."

The door groaned as John tried to open it quietly. He shut it and looked around, his eyes adjusting to the room's darkness, lighted only by the glow of a single candle at his father's bedside. Suddenly, from the corner of his eye something dark and looming made him jump and his heart race even faster. He took a deep breath once he realized the horrific-looking monster was the mere shadow of the tall, solidly built highboy, jerking against the wall from the candle's erratic flame. Distorting its silhouette was the bulk of his father's great black coat hanging from an adjoining peg.

At the four-poster bed, the boy looked down at the man who had given him life and his name. The man didn't really look like his father. There was a resemblance, but not really. This man had no vitality about him. Not like Father.

"Father?" he whispered so quietly even he could scarcely hear.

John sat and waited as he had been told.

He could feel his breathing come easier and his heart resume its normal pulse. He pushed his straight black hair away from his face. It fell to the top of his collar. He combed it straight back, but no matter what care he took, it was forever falling down in front of his eyes. Especially today.

His mouth was dry. He wished he had taken a swallow of ale or tea or something before he came in. But he didn't remember being thirsty then.

"Son," his father said.

John jumped. He wasn't aware his father had awakened.

"Come close, John." He leaned down to his father to hear more clearly.

"I know this is not easy for you, John, but you must realize that the time of my departure is near."

The boy felt the blood drain from his head until he was surely as pale as his father. *Dear God in heaven, do not let me swoon,* he prayed. He shook his head to clear extraneous thoughts.

"This is not a time of sorrow, John, because I will be with our heavenly father. I have seen his light, and I know God will grant me the grace to be with him. You must rejoice that I will be with God and Jesus. You know there is nothing in heaven but joy. So, be happy for me."

The silence that followed filled John Junior with raw terror. He couldn't say a word. Was he supposed to say something? He couldn't even bear to look at his father any longer. Instead, he squeezed his eyes shut tight to stem his tears as they began to flow. He saw a million little red and blue spots with his eyes clenched so. A sob sounded from the depths of this young man who didn't know he had such depths.

"John," his father said, "you are now seven and ten. I know you are not yet a man, but unfortunately, you must now become a man. On this very day. And, as a man, you must help your mother in any way you can. Now that your sister Deborah has married, she cannot be such a support to your mother as she was before.

"John, it is your duty and responsibility to be the man of this house and help your mother raise your younger brothers."

John Junior's shoulders shook, although he made not a sound—his first sob had scared him so. He did not want to cry, but he couldn't help himself. He did not want to be the man of the house. He wanted his father to be well and head up the family. He wanted to see his father sitting at the head of the table saying grace with every meal. He wanted to see his father sit before the fire and hear him read from the Bible. He wanted to walk beside his father as they walked to church one more Sunday. Just one more Sunday.

Dear God, please make him well so we can be together for a while longer. I promise, dear God, I promise that I will be good, I will be the best son possible. And I will devote my life to you, dear God, if only you let my father live. Please, dear God, let him live. He felt panic building from within.

That terrible-sounding sob sounded again.

John Junior fell to the floor on his knees and laid his head on his father's bed. John Senior smoothed the black head of hair that had once been so small it rested in the palm of his hand. Now it was the head of a man. Rather, a boy Providence required to be a man.

"I know 'twill not be easy for you son," John said, taking the boy's hand in his. "But always remember that I am in heaven looking down upon you and giving you support. You will have two fathers in heaven instead of just one.

"Do you hear me son?"

"Yessir," John whispered.

"Do you understand me?"

"Yessir."

"Tell me what you understand."

John lifted his head and cleared his throat, and with the back of his hands roughly swiped at the tears on his cheeks and in his eyes. He wiped his nose on the sleeve of his shirt where it flounced beneath the cuff of his coat.

"I understand, Sir, that you are dying and that I am to be the man of the house and help Mother raise my brothers."

"And?"

"And, Sir, that you and God will help me from heaven above."

"That is exactly right.

"John, about our plans to emigrate to America with Grandfather Bachiler. Though I pray you will still go, those plans may change now, and you and the family might well live in Holland. But, Son, wherever God calls the family, you will have to be a man. To cross the Atlantic and settle in the wilds of a new country would be trying for your mother, what with the little boys and all. Above all else, John, your mother must be able to rely on you wherever you might live, but especially if you emigrate."

With his eyes closed, but his ears and heart open, John Junior foresaw what was to be: He saw an ocean of blue water, a shore of gleaming white sand, a forest dense with trees. The scent of pine filled him. He saw himself helping his mother and young brothers from a ship whose sails were furled to their masts. He saw Grandfather Bachiler between the stark masts. Now ashore, he smelled the sweetness of a new, clean Earth.

His father spoke again and the scene blinked away as quickly as it had appeared.

"I love you, John. My son. I have faith you can bear this burden."

Chapter 23

London
1630
Deborah

John died quietly at mid-morning the next day, with family and close friends gathered around.

"I think Father is sleeping," Matthew whispered from his mother's arms as she held him. His arms were wrapped around her neck and he laid his head on her shoulder.

John did look peaceful. The pain that had pervaded all summer and etched its presence onto his face was gone. It had been instantaneously replaced with serenity. His loved ones watched it happen.

*　　　　　　*　　　　　　*

Now, a few hours later, Deborah stood alone with her husband for the last time. She looked at him. He laid so still. He was so white. She cocked her head as she heard the bells of St. Mary Aldermary's Church tolling the passing of a soul from this world to the next. She knew all those who heard the bells would pause to say a prayer for the one crossing over.

She took comfort knowing that Printer Dawson, John's publisher, would pause to say a prayer; that the baker where she bought bread this past while would offer a word on John's behalf; that members of St. Mary's would pray for her beloved John. She had uttered those prayers herself whenever she heard the bells tolling for someone's dearly departed.

Deborah had prepared a bathing mixture of herbs to ready her husband for burial. She was mindful of the women who went to Christ's tomb to ready his body for burial, only to discover he was not there. Usually women of the church would have completed this task, just as women had done for centuries. Deborah appreciated the offers of others, but she wanted to prepare her husband's body by herself.

The fragrant water pleasantly scented the room. Rosemary was the predominant herb, the herb of remembrance, as Goody Hilliard had taught her. The warm water felt good on her cold hands. She wrung out the cloth.

This is the last gift I can give to you my sweet heart, she silently said as she slowly and lovingly began to wash John's body.

She washed his face and said, *I'm going to miss that smile of yours, John Wing. But I will remember it always. And whenever I think of you and your smile, my day will be filled with sunshine. Your smile was truly a gift from God. I imagine you are smiling at our blessed Lord this very moment. Yes. 'Tis true. That's why you look so peaceful. You are at peace.*

She washed John's closed eyes. *Who closed them? Oh, yes, Doctor Millstone closed them.* She washed either side of his nose. His lips and chin. The folds in his ears. A soft smile crossed her face as she washed behind his ears. She began to hum like she did when she had bathed her newborn babies.

She dipped the cloth into the warm, scented water and wrung it out.

She washed his arms and hands, finger by finger, and was struck anew by how thin he had become since he caught a dreadful spring cold that simply would not go away. She remembered his arms strong, gently carrying his babies, baptizing the babies of his parishioners.

She washed his chest blackened with curly hair. She remembered laying her head on that chest and teasingly pulling those hairs after they made love. She tugged at them now and smiled.

Again, she rinsed her cloth and wrung it out. It was good to have something to do. Something constructive.

She washed his legs and feet and thought of his great stride. She closed her eyes and saw him coming home from a day of calling when they lived in Holland. The closer he came to the house, the longer his step, until he was nearly running. She saw her children scrambling to greet him and saw them all tumble to the ground under their rambunctiousness. She could hear them laugh. She could. It was the most beautiful sound in the world.

She dipped and wrung.

Lovingly, Deborah washed his genitalia and was grateful again for the five children he fathered. Those children were truly a part of him. A continuation of him. John Junior was especially like his father. They looked a great deal alike. Their mannerisms were much the same, this father and son. There was no doubt that within a few years son John would have a gait long enough to equal that of his father's. And, Deborah knew, this second child of theirs would one day become a loving father just as he was now a loving son. She wondered if he, too, would become a minister. In the deepest reaches of her soul, where she would not own up to its honesty, she hoped he would not. The mother wanted her son to be a man of God, yes, but not a minister. There was so much grief associated with being a minister in these turbulent days.

Deborah lathered and shaved her husband's face, being careful not to nick him. When she shaved his throat and under his chin, she wished she could hear his voice again. She knew if he could speak that he would say, "Absolutely not, Deborah! Absolutely not." Never, ever would John let Deborah shave him, even though she coaxed him time and again when they were newly wed. Thoughts of those scenes brought another smile to her face.

She dipped and wrung.

With some difficulty, she rolled John's stiffened body on its side and held him steady while she washed his back.

She laid him down again and brushed his hair. She liked the way it curled down over his ears. It was sad to see it so lackluster when it had always been so thick and shiny.

Deborah knew her time with John was fleeing. Soon Edward would arrive with others, come to wrap John in the swaddling cloths and lift his body into a casket made of the finest walnut. Then the house would begin to fill with people, a constant stream of people, come to view the body and pay their respects to his widow, who by then would be dressed in black. A friend was even now seeing to the purchase of proper mourning weeds for the Widow Wing. Relict Wing.

Not yet. Not yet. She did not want anyone to come into the room. She did not want them to knock on the door and ask if she was ready. She was not ready. Not yet. Again, in the still of the room, she heard that roaring in her ears. Like yesterday.

Deborah climbed atop the bed and lay down next to John and was still. She closed her eyes. Her right arm crossed his body as it had so many times before. But it felt heavy, foreign, out of place. Because there was no response.

Slowly, she sat up and knelt beside him and bent down to kiss him on each eye, on each cheek. The tip of his nose. His lips. She touched his hand for one last touch.

"Oh, John."

Chapter 24

Holland
1631
Deborah

The red blotches on Stephen's face defined his anger.

"Deborah, what about you?" he said, fixing his burning eyes upon his eldest daughter. Never had her father addressed her in such a tone. "Do not forget your sister Theodate. She's expecting us."

No one dreamed of suggesting that Stephen sit elsewhere than where he was—at the table's head. This might not be his house, but he was head of this family and of course he should sit there. Deborah took her place at the table's foot.

Stephen was holding forth over this gathering of Bachilers as they sat around Deborah's table in the great room of her Flushing home. Helena, Stephen's third wife, sat to the right of her husband, of course; then, filling the benches on either side of the oblong table were her widowed sister Ann; Samuel and his wife Honor; and Nathaniel and his wife Hester.

And, John Junior.

Just as the morning's session was about to start, John had walked into the room and confidently made a place for himself at the table, the others squeezing together to make room. Knowing looks and gentle smiles were passed around. John had grown to be the adult his father had groomed. At eight and ten, he was sufficient in age and maturity to assume a position at the table.

The only Bachiler not present was Stephen Junior, who, after his dismissal from Oxford, resigned all ambitions of the ministry. He turned his energies elsewhere and was now a successful London merchant who had no intentions of going anywhere. And, of course, Theodate and Christopher Hussey, who were in America. Waiting.

The Husseys had crossed the ocean more than a year ago, assuming Stephen would join them post-haste with his congregation and family in tow. That was also Stephen's assumption. Then one thing and another happened, and now here he was, ready to sail—but faced with a reticent family. First, it seemed, he must re-convince his sons and daughters to emigrate because, obviously, their journeying together was not the foregone conclusion he had assumed.

That's why he called this meeting at Deborah's.

Deborah and her sons had returned to Holland when the last of John's affairs was concluded. Holland was home now, where John wanted the family to live. For the past year, Deborah and her sons had grown to depend only upon one another, getting used to life without John. Certainly they missed him, but Deborah sometimes astounded herself at how capable she was becoming, how able she was to fend for herself and her family.

Then this.

Stephen, Helena and Ann and her children had all applied for and received licenses to cross the Channel to visit her, and Stephen made arrangements for Nathaniel and Samuel, who both lived in Holland, to gather for this conference.

This was Wednesday, their second day together. Yesterday, after their warm greetings of hello, the day dissolved into stares and glares without much said. Yesterday their father applied the techniques he used to convince sinners to change their ways and follow the Lord. And, like the most debased of sinners, the Bachiler children did not think their ways needed changing.

Today, boldness was setting in and words were exchanged. Some heated.

With Reverend Bachiler's admonition that Deborah remember her sister in the wilds of America, Helena, and Hester and Honor, the two daughters-in-law, fidgeted. But each blood-filled Bachiler remained still. Stoic.

The patriarch stood up, knowing his children would have to raise their heads towards him. He grasped either side of the table with his enormous hands and leaned towards Deborah at the opposite end.

"Well?"

Deborah swallowed, but did not blink. She did not back away from her father's probing eyes. She would not be rushed with her answer. She sought the exact words she wanted to say. She was perplexed; she had never been in this position before. Here she was, still grieving for John, striving to persevere without him while doing her best to maintain a home for her sons. And now she was facing her confrontational father who had always, since the day she was born, been her ally.

Deborah thought of Theodate. She uttered the prayer that was continuously on her heart for God to protect her sister and that all be well with her and hers.

Deborah's confusion was compounded: where did her responsibilities lay? Her loyalties?

Looking at her father, eye to eye, she said, "How can I possibly forget Theodate?" If Stephen had been really listening, he would have heard a tinge of sarcasm sounding.

"Well?"

"Father, so much has changed since we first decided to go to America. I no longer know if emigrating is the right thing for me to do, now. Considering."

"Considering what?"

Deborah felt her face flush. Stephen was quite the adversary. Just as strong an opponent as he was a protector.

"Considering that John is gone, of course. I have to consider my children in a different light, now," she said, trying to be pragmatic and not argumentative. She did not look at John Junior, but she felt his presence at the table.

"John wanted to go to America," Stephen said. "You know that."

"Yes, I know that."

"He wanted religious freedom not only for himself but for his children, too. Is

that not right?"

"Yes. That is right."

"We Puritans have fought dearly for this opportunity, have we not? We have been excommunicated. We have been imprisoned. We have been exiled. We have had our ears lopped."

The following silence was stunning.

"Is that not right?"

Stephen slowly enunciated each word and spoke loudly, as if talking to a deaf person; his tone was cross, as when he had scolded them as youngsters.

Not a word was said in reply.

"Well?"

"Father," Samuel said, interrupting. "I want to say something. You are not being fair to Deborah, interrogating her like this. Inquisitions are no longer fashionable."

Deborah looked at her brother with relief. *Samuel, bless your heart,* she said to herself. She could have hugged him for diverting their father's great probing eyes to someone else.

Indeed, Stephen's eyes darted to his youngest son who had followed in his footsteps and was now a minister to the English in Gerischem, Holland.

Stephen sat again, heavily.

"You know Theodate and Christopher are in America waiting for us because of you," Samuel said. "They are there because otherwise you would not have given them your blessing to marry. If they wanted to be husband and wife, they had to immigrate to America. Simple as that."

Stephen frowned at his son, his eyebrows coming remarkably close together in the center of his face, all but obliterating the creases above his nose. He said nothing. There was nothing to say. Samuel was correct. What he didn't understand was the tone. It implied, that he, Stephen Bachiler Senior, Theodate's father, had erred with his conditional marital blessing. Nonsense. That was his prerogative.

"And," Samuel continued, "we are not there because of John Wing's death and John Sanborn's death, and because your venture with the Plough Company fell through."

"Samuel is right on both counts, Father," said Nathaniel. "You lost a great deal of money when your company members defaulted on that patent in Casco Bay, up in Maine."

Deborah saw her father blanche at the mention of the Plough Company and her heart went out to him.

"Father, I know how distressing that loss was to you," she began.

"Daughter, you have no idea! You cannot possibly know. That patent represented my life's blood. My Wherwell congregation, which has been so supportive all these years, was set to sail with me. Together, you, they and I met all qualifications to populate a township. I would have been the minister required by each patent. We had worked on this and planned on this for such a long time."

His voice faded. Everyone was silent. No one looked at him.

"I will tell thee what this emigration means to me," he said at last. "Casco was the star that has guided me these past years. I wanted to follow that star to a new Israel. Just like the wise men who followed the greatest star of all time, I wanted to follow my star, that, like the Magi, I would see our Savior who is waiting for me on New England's soil."

Stephen's children stared at the table or their hands or the wall opposite them. They stared at anything to avoid looking at each other or their father whose eyes had brimmed and spilled.

The glow of Stephen's star had flickered and was all but snuffed out when his kinsman Richard Drummer and Plough partners John Dye, John Roach and Thomas Jupe deemed the land at Casco unsuitable and surrendered their patent.

The Plough. The significance of the plough was dear to Stephen. The ship on which the others sailed to America was christened The Plough. His parishioners presented him with a coat of arms with a plough and a rising sun. Ploughs cut straight furrows in preparation to sowing. The seeds he'd sow, of course, would be blessed words to bring sinners to the Almighty. And the new sun arising would nurture those seeds to fruition.

But then those miserable people whom he trusted to put things in order in Casco had let him down and surrendered their patent before he could survey the situation.

"I have been dismayed," Stephen said to his children. "I have been outraged. But I will not be deterred. I have enough money for another patent. And I thought we would all go now, just a year or so later than we planned. It never occurred to me that any of you would renege.

"Only a year has passed since you were all so anxious to leave. What is your hesitation? I simply do not understand."

"Father," Deborah ventured. "There is another factor which we have not discussed. You are no longer a young man. In fact, dear Father, you are aged. You turned seventy this year. Emigration is for young people," she said gently, "not a man of advanced years."

"I need no reminder of my age, thank thee very much," Stephen roared, his voice raspy. He looked around at these children of his and shook his head. A sorry lot they were this day. He checked his anger before speaking again.

"Helena and I are going," he said. "There is nothing further to say on that fact.

And, we want each of you to come with us. Just as we planned." Stephen's frustration was evident in his voice, just as his anger was spelled out on his face. "For the life of me, I do not understand why we are having this discussion. We have had this plan all along. And, as we have said, Theodate and Christopher expected us last year. We cannot disappoint them further."

Uneasy about starting the marathon in full swing again, Samuel spoke softly: "Father, Honor and I are happy here in Holland." He was silent; he knitted his fingers together and stared at the thumbnail on his left hand. This was hard. Speaking out against your father was hard. In his head rang the words, "Honor thy father…" Still, he continued: "Father, I do not want to hurt you, but now that I have been apart from you and your influence these past few years, I am no longer filled with the fury of injustice as I once was. I have a successful ministry here. I am following God's edict in this country."

The blood drained from Stephen's face. He looked as though someone had slapped him in the face. And that someone was his own son. Samuel, whom he thought would never fail him since they shared the common calling of the pastorate and all that went with it, good and bad. The hairs on the back of Stephen's neck sprang to attention again. They had been up and down ever since he arrived at Deborah's, but they were now stiff once more. They pricked.

"If we can't worship the way we want in England," Samuel continued, "then we will live in Holland which has become home for us. And, Father, as my dear Honor says, Holland is much more civilized than America will ever be."

Nathaniel spoke next: "Hester and I do not want to subject our children to the rigors of what we might find in that wild country. We do not know what lies ahead of us in America, but we know what our lives are like here. For one thing, we are safe. I could not subject my family to unknown dangers and terrors and deprivations." Nathaniel stopped only long enough to swallow. Hard. "My neighbor was told by someone just returned from America that the Indians walk around naked—in front of women and children—and carry small hatchets with them at all times. More than once, the godless wretches have buried those hatchets into the skulls of God-fearing English men and women—and children."

"Nathaniel, I am surprised and disappointed in you," Stephen said. "I would have expected you to moderate the reports you hear. The dispatches I have heard tell of great expanses of space, of fertile land so rich it will grow any food you plant. I hear, Nathaniel, that men are free to be the Lord's ambassadors and that there is no one to spy on you or tell you what you can and cannot say.

"That's what I hear.

"And don't forget the glowing descriptions from Theodate and Christopher.

"You didn't feel that way last year!" Stephen barked. He pounded his fist on the table at the injustice of his children's arguments, causing his pewter mug to bounce, slopping its dark ale.

Nathaniel spoke: "A year's passing has given us just that much more time to think things through. We have had the benefit of a year to face this decision with that much more thought and prayer."

Stephen glared: "So, there's nothing I can do or say to change your minds?"

The brothers looked their father in the eye and respectfully declined with a shake of their heads.

More silence.

"As Nathaniel and Samuel said, we have religious freedom here," Deborah said.

"God's teeth!" her father exploded. Everyone at the table jumped. Never, ever had any of Stephen Bachiler's children heard their father express such blasphemy. They all stared at him, their mouths agape. "Staying here for freedom of worship is a compromise." he ranted. "Here you must be Congregationalist or Lutheran or Presbyterian. In America, you can be a Puritan. Just as I am a Puritan and just as John was a Puritan.

Just as your sons are Puritans," he said, looking directly at Deborah. "Just as you are a Puritan."

Deborah, who grew up hearing stories about the hair on the back of her father's neck, could feel her own hackles rising.

"Father, I would have to leave Deborah. I would never see her again. I had to give up John but I don't have to give up Deborah. I don't know if I could."

"You left your mother when you married John, I believe. That's the order of things. Children leave their parents when they marry."

Stephen did not see the muddle of his argument and no one wanted to point it out to him just now.

"What did you tell me John said to you before he departed?"

Deborah took a deep breath. She could feel herself trembling. She concentrated hard to transfer the tremble from her voice to her hands which she clenched together under her apron, giving it a life of its own, just as it had when she was pregnant. She was angry and her voice was low and steely in its anger.

"Truly, you know he said if your plans to emigrate fell though, that I was to bring the children back to Holland."

"Yes. Well, our plans will now be restored. And I want you with me. By my side as I fulfill the directive God has laid out for me."

"Father, you have Helena by your side," Nathaniel ventured.

"I do indeed have Helena, but I want my children there. At least those who are not afraid to go."

Ignoring the insult, Samuel said, "There is one more consideration for you to examine before you cajole Deborah into submission, Father. Honor brought the subject to mind in a conversation we had last night, after we retired. Here, in Flushing, Deborah has a lovely home, handsome furniture, fine pieces of silver. She has a woman to help her with the cleaning and to care for her sons. She has dear friends here. And we are close by, Nathaniel and I. In America, Father, it is doubtful she will ever have any of those things again."

Deborah looked at Samuel, four years her junior, and smiled warmly. Bless your heart, she said with the glow from her eyes. Certainly, sacrifices had occurred to her—more than once—but she said nothing. It would have been unseemly to do so. Every emigrant would make sacrifices and complainers would not be welcomed. Especially not a woman. As it was, she had already ventured further onto the proverbial thin ice than ever before, disagreeing with her father the way she had.

Stephen was unmoved by Samuel's petition. It became evident no one was going to say anything further. A stalemate was silently acknowledged.

Finally, Samuel offered, slowly in a husky voice: "I think 'tis time we have a meal. After we have staved off hunger, maybe we will be able to think with clearer minds."

*　　　　*　　　　*

"Excuse me, may I speak with you?"

Deborah spun around to face her questioner. It was John. Her son. For a haunting, fleeting instant she thought she heard her husband speaking. Their voices were so much alike, her son's and his father's.

Deborah left preparation of the meal to the other women, grabbed her bonnet and a lightweight shawl and followed John out the door. Great cumulus clouds billowed in the sky, changing their shapes ever so slightly as a gentle June breeze nudged them along.

Mother and son, he now taller than she, walked down the road until they came upon a bridge that crossed a canal. Without crossing and ignoring the ground's dampness, they sat on the tall grass alongside the canal, not far from the road. The sweet scent of spring grass and tiny, colorful, fragrant wild flowers greeted them.

"Mother," John began.

Deborah looked at this son of hers. *Why, he's a man, now. No doubt about it,* she thought. *He should still be a boy, but 'tis comforting he is grown and has such a sensible head on his shoulders. Just as his father had. I do rely on him for so much. Even his advice.*

"Mother," John started again. This time Deborah cleared her mind of sentimentality, looked at her son with attentive eyes and listened.

"I think we should go to America with Grandfather," he said quietly.

"Why is that, John? Why do you think we should go?"

"I think Father would want us to go."

Deborah blinked twice and looked anew at her boy. "Why do you say that?"

"That time when I went into Father's room by myself, the day before he passed, and we talked, he and I, remember?"

"Yes."

She looked away from John, her eyes drawn to the canal where two majestic white swans arrogantly glided downstream, their feathers glistening in the sun.

"Father said I was to become a man that day, that I was to help you raise my younger brothers. He said he hoped we could go to America, and if we did, I would for certain have to be a man."

As John sat on the ground, he rested his chin on top of his arm, which, in turn, rested on a bent knee.

"Mother, when Father talked of our going to New England, I closed my eyes and…" He averted his eyes from his mother to the grass where it sprung up between his legs. He pinched off a single, long strand of grass at its base and ran his fingers along its length.

"Mother," he said quietly, "I had a vision that day."

Deborah looked back from the mute eloquence of the swans and into the glorious keenness of her son's dark eyes. A chill enveloped her and she wrapped her shawl a little snugger around her shoulders.

"When Father talked about our emigrating that day," John said, "I saw what was to be. I saw us on a ship, its sails filled with the wind as it headed west. I saw the sea's white caps as that ship parted its waters. As we neared land, I saw the shore glistening in the sun. I saw forests so dense it wasn't possible to see beyond the first of the trees. And, strangest of all, Mother, I could smell the land's sweetness as we neared it. The trees gently blew that scent out to sea to welcome us.

"I saw us, Mother, all of us—you, me, Daniel, Stephen and Matthew—as we

walked down the gangplank to the dock. You were carrying Matthew in your arms and I was there, by your side, my arm under your elbow, helping you. And Grandfather Bachiler was there. And, there to greet us was Aunt Theodate and Uncle Christopher."

Deborah closed her eyes and realized her face was wet. Unbidden and unnoticed tears had spilled.

"John, are you certain?"

"Mother, I am certain."

"'Twill be a hard life, John. It will be like nothing you have ever experienced."

"I know, Mother, but this is what Father would have done. 'Tis what he hoped we would do if it were possible, and Grandfather has made it possible.

"I believe it is foreordained that we go."

As mother and son looked at each other, they clasped one another's hands and were all but overwhelmed by the emotions of their own private dramas.

"Mother," John said at last, "Father assured me that he and our heavenly father would always be with us. Wherever we are. They have been with us and have helped us thus far. We must trust them to help us further."

Chapter 25

Thames River Dock
1632
Deborah

"This March wind chills my bones to their very core," Deborah Senior said as she and Deborah Junior huddled together, their hooded cloaks drawn tight.

"Deborah," the mother said, "your hands are shaking; let me hold them and warm them."

"Their shaking has nothing to do with the cold," Deborah Junior said. "I so wish thee weren't leaving, Mother. We will likely never see one another ever again." She swiped at the tears that spilled down her face.

"We agreed we'd have none of this," Deborah gently told her daughter. "Besides, one should never say never. Who knows what might happen in the future? I've had not foreshadowing, have you?"

Not answering her mother's question, Deborah Junior said, "'Tis as though you and my brothers and grandfather will be dead to me," Deborah Junior said between sobs. She dropped her chin to her chest. "I've not enough nose cloths and my nose is dripping." Both Deborahs chuckled at the predicament.

"I have an extra," Deborah said as she searched for her pocket in the vast fabric of her cloak. "There's so much I wanted to tell you, but there's no longer any time. We did discuss much last night, didn't we? Did you note the time when we finally went to bed?"

"It was half three," Deborah Junior said. "'Tis no wonder our eyes are so high-swoln this morning."

"Ladies, Cap'n says it's timeful to board," a disheveled shipmate grumbled as he hobbled by, one leg dragging a step behind. "Let's get along."

Deborah and Deborah hugged one another, melding together as one.

"Let's be on our way," the impertinent sailor barked as he made the return trip along the length of the pier. "Anyone fer the William 'n' Francis better be climbing the gangplank now."

Deborah took her daughter's face into her hands and looked deeply into her eyes. She placed a quick kiss on Deborah Junior's lips, and abruptly turned and walked away without uttering a word or stealing a backward glance. Her sons waited aboard for her, and John Junior met her as she crossed the bridge from solid Earth to the ceaseless rocking of the ship, its wooden joints forever complaining. It would be months before they would next feel the solidity of ground underfoot.

Deborah kept vigil at the ship's stern, waving her white cloth, watching her daughter's white cloth waving in turn until she could no longer see it. Her heart hurt and she could not swallow for the tightness of her throat. *My darling daughter,* she thought, *you will always be in my heart if not my eyesight.*

Her father joined her, his arm gently wrapped around her shoulders. She leaned heavily into his arms.

A sudden blast of wind lurched the ship forward as it twisted its way down the River Thames to the English Channel and the Atlantic Ocean. Deborah and her father stumbled to regain their footing.

"'Tis an ill wind that blows no good," her father said. "The more wind, the faster we will sail and the sooner we will be in our new land of opportunity. Yes, my dear, let us pray for a good, strong wind."

Chapter 26

Aboard the William and Francis
1632
Deborah

Deborah watched as her father braced himself and spread his legs wide against the ship's violent pitch as he worked his way towards her and Matthew. He stopped, raised his hands and prayed for all to hear: "Heavenly Father, we entreat Thee to calm these seas."

A deafening bang of thunder answered the plea as though it were trying to engulf them. "My friends," her father said, "we have come too far, we have struggled too long to allow a mere wind deter us. I am but an aging Puritan priest, but I know our Father will allow us to reach our destination. I, for one, intend to spend what is left of my life to worship without restraint."

At Deborah's side, he tousled Matthew's hair, to which the boy said, "Grandfather, I fear I'll be sick again if you rock my head anymore."

Stephen laughed, picked Matthew up and wrapped an arm around Deborah: "Let me walk you home." As they approached their "home," a few boards of space, her father said, "I do believe our close quarters help keep us warm." Deborah sank next to where her sons sat.

Her three older boys eyed their grandfather from beneath heavy lids, but said nothing. There was nothing to say. Children, no matter how old—or how ailing—were to be seen....Still, young Stephen Wing, named for his grandfather, hissed to his older brother, John, "I'd just as soon leave it be a bit colder and have more room."

Deborah patted John's back, rubbed an open palm over Stephen's shoulders and asked Daniel about his ailing stomach. She passed hard tack all around. Matthew grabbed his dry cracknel, as though it were a warm slice of his mother's delicious bread, hot and fresh from the oven.

"Eat it slowly," she cautioned. "Just nibble. And when you lie down, don't close your eyes. 'Tis best to leave them open a bit and fix them on a steady object." As if there were such objects, she added to herself.

"I'm off," her father said, "People to uplift."

Deborah made a makeshift table with her arms, crossing them atop her bent knees, to rest her heavy head. The stifling air trapped in her skirt folds was not pleasant, but better than the air at large. Like everyone aboard, she was making the crossing wearing a single set of clothing. Will it ever be clean again? she wondered. It was the sadd shade of mauve, the first color she'd worn since packing away her black mourning weeds.

As the trip and relentless storms wore on, the dress had become roomy. Long ago she had solemnly removed her mourning ring and safely tucked it away lest it fall from her now-bony finger.

Not heeding the advice she gave her sons, she closed her eyes and concentrated on not thinking about the stench. If she permitted the offensive assault to her nose to penetrate her consciousness, she would be overwhelmed. There was no escaping the acerbic odors of vomit and urine and the odious smell of bodies too long unwashed. She would give most anything just now for one deep, cleansing breath of fresh air.

This ship creaks and groans as though it were as old as Methuselah, Deborah thought as she listened to its grumbling.

Oh, John, my dear departed husband, she prayed. How I wish you were here, beside me, so I could rest my head on your shoulder and hear your heart beat and listen to your assurance that all will be well. There are times when I question what I have done, taking our boys across the sea like this. Leaving our daughter behind. I fear for the danger of what lies ahead—if we ever do land in this new, wild country where you so wanted to live.

With the next slam of thunder, her father was back. "'Twill be all right, Deborah," he said, wrapping an arm around her. The dark of the ship sounded of groans. "God will see us through this storm—and the next. You know that." And, as if he read what he thought was on her mind, he added: "You know 'tis too dangerous to be outside. I know it's unpleasant to breathe down here, but we must stay. The Devil himself could not ride these winds without help from the Almighty."

Again Deborah heard the sounds of ailment and fright all around her, but that was good, at least those who complained were alive. Everyone now was pasty white in complexion. She gathered a moaning Matthew into her lap and wrapped her cape around him. She pressed her son's sweaty head against her small bosom and shush-shushed him into quiet. Likewise, Stephen Bachiler gently pulled his daughter's head so she could rest it upon his strong shoulder.

"Oh, Father, what on earth are we doing?" she whispered. "I wish we had never left England. What if my children perish in this black, bottomless ocean? Sometimes I fear we'll never set foot on land again."

"Dear Deborah," her father quietly, gently chided. "Where is your faith?"

Deborah sighed, her heart dropped. *Oh, Father,* she thought, *where is my faith, indeed.*

"I have faith, Father," she said, unable to swallow the testiness in her voice. "God knows I have faith, else I would not be here with you on this vessel, fearing for the lives of my children."

She breathed deep and vowed not to speak again until the abruptness was gone from her voice. Out of love and respect for her father, she tried to disguise the rancor she felt. She wanted to avoid another war of words.

Neither Deborah nor Stephen liked quarreling, but it seemed lately that they were often at odds, which weighed her soul down with guilt. She had been taught to honor her mother and father. Love, honor and obey. This new, alien relationship with Stephen was not right. God would not be pleased, she knew, but still she could not, would not, return to the docile daughter of her youth. Not only was she now a widow with five children—with four sons to raise alone—but she had buried her husband and mother. And her father had chosen a new life of conflict and immigration and dragged her along with him through it all.

If I am rebellious, 'tis he who created the rebellion, she argued with herself. *How dare he question my faith?*

She answered her father's chastisement: "For years, I've watched you rebel against church officials. You were an example of how to face your foes and retain your dignity.

"Faith has seen me through exile, through the death and burial of my husband, through leaving my daughter as she stood so alone on that London pier—all to traipse off to an uncivilized country far beyond this endless sea, through one terrifying storm after another.

"Where, indeed, is my faith?"

Faith, she knew, would be her steadying force in this new world of hers. Things on Earth would always be in flux, but not God. God was unchanged. Would never change.

And the thunder sounded again.

*   *   *

"Deborah, forgive me, but do you know where your father is?" It was Helena.

"He left a moment ago to comfort some of the passengers."

Helena sat down. "He's probably tending to old Goodwife Pugh."

No doubt, Deborah silently agreed. *Or some other woman. They're all becoming such pests. They'll bring nothing but trouble upon Father's head.*

She and Helena, her stepmother—oh, how that word stuck in her craw—were so close in age that both were uncomfortable. But, in spite of herself, Deborah felt a rush of sympathy for this woman whose very existence was a daily irritant to her.

Is this failing of his never going to end? Are we to be plagued for the rest of our lives with his wantonness? How did Mother live through that? She never let us children know anything was amiss. But I knew. I didn't want to know, but I did.

As Deborah considered the shipload of good-wives, their flirting and fawning so blatant, she experienced a renewal of shame at the old charge of her father's wandering eye. Did Helena know the stories and charges? Deborah would never divulge her dirty secret. Humiliation prevented her from revealing the distrust she harbored about her father. She still felt compelled to shield her mother, now long in her grave. And, yes, Deborah had to admit, she was also protective of her father—and even her own self.

For such a learned man, Father could be so thickheaded. He acted as though she knew nothing. The memories of his meandering eyes and hands could not be buried deep enough and they flooded to her mind at the least provocation, sickening her with each image. Her mental agony became a physical hurt. Her chest ached so she thought her heart would surely break. *Please, dear God, do not let this sin revisit us,* she prayed.

"It's just that Goodwife Pugh is always asking Stephen for special prayer to calm her nerves," Helena answered, jarring Deborah into full consciousness. "And Goodwife Smithers is no better. Those two women simply will not leave him alone. I fear their husbands will mistake your father's ministry towards them."

Deborah saw Helena look at her hesitantly—as though she wanted to ask a question, but thought better of it. Instead, Helena quietly said, "I overhear snippets of conversation now and again about the spiritual guidance Stephen ministers to all the women."

Deborah's eyes darted over her stepmother's ashen face, which, in turn, grew more confused with each second that passed in silence. *Should I say anything to her,* Deborah wondered. *Should I tell her and promise to be her stalwart friend should she ever need one? Is it my Christian duty to do that?*

"My Love," Stephen greeted Helena as he lowered himself to the floor, ceasing any further conversation. He planted a kiss on his third wife's cheek.

"Deborah," he said, acknowledging his daughter.

Deborah looked at her father, trying to see him through the eyes of his older women parishioners.

It's his size that's comforting, she thought. *A man as large as Father cannot be undone.* She looked at him anew. *He's a handsome man. His wavy white hair is most attractive, even when it circles his head like a halo.* She smiled at the image. *He appears downright saintly then. But there are terrible times when he is not saintly; when he is anything but.*

*   *   *

Yesterday's storm had been bad, but today's was even more horrifying.

Deborah closed her eyes. *As long as Father remains strong and his voice remains strong—and his halo doesn't slip too far—we will all feel safe. I pray Heavenly Father that it is so. Please deliver us from the middle of this ocean.*

She felt her father's hand against her head, practically commanding her to relax; she closed her eyes—*only for a minute,* she thought.

Just then a terrible loud crack sounded overhead. Deborah was startled wide-awake. In the time it took to catch her breath, adrenaline rushed through her veins, flushing her face and tingling her fingers, sending her heart pounding at a frightening rate. The sickening noise came from topside, far above the main quarters.

"Father?" Deborah questioned.

"Mother?" her children questioned.

"Pray, children," Deborah said. "Pray."

Chapter 27

Aboard the William and Francis
1632
Stephen

Stephen braced himself against a post inside the ship's bowels that were dank, smelly, and as black as ink. His mood, however, was so glowing, that, had he been a lantern, the entire place would have shone as bright as day. He eased down to sit next to Deborah and said, "Visitation is done. I've spoken with every family." A baby whimpered unceasingly from the further reaches of the "cargo" hold where the 60 passengers lived, each family with precious little space.

"So, Daughter, what do you think of your father being the modern-day Moses?" Stephen asked. "I doubt Moses and his people could have had any greater hardships and challenges to their faith as I and my faithful followers have."

"I pray, Father, that you will be more blest than Moses," Deborah said.

"I feel assured that God will not deny me entrance into this new paradise that we have desperately sought for so long," Stephen said. "In due course, we will dock at the new Promised Land. I know it! We shall rise from the darkness of this hold to build a church atop a hill as a light, a beacon, to show man the way to salvation."

The hairs on the nape of his neck stiffened. Prickled.

Then, thunder banged against the hold's door and passengers renewed their cries of fear: "No, dear God, not again." "Save us Father." "My babies, my poor babies." One after one, the children cried until the place was filled with tormented sounds, pleas to God to not forsake them.

"Faith, my people," Stephen cried out, standing again. "Have faith." *Why do these parishioners of mine not exhibit more faith,* he wondered. *Have I not taught them well enough?*

"This thunder that frightens you so is no more than God's voice," he called out.

loud enough to be heard over the crashing clouds in the sky. "God answered Moses in thunder, and so He is speaking to us. We must stop our wailing and listen."

And, as if on cue, the sound of cracking lightning answered the minister and the weeping began again.

"Please, my friends: the lightning is nothing more than God calling to gain our attention.

"Ask, ask, and God will provide."

Now undistinguished voices turned to quiet prayer: "Hear us, o Lord…" "Heavenly Father, I pray…" "Grant to us a quieting of the wind…"

The hysteria began to calm.

*   *   *

After the storm abated, Stephen and a few of the stronger passengers emerged atop of the ship for fresh air.

Stephen and Thomas Wedde, also a Puritan minister, stood by the ship's railing. Wedde's face was nearly green in color. "You know, Thomas, William Bradford and I have corresponded for some time," he said as

Wedde renewed his grip on the railing. "To think, Sir, this long-time acquaintance of mine is now governor of the colonies."

"Ah, yes, so you have told me—a number of times," Wedde said. "Stephen, tell me your opinion of the Separatists. I, for one, find them much too rigid and unrelenting. How much contact do you expect we will have with them?"

"I doubt we see much of them," Stephen replied. "I must say, though, I feel a kinship with them."

"A kinship?" blurted Mister Wedde, startled momentarily out of his seasickness. "How can you say such a thing? That's preposterous. We're nothing like them."

"I'll always be beholden to them," Stephen replied with a smile. "They made it possible for us to leave England. You did want to leave, did you not?"

"Of course," Thomas said. "Don't ask such fool questions."

"We're all in the same pickle barrel, so to speak," Stephen continued. "If the Separatists hadn't first fled England and Anglican Church officials, 'tis doubtful we could have." He thought a moment. Then: "Do ye ever consider a comparison to this thing we're doing to Martin Luther nailing his theses to the church door? Or John Calvin converting the Catholic French to Protestantism?"

"Come Stephen," chided Thomas, "Let us not compare our lowly efforts to those of the saints."

"Certainly not," Stephen blustered, his face all of a sudden the shade of a ripe tomato. "I intended no such comparison to us as men, rather, to our mission. It took all the saints, and the Separatists, too, for us to dare venture to this new land to spread our Gospel wings, so to speak. I do believe, however, there are among us saints-in-the making, Reverend Wedde. Don't you agree?"

But Wedde was no longer listening. The ship's roll heightened as it fought the fitful seas and he had turned green.

"We will be safe once we touch land," Stephen said, clapping his friend's shoulder. "God will grant us safe passage. 'Twill all be worth it, Thomas, 'Twill all be worth it. Why, ever since those Separatists dared leave, England's shipyards are in danger of being buried beneath mountains of sawdust, the residue of logs sawn into lumber to build ships at an unprecedented pace."

"Yes, it seems every other Englishman wants to emigrate," Thomas said half-heartedly, then turned his back on the enormous white caps and to look heavenward, as if to search the dark, clouded heavens for a glimpse of God himself, to beseech Him, face-to-face, for better sailing weather.

"'Twill be a gift from heaven," Wedde said wearily, holding his stomach, "not to deal with the foppery of rituals and all the finery we put up with for so many years." But his heart wasn't in his rhetoric. His words sounded hollow.

Stephen clapped his friend's shoulder a second time, ignoring the man's predicament of a sick stomach: "Ah, yes," he said. "The Separatists' fought their way from England to Holland, and on to this wild, untamed country we're headed for might seem drastic to some. But we understand, don't we, my friend? Like us, Separatists must worship God as God directs. Simply. Anything more is extravagance, a device of the Devil. Puritans are not so stiff-necked as Separatists. Separatists want to have nothing to do with the Church of England or England itself. They want to separate the church entirely from the government. We puritans don't go that far. We simply want Anglican authorities to do a bit of housecleaning and rid the church—and themselves—of the clutter that comes between them and God"

"'Tis so, for the most part," Wedde said, nodding his head and instantly regretting it. Again he looked upwards to avert his eyes from the seas. "But I am displeased with their too-stringent ways. Plus, they're going too far in separating church and government."

"'Haps so," Stephen said, now looking heavenward, too, "but I understand these Separatist brothers and I sympathize with them." *What's*

Thomas looking at? Stephen wondered. "I am humbled to follow them, soon to join them. Yes, indeed." *Does the man have a nosebleed?* He looked keenly at his friend's nostrils. *No, his nose is fine.* "Our paths are similar to the Separatists. Very similar. Why, even the William and Francis, this fine ship we're sailing upon, is similar to the Mayflower which carried our brethren to a New World. Yes sir, 'tis the same type of ship made by the very same shipbuilder for the same company. 'Tis about the same in most every detail. God blessed the Mayflower and He will do no less for the William and Francis."

Stephen looked at his friend again.

"Thomas, are thee ailing?"

With a less-than-saintly look directed at Stephen, Thomas turned and hung his head over the rail.

I won't ask the Lord any more for such strong winds to carry us along, Stephen thought. *Instead of making time, we seem to be losing it.* He patted his friend on the back and set out to find other company just as the wind picked up again.

Chapter 28

Aboard the William and Francis
1632
Deborah

"Just feel that sun," Deborah exclaimed to Helena. The two women, along with most passengers aboard the William and Frances, were topside. Deborah closed her eyes and turned towards the radiance, letting it fall full on her face. "Is not the sun God's most wonderful creation?"

"'Twould seem so," Helena agreed.

"It's especially wonderful, after all this time without it," Deborah added.

"But Deborah," Helena cautioned her step-daughter, "mind your skin. You know the sun is harmful. It will turn you skin red, or even brown. That's why we wear bonnets."

"I know," Deborah said evenly, choosing to ignore the unwanted motherly concern, "but it feels so good. I've missed it so. I do believe it even warms my very soul."

This turn in the weather was a welcomed change from the bite of March winds and April's gales. Today God provided perfect weather. Besides the shining sun and bluer-than-blue skies, there was enough wind to fill the sails so the ship skimmed along but not so much as to toss it about. That's why the open deck was crowded. Everyone with strength enough had climbed up from out of their wooden cave to breathe clean air, warm their aching muscles with the sun's rays. And smile. Everyone was smiling.

Deborah opened her eyes, turned and saw her father talking with Esther Pugh and Ruth Smithers. Where one woman was, there was the other. The two traveled as one, often with linked arms. Deborah turned her back on the scene of Stephen, his hands on the women's shoulders, offering prayer for them.

"Excuse me, Helena. I'm going to walk about the deck a while."

She made her way to the ship's bow and crossed over to walk the length on the other side. She stopped near the galley and looked over the railing, paying no mind to the activity going on there.

Bless you Father in heaven, for this glorious day, she prayed silently. *It fills me with hope. Blessed hope.*

Deborah became aware of a soft, murmuring voice. She turned but didn't see anyone.

"Reverend Bachiler," she heard. It was Patience Eccles, a girl of eight and ten. "Reverend Bachiler, I wish to talk to you a moment. I want to tell you of my great love and admiration of you."

Immediately, Deborah's stomach churned as she turned further and saw them. There they were, standing behind a lifeboat, nearly out of sight, facing the water.

She heard her father's voice acknowledging the gratitude, which was hushed by Patience's girlish tones.

"I have been so frightened ever since we left home, but you have given me strength, Pastor. I would have perished of fright had it not been for you."

Deborah wanted to escape but her feet remained planted as she watched and listened in horror.

"I want to repay you for your kindness," Patience said, reaching up and pulling Stephen's face close to hers.

"No, Girl," Stephen said.

"Yes," Patience said and kissed her minister fully on the lips. And in the breath of a heartbeat, Deborah saw her father return the kiss.

She involuntarily gasped and Stephen looked up and saw Deborah. Their eyes locked.

"Daughter," Stephen began, his voice and demeanor shouting his guilt.

Deborah turned and walked off.

She had hoped, prayed, America would be a fresh start for her father, that the slate of any real or imagined wrongdoing about past dalliances, or even an appearance of dalliance, would be wiped clean. She had so prayed nothing of this sort would happen in the New World. But now she realized her father's sin would make its presence known time and again, just as before. This was one more ugly secret she would have to bottle up.

But she would keep the secret. *Mother, bless her heart, had kept the secret, and so shall I,* Deborah thought. But it wasn't easy to excuse what she had just seen.

The sound of Stephen's voice drew Deborah's attention and she saw him walking toward Captain Thomas. Patience had scooted away, evading Deborah's smoking eyes. How could he be of such good humor? Did he have no shame at all? She saw him clap the captain's back and watched as they turned and walked towards her, talking. Deborah wanted to take flight, but there was no way to escape them. Stephen's face broke into a beam as bright and inviting as the sun itself. His halo of white hair shone.

"Daughter," he said, looking cautiously at Deborah, carrying on as though there were nothing amiss, "I want you to hear this. Go on, Captain, tell her what you just told me."

Deborah firmly pulled her elbow free from her father's hand and moved a couple steps away. She was trembling, regardless of the warming sun.

"Goodwife Wing," Captain Thomas greeted her, touching the rim of his tri-cornered commander's hat, its ostrich feather fluttering in the breeze. "I was telling your father I believe we shall sight land today—or tomorrow at the latest."

Deborah couldn't clear her mind. It was so cloudy and dark she couldn't focus on the conversation at hand. Finally, she managed, "That is wonderful to hear." Tears sprang to her eyes. "Thank you, Captain Thomas."

"Yes, well, we—the passengers and the crew and the ship—have managed to weather it all, have we not?" the captain asked, pride sounding in his voice.

"We certainly have," Stephen boomed, "thanks be to God." He smiled at Deborah and raised his eyebrows as if to plead forgiveness.

"Ah, yes," the captain replied, "and my mates, as well. Now that we are safe, I guess 'twould do no harm to tell you how anxious we were last week when the main topmast was nearly split asunder. That squall of a sudden, atop those horrific winds, liked to snap the mainmast in two. We might well have sunk straight to the bottom of the sea."

"Thank God we did not," Stephen said. "We have much to thank Him for."

Just then Mister Gimp walked past and muttered a bitter something under his breath; something like, "'Twarn't God who climbed up the mast to rig it up and 'twarn't God who got nigh blowed off. No sir, 'twarn't God a-tall."

"During prayers on deck this morning, we praised God and your crew of fine, brave sailors for seeing us safely thus far," Stephen assured the grumbler and his captain, but Mister Gimp had already stomped on and didn't hear the reverend's praise.

"Hi ho, Mother," Matthew called out as he and a clutch of boys raced by. Their rambunctious nature revived with the good weather and they were in hot pursuit of a barking, mangy-looking dog, which was in pursuit of one of the ship's many cats. Dodging masts, ropes, kegs and legs, the noisy, laughing, yapping entourage tore down the steps of the poop deck (where, because it was above the captain's headquarters, they shouldn't have been in the first place) to the quarter deck, across it and down half a dozen more steps to the upper deck to run the length of the vessel, bound pell-mell for the forecastle.

Deborah's spirits lightened at the sight of the young boys. "I am so grateful to see the children teeming with energy again," she said, and with a laugh, added, "never did I think I'd hear myself say that."

The captain smiled, tipped his hat and returned to his post.

The disposition of everyone but Mister Gimp, it seemed, was as sunny as the cloudless sky. And why not? The day dawned with the promise of good tidings. And, as the sun rose, the shipload of bedraggled passengers, one after the other, used what little strength they had to climb up out of the ship's belly to the deck, awash in sunshine.

"'Tis like a bunch of moles comin' up outta their hole, squintin' at the light," Mister Gimp had grumbled.

Turning to watch the captain walk away, Deborah inhaled deeply, turned her nose upward and sniffed. Her father reached for her hand, but she jerked it away.

"What is that delicious smell, and where is it coming from?" she asked. "I haven't smelled anything so glorious since…I don't remember when."

"'Tis dinner, Daughter," Stephen said as if he had stirred the pot himself. "The captain ordered the sailors to kill his last pig, the runt of the lot, and cook up a soup for everyone."

"Soup. Meat. Oh, that sounds delicious," Deborah said. "'Tis been such a long time since we have had a hot meal and even longer since we've had a bite of meat."

"This is the first weather in a spell that's been calm enough to build a fire for cooking," Stephen said. "It will be a fitting way to celebrate what we pray will be our last full day aboard ship."

"I hope not to eat cheese and hardtack again for a long, long time," said Helena as she joined them, "and never again do I want to taste that horrid salted beef or pork…"

"Salt horse," Stephen replied. "I've grown rather fond of it myself. The fact is, we haven't even had much of that to eat the past while."

Deborah took her leave, not speaking to anyone.

*　　　　　　*　　　　　　*

It was early evening, but no one made a move to go below. No one wanted to surrender a single moment of daylight. The sun would set soon enough leaving Venus visible in the evening sky. But until the pale sun dropped totally from sight, until there was not a ray of light left for Luke to see, perched high above in the crow's nest, up where the wind filled the sheets of sail, no one moved.

Luke held the spyglass against one eye and squinted shut his other eye. For nearly four hours Luke had been on watch, all but soldered in the same position—leaning out of the mast as if the added inches would make him closer and help him see better.

As long as one tar or another had been in the perch looking out, passengers and sailors stood below, gaping up.

"Do ye see anything, Mate?" Mister Gimp yelled up to Luke.

"Nothing. I don't see nothing," Luke called down.

A disappointed groan sounded from the forecastle to the poop deck and back again.

"Wait. Wait."

"What's that ye say?" Mister Gimp hollered.

A great inhale of breath sounded as everyone aboard gasped and held their breath, waiting to hear Luke's next words.

"What is it Mother?" Matthew asked. "What is it?"

"A moment," Deborah answered, impatient, intent. "A moment, Matthew."

"Land ho!" Luke cried out. "Land! Land! I see land."

"Are ye sure, Son?" Captain Thomas called up to his youngest sailor. "Are ye sure?"

"I'm sure, Sir. 'Tis land."

"Praise be to God," Reverend Bachiler said. "Praise be to God."

As one, every soul—man, woman, child, traveler and sailor (except Mister Gimp)—fell on bended knee, bowed their heads to thank the dear Lord above.

"Mother?" Matthew asked. "What's happening?"

"It's land, Matthew," Deborah said, hugging him and kissing the top of his head of thick, black hair. "Blessed, unmoving, steady, solid land! Tomorrow, we will walk on solid ground." *Pray God it's so,* she said to herself.

Even as she praised God for granting their arrival, Deborah felt the urge to turn, and there, behind her, was her father and Patience, their heads close to one another. In prayer?

The tremble from earlier in the day returned, and Deborah was sick.

Chapter 29

Aboard the William and Francis
1632
Deborah

The sun hadn't quite cleared the horizon on June 5, 1632, than each bone-weary seafarer clambered topside with renewed vigor to crane their necks and strain their eyes to recognize something from the blur of land that lay ahead.

Then, as if following the baton of a music conductor, first one head tilted upward and another and another and another—until every neck aboard the William and Francis was heaven-bent—sniffing. Stabbing, tentative, questioning sniffs gave way to big, audible, lung-filling gasps inhaling sweet air. Everyone breathed deeply the magnificent scent that filled them deliriously.

"Mother," John said quietly to Deborah, "it's just like my vision. Remember? I told you I could smell the sweet fragrance of trees as we neared the harbor. And I can. We all can. 'Tis just as God promised."

The clean, fresh scent of pine trees greeted them—as though God were delivering a whiff of encouragement, telling them their journey was nearly complete. Another few hours and these people who had been cooped up

175

with one another for eighty-eight days without sight of land, without enough food, proper sanitation, privacy, a bed to lie upon. Without even the meager basics of civilized living—these people would see with their own eyes the forest that delivered its welcome upon the breeze.

Deborah looked into her son's eyes. They were big and round. Like a child's. He looked like her little boy again and not a near man. He was excited, breathing rapidly. Deborah took him in her arms and hugged him.

"Yes, John, 'tis just as you said. 'Tis just as God told you it would be."

*   *   *

"There's Aunt Theodore," Daniel called from his vantage on the half deck. "See her, Mother?"

"No, I don't see her. Where are you looking?"

The ship's sails had been furled, all but one, as Captain Thomas guided the vessel towards a dock. The William and Francis deck crackled with expectation and anticipation. Every passenger was topside, anxious to lay eyes on this new country, to see just what it was they had left home for.

"Mother, now do you see them, Aunt Theodate and Uncle Christopher?" Daniel cheered. "Grandfather, you see them don't you?"

"Yes, indeed," Stephen boomed, three people back in the press of humanity. "God be praised. There they are." Tears flowed unchecked from his eyes and down his cheeks. "God be praised."

"I can't see," Matthew wailed, jumping up and down. "I can't see."

John picked up his little brother and lifted him above his head to ride his shoulders. "How's that?"

"Yes, yes," Deborah exclaimed, "now I see Theodate. There she is." She waved furiously. At least Deborah thought it was Theodate. There were so many faces to sort through on the pier.

As they drew nearer, Deborah feared the dock was in jeopardy of sinking from the weight of well wishers. And scores of people lined the shore.

All of Boston, it seemed, were there to welcome another ship from home. Everyone was cheering, waving hats, nose-cloths. And the passengers waved back.

Tears, too, were unanimous: those on board shed tears of thanks that God helped them weather the storms and at last delivered them to their new home; those on shore wept grateful tears that their loved ones had not been lost at sea as feared.

A scene of this sort repeated itself with every arrival from home, although a collective sigh of relief was uttered that this particular ship was finally docking. Not many, thank God, were this long at sea in crossing.

The arrival of each ship meant word from loved ones an ocean away. Letters were a ship's most precious commodity. Also aboard were seeds for planting, fabric for sewing, furniture to help transform an immigrant's house into a home. And, a store of London's latest fashions.

But best of all, the ships brought people. Family. Friends. Workers. Healers. Tradesmen. Leaders. Spiritual guides. More citizens to help form a new England.

"Father, Deborah, here we are. Here we are." Theodate jumped up and down to be seen amid the crowd.

But the family was stalled on the gangplank, stuck in the midst of an unmoving clog of humanity.

"All right, all right," barked Mister Gimp, elbowing his way through the sea of passengers. "Make way. Make way. Say your helloes when you're on dry land, not midway 'tween the boat and the dock. Make way. Make way."

At last Stephen and Helena were on the pier. Having seen others falter as their sea legs gave a rubbery way to solid footing, John, Matthew still astride his shoulders, took hold of Deborah's elbow to steady her as she set foot from the ramp's last plank to planks on the dock.

Deborah looked at her son and smiled. *How like your father you are*, she thought.

Then she was in the arms of her youngest sister.

"Theodate," Deborah said. "Deborah," she heard in return.

"And who is this?" Deborah said, finally seeing the child in Theodate's arms. "Oh, Theodate, what a wonderful child God has blessed you with."

Everyone was laughing and crying at the same time. Christopher Hussey worked to move the huddle away from the path of other greeters.

"Reverend Bachiler, Reverend Bachiler."

Stephen looked around and broke away from his children. "Governor Winthrop," he said.

The two men shook hands.

"I am most happy to see you, Reverend," said John Winthrop, Massachusetts' first governor. "We have been sorely concerned for your safety. Not a day went by that we didn't remember you and yours in our prayers."

"'Twas a most grievous trip, Governor," Stephen said, "but not a soul was lost. God fulfilled his promise and safely delivered us to this blessed land."

"Stephen, let me introduce you to Aaron Dudley, my deputy; my son, John Winthrop; Reverend John Wilson, and William Blackstone, who has the distinction of being Boston's first white settler."

The men shook hands all around.

"Stephen, how fit you look," the governor said. "I must admit I had some misgivings about your undertaking this journey at such an age."

Stephen bristled.

"I am but one and seventy, Governor, and God has granted me fair health. There was not one aboard our ship who can boast of a constitution such as mine." Softening his tone, he added, "But I do thank you for your concern. I realize you meant no ill will."

Winthrop reddened at the rebuke.

"I won't keep you Stephen," he said. "But I wanted to deliver my greetings personally—one Puritan to another. I know you have suffered much at the hands of the bishops at home, but I pray your life here will be more blissful."

"Bless you, Sir," Stephen said. "I pray so, too."

"What are your plans, now?"

"First we want to renew our acquaintance as a family," Stephen said. "We will spend a while in Saugus, with my daughter and her husband, Christopher Hussey, and yet another namesake of mine."

"When you're in Boston again, Stephen, come see me and we'll have a nice long visit."

Governor Winthrop and his entourage moved on to greet other passengers and Stephen returned to his family. Once certain he was out of Stephen's hearing, Winthrop said to those around him, "It's true Bachiler had a rough go at it in England, but some of it might well have been of his own doing. We'll have to wait and see what happens here. Maybe all he needs is a fresh start. We'll check our judgment for the time being."

Chapter 30

Saugus, Massachusetts
1632
Stephen

Stephen closed his eyes, hoping his daughters would think he was meditating, not sleeping. It was true—he was meditating, and praying, but as much as he didn't want to admit it, he was exhausted and nodded off from time to time during his conversation with God.

Dressed in shirtsleeves, his coat jacket hanging on a peg by the door, Stephen slumped in the ornately carved white oak chair with its worn leather, horsehair-filled, seat that had been his father's before him. Stephen stretched out his legs full length, one crossing the other, his feet close to the fire. His chin rested on his chest.

That was some ride across the ocean, Father, Stephen prayed. *Some ride, indeed.*

It was Sunday, the Reverend Stephen Bachiler's first day of worship in this paradise he had prayed about so often for so many years.

Bless me, Father, he prayed now. *Give me strength to shepherd this group of devoted saints who crossed with me to worship you in the manner you have directed us.*

Aye, God, I am weary, but I'm devoutly happy. I'm anxious for my first worship service to be underway. Oh, blessed Jesus, son of God, no more bishops dictating what I can and cannot say, no more demanding, pompous Canterbury officials threatening expulsion, no more antichrist pope. No more Little dictators. No more arbitrary laws. Freedom of worship. Yes. Freedom of worship.

This was the day Stephen had long awaited. It seemed a lifetime. His eyes closed. Just a few moments to rest: *Nothing can spoil this day. Not a thing.*

I feel a little light in the head, heavenly Father. The room, it sways, like aboard ship. I pray for your divine healing touch that I may be as whole and fit as ever I was.

He snoozed, his breathing deep and rhythmic. A deep breath filled his cheeks and escaped through his lips, blowing out, reverberating, staccato-like.

*   *   *

The William and Francis had docked in Boston a few hours after midday the previous Thursday.

The next morning Stephen arrived at the pier in time to watch the sun rise and the ship be unloaded. He wanted to gather his goods along with those of Deborah's and his parishioners'. He wanted to supervise transfer of his group's paltry possessions to the boat that would ferry them across the bay to Saugus later that morning.

The high-pitched screech of sea gulls was the only sound to disturb the early hour's quiet. The pier was empty of visitors and the seamen went about their work without speaking. They, too, sagged from the voyage some thought would never end—and now that it had, there was one more immediate job to do and they wanted it done.

A gentle salt breeze accompanied the pastel pinks and yellows of sunrise, bringing with it the unmistakable whiff of fish not rinsed away by the cleansing breath of the previous night's rain.

Stephen watched the scene: On adjoining piers, fishermen shoved off, bound to catch their day's earnings. The noisy gulls escorted them to sea, anxious for their return, their boats heavy with dinner.

Stephen looked at the William and Francis. The ship looked so small, its sails furled. It appeared almost foreign as he walked the pier's weathered-gray planks, looking up at it rather than down from its deck. He much preferred this viewpoint.

He located the four hogshead of peas he'd brought as part of The Plough's bounty. Now, it would see his family and others through their first winter and then be planted next spring. He pried open the barrel that contained the twelve yards of fabric and two hundred yards of list. Even though the store of goods wouldn't be used by Plough households, they would not go to waste. He rifled through the fabric and what had been his neatly folded white linen shirts looking for his precious contribution box, a token from his first days in the ministry.

Where is it? he thought, consternation written on his brow. *I packed it mineself. It has to be here.*

Stephen's father had presented him with the box upon his graduation from Oxford.

His pawing stopped with the feel of hardness. There it was. He pulled it out, relieved to see the intricately carved oak box was safe and whole.

Stephen ran his long, slender fingers with their arthritic, knobby knuckles over the carved scrolls and spiraling vines and grapes that entwined a cup, representing the chalice Christ drank from during his last meal. At each end of the box, contrasting the intricate side carvings, was a stark, simple cross, the definition of every Christian's faith.

The raised designs were worn, rubbed smooth, and darkened, these many years later from being passed how many times from one parishioner to another, for each to drop in his dearly earned tithe.

Stephen recalled the day his father gave it to him.

"Carved it myself, Son," Nathaniel Bachiler had said. Stephen could hear his father's voice speak to him from a lifetime ago. "Carved it from the finest oak. I made it long enough and deep enough to hold what you will need to support your ministry."

Stephen's inner eye saw himself as five and twenty, holding the rectangular box, some three times as long as it was wide and deep. The emotion he felt then—when the box was light-colored and he was an eager, clear-eyed young man with a mission to accomplish—came rushing back now as he lovingly felt the rich symbolism so artfully crafted.

"'Twill be perfect," he had told his father in a choked voice. "I pledge to thee and to God that I will use it wisely."

Now an old man of one and seventy, Stephen smiled as he gently replaced the collection box into the shipping crate.

I haven't recalled you for such a long time, Father, but I thank you again now, today, for this most precious gift.

Stephen stood, looked around and started to search for his furniture. He especially wanted to find the chair that had belonged to his father. It was the one luxury he had allowed himself to transport across the sea.

"Got it all?" a dark voice snarled from behind, startling Stephen. It was Mister Gimp. "Rest assured no one save the rats have had a gander at a solitary t'ing, not since we set sail back there in London. No sir, only the rats and there's no accounting for them. No sir."

Does this man ever speak without grumbling? Stephen wondered.

Stephen turned and faced Mister Gimp, the sailor with no proper name, and saw an unusual amount of pain written on the man's craggy face.

"I'm certain 'tis all here, Mister Gimp," Stephen said. He thought of turning back again from this bedeviled, rancorous man who had been such an annoyance for such a long time. Instead, he was drawn to say, "I want to thank you, Mister Gimp, for your assistance in crossing the Atlantic. You are a fine sailor and we were blessed to have you aboard."

The old salt narrowed his eyes and frowned. He warily sized up this towering religious man, making certain he saw or heard no sneer or mockery. The aging, aching sailor shifted his weight to his good foot so he stood taller. In a sudden rush of movement, he doffed his rank stocking cap and held it in two hands behind his back and said, looking directly at Stephen, "Me Christian's name's Jonah, like in the Bible, the fella what got swallowed by the whale. That's what me dear mum called me a'fore she passed over and become an angel just moments after I was borned. Jonah weren't asceered of no waters. And neither am I. Just wished me dear mother'd named me Noah," he said with the hint of a grin, "then m'ybe I'd be cap-t'n of me own vessel." At that, Jonah turned his head to spit the juice chawed from the wad of tobacco pouched in his cheek. He looked back at Stephen and grinned, baring his brown teeth. "Yessir, the moniker Noah might a brung me better fortune. Still, Jonah's done right good by me. But don't no one call me that no more."

Stephen smiled. In the eighty-eight days he had been cooped up with Mister Gimp—Jonah—he had not heard him utter as many consecutive words as had just now flowed from his mouth—and not a one of them morosely muttered.

"Jonah, I thank you for sharing your story with me, and I will remember you in my prayers, Sir. I will ask God grant you safe passage wherever the winds may take you. And, I pray you will come worship with us whenever you are near." Stephen offered his hand. "May the good Lord cause his eyes to shine upon you."

Slowly at first, then vigorously, Jonah swiped his right hand, front and back, on the seat of his britches and shook the minister's hand.

"Bless you, guv'nor," Jonah whispered, awe struck, "ain't nobody ever blessed me a'fore." He turned and hobbled as fast as possible up the gangplank. There was work to do. No time for sniveling.

*　　　　　*　　　　　*

"Father," Theodate whispered in Stephen's ear as he dozed in front of the Hussey's fireplace.

"Father, I'm sorry to disturb you," she was saying. Theodate, this youngest child of his, so resembled his beloved Ann. She was short, petite, like her mother and had inherited Ann's iris blue eyes. Her soft voice even sounded like Ann's. Her personality, too, was much like her mother's. For one thing, she was agreeable, pliable; whereas Deborah, who more resembled him, could be irritatingly headstrong.

"People continue to arrive to worship with you this morning," Theodate said. "But there is not enough room in our house for everyone."

"Praise God!," Stephen said, immediately renewed and rejuvenated. "We will meet outside, under a canopy of trees."

Stephen stood, stretched, smiled broadly, retrieved his coat from the peg, grabbed his hat and went to greet his waiting congregation, making sure he ducked to miss the doorframe. The head smack he'd received when he entered his daughter's house the first time was reminder enough of his height versus the doorway's sharp, unforgiving opening.

"'Tis a good thing God gave me such a thick head," Stephen had wryly laughed when his hard head met the even harder wood. "That's what your mother always said."

"Daughter," Stephen called back to Theodate, "bring along your basin and a pitcher of water. There are babes to be baptized."

At the sermon's close, Stephen asked the parents of the babies, two already two years on this Earth, to come forward for the rite of baptism, his own grandson included.

Theodate and Christopher had named their first child Stephen. Indeed, Grandfather Stephen was honored and anxious to reflect his gratitude.

Four sets of parents made their way towards the first minister they'd heard since the town was formed a few years earlier. Stephen smiled benevolently at three, but beamed broadly as he took toddler Stephen from Theodate's arms.

"Of all the privileges bestowed upon a pastor," he said for all to hear, "the ancient rite of baptism is the most blessed and happiest of all occasions, especially when it's babes being born again in Christ."

Stephen directed the plain white porcelain basin and pitcher be brought forward.

"Reverend Bachiler," Ezekiel Newhall interrupted with a hoarse whisper, taking his child from his wife's arms. "May I ask what you are doing?" Astonishment filled his voice.

Stephen's eyebrows knitted together in annoyance at the disruption of this holy event. "What do you mean, Sir?" Stephen mumbled back, "I am going to baptize these children of God. You know that. What say you?"

"Are you baptizing the Hussey baby first?"

Newhall hissed his words. The people closest to the scene began to murmur. Others in the back could be heard to say, "What's happening?" "What's the hold up?"

"Of course I am," Stephen said, forgetting to keep his voice down. "He is my grandson!"

The men relinquished any pretense of religious decorum.

"Our Thomas should be the first child baptized," Ezekiel Newhall said, turning to the worshipers as his audience. "Our Thomas was born four days before the Hussey baby—the first white child born in Saugus. 'Tis his birthright to be the first child baptized in this town. His birthright!"

Stephen felt his hackles rise.

"Sir, I cannot believe you would deny me the right to baptize my own grandchild, my own namesake, before I anoint the soul of a stranger's child."

Mistress Newhall began to cry as she retrieved Thomas from her husband's arms. Ezekiel was holding the youngster so tight she was afraid her son would be squashed. "Ezekiel," she whispered, "'Tis all right. I pray you, do not make a fuss."

Thomas began to whimper. As the tension grew, his whimpers turned to squalls.

"Mister Bachiler," Ezekiel persisted loudly, "I insist Thomas be baptized first."

"Goodman Newhall," Stephen retorted even louder, "I will baptize Stephen Hussey first. Of that, there is no argument. I will baptize your son next—and if that is not to your liking, you are free to wait and have him baptized by another minister at another time."

Theodate attempted to take Stephen from her father, but he tightened his grip on the youngster and scowled at his daughter.

Stephen Hussey yelped at being the object of this tug-of-war between his mother and this strange man who so recently entered his small sphere of awareness.

Theodate retreated.

"Come, wife, this man—this minister," Ezekiel spat out the words— "has not even been duly authorized to form a church here, at any rate. No doubt the baptisms will be null and void."

"Husband," Goodwife Newhall pleaded, "Thomas must be baptized today lest something happen and he perish before another minister visits. We cannot condemn our son's soul to the flames of eternal hell because we did not have him baptized. First or second, it matters not, but he must be blessed today with holy water."

She thrust a wailing Thomas back into her husband's arms.

Ezekiel Newhall stood, son in arms, glaring at Stephen, who continued to hold Stephen in his arms.

By then, Thomas and Stephen were both vociferously screaming their objections to the yanking, clenched holding, passing back and forth. They understood nothing but the anxiety coming from arms which usually comforted them.

Their cries of protest were contagious and soon all four children awaiting baptism were bawling a chorus of complaint at the top of their tiny lungs.

Neither Ezekiel nor Stephen moved. Neither man averted his eyes. At last, Newhall stepped back.

"Baptize your beloved grandson first, sir." Ezekiel Newhall snarled. "But we shall see about this." The color drained from his face, his voice trembled in anger. "We shall see."

Chapter 31

Saugus
1632
Stephen

Early the following morning, while the rest of the family remained bent over their wooden trenchers heaped with gruel, Stephen stood, ready to start the day.

Since the table was not long enough to accommodate the Hussey's newly expanded family, John, Daniel and Stephen Wing propped themselves up against a wall, balancing their breakfast as they ate; Matthew Wing and two-year-old Stephen Hussey sat cross-legged on the floor to tackle their bowls.

"I'm going to walk about town," Stephen announced. "I've decided we will make Saugus our home and the first order is to find a lot upon which to build a church."

Deborah looked up sharply at her father's pronouncement, made as he pushed himself away from the board table with its one chair for the man of the house. Christopher Hussey, whose table it was in whose house it was, obligingly seated himself at the opposite end, sitting atop a keg.

Stephen stood with his legs spread far apart, his hands on his hips. He smiled expansively.

"I thought we were to settle in Newhouse," Deborah said to him, somewhat sharply. "That's what was decided before we left home."

"Aye, Daughter, that's true," Stephen replied. "Our destination was indeed Newhouse, but several in attendance at our worship service yesterday spoke to me about ministering right here. Until yestermorning the citizens of this God-fearing but church-less town had not heard a proper sermon since they left England's fair shores nigh two years ago. And, after all, what does it matter to us if we live in Newhouse or in Saugus? Surely, one is the same as the other."

"But Father," an exasperated Deborah continued, "we haven't discussed it. Don't you think we should talk about this? Don't the rest of us have a say in this matter?"

"What possible difference can it make to you?" Stephen said, knitting his eyebrows together, returning his daughter's curt tone. They were two razor-sharp swords poised to clash in scrimmage. Sparks flashed from one set of dark eyes to another. "Even those who came with us from Wherwell offered no objection," Stephen continued. "In fact, they were in agreement. This town suits them fine."

Deborah, her lips taut, rimmed white with anger, said nothing but continued to stare at her father.

"Deborah, move to Newhouse if you must, but I have received a call from the good people of Saugus—and from Almighty God—to preach here, and here is where my good wife and I will reside."

Helena ducked her head, seeking refuge from the skirmish between her husband and his daughter. The two women continually skirted around one another. There had been tension between them since Day One, when Stephen unabashedly introduced them as Mother and Daughter. Ever since, it had been a troubled relationship, try as they sporadically did to rectify the situation, and Helena did not need Stephen to now position her directly in the face of Deborah's ire.

Stephen turned on his heel, strode straightaway across the room, grabbed his coat and hat and was out the door before another word of protest could be uttered. The only noise heard was the crack of Stephen's head as it smacked the door frame, followed by an extra forceful slam of the door as he vented his anger over his daughter's obstinacy—and his sore pate.

Theodate reached across the table to take Deborah's hand, clenched tightly about her spoon, holding it upright as though it were indeed a sword. "Never mind, dear. We have found Saugus to be truly a comely town, and most of her residents are fair-minded, God-fearing folk."

Theodate wanted to offer more reassurance, but hesitated when she saw Deborah's outrage continue to crackle in those wide, dark eyes of hers.

"Deborah," she ventured, "what is wrong between you and Father? Why do the two of you confront one another so?"

Deborah rose, excused herself and made her way to the door. As she was about to leave, between clenched teeth, she said, "I'll be back. I must be alone for a while. I have much to think about."

The last two sentences were spoken to herself, even though they were uttered for all to hear.

*   *   *

"Theodate, I'm famished," Stephen said as he burst into the house later that afternoon, remembering to duck in the nick of time. "Fetch your ravenous father a bite to eat, if you please, Daughter. My, but I've had a productive day."

He continued his non-stop conversation to a house-full of family but to no one in particular. He had forgotten—or chose to ignore—the hostility he'd slammed the door on a few hours earlier.

"I've found the perfect place to build our church and the town fathers are willing to offer it to us if we but stay. It's the lot on the northwest corner of Shepherd and Summer streets. It means we must build in a small hollow and not on a hillside as I'd prefer—let our light shine and all that—but this way our house of God will be better protected from the winds and weather. I understand winters here can be devastatingly wicked, and I'm told a church built into Mother Earth will offer us much more shelter. So, for protection from the elements, we will build our church into the Earth. Instead of praisefully climbing stairs to enter God's house as we normally would, we will humbly step down three or four. What think you, Christopher?" Stephen demanded.

"Yes, 'twill be a fine location," Christopher agreed. "And that's a sensible idea for building in this country."

No one else said anything.

Stephen looked around. "Where's Deborah?" he asked.

"She went for a walk of her own right after you left, but I expect she will be back in time for tea," Theodate said.

"Splendid," Stephen returned brightly, "she will see for herself what possibilities lay ahead for us here. I believe 'twas Providence that led you and Theodate to settle in Saugus, Christopher. Yes, indeed, it must have been Providence. The good Lord's eye is indeed shining upon us."

Chapter 32

Saugus
1632
Deborah

Deborah ran from her sister's house. Frustration fueled the anger raging in her, propelling her onward. She ran between the ruts of a road, bunching the skirt of her dress in one hand so as not to trip, and brushing tree branches from her face with the other. At last she was forced to slow to a walk and, finally, to stop.

Her chest heaved. Her heart beat harder than she ever remembered, rhythmically thudding in her ears. She bent over at the waist. Hands on her hips, she panted for breath.

How long had she been gone? How far had she run? She believed she'd run south. She looked all around. Of course, nothing was familiar. Was she lost?

On her left was the endless ocean she had so tortuously crossed. But here, she noticed the waves broke calm. A great expanse of a white, sandy beach spread out far below her.

This must be the bay Christopher talked about last night, Deborah thought. *What did he call this place?*

Nan. Nah. No, no, no. That's not right.

An Indian name. Nahant! That's it. Nahant.

Once her breath came without pain, she walked on. The wind had rearranged her hair, her cap having been snagged away by a branch long ago.

"Oh, my dear God," she said aloud, looking at the scene before her, "this is the very definition of beauty." The run had deflected her outrage, and was now put aside.

From the sea, Nahant appeared to be an island, but in reality it was not. Below, against the great cliffs, waves crashed as though they were as angry as Deborah had been a short while earlier.

In 1614, once his Virginia colony had been established, Captain John Smith surveyed this part of the coast. He described this land as the "Pieramides of Egypt."

As she explored, Deborah discovered Nahant sat majestically atop steep, craggy cliffs which rose upwards above the tide between twenty feet and sixty feet, with the water falling deep at its base.

Oh, my, just look at God's beauty, she thought. At her feet were small stones of white, green, blue, red, purple, gray. The spring grass was verdant and the flowers were white, bright and cheery.

Deborah continued her walk, now slowly, her anger spent.

She wound her way to the southeastern part of Nahant to what she later learned was aptly named Swallow's Cave. Here countless graceful birds swooped to and from, in and out, above and around the great rock and its protective irregularities that made nesting there so perfect.

Deborah strolled, now eastward, her aching heart mending itself with the salve of the magnificence surrounding her.

"Behold the beauty of the Lord," she quoted from Psalms. Then, from nowhere, another verse popped into mind: "Cease from anger."

Before her stood an odd-looking, formidable formation: Pulpit Rock, she was later told. She stopped to stare. It stood boldly out in the water some thirty feet tall, solidly impervious to the waves crashing upon it. It was nearly twenty feet square; nature had piled one rock atop another until it resembled a great stack of books. On top was an opening that formed a seat—but to reach it would be to take one's life in one's hands.

Deborah studied the rock, awed by its stark beauty. A sweet smile gently erased any furrows that remained on her face. A sharp gust of wind billowed the fullness of her cape and dress behind her. It blew her hair away from her face now wet—from sea spray, not tears.

She sat upon the wind-swept grass and stared at the great, exaggerated shape so familiar to her in its man-made form.

John, I see you there, atop that rock God made into a pulpit, and I hear your voice above the deafening sound of these waves.

Exhaustion overpowered her.

John, what am I doing here, she asked. *Across this water is home, is Deborah. Across this water is civilization.*

John...

She didn't know what else to say. To think. No words could express the hopelessness that gnawed at her.

She lay back on the long, soft grass and breathed in its cool, sweet smell. She stared up at the bulbous white clouds made even whiter by the bright blue of the sky.

What a vexing dilemma this is, Deborah thought. *I can't go back and I don't want to go on. Oh, Heavenly Father, help me.*

She closed her eyes.

*   *   *

A fortnight later, Deborah walked the short distance from Christopher and Theodate's house to the property she—and her son John, as head of their little household—had bought that morning.

My, just look at these trees, she said to herself, turning in a complete circle. *They're mighty beautiful. 'Twill be sad to cut them down to make room for a house and then use them to build that house with.*

She sat on a fallen birch and listened to the sweetness of a bird's song.

Dear God, she prayed, *how will we ever manage? How does anyone over here manage? How can my boys build us a house when they have never, ever, done anything close to that in their young lives?*

Oh, Father in Heaven, what have I done? What was I thinking of? What have I brought upon my sons?

Deborah's prayer was interrupted by the gentle sound of scurrying as a squirrel darted in front of her, traveling from one tree to another. The squirrel stopped midway to take in the sight of this woman, this aberration. And Deborah stared back. Neither creature blinked.

Aren't you the most beautiful critter? Your bushy tail is a thing of comeliness, she said to herself, not speaking aloud for fear she would scare the animal away. She wanted the blissful moment to never end.

But the squirrel, at last feeling safe, turned and scampered away. *"God love you,"* Deborah said, watching as it whisked up a tree and out of sight.

Visits from God's creatures were something she and John had enjoyed as a couple.

Oh, John, I miss you so. There's not a day that goes by that I don't think of you. I miss your guidance, but then I find you and hear you in times like this—when I least expect you. I feel you are still with me, helping me through each day.

Bless you for helping me that day when I was so upset with Father. I felt your presence beside me when Father said—no, when Father mandated—we were to stay in Saugus.

She closed her eyes.

"Deborah?"

Deborah jumped as though she heard the voice of her husband. Instead, it was her sister's.

"Theodate," Deborah said, "you startled me."

"I'm sorry," Theodate answered, "but I am happy to have found you. Sister, are thee well? Are you troubled?" She paused a minute. "You cause me to be troubled."

"I am just fine," Deborah answered testily. "Why wouldn't I be?"

"Don't be angry," Theodate said. "Confide in me, Deborah. Tell me what is troubling you—like you had me confide in you when I was a child and you were the elder sister. I'm all grown up, now, Deborah. Let me be the elder sister this time."

"Oh, Theodate, I do need a sister, or a mother—or a husband."

Theodate sat next to Deborah and wrapped her sister in her arms.

After a few moments, she took a deep breath and began: "I was so angry when I stormed from your house a fortnight ago, Theodate. I was angry at Father because he decided on his own that this is where we would live, rather than discussing it with us."

She retrieved a nose cloth from the wrist of her dress A sob rattled deep from her throat. The noise surprised both sisters and they laughed in surprise.

"I've also been angry at John for dying and leaving me alone," she said. "Isn't that ridiculous? Plus, I ache for my daughter."

"Where did you go that day?" Theodate asked.

Deborah stood and looked about her. She wiped the tears from her face.

"Do you think the boys will be able to fell these trees by themselves?"

"Yes," Theodate said. "And Christopher and others from town will help. Your boys won't have to build the house all by themselves."

Deborah was silent, still looking at the land she now called her own.

"Do you think 'tis right, that we buy this ground from the English government, when it clearly belongs to the natives? Why don't we pay them for it?"

"Deborah, those transactions are not for us to question," Theodate said.

"Why?" Deborah retorted. "Because we are women? 'Tis my money that is paying for it, and I have a right to know if it's being spent properly."

The two women stared at each other in the still forest.

"Theodate, I apologize. I'm well strung; full of nerves this past while. Ever since we left England, actually. There is just so much happening. There is so much new territory for me to explore and understand that 'tis near overwhelming. I'm doing my best to be its equal, but sometimes I weaken and feel so frail."

She returned to sit by Theodate again.

"On the day I stormed from your house, I ran 'til I could not take another step. I finally found myself sitting on a lawn as lush as any we'd seen in Holland.

"Theodate, don't think me mad, but I found John there. Atop Pulpit Rock. John and God. I heard him that day—John Wing. And God. And I listened. I heard John tell me that 'Love is patient and kind.'" Deborah hesitated. *How much does Theodate know about Father?* She wondered. She plowed ahead, bumbling, feeling her way. "Theodate, I know Father needs me—us—to be patient and kind, but sometimes 'tis difficult to love him these days, let alone to be patient and kind."

She stopped and waited for a response.

"I know, Deborah," Theodate said in a barely audible whisper. "I know."

"What do you know?"

"I know about Father and...," Theodate stumbled. "...and...Don't make me say it, Deborah."

The sisters looked at one another and then hugged tightly.

"And women," Deborah said. "Father and women."

It was Theodate's turn to weep.

"Sometimes 'tis as though he's not the same father who raised me," Deborah said. "He's not the same man who took my small hand in his huge one and walked me to town for a sweet biscuit at the baker's. Now, he's different, somehow.

"I can hardly look at him with Helena," Deborah said. "I have tried so hard to love Helena. I know 'tis not her fault that I feel this...this resentment towards her, but I cannot help myself. At first, I thought I would try to love what Father loves in her. But, of course, that's not possible."

She smiled sardonically at Theodate, whose returned smile was wan at best.

"I don't understand Father any more," Deborah said. "'Tis like he is a child again. I feel as though I am the parent and he is the child."

"Yes," Theodate said. "Yes, that's it exactly."

"Sitting on the grass that day by Pulpit Rock, I recalled a sermon John once preached on patience and self-control. I could see him, John, standing up high in the lectern and I heard him saying, 'The fruit of the Spirit is self-control.'"

Deborah rose and took Theodate's hand and pulled her up beside her. "I've been told that houses are set north and south in this country—with the front facing south to capture the warmth of the winter sun—and to serve as sundials to mark the nooning hour on a clear day.

"Where do you think we should 'plant' our house, Theodate? I brought tulip bulbs from Holland with me. I do hope they take to this climate for they are the most beauteous flowers. And a dear friend gave me starters of plants and herbs from home."

"I, too, brought plants from England," Theodate said. "Little reminders of home can be a great support when longing cannot be put aside.

"There were days when I worried that Father and you would never come. When we heard your John had passed, I was so afraid you would change your mind.

"'Twas selfish of me, wishing John to be alive just so you would come."

The women hugged again.

"On those days, flowers from home meant so much."

"Theodate, when I'm troubled, I take comfort in these words John once preached to his parishioners: 'I feel your presence in the fullness of joy.' When I was so filled with despair that day I ran away 'twas John's memory that gave me the fortitude to say, 'All right, Father, we will remain here. We came here with you and we will stay with you.' It wasn't easy, Theodate, but John's spirit helped me."

To herself, Deborah added, *Please, my dear John, my loving husband, I pray thee, always be near.*

Chapter 33

Saugus
1632
Deborah

"I can do this," Deborah said to Christopher, rolling up her sleeves and nudging her brother-in-law aside to free him for heavier work.

Deborah had watched the men wattle the Wing's house, Anglo-Saxon in design and identical to most in Saugus. It was framed with the small tree trunks of birch and beech they felled on their land.

Wattle—weaving twigs, branches and reeds between the poles—bound the house together. Once in tact, the wattle would be sealed with daubs of mud and clay, inside and out.

"I can wattle as easily as you," Deborah said with a smile, "but I can't root out stumps. So, let me do this."

"You don't think it unseemly?" Christopher asked.

"My dear brother-in-law, I would not, could not, do this in England, but 'tis different here. We must all do what we can to make this Great Experiment work—and this is something I can do."

When the wattle was completed and it was time to daub, Deborah, sleeves rolled up, couldn't help herself: "Phew," she said, looking at her hands coated with grime that instantly fastened itself to the underside of her fingernails. "'Tis a frightful smell," she said, smiling at Christopher. "You guarantee 'twill wash off?"

"Guaranteed," Christopher answered. "But you don't have to do this, Deborah. We can manage fine."

"Absolutely not," Deborah said. "This is where I want to be and this is what I want to be doing. You go on and leave me be. I'll be fine."

"Mother, let me help, too."

It was six-year-old Matthew.

"Darling, I thought you were with Aunt Theodate. This is no place for you. You will just get underfoot."

"Sorry, Deborah," Theodate said as she joined her sister. "We just came down to take a look at the progress and he got away from me and scooted ahead."

"Look, Mum," Matthew continued as if Deborah had been speaking to the wind. He showed her his small hand filled with mud: "See, I can put this between the trees. Just like you. Let me stay, pleeeese."

"All right," Deborah said, caving in. "But no complaining, mind you."

"Mother? Is that you?" Daniel asked, unable to stifle a laugh. "Beneath that coat of muck and mire is my mother?"

"Never you mind," Deborah scolded good-naturedly, wiping strands of hair away from her face, thickening her makeup of mud even more. "Matthew and I are making fine progress. We may look a tad untidy, but we are getting better with each handful of this muck. Now you just get along and tend to your own knitting."

Daniel guffawed and left. Soon both John and Stephen found an excuse to come to the front of the house to see their mother daub.

She pointedly ignored them, but out of the corner of her eye she caught a glimpse of admiration coming from their way. She knew they were as proud of her as she was of them.

It had taken the Wing family—Deborah, and John, nine and ten; Daniel, seven and ten; and Stephen, two and ten—a fortnight alone to clear the mini-forest of elm, maple, birch, oak and bushes and boulders to make room for their house.

Then, with guidance and direction from their Uncle Christopher, John, Stephen and Daniel began apprenticing the craft of carpentry.

"'Tis but a rude house," John apologized to his mother as he clambered down the makeshift ladder after a stint of thatching the roof. "But it does have a loft," he said, shading his eyes for a look at the on-going work. The loft, resting on rafters, would be sleeping quarters for him and his brothers. "'Tis obvious we Wings are not carpenters."

"Never you mind, Son. I fancy, come winter, we will consider this 'rude house,' as you call it, to be as fine as any lord's castle."

Finally came the day when the house was finished.

"Close your eyes, Mother," Stephen said.

"Are they shut tight?" Matthew demanded. "Really tight? So you can't see a wink?" He could barely suppress the giggles that wanted so much to escape his mouth.

"They're shut as tight as I can shut them," she said.

"Here, take my hand." It was John.

Her four sons led her down the lane. When it was time to turn off the path, John said, "Mind your step."

"And, how am I to mind my step when I cannot watch my step?"

"We're almost there."

"Wait," Matthew said. He seemed to be leading the contingent. "Wait."

Deborah heard a heavy door open.

She was urged forward a few more steps.

"Stop!" Matthew again.

"All right, Mother, open your eyes."

"Welcome to the Wing House," John said. "Our new home."

Deborah stepped over the threshold and looked lovingly at the solitary room she happily called home.

Deborah gasped at the sight. She blinked rapidly to chase any tears away before her sons saw them.

"Sorry 'tis only a dirt floor," Daniel said.

"The floor is fine," Deborah answered. "'Haps next year, planks can be cut and laid, but there's too much to do this first year to worry about the nicety of a proper floor."

"Yes," said John, "we still have Grandfather's house to finish and fall is upon us."

"We'll pack down this dirt so 'tis hard as rock," Deborah said. "It will look like a brown carpet. You'll not be able to tell the difference."

This home in New England was far different from the many rooms and fireplaces that had been their home in Holland. She loved that grand house, but for different reasons. This house was not so large or fine and it lacked all but the most rudimentary furniture. But it was all truly theirs. Made with love from their sweat and muscles.

"At least, Mother," Stephen jested, "there's no fear of getting lost in this new house of ours."

"The important thing is that we have a place to call our own, no matter how primitive," Deborah said. "Boys, I love our home. And I love you—all of you. You make me proud to be your mother."

"Oh, Mother," the older boys groaned together.

*　　　*　　　*

That evening, as she stirred their kettle of fish stew, Deborah said to her sons, "I must say you did a fine job building this fireplace. I know it wasn't easy."

The chimney had drawn the smoke up and out just as it was supposed to. The boys had laboriously unearthed, cleaned, chiseled, laid and cemented the stones together, with the help of their Uncle Christopher. Deborah had worked with them, side by side, building this house, but it warmed her heart to award them the credit.

Deborah hoped to always remember their first night in this new home.

John, Stephen, Daniel, Matthew and she sat on the floor in front of the fire for the longest time, content to silently watch the flames flicker into cinders. Matthew's eyelids refused to stay open, no matter how he fought, until at last he surrendered, laid his head in his mother's lap and slept. She ran her hands through his hair. Absently. Again and again.

At last, as one, the family was ready to retire. John leaned over and took his mother's hand into one of his, grabbed Stephen's hand with his other, gave them a gentle squeeze and quietly and reverently said, "Amen." Deborah looked at him and added, "Amen." Stephen and Daniel, too, uttered a quiet, prayerful, "Amen." "Amen."

Chapter 34

1632
Saugus
Deborah

.

"They are such handsome lads," Theodate told her sister. "The three eld-est are like peas in a pod."

Theodate and Helena were helping Deborah candles, her first experi-ence at this age-old craft.

"But their personalities are markedly different," Helena said. "I dare say John Junior will be the fearless, practical pioneer of them all; Daniel, methinks, will be a man of religion and an idealist; and Stephen? He looks to be a man of affairs."

"And Matthew?" Deborah asked, amused at their characterizations.

"'Tis too early to tell," Helena said, "but for certain he will grow to be as fine a man as his three older brothers. They will teach him all he needs to know."

"For which I am especially grateful since he will remember so little of his father," Deborah said quietly.

They worked in silence for a few moments.

"Candle-making isn't hard in the sense of waddling a house," Deborah said. "Not hard like that. Still, it does make one weary." She lifted her apron to blot the sweat beaded on her forehead and upper lip.

"I warned you that candle-making is sevenfold worse than your worst laundry day," Theodate said.

"I vaguely remember Mother dipping candles," Deborah said, "but by the time you were born, Theodate, she had taken to buying them, like most village women. I had no idea what a luxury John was affording me until this very day. This very moment." She plopped down on a tall, crudely made three-legged stool in the stark room with its floor tamped as hard as a rock. "I cannot tell you how much I appreciate your help, Helena and Theodate. You are truly dears."

"Just wait," Theodate said, "it won't be long 'til you will help us with the same project. Doing it together makes the day pass faster and the work seem less toilsome."

"It must have been hard on you, Theodate, to do this all by yourself the first year you were here," Helena said.

"Yes, but there were women who gave me wonderful advice—like candling in the autumn because they cool better then. Candles will last up to nearly a year if they're stored properly in a cool room.

"And," Theodate continued, relishing her position of instructing these two older women on the whys and wherefores of keeping house in this new land, "melting beeswax with tallow cuts down on the dripping and they will burn a much clearer light.

"'Tis ironic," Deborah said, smiling at Theodate, "to have you, my little sister, giving me household hints. But then, everything in America seems to be topsy-turvy. Here, Theodate, with your two years' experience, you are the expert."

Theodate beamed.

"I never imagined myself doing chores like this," Deborah said. But 'tis a fine thing to be self-sufficient. I knew we had to be independent, but still I am greatly relieved that we can do it."

"What's the hour?" Helena asked suddenly. "I must return home to fix the reverend's noon meal."

"And I must go too," Theodate said. "Can you manage alone now?"

"Of course," Deborah said as the women left. "Bless you both for your help today. And I will be more than happy to return the favor. This has been a most-pleasant day."

All told, I'd guess there must be some fifteen pounds of candles, she said to herself, looking at their handiwork. *That should be enough to light away winter's gloom.*

Deborah placed the palms of her hands on the small of her back and leaned backwards, letting her head drop towards her spine. She ached in places she didn't know were there to ache. She hunched her shoulders forward and her neck back. Righting herself, she caught sight of the mini-mountains of candles, and a small smile crossed her face, a reflection of the satisfaction she felt about the day's accomplishment.

Thank goodness for Theodate's tin molds—and Theodate herself, and Helena, too. *They saved me untold hours. I'm glad that Helena and I have become friends. It's so much more pleasant to love a person than to be at odds with that person. Shame on me for taking so long to warm up to Helena.*

She tucked back the strands of hair that had strayed from her close-fitting white hood tied beneath her chin. *This is truly long, hard, dirty work,* she complained silently, scraping the wax stiffening her fingers. The minute lines her fingers had formed on the now-cooled wax intrigued her. *Hmmm, isn't that something?* She hummed an ancient, ageless tune.

*   *   *

That afternoon, the Wing's door, with its double thickness of wood, stood open, inviting fall's cool fragrant air to freshen the house of a single room. An occasional breeze blew in a few newly fallen leaves of golden yellow, pumpkin orange and flame red. Outside, nearby, her boys worked together with the spirit of comrades.

It was a gorgeous day: A perfect autumn day. The sun was warm, but the air felt cool; a flawless combination.

She looked about her. *John, my dear husband,* she said in her heart, you would be so proud of your young sons. *This day gladdens me so. You are truly a fortunate woman, Deborah Wing.* She studied the array of candles and felt good. Achy, maybe, but good. She sighed and leaned against the table—three planks atop saw horses.

"'Tis time for a cup of tea," she said aloud.

She rose and moved to the fireplace that covered most of one wall. She swung the crane holding the copper teakettle so it was directly over the continuous flame.

When steam rattled the kettle's ill-fitting lid, she fetched a teapot and five cups from the shelf, set the tea to steeping and went to call her sons.

"Are ye ready for a cup of tea?"

The boys were digging a root cellar to store vegetables and fruits and dried meat for the winter. At the moment, however, Stephen was teaching Matthew the game of handydandy. He'd shake a rock in the pocket of his two hands closed together before making each hand into a fist, hiding the stone in one. Matthew then had to choose which hand held the rock.

"Be right there," Stephen answered after conferring with the brothers inside the cave they were carving into the bank.

Deborah returned to slice bread for their mid-afternoon tea. She bent down to pick up the leaves that had rustled into the house, intending to toss them out the door. Instead, she held them in her open palm and looked at them, then she clumped them together by their stems.

"Well, if your don't make the prettiest bouquet I've seen in many a day," she said. She went outside and selected half a dozen more, picking the brightest and prettiest, returned to the house and retrieved a squat, short-necked vase of pottery. She was mindful of the leaves' fragile crispness as she arranged them into a dried bouquet of New England's fall colors of bright yellow, dark red and rich brown.

Deborah swallowed and was surprised at the lump that had formed in her throat. She realized tears threatened to spill. *I must be weary,* she excused herself. With each leaf she added, she saw a long-stemmed tulip from the bouquet John had presented to her so many years ago.

Well, if this isn't the silliest thing, she scolded herself. *Save your tears for something important,* she thought, mimicking her husband's tone. She recalled that voice well enough, having heard it time and again during the first years they shared. *I'm certainly not going to shed tears over a handful of silly leaves. Leaves whose beauty is in its season of death.* She placed the bouquet in the middle of the table, next to the bowl of quince jelly, and moved on to slice the bread.

Another smile crossed her face, remembering John's passion for her bread.

"That looks good, Mother," Daniel said. "I'm as hungry as a bear coming out of hibernation."

Deborah jumped, nearly slicing her hand.

"Did I frighten you? Sorry."

"No, no, of course not," Deborah said. "My mind was an ocean and years away. Come, boys, sit down. I have our tea all ready."

*   *   *

"Aye, Grandfather, welcome," John greeted Stephen as the minister ducked his head, removed his hat and entered the room in a single motion. "We've all but finished our tea, but join us. Sit down, and Mum will fetch ye a cuppa, I'm sure." John spoke from where he sat at the head of the table, a position he had assumed without a word of discussion with anyone. He was, after all, now the head of the Wing household. Man of the house.

Deborah and Stephen exchanged slight smiles and blinks of winks at John Junior's comfortable confidence. It pleased them he so instinctively assumed his role.

"Father, you look piqued," Deborah said. "Would a cup of tea be welcomed?"

"Indeed," Stephen answered. "Daughter I need a word alone with you."

At that, the brothers rose. They understood, without being told, that this conversation was to be private. They brushed the breadcrumbs from their hands and the front of their pants and excused themselves to resume digging in the daylight that remained.

"What is it?" Deborah swung the kettle back over the flame. "You look troubled."

Stephen sat in silence for the longest time. His head was bowed and he stared at his hands, his fingers knitted together on the table in front of him, as if in prayer. When at last he looked at Deborah, tears stood in his eyes.

"I've been summoned before the General Court in Boston," he said in a barely audible voice.

Deborah rushed to his side, put her arms around his shoulders that didn't seem so broad anymore; she held him tight and laid her head atop his. "Whatever for?" she asked.

"First off, they're saying ours is not a proper church, that we're not a legal church, that I did not properly apply to preach here, so therefore I've no right to minister to anyone here. Next, they're saying I am under suspicion of having independent ideas, and that I'm not willing to yield to the dictation of others." He spoke as though his heart were breaking. "Newhall, that confounded rascal, issued a formal complaint about my baptizing Theodate and Christopher's son before theirs." Stephen cleared his throat and his voice began to regain its former strength fed so many years by his anger of injustice.

"My own grandson; my namesake, born only days after Thomas Newhall, and they raise a fray simply because I anoint my own flesh and blood minutes before their child. 'Tis not as though either babe were in danger of perishing and falling into the fires of hell before the rite of baptism could be administered."

Her father heaved a great sigh and looked into her eyes as she now sat next to him, her hands covering his, still entwined. It saddened her to feel the gnarly knots that were misshaping her father's aging hands. Deborah realized in her own frustration she was clenching her father's hands too tightly.

"Is the strife I suffered so long at home to haunt me even over here? Clear across the Atlantic?"

"Father," Deborah said quietly, "remember what you asked me on the ship? 'Where is my faith?' As you rightly said then, everything will be all right.

He looked at her. "I asked you that, did I?" He removed one of his hands from beneath hers and placed it on top of hers. "I apologize. Of course you have faith. And I have faith. And this, too, shall pass and will work out to the betterment of God's plan."

The silence around them was healing.

"It seems as though the Devil himself has made it his personal mission to make my life on Earth a miserable, living hell unless I submit to him. Surely, hell can be no worse than life at this very moment."

His voice trembled; he felt the hairs of his neck start to stiffen—and then fall slack. He laid his head on his hands and let out a sob that wrenched Deborah's heart.

"I miss your mother so," he said, sounding like a child hidden inside the aged man crying out for comfort. "I wish she were here. Here by my side. I need her calm and her wisdom. Without her, I cannot continue."

"Of course you can," Deborah scolded, wiping away her own tears. "Don't talk of such nonsense. You are Stephen Bachiler, Man of God, Saver of Souls. You crossed an ocean as wide as eternity to come to this new land for the sake of God. You cannot give up now. Giving up now would be to succumb to the Devil."

Deborah swallowed and continued her role as minister/parent/daughter. Gently, she rubbed her father's shoulders and spoke softly: "You have oft preached that character produces hope. 'Christ in you is the hope of

Glory,' you have said." She tried to recall other pertinent biblical passages. "Christ Jesus is our hope."

*   *   *

The next session of the Boston General Court ruled: "Mister Bachiler is required to forbear exercising his gifts as a pastor or teacher publicly in our patent, unless it be to those he brought with him, for his contempt of authority and 'til some scandals be removed."

Chapter 35

Saugus
1633
Deborah

Stephen and Helena blew into the Wing home in a frenzy that was as blustery as the stinging, whipping March wind they shut out as they closed the door.

"I have great news, Daughter," Stephen roared with enthusiasm.

Deborah hurried to greet them.

"Let me have your wraps and you go stand by the fire. 'Tis a chilling air out there."

She shook the cold and dampness from their surcoats and hung them on pegs by the door.

"Now, tell me, Father, what has you so excited? I haven't seen such a happy smile on your face in I don't know how long. What is it?" Deborah looked quizzically first at Stephen, then Helena, who obviously was not going to spoil her husband's surprise. Deborah's face began to mirror theirs.

As a unit, John, Daniel, Stephen and Matthew moved to join the trio by the fireplace.

"What is it, Grandfather?" John asked, his face breaking into a smile without bidding.

"Tell us, Grandfather," Daniel said, "we could use a bit of good news—and, obviously, you have good news."

Matthew jumped into Stephen's arms and hugged his neck.

Stephen returned his young grandson's hug, tousled young Stephen's hair and slapped John and Daniel's backs in a congratulatory manner, everyone smiling and laughing all the while.

"Life is good," was all Stephen would say. "God is good."

"What is it?" Deborah asked again. She was still smiling, but tension sounded in her voice.

Stephen put Matthew down and turned to warm his backside by the fire, his smile growing even broader. He was enjoying himself immensely. He lifted the back of his jacket and bent over so the heat would get to the heart of his cold bottom.

His smiled turned sly. A mischievous twinkle sparkled from the eyes that had appeared so sunken and dark of late. Stephen delighted in his teasing, prolonging the suspense, savoring every moment his daughter and grandsons agonized over his untold news.

"I hope you don't mind," Stephen said, looking at Deborah, "but I've invited Christopher and Theodate and a few others to bring their supper with them to your house so we can celebrate this revelation together."

Stephen's face reddened with excitement. The puffiness beneath his troubled eyes that had been there yesterday was gone today. Excitement filled every fiber in his body. Even strands of his white hair, charged with electricity generated by his hat, waved in wild disarray atop his head. Deborah couldn't help but smile—not only at whatever his good news might be, but at his personage, as well.

So his grandparents could warm themselves in comfort by the fire, Daniel trucked over a slab bench he'd made from a piece of hewn lumber supported by forked branches.

"Bless you, son," Stephen said as he gingerly sat down. This homemade New England furniture was not to be compared to what had been left behind. Still, these makeshift pieces served their purposes and far be it for Stephen to complain.

He took out his nose cloth and noisily blew his nose. He sought Deborah's eyes above the square of fabric embroidered with his initials. He winked at her.

Deborah clapped her hands together.

"I know. I know. I know. Oh, Father, I am so happy for you."

She was immediately at his side, her arms hugging him as she had the day he received the horrid news he was to cease preaching to any but those who came to America with him. The scent of damp wool from his suit filled her senses. She laid her head atop her father's like she had that other day. With one hand, she tried to still the straying strands of hair that stuck up and tickled her face, and with the other hand she patted her father's face. He put his hand around her waist, swung her down to his lap, hugged her close to him and the two enjoyed a moment of intimacy amid the clamor of the boys' cheers of congratulations—even though they were unsure just what it was they were celebrating.

"What? What? What?"

By this time, Christopher and Theodate and parishioners and friends and neighbors had let themselves into the house. Word quickly spread that their pastor had good fortune to learn at the house of Goodwife Wing. There was a cause for celebration!

At last, Stephen removed a folded letter from an inside pocket of his coat.

"The governor has written me a letter, handed to me less than an hour ago, informing me that now, five months after the fact, my prohibition has been lifted and I am here-to-forth free to legally petition to start up a church anywhere in the Massachusetts Colony."

The room erupted as celebrants began to laugh, talk, fill mugs of wine and beer to toast the governor, the councilmen who at long last righted their wrong. And of course, over and again, they toasted Stephen, the beloved head of their family, their much-loved pastor. His redemption was theirs as well.

"What reason did they give for rescinding their ridiculous edict?" called out a neighbor standing shoulder-to-shoulder amid those now jammed into the Wing's house.

"Actually, they gave no specific reason," Stephen said. "But they acknowledged the charges were ill-founded and that Master Newton's complaint was solely of personal nature, founded on spite and jealousy, that he sought revenge because his son was baptized second instead of first."

Stephen shook his head. A brief look of puzzlement crossed his face, but instantly he replaced it with the smile that was now causing the muscles in his face to ache.

"What matters is that our church has been officially recognized. Nothing can stop us now."

Christopher jumped atop a stool, raised his hands above his head, clanked a knife against his dull-gray pewter mug, and asked for quiet.

"Sir," said Theodate's husband, who defended his father-in-law as though they were blood kin, "may this be the last of any religious persecution ever brought against you. From this day forward, may you enjoy the freedom from restraint you—and we—have so long sought."

"Christopher, children, friends." Stephen called out. The room was instantly quiet. All eyes were upon him. "I cannot express to you what is in my heart at this moment. You persevered and stood by me whilst others stoned me with cruel words. Thank the good Lord it was mere words they hurled and not actual bone-splintering, head-bashing stones like those thrown to slay Stephen—Stephen, the saint whose name I have the honor to bear.

"Nay, the evil, wrong, hurtful words flung at me by ignorant people did not slay me." He smiled again. "Nor did they still me. I knew God would exonerate me so I could continue my mission of cleansing the church and its people."

Stephen looked at the faces looking at him. There wasn't a dry eye in the house.

"I am so happy and proud to call all of you my children and to know that your trust and love is steadfast. Mayhap, at this moment, I am the luckiest man alive."

Deborah recognized her father was losing composure. Too much wine or ale made him weak in spirit, turning his emotions and words to mush. So, she called out, "Everyone, hear me: No more toasts. 'Tis time to eat. Come, put down your mugs, pick up a trough and we will eat to our fill. Between our several families, we have a veritable feast in front of us."

"A moment, Mother," John said, taking his turn atop the stool. Everyone quieted again and looked at Deborah and John's oldest son. "Grandfather, I want to give you the blessing you have intoned on so many of us. As you have pronounced so many times: 'May the good Lord cause his eyes to shine upon you.'"

"Bless you, son. Bless you."

"Amen," was the unified response.

Chapter 36

Saugus
April 1633

"You, Thomas Dexter," rang out the voice of the town crier as he read the pronouncement quilled on a scroll, "are to be set in the billows, disfranchised and fined forty pounds for speaking reproachful and seditious words against the government here established."

All of Saugus had turned out to see the spectacle of a leading town citizen be cramped and trapped into the pillory. Some came to make sport of the humiliation inflicted on a fellow human being, others to support Farmer Dexter if only to stand by helplessly as he was indignantly forced into the stock next to the church, which doubled as the town's meeting place.

In most villages, stocks were placed midtown, next to the meetinghouse, as a visible reminder of the punishment that awaited those who dared question the government. Or who were spotted chewing tobacco or who nodded off during a Sunday sermon, never mind it might well drone on for two hours or more.

A group of families—the Wings, Husseys and Bachilers among them—stood apart from the rest of the townspeople, bolstering their mal-treated friend.

A core of solidarity bonded these dozen Saugus families, and friends did not turn their backs on friends in times of trouble. There were others, however, who delighted in taunting the hapless Thomas Dexter.

Prisoner Dexter was aware of no one except his captors—and he was not going to be imprisoned quietly in the evil contrivance. He dug his heels into the ground as the guards yanked him towards the dreaded stock. His well-muscled arms wrestled about, trying to escape his captors.

"Here, here, you rogue, you rascal. Be peaceful and 'twon't be near so hard on ye," an officer barked.

The more Dexter and the soldiers sparred, the louder the crowd cheered.

He was dashed to the ground on his back and held firm by two soldiers while another two grappled with his kicking, thrashing legs to sequester them in the bottom-half of the pillory's two hewed-out circles. The top was slammed down and locked into place.

A soldier grabbed Thomas by the back of his shirt collar and hauled him upright, gagging him, choking the breath out of him, while other soldiers captured his flailing arms and hands and roughly forced them into the wooden contrivance that already held his feet. The top was loudly clapped down and a great display made of turning the key in the lock.

"There," growled the turnkey. "'Tis not too good for the likes of you."

Judith, Dexter's wife, appeared from the edge of his supporting friends and begged the soldiers to "please let my poor husband sit upon this stool."

Boos and catcalls sounded from his foes that Dexter should be allowed any comfort of any kind.

"This is truly a disgrace," Stephen fumed, loud enough for those sanding nearby to turn and look at him. "These pillories are a disgrace! Why should a fine Christian man, such as Goodman Dexter, be so ignobly confined? Just for speaking his mind. Here, in this country, in New England!" Stephen's voice carried the tone of disbelief and discouragement that was so visible on his face. He shook his head.

"How can it be? If every man who spoke his true mind against the government were to be thusly punished, there would scarce be enough trees to cut down to make into pillories," Stephen said, again shaking his head as though he could make no sense of this humiliating scene.

"Father, in the name of all that is sacred, keep still," Deborah hissed.

Helena discreetly tugged at the sleeve of her husband's coat. "Stephen, please, for my sake, mind thy tongue."

Stephen frowned at his wife, but stopped wagging his tongue.

"What did Goodman Dexter say that landed him in such ado?" Daniel asked.

"Who can say for certain," his Uncle Christopher answered. "We've not yet been told the particulars, but Goodman Dexter has himself a hot temper and a contrary nature, and this is not the first time he has been given cause to rue that sharp tongue of his."

The fine mist that had greeted the villagers in the early hours of the day now began to fall in thick drops. Still, the crowd made little effort to move.

At last, deciding there was nothing more they could do to boost the morale of the dejected Thomas Dexter, the Bachiler entourage began to leave, Christopher, steering his gang of nephews away from the scene and towards home. The April chill was enough to cause one's bones to brittle.

"We'll say a prayer for thee," Deborah said to Thomas Dexter as she passed in front of him. "Keep up your courage."

The family made its way down the path of trampled weeds and grass, just now beginning to green again, oblivious to their awaited fate of being trodden down yet another season.

The rain made the earth smell fresh and clean as opposed to the dirty scene the Wings, Bachilers and Husseys left behind them. The rain would also help melt the remaining snow and ease the memory of the months of bitter cold, which might have frozen the spirits of a less hearty group of newcomers. But not the Bachilers, although they could not deny it was the coldest winter they'd ever known.

Matthew didn't mind the weather, no matter its form. The great snow, more than ever fell in England or Holland, provided a world of new fun and games—snowballs, forts, plunking down backwards and "winging" his arms up and down to make angels. And today's rain was perfect for the spring sport of splashing. He was teaching his toddling cousin, Stephen Hussey, the skill needed to make the biggest splash possible: run, jump high and hard and land smack in the middle of the puddle with both feet. The lesson was cut short when Christopher scooped Matthew up and over his shoulders and grabbed his son Stephen, stuck him under an arm, and toted him on home, wailing all the way like a squealing pig.

In front, beside and behind Christopher, were his other Wing nephews: John, Daniel and Stephen.

Now, as they walked, Christopher explained the fate of New Englanders dareful enough to break the rules set by the Mother County an ocean away.

"Goodman Dexter's first offense, the one that singled him out as a potential trouble-maker, was when he purchased the land called Nahant from 'Black Will' for nothing more than a mere suit of clothes."

Deborah's ears perked up at the mention of the word Nahant, the place where she'd come to terms with herself last fall.

"Black Will?" questioned John. "Isn't he Poquanum, the Indian chief?"

"The very same," Christopher said, pleased with John's quick mind. "The sale cannot be considered legal. As much as I admire Thomas Dexter and all he's done for Saugus—building the mill and the dam to run it— 'Twas not a fair nor Christian bargain he struck with the unknowing and trusting Indian. In time, there will be trouble settling the sales account. Nothing's been officially said about it yet, but mark my words, there will be trouble. 'Tis not right to take such advantage.

"Still, 'tis a sorry thing that Farmer Dexter will now have his freeman's privileges stripped. And for speaking words rather than the fisticuffs of other troubled times."

"Fisticuffs?" prodded Stephen Wing, anxious to hear the most dreadful of details to satisfy his young, morbid curiosity. A rough-and-ready, stowed-up bundle of energy, Stephen could easily imagine a bout of fisticuffs: he'd boxed the ears of his friends and brothers enough times, as well as having had his own boxed a time or two.

"Well," his uncle replied, "last year there was an unfortunate situation in which Master Dexter caused John Endicott, the magistrate from Salem, to lose his temper and beat upon Master Dexter. Not once, not twice, not even thrice—but mayhap a half a dozen times or more. Goodman Endicott was recently married and had put out to sea to cross to Mistic, but a great storm, the wind stiff against their sails, drove them back to shore. That's where his trouble with Thomas Dexter began."

By this time, Christopher and the boys had reached the Hussey home. They looked around and found themselves alone, Theodate waiting at the opened door. Deborah and Theodate, who quickly became more interested in staying dry than hearing a recount of Goodman Dexter's tribulations, had quickened their steps once the rain began to pelt; Stephen and Helena had earlier ducked their heads and made straight away to their cottage for dryness and warmth.

Christopher and his group of entranced listeners had been left to lag behind, oblivious of being sopped, wet to the skin. Now Deborah called for her sons to hurry their steps and come along.

"Uncle is telling us such wonderful tales," Daniel called back to his mother. "Can we stay a while to hear the rest?"

"Don't be long," Deborah called back. "'Tis likely to really storm."

Inside the Hussey's house, prototype for the Wings' and Bachilers' houses, the boys dropped their coats and scarves and mittens by the door and gravitated to the fire to warm themselves and hear the rest of Uncle Christopher's tale.

"Go on," the boys said. The image of the maligned Dexter, who was even now being so indignantly punished, was fresh in their minds.

"Well, Farmer Dexter complained to the court in Boston about Endicott beating him—and rightly so. Endicott, however, took umbrage and said he had good cause for him to lose his temper and strike out.

"You see, 'tis not legal for a magistrate to strike another person, and Endicott knew he could very well find himself in a kettle of hot water for allowing himself to be reduced to the level of a common waylayer," Christopher explained.

He raised his voice to a whine, imitating Endicott when he pleaded his case to Governor Winthrop: "If you had seen the manner of his carriage, which such daring, his arms akimbo, it was enough to provoke even a patient man." The boys began to roar with laughter, "Were it lawful for me to try it at blows, and he be a fit man for me to deal with, you should not hear me now complain."

Christopher's voice returned to its natural level: "That time, grant you, the governor and court officers sided with Goodman Dexter and allowed him damages of nearly ten pounds, a hefty amount, indeed."

"Is that all? Are there more stories?"

"Boys, we should not gossip."

"Oh, 'tis not gossip," John rationalized. "We need to know these things in order to conduct ourselves in a proper manner."

Christopher smiled and continued:

"Well, there was one more time. Although Farmer Dexter is most often a man of control and Christian attitude, he does at times not stand for the proper points of etiquette and he does have occasions of irritability. More so than most rational men.

"A while back, he felt a slight of some sort by a neighbor."

"Who?" "Which neighbor?" "Tell us," the boys all interrupted at once.

"I'm not going to tell you who it was, but Farmer Dexter kept thinking about this slight, and thinking about it. He let his feelings fester and fester until finally he was nigh beside himself in anger he built up needlessly.

"As luck would have it, one day he happened to meet this neighbor on the road, and Dexter, jumping from his horse, bestowed some twenty blows on the neighbor's head and shoulders."

The boys were awed, fascinated, at hearing the dark side of the man in stocks, who, by now would surely be drenched.

"Nothing came of that offense, but alas, this time, Goodman Dexter's sharpness has cost him dearly. His punishment will likely cause him to think twice before speaking again so rashly. One hopes by now he will have at last learned that a fly flies not into a closed mouth. The moral of this tale, lads, is that you must mind your tongue, lest it cause you great harm. There are ears everywhere, and, sad to say, one neighbor may very well set upon another."

Chapter 37

Saugus
1635
Deborah

"Bless this food, Heavenly Father, and the hands that have lovingly pre-pared it," Stephen Bachiler prayed by rote. Instead of its usual exuberance, his voice was sad. "May it nourish our bodies as we seek to nourish our souls in order to serve thee to the fullest."

With Stephen's "Amen," Deborah looked curiously at her father but said nothing.

"That's the shortest prayer Grandfather's ever said," hissed Matthew to his little cousin Stephen sitting next to him, forgetting his mother was sit-ting on his other side.

Deborah frowned at her youngest son and firmly pressed her foot on top of his, out of eyesight of the other family members. Matthew swal-lowed a "sorry" and wiggled his foot free.

It was a solemn extended Bachiler family that gathered at the Wings' home this blustery March Saturday in 1635. Two trestle tables were placed end to end so the entire family might sit together. They regularly gathered at one house or another for a meal, but usually didn't bother with extra tables, leaving the children and young people to sit or stand however and wherever they pleased.

The severe winter, however, which dumped snow knee-high and froze rivers solid made Deborah and the other women long for the warmth of family. So, with the first possible Saturday when slipping in the snow was no longer a threat and tables could be transported with relative ease, plans were made to convene for a meal to warm their souls even if their bodies must still fight the cold.

There had been much hilarity that morning as the older Wing boys hoisted Hussey's plank table upside down over their heads and rowdily made their way down the paths from Aunt Theodate's houses to their house. Matthew and Young Stephen hitched a ride on the tables, hanging on dearly so as not to be bucked off as the older boys purposely jostled them about.

The boys had sounded no warning that Grandfather Bachiler was "in a pique," and the anticipated festive meal soured with Stephen Bachiler's entrance across the Wing threshold. The carriage of his body and the countenance of his face spoke volumes even though he said not a word. The wind that blew in with him was nowhere as penetrating as the sorrow Deborah saw in her father's eyes.

Her heart sank. *Not again,* she thought. She knew only too well the pained expression that etched itself on her father's face. *Oh, dear Lord, not again.*

*   *   *

Just that morning, during her devotional time before the rest of her family roused, Deborah praised God for all the good that had come into their lives in the recent past, and for the further goodness she felt awaited them.

Indeed, the entire family had felt God's graciousness would be recognized in its fullness this year. For the most part, events had been peaceful the past while. The rancor that had tainted so much of their daily lives for so many years seemed to be in abeyance.

Deborah had rekindled the night's embers into crackling flames before she retrieved her Bible and pulled her chair close to the fire for her time of meditation. The chair was the one she had bought John when he began his ministry. Both the chair and her King James Bible, a wedding gift from John, were showing their age. She ran her hand over the Bible's black leather cover, and with her thumb contemplated the spot made smooth from its daily use. Her other hand automatically caressed the leather chair's arm that John had darkened and worn smooth.

A smile crossed her thoughts and lightened her spirits. She treasured the small reminders she found of her husband in her every-day life, even from where she buried him. Her husband's grave appeared in her mind. She closed her eyes. "Rest in Peace." She could feel her eyes move back and forth as she silently read the inscription. "Rest in Peace."

Deborah quieted her mind, emptied her thoughts of any distraction, including the tasks that awaited her final "Amen," and opened her Bible to Psalms 29 and read, "Give unto the Lord, O ye mighty, give unto the Lord glory and strength." She considered each verse of David's until she read the 11th: "The Lord will give strength unto his people; the Lord will bless his people with peace."

Oh, 'tis so true, she thought and began to detail the family's recent sorrows versus its even more recent blessings. At long last, her family was being blessed with peace.

The previous year, Thomas, the Hussey's second child, died at childbirth. The delivery, like the travail, had been long and tedious and the infant wasn't strong enough to survive the trauma. Theodate, herself, nearly passed with her babe. But instead, praise God, she had regained her health and only a fortnight ago announced she was with child again, and was feeling fit.

Deborah warmed her bones and her soul before the crackling fire and thanked God that her sons were proving to be such excellent students under her daily tutelage. John had "graduated" from his mother's sessions and had taken to farming.

Even father's life seems to have planed itself an even course, more or less, Deborah thought. Once the court ruled his "scandals" were nothing more than his bent to be less than truly orthodox, less than truly conformable to the rules and orders of the church, his life seemed to have found an easier path to follow—one without so many slippery stones to skid upon.

And for that Dear God, I will be eternally grateful, she prayed.

In short, Stephen's scandals were nothing more than a repeat of the misunderstandings he'd encountered with church officials as far back as Deborah could remember.

In fact, Deborah noted, *things could hardly be better these days. Since the court's ruling, Father's peers have included him in the colony's conferences of ministers. Father does enjoy being consulted on matters of import.* She smiled to herself.

Stephen first met with the conference on September 17, 1633, to consider the settlement of Mister Cotton. And, just last month, the biblical scholars reconvened to consult with one another about two more weighty issues: what course of action ought to be considered: should a general governor be sent over from England, and whether it should be deemed lawful to carry the cross on church banners.

Besides which, Deborah told God, *Father will no doubt soon be made a freeman of the Massachusetts Colony.*

She was happily aware of the marked difference in her father once the court made its ruling these two years past: His step once again had its spring; the twinkle sparkled in his eyes again. He was his jaunty old self.

But now this.

*　　　　　*　　　　　*

It was time to eat. Deborah called the family to sit down. As she watched them seat themselves, she worried they would come away from dinner with colic stomachs instead of pleasantly full bellies.

Everyone had looked forward to an afternoon of laughter, cheers and anticipation of God's blessings they were certain would blossom along with the spring flowers. Instead, Deborah feared, the meal would be eaten in silence or with forced conversation.

For several months, Stephen—indeed, the entire family—looked the other way, turned a deaf ear, trying to ignore the rumblings being renewed amid a corner of his congregation. But instead of lessening, the whispering attacks were becoming more heated, more volatile and Stephen could no longer ignore them. He tried to reason privately with those who talked against him; he preached one Sunday about the sin of bearing false witness.

But the ugliness continued. Even this morning. At the Saturday market, Stephen had been reproached by a group of men who turned on their heels when he neared.

"Father," Deborah asked, "would you do the honors of slicing the gander? And, John, you can pass the ribs and horseradish. Christopher, help yourself to the carrots. I drizzled them with honey, just the way you like them."

Deborah was determined this celebration, this longed-for meal, would not be daunted by unvented frustration: Her father at the gnarling element in his congregation bent on his dismissal and his family on his behalf.

"Eat your fill, but save room for dessert," Deborah cautioned, "we have pumpkin and minced pies, gingerbread, and Theodate sugared and glazed a pan of almonds."

"Daughters and wife, you have out-done yourselves," her father acknowledged to his women folk. "This is indeed a feast."

"Aye," the children chimed, relieved their grandfather had at last cut the tension as well as the meat.

"John," Stephen said, holding up his empty ewer, "I believe we could all do with more ale."

Finally, when the last child swallowed his last bite, the older children were told to take the younger ones to the Hussey house and tend them there.

"Now, Father," Deborah said once the clatter of the young ones moved down the way and the adults congregated on either side of one table, "let's discuss this situation rationally. Tell us exactly what is going on."

Stephen looked up at his wife, his children and their spouses and at his grandson, John Wing. Now that the young ones had left, the aging minister allowed his shoulders to sag as though he would never shed the constant weight that pinned him down.

"It's begun again," he said. "The whispers. The accusations. The persecution. It seems I am never to be at peace. What is it about me that invites such attacks?"

"No! We'll have none of that," Deborah scolded as though Stephen were her charge. "There is no room for self-pity. We did not very nearly lose our lives crossing that dreadful ocean in search of peace for you to so easily surrender to those who disagree with you. If you were going to give in, you might as well have done it years ago. At home."

"Deborah's right," Christopher Hussey said. "We came to this country with an objective and we cannot let a few intolerants set us back."

"Grandfather," John said, "you are our leader in more ways than just as the head of this family. It is you—and, of course, my Mother and Father—but mostly you who taught me—us, all of us—about God and God's will. Through you, we know God's will is pure and just."

Deborah picked up on her son's thought.

"We know it is God's will that you be here, Father. That we be here. We know God is right. We know you are right."

Stephen rubbed the back of his neck with an expression on his face that something felt queer. He moved his head back and forth, up and down against his collar. A wry smile ticked at one corner of his mouth, as if to say, things were right.

"I feel God is speaking at this minute," he told his family in a whispered voice. "God is speaking to me through you."

He slapped his open palm on the table.

"You are right. By God, you are right."

Everyone fairly jumped at the sound of Stephen's transformation. The pewter mugs teetered with the reverberation of Stephen's smack.

His family looked at one another, startled by the turn-about. Pleased. Relieved. But startled.

"So, what do we do?" Theodate asked.

"Yes," Christopher added, "some action must be taken."

"Specifically, Father," Deborah said as she rose from the table and walked to one end of the room, "what is being said? Who is saying what?"

When she returned to the group, she had with her a bottle of ink, a quill and a piece of paper as if to take notes of this family council.

"That's the rub," Stephen said. "I ask one person and they say another person is saying this. I ask that person and they say, 'Oh, no Reverend, I would never say that, but I heard So-and-so say this.' I go to that person and 'tis the same run-around. The crux is, I do not know who is saying what or why. I only know that a certain few are trying to undermine mine authority and have me ousted. They, whoever they are, still insist ours is not a proper church and that I am not a proper shepherd to tend the flock."

Everyone sat in silence, perplexed about how best to tackle the elusiveness of hearsay.

Deborah fussed with the pen's feather, twirling it about with her fingers, unmindful of the drops of ink flying from the nib. She cleared her throat tentatively.

"Father," she began somewhat meekly, voice trembling. "I daresay I hate to bring this up, but are there complaints among the husbands in the congregation?"

"What?" her father blustered. "What?"

His face flamed as though the blood in his veins would burst into beads of red sweat.

No one said anything. The room was filled with a deadly silence that threatened to suck the oxygen right out of the air.

Theodate hid her face in her hands.

Stunned, Helena looked at Deborah and then at Stephen. She retrieved her nose cloth tucked into the sleeve of her dress at the wrist and quietly wiped the tears that sprung from the corners of her eyes.

"I've heard some rumblings," Stephen finally owned. "But, like all the other charges, they are baseless. I have harmed no man—or woman—in either thought or deed. If someone says otherwise then let him speak to me. So far, not a man has made such a charge against me."

Again silence.

"I have an idea," Deborah said at long last, slowly whisking the quill's feather back and forth across her chin. "Maybe it's the teacher in me, but why don't you ask your parishioners to make a list of their complaints? Nothing can be gained if you continue to talk of chalk while they talk of cheese. It's difficult to fight a battle if you don't know who your foes are or what ammunition they're firing."

Everyone turned to Deborah, then to this aging father and husband. Smiles began to appear on their faces as the dawn of hope illuminated itself. It was as though Deborah had lit a torch whose blaze instantly cast a light on the path that had been shrouded in darkness for many months.

Chapter 38

Saugus
March 1635
Stephen

"I am heartened to see such a great turnout today," the Reverend Stephen Bachiler greeted his parishioners. A smile suggested itself on his face, but it was without warmth.

In fact, his demeanor was nearly as chilly as the church itself this March day. The women warmed their toes atop small foot burners filled with hot coals and wrapped their hands around hot potatoes tucked inside their muffs. Some men brought their wooly dogs to lay atop their feet to keep them warm and their blood circulating.

Once everyone was seated Stephen continued:

"We all know the village has been astir with rumors since it became known I called this meeting," he said. "And, I am aware that some of you have fermented that turmoil.

"I also know something you do not. You have no idea what this meeting is about. You may think you do, but believe me, you do not."

The men looked at one another. What's this man up to, now, was the consensus of their expressions. The women peered at their husbands across the aisle to read their faces.

Although both men and women sat in silence, it was obvious there were two mind-sets in the audience, split by gender.

"I have heard," Stephen said, his voice rising, "some of you think I am going to do as you have asked and resign my pastorate today and step aside for this congregation to call another minister."

There was nodding of heads in one camp, shaking of heads in the other.

"Well, sirs, I am not!"

His fist ferociously slammed the pulpit. His congregation literally jumped in their seats. Stephen's emphatic proclamation caused an immediate stir: grumbling from the men, whispered prayers of "God be praised" from the women along with muffled applause of several pairs of gloved hands clapping. The men cast stern glances at their womenfolk who smiled and looked straight ahead at their beloved religious leader, ignoring their marital leaders.

Deborah shook her head at the divided response and Helena blushed and ducked hers.

"We can no longer have Satan sundering this congregation," Stephen continued, the tremor in his voice matching his emotions. "Unless we are unified, we shall sink in the mire of discontent.

"You have asked for my resignation without giving me the courtesy of telling me why. Well, sirs, I will give you some 'whys' of my own: Why would any sane man think another sane man would relinquish his post, any post, without hearing the charges brought against him? Why would any man with the least bit of a conscience visit such grief upon another, especially when that man is his minister, a courier of God? Why would any hard-working man, as truly all of you are, spend such draining energy to wrongly accuse another? And, maybe most importantly, why would you surrender your lives in Mother England to travel half way around the world in search of religious freedom and then deny its happening?

Stephen paused. "Have you no answers?" he thundered, enunciating each word as though it were a sentence unto itself.

The room was silent. It was as though frost could be heard forming on the windows. No one moved. Not a soul moved. Then the fidgeting began. Men twirled their hats, pulled at their collars for extra breathing space, inspected the toes of their shoes. Women wiped away tears . Blew their noses. The men looked at one another. Obviously, they had not elected a spokesman among them to respond.

"No one wants to speak aloud?" Stephen asked incredulously. "No one wants to speak to my face? Only behind my back?"

Silence.

"So be it. If you are to be such cowards," he roared then lowered his voice to a mere whisper: "I will give you a coward's way of addressing thy grievances."

The men squirmed. The split-and-planed log pews they sat upon were growing harder and more uncomfortable by the minute. They held not an ounce of give.

In his normal voice, Stephen continued: "Members of my family and a few beloved, trusted friends are going to walk among you to hand you pieces of paper. I want you to take these pieces of paper and go to the back of the room where we have plenty of quills and pots of ink set up. I want you to list your complaints. Number them for me. One by one. If more paper is needed, it will be provided. Tell me specifically how I have wronged you." He dropped his voice dramatically: "But tell me honestly. List the dates and times of the truth as you see it. You need not sign your name after your complaint."

No one moved.

"Please gentlemen, let us get on with this business," Stephen coaxed wickedly. "We do not want to be at this all day."

Still not a man rose to file to the back of the church.

"What?" Stephen asked, sarcasm oozing. "What? Where among you are those who have been so quick to speak in town? I plainly see you sitting here in front of me. I know who you are. You cannot deceive me on your identities. Therefore, can you not comply with this simple request? Would you rather gossip like a woman than face the one you accuse like a man?"

Again, a dramatic pause.

Deborah winced at his comparison, but swallowed it. Still, she paused to sort her thoughts about what her father had just said and was surprised to discover the depth of her exasperation. A few years ago, a statement categorizing all women as gossips would not have penetrated any thoughts. It was simply something men said. She and other women friends might have even 'tee-heed' about it, even if they might have been a bit annoyed.

But that was then and this was now—and now, the reference was offensive. Now, she resented the notion of any woman being depicted as a cackling hen, scratching about a chicken coop, clucking the latest gossip with her feathered friends. The very idea! She could just see the cock strutting about, which infuriated her even further.

But now was not the time for such thoughts. Later. She'd think it through further later.

"Well, then, if there is to be no help forthcoming from you, my congregation, regarding this point, let me tell you now what I intend to do. There is no doubt that this problem must be resolved. You have said there is Godlessness in our midst. At first I denied it. Such a thing was not possible in this church of God. In this congregation of God. But the more I prayed about it, the clearer it became that you were right. There is Godlessness amongst us. But it comes not from me, gentlemen. I have searched my conscience and know it to be clear. You—the people I pray for continuously, the people I am trying to lead to salvation—you have caused me woeful anguish in a most unchristian-like manner. Until now, I would not have believed it possible to be God's servants and treat another human being thusly." Stephen looked at the men, leaders of a vocal minority in the congregation He longed to search their faces for contrition, but to see remorse, he would have to see their eyes and all eyes were lowered. "Therefore, considering your sin against me and against God, I am going to write to the Massachusetts church leaders and ask that each of you be excommunicated!"

The room exploded.

"You can't do that."

"Who do you think you are?"

"You must certainly be Satan's minister."

Without saying a word further, Stephen straightened his frame to its tallest possible height and strode down the center aisle between the pews. His white mane haloed magnificently above his head. When he reached the doors, grandsons stood ready to open them so he could continue his exit without breaking stride, followed by his family and others of his old Hampshire congregation.

*   *   *

"Come," Stephen barked from behind his desk, in answer to the rap on the church door. His great eyebrows furrowed into a frown. He was studying, preparing for the following Sunday's sermon, and was annoyed at the interruption. All who knew Stephen knew better than to disrupt him when he was burrowed deep into his books and Bible.

As the door opened, the wind gusted into the building, bringing with it an immediate drop in temperature and a generous sprinkling of the snow now in its third day of falling.

"Hello, Stephen," greeted the Reverend Adam Bartow, a friend and fellow cleric on the Massachusetts Board of Ministry.

"Adam, my friend," Stephen said as he arose and went to shake hands with his visitor. "I've been expecting you. Or someone from Boston, at any rate. It's been a fortnight since I addressed my concerns in a letter to the board. 'Tis good to see you."

"You are studying. Should I come another time?"

"No, not at all. This is as good a time as any. Would you care to walk to my house and have a cup of hot tea while we visit? Helena would be happy to brew a pot and to see you. Besides, 'tis warmer there."

The men gathered stares and created chitchat as they walked the short distance to Stephen's house, snow crunching under foot.

Once inside Stephen's home and cozied up to the fireplace with steaming cups of tea in their hands, Bartow divulged his mission:

"Your letter was read aloud at the conference lecture where elders of every church were present. To a man, we were greatly concerned about your dilemma but decided it would be prudent for us to hear both sides of the issue. That way, perhaps the matter can, once and for all, be laid to rest."

Stephen heartily agreed: "Of course, Adam. Absolutely. I have no quarrel with that approach at all. And after you hear from the 'other side,' you will no doubt see my point of view even clearer than you now do. 'Tis impossible for me to do justice to explain their wrath."

"Excellent," Bartow exclaimed, "then, next week, two elders from each church in the district will gather at Saugus to consider the problems—and find a resolution."

"As you say, Adam, 'excellent'," Stephen agreed.

Chapter 39

Saugus
May 1635
Deborah

As Deborah and neighbor Hepsobah Collins neared the village square, Deborah sensed the scuffle of movement. She stopped, squinted her eyes to peer harder and quickened her step, leaving Goodwife Collins behind.

She heard grunts and saw flailing arms and kicking legs—and winced at the audible punches of a fist hitting a stomach or the hard bone of cheek.

"What on earth? Stephen? For heaven's sake, what are you doing? Stop that! Now!"

"You take that back, Jeremiah Spooner," Stephen panted to his opponent. Both nearly breathless, the boys continued to swing wildly once they fought their way back to upright positions.

Deborah plowed in betwixt them, only to receive Jeremiah's left hook to her right eye. She went down.

"Mother!" Stephen cried.

"Goodwife Wing, I am truly sorry," Jeremiah stammered.

The two boys helped a stunned Deborah to her feet.

"Please, Ma'am, I meant not to harm ye."

"Just my son?" Deborah answered, coldly, patting her eye. "And, you, Stephen, you meant harm to Jeremiah? I thought you two were friends. We do not deliberately set out to hurt our friends. If we are to love our enemies, then we most certainly are to love our friends.

"Goodwife Collins, I apologize for this spectacle," Deborah said to the woman looking aghast at the scene. "Stephen, you and Jeremiah also apologize to Goodwife Collins."

"Sorry, Ma'am," the boys said in unison.

"Come, Stephen, walk me home," she snapped to her young son who was now, at four and ten, as tall as she. "We'll be done with the village this day. And, Jeremiah, I suggest you, too, head for home and tell your mother about this fracas—about you and Stephen acting like a couple ragamuffins."

Deborah trod a fast pace down the road, beneath the canopy of leaves beginning to leaf out on the many and various deciduous trees. Ordinarily, she would have stopped to admire their beauty and to thank God for his creation. But not today.

She walked so fast Stephen had to skip a step now and again to keep up. They walked in silence. The only sound made was the swish of Deborah's skirts and the fabric of Stephen's pants rubbing together at his thighs. Stephen knew better than to speak. He couldn't remember when he had, ever seen his mother so angry.

"Just look at yourself," Deborah said at last. "You are mud, head to toe."

More walking. More silence.

Finally, they reached home.

Stephen skittered in front of his mother to open the door for her. She frowned at him as she brushed past. Matthew was sitting by the fire, reading his primer.

"Matthew, if you please, go to Aunt Theodate's house and stay there until I come for you."

Matthew looked at his mother, then his brother, and without a word, dropped his book on the floor and scuttled out the door.

"Now, then," Deborah started, removing her cloak and hanging it on the doorway peg. "May I inquire as to what was going on? Why were you fighting with the Spooner boy?"

Stephen stood by the fire and wiped at his pants. He hung his head.

Deborah gathered a cloth and a bowl and joined her son at the fire. She poured hot water into the bowl from the kettle steaming over the fire and dipped the cloth into the water.

"Stephen, I would like an answer and I would like it now," she said as she began to wash away the globs of mud hiding his face.

Stephen looked at his mother, then down at his pants and brushed at them some more.

He winced at her ministrations.

"Leave your trousers alone," Deborah said, softening the edge of her voice. She also lightened her touch as she washed his face, scraped as it was. "We'll worry about the dirt stains later. I want you to talk to me now."

Stephen lowered himself on a stool and placed his head in his hands. And said not a word.

Deborah found herself a stool, pulled it up and sat beside her son, the son named for her father.

"What is it, Stephen? Tell me."

"I cannot, Mother. I cannot tell you."

"There is nothing so dire in this world that you cannot tell me about it, Stephen," Deborah said. Worry replaced anger in her voice.

"I am truly sorry, Mother, but I can tell you nothing."

Deborah waited.

Then to fill the silence between them, he said, "What started out as horse-play turned ugly. 'Twas nothing more than that."

With the back of his hand, he swiped his eyes, angry at the appearance of a tear.

Deborah looked long at her child, her fourth, and sighed. "I would just as soon wrestle with the Devil as to see you in such pain, son."

"My scrapes are nothing. They will heal."

"I'm not talking about your bruises." She took his hand and held it with both of hers.

Stephen looked into his mother's eyes, recognized her anguish, and looked away.

"Truly, Mother, 'twas nothing. I am deeply sorry to have troubled you. 'Twill not happen again."

"So," Deborah said slowly. "You have nothing to say to me?"

"No Ma'am. Nothing. Except I'm sorry to have fretted you."

He looked at her again. A sheepish grin crossed his face. "Mother, you have quite a sore eye, yourself. Does it hurt much?"

Deborah's hand automatically felt her eye. She cringed. "'Tis a bit sore, but it will be fine. I must say, 'tis the first black eye I've ever had." She smiled at Stephen. "But it's not my eye nor your lacerations I worry about, Stephen."

"I know, Mother. I know. But, truly, 'tis all right."

*   *   *

"Theodate," Deborah called, entering her sister's house, "are you home?"

"Here I am," Theodate sang out, emerging from the room Christopher had recently added to the house, baby Joseph riding her hip. "Deborah, how good to see you."

"Matthew," Deborah said to her son, who had been his Aunt Theodate's shadow but ran now to greet her. "Please return home and tell Stephen I said that he should listen to you read your primer."

The sisters met in the middle of the room and exchanged hugs and Deborah removed her wrap.

"I know I've said it time and again," Theodate said as she laid the baby into its cradle, "but 'tis true. I love our visits. Just the two of us. 'Tis as though we are making up for lost time when I was so young and you left home to marry John. I've always 'known' we were sisters, of course, but since we've been here, together, this past while, I've grown to 'feel' like we are sisters. Listen to me go on. Have you been to market? Matthew said you were upset about something."

"Yes," Deborah answered. "I was almost to Town Square when I was stopped by the queerest exchange. Brew me a cup of tea and I'll tell you about it and you can tell me what you think."

Theodate swung the kettle across the fire.

"I was off to market, walking with Hepsobah Collins—the wife of the starch maker; they live on Exeter Street—anyway, she was asking if I would consider teaching her children along with ours, when I heard a terrible commotion.

"As we drew near, I saw that Stephen was in a melee, pummeling the daylights out of the Spooner boy who was swinging his arms around and wailing as though he were being murdered."

Theodate poured boiling water into the teapot

"Stephen's face was smeared almost beyond recognition. It was obvious he'd been crying—although he wouldn't admit to it—and his tears had made muddy streams through the dirt caked to his cheeks. The sight of him nearly broke my heart," Deborah said. She straightened her spine and continued, "But I was also so angry with Stephen that he should be fighting."

"What were they quarreling about?" Theodate asked

"He wouldn't say. He said ne'er a word, but I have my suspicions." Deborah looked directly at Theodate. Into her eyes.

At first, there was no recognition. Then Theodate's eyes registered the briefest acknowledgement before she averted them. "Surely not," Theodate said. "Surely not."

"Truly," Deborah answered. "I truly believe the gossip surrounding Father has reached our children."

Both women sat and stared at the fire, their fingers wrapped around their cups of steaming, un-sipped tea. They ignored the wafts of steam as they lifted the fragrant scent of their tea up to their nostrils. The women stared at the fireplace, which was never without burning embers. Neither moved. It would soon be time to fix the noon meal, but still they sat.

"What are you going to do, Deborah?" Theodate said, her voice trembling. "I know thee will, indeed, do something."

"I don't know," Deborah answered. "I simply do not know. But I do know I will not have my children suffer the consequences of their grandfather's philandering."

"Deborah," Theodate gasped. "Mind your words. You know very well that none of those woeful tales about father are true."

"I must be alone to think," Deborah said. Slowly, and without another word, she rose, and, with a determined look, she sat her still-filled cup on the table, gathered up her cloak, and without a word, opened the door and walked from Theodate's house.

Chapter 40

Saugus
May 1635
Deborah

Deborah walked briskly from Theodate's house, her head lowered, until she reached Nahant where she broke into a near run before stopping at the pulpit of stones. John's pulpit of stones. She'd adopted the solid rock formation as symbolizing her husband. It was ever bit as unyielding as he had been.

She looked at that powerful formation defying the thunderous waves that would erode it if only they could, and felt John's presence. She admired the dainty, hearty, spring flowers at her feet, and her daughter Deborah sprang to mind.

Nahant had become her solace.

Deborah removed her bonnet and released her hair to the constantly blowing wind. It felt good to let it escape the confines of her bonnet and "breathe" unfettered. The wind blew her hair and cleared her mind. Spray from the sea, carried on the wings of the wind, whipped her face and cleansed her soul.

Nahant was her home away from home.

I love the sea. She sensed the words within her, rather than actually forming them in her mind. *I love the sea and its unpredictability when its waves rage as though it were going to swallow the world and all that's in it, or when its waters are calm and still enough for a sea eagle to eye a fish and dive for its dinner.*

I love the sea for the calmness it sets upon me, for all its roaring that drowns out the roaring inside of me.

It's here I sort my feelings.

Amen.

Deborah eased herself to the ground, pulled a white daisy from the green grass next to her, drew it to her face, inhaled its fragrance and stared at Pulpit Rock.

She sat mesmerized, forgetting time. Forgetting anxieties.

Letting her mind get lost in the blue, blue sky, that magnificent rock, and the green, foaming sea; the smell of the ocean, the touch of the mist on her face, and the beguiling sounds of gulls flying overhead. She let her mind turn itself off and basked in the sun and the sky and grass and the sounds of the ocean—and was at total peace.

*   *   *

"Mother."

Deborah bolted upright at the sound and turned around. It was John.

"Mother, we've been worried." He sounded cross. "You've been gone such a long while. We went in for the noon meal and you weren't there. The fire was cold and nothing was prepared."

Deborah smiled, reached up with her hand, took hold of his and pulled him down, next to her.

"I'm sorry, Son. Truly. I lost track of time. Did you boys fix yourself something to eat?" The crossness in John's voice softened. He grinned at her. "Yes, Mother, we had something to eat. We are not totally helpless. We are, after all, your sons—perfectly capable of doing most any thing that needs to be done. You can hammer a nail, we can slice bread. But you did have us in a fret. It's not like you to leave without a word."

John waited and when he received no response, he quietly asked, "What's bothering you, Mother?"

After another moment, Deborah said, "John, remember the day we sat by the canal in Holland, you and I, and you told me of your vision? About coming to New England?"

John nodded.

"Well, I believe I've had a vision of my own. It's not as crystal clear as yours, but I do believe I've learned what it is we should do here, in this country."

Petal by petal she separated the daisy. One by one the petals flew from her open hand as a breeze caught them, and when one lingered, she gently blew until it sailed off.

"I have sat here all this time perfectly still. Quiet. At peace. I said not a word in that time—not aloud, not in my mind. But, John, I do believe I received answers in my solitude."

"Tell me," he said.

"First off, I truly believe it's right that we are here. You see that rock, John?"

"Pulpit Rock?"

"Yes. Pulpit Rock. Your father was like that rock. Your grandfather is like that rock. As are you. And I. We are strong people, John—as strong as that granite. We will not let our beliefs be undermined. We—your father and I—spent our entire married life together looking, searching, for religious stability; something secure where we could anchor our faith without someone threatening us. Peace. That's what your father and I wanted, John. Peace. It was wrenching being forced to leave England, our home, our families, in search of that freedom. That peace." Her eyes clouded with painful memories. "Well, we've left home, again, haven't we? This time, we went so far as to cross an ocean—you, your brothers, your grandfather and I—once again in search of the sureness to worship God as we believe. I want that for you boys more than anything in this world, John. For the four of you to have the freedom to worship God as you believe, as your father and my father believed and have taught us. God wants that for you, your father wanted it for you and I want it for you."

Mother and son sat, side by side, and stared out at the endless sea. Deborah laid her head against his arm.

"John," she finally said, "there's more."

"Yes," her son answered.

Her mouth was dry, her voice hoarse as she spoke: "You will not have that peace, that serenity, that freedom of worship as long as we follow my father in his ministry."

John turned and looked at his mother. Her voice and her face were filled with sadness.

Deborah turned away from him. She picked another daisy. "Your grandfather was sorrowfully mistreated by the magistrates in England and now by the authorities here in New England." Her voiced dropped to a hush. "I am indeed sorry for your grandfather's woes, but I can no longer weep for him."

"Can you tell me why?" John asked, his breathing quickened.

"No, Son. I cannot and I will not."

"What do you propose we do?"

"Later this month, Father is to be admitted as a freeman—and life should be easier for him. He will be a more respected member of the community. He will be able to vote. But, John, this trouble in his congregation is not going to go away. It's only going to get worse. It will drag him down and all those with him."

"We can't desert him, Mother," John protested.

"We shan't desert him, Dear," Deborah replied kindly. "But he does not need us. Me. He does not need me. He has Christopher. And Theodate. And Helena. He does not need us, John. Your grandfather and I only serve to antagonize one another, and that is not good for either of us."

John said nothing, waiting for his mother to clarify this mystery.

"John, you boys are my concern. It is for you that I was born. It is for you that I am here. It is for you that I left Deborah. Your father, too, fought for you boys, our sons. I am in search of peace for you. And for me. Your grandfather's search is not our search. We will always love him, John. We will forever be devoted to him and be loyal to him. We will forever be his standard bearers. Whenever he needs us, we will help him, as we always have. But we need not follow him like a dog scratching a pesky flea. I believe, in his advanced years, that your grandfather grows confused, but I do not think we need take up that burden as our own. He prefers the solace of Helena and Theodate to mine." She smiled ruefully at her son. "Methinks perhaps we are too much alike, he and I. John, I want our home to always be open to him. But I want him to live in our house, not us in his."

Chapter 41

Saugus
August 1636
Deborah

Deborah sat straight up in bed.

Something was in bed with her.

She stifled a scream.

It wasn't a something. It was a somebody—six-year-old Matthew.

"Mother, can I please sleep with you?"

"Of course, Darling. What is it? What's troubling you? Did you have a nasty dream?"

"No, Mother. The noise scared me. It really scared me."

"Noise? What noise?"

Just then, as if to answer her question, a whistling howl wrapped itself around the house. Thunder punctuated the wind with a boisterous peal. Rain began to pelt the roof.

"That noise."

Matthew's voice rose to a panic as he burrowed his head in his mother's bosom, knocking the two of them down atop the straw-filled mattress.

Deborah sought to reassure Matthew as her heart resumed its normal beat. She enveloped him in her arms and held him close: "'Tis only the wind, Matthew. It won't hurt you."

Her optimistic words, however, collapsed with a great clap of thunder that sounded as though it were forcing its way down the chimney. That, and the accompanying blast of wind, brought John, Daniel and Steven bounding down the ladder from the loft, not one of the three pairs of feet touching a single rung.

"What was that?" Stephen asked. "What's going on?" questioned Daniel.

In four loping strides, John pounded to the door, opening it to check the weather, only to fight the heavy door shut again. Daniel ran to help shoulder it closed.

"What's the hour?" asked Deborah.

"I'm not sure," John answered, "but 'tis still dark. I suggest we all get dressed. By the looks and sounds of it, methinks we're in for a day of it."

The boys slid the heavy wooden bolt back into place.

"I'll stoke the fire," Stephen offered.

"No!" John barked. "We'll have to put out what's left of the fire. The wind would drive the smoke and flames inside. There'll be no fire today. And, like as not, no warmth."

"The water in the kettle will still be hot," Deborah said. "I'll fix us some gruel."

Once dressed, they ate their meal in silence, listening to the ferociousness of the screeching wind shaking their house—their bones and their souls.

"I've never heard anything like this," Deborah finally said. "Not in all my years. I'm concerned about your grandfather and Helena. I pray they are safe. In fact, boys, let us get on our knees this very moment and ask God Almighty for his divine protection over us—all of us, the entire village."

The Wings rose from their place at the table and knelt in a row along the bench where they had sat.

The "Amen" had not yet been said before a pounding on the door caused the family to rise. It sounded again.

"That's more than the wind, John," Deborah said. "Someone's here."

Even as she spoke, John and Daniel were at the door, sliding back the bolt.

It was Christopher.

"Come, John and Daniel—and you, too, Stephen," their uncle said as he entered the room and backed himself up against the door, forcing it shut. "We need your help. Get your warmest coats. You'll need to be bundled up, August or no. 'Tis raining and blowing as though it will never stop."

Christopher was panting, as if the wind had been blown out of him.

"Christopher, what is it? Father? Theodate? Are they all right? Tell us of the storm."

Deborah searched her brother-in-law's unshaven face for answers but found only questions in the uncustomary stubble. He was obviously as bewildered as she was.

"We are fine, as I trust Reverend Bachiler is, and as I trust you are," he answered. "God be praised. But others in Saugus are not so fortunate. Some houses have been toppled and others have lost their roofs, blown clean away as though they'd never been attached. Are ye ready yet?" Christopher called out. "We have no time to waste."

"Coming."

"I'll come, too," Deborah said, reaching for her wrap. "I can help."

"No, you stay here," Christopher said. "You have Matthew to tend. No, I know. You and Matthew go stay with Theodate and the children, and I'll send Stephen and Helena there to be with you. I'm off to their house, now. Come with us. We'll help you to our house."

"No, you go on," Deborah said, picking up his anxiousness. "We're not ready and I don't want to stay you. We'll be fine. Go on with you—and God be with you."

"Promise me you will go," Christopher said. "It will be less worrisome for us if you are all together."

"We'll go. We'll be there. We'll be fine. Don't worry."

They were out the door, pulling it from the outside while Deborah pushed from the inside.

"Come, Matthew," she said, lightening the tone of her voice. "Get your coat and I'll gather some food in my basket and we'll go visit Aunt Theodate."

She looked at her son whose skin had blanched as white as her under-petticoat, and whose black eyes had opened as wide as the saucers of the teacups she left in Holland.

"Oh, Love," Deborah said, going to him, kneeling and pulling him next to her. "It will be all right, Matthew. Please don't fret."

Matthew was shaking like tender leaves fluttering on an aspen tree in a spring breeze.

"You remember how the wind blew when we were on the ship, Matthew? Remember? It blew and blew, and we were all so afraid. But everything turned out safely. Didn't it? Look at me, Matthew. God took care of us then and God will take care of us now. But, we must go to Aunt Theodate's and help her with her little ones. You're older than they, you're a big boy, and you can be a big help. You can play with them and bemuse them so they won't fear the storm. You can do that, can't you?"

*   *   *

"Where do you suppose Father and Helena are?" Deborah asked. "I'm worried, Theodate. They should have been here long ago."

"I know, Deborah," Theodate answered. "I would have thought they'd be here by now." She was nursing John, trying to no avail to quiet his fussiness. "My milk is apt to colic him, I'm that upset," Theodate said, "but he must eat. If only he would sleep."

Deborah stood at the small window and peered out. Whenever rain-filled gusts of wind eased, she could see fallen trees all around. She was still shaken by the mammoth fir that uprooted and fell not ten feet behind her and Matthew as they had ducked into Theodate's door. Had they left home even a moment later, they could have been crushed by the tree that God had planted scores of years earlier.

"I'm going to look for them," Deborah announced to her sister as she rose and donned her cloak. "Something must have happened. I have to go look. Father could have fallen and Helena might not be able to help him up."

"Deborah, you can't. It isn't safe. What if something happens to you, too? Then what?"

"Care for Matthew," Deborah heard herself say.

*   *   *

The wind blew so hard that Deborah was nearly upended. She wrapped her cape close so the wind wouldn't catch in it and billow it out behind her, slowing her pace even more. She was nearly bent in half, her head bowed into the wind as she waged against it. The rain stung her face as it blew at her full force.

You know 'tis a strong wind when it blows horizontally, she remembered her mother telling her as a youngster. *'Tis blowing horizontally,* she wanted to tell her father now.

"Father, Father," she cried out until she realized her voice couldn't be heard by any ear—not even hers.

The air sounded with the whipping of wind and the groaning of great tree roots reluctantly giving way and the heart-sickening thud as the once magnificent creations collided with the ground.

If only the wind would stop, she thought as the sound filled her with fear.

Uprooted, broken and mangled trees littered the countryside.

Deborah yanked at her cumbersome dress that caught on a branch as she straddled the girth of a tree, trying to reach its other side. The pine, which had swayed in breezes for eons before being felled by this storm was too long to walk around. It would have taken her deep into the forest.

There was no respite from the wind. It roared ceaselessly as it blew carnage all around.

Once-tall grass lay crushed; flowers beaten down, their color washed away. The sight of Matthew bringing her a handful of smelly, yellow sunflowers yesterday flashed through her mind. This was probably the field where he'd picked them, but now, nothing was standing.

Deborah looked at the other side of the road—at what had been Farmer Hubertson's cornfield. Yesterday, it had been filled with tall, proud stalks of corn ripening to perfection, their ears bursting with silk. Today, it was nothing more than a flattened field. Even its yellow color had been robbed from it, leaving in its place, a muddy brown.

She felt sickened.

Oh, the corn, she thought. *Those stalks will never rise more.*

It was dark, even though it was not yet the nooning hour.

What was that? I heard something. "Father? Father?"

She lowered her head further and shielded her face from the driving wind and rain by placing one arm in front of her. She might not be able to see as well with her face covered, but it was a bit of protection. She knew now why Christopher had been so breathless.

Lightning zigzagged through the sky, one flash after another, topped by one deafening clap of thunder after another.

Deborah jumped.

Where am I? She stopped to take stock of her position. *Where is Father's house?*

"Father," she cried out. "Father."

Am I lost? She looked around her. Nothing looked familiar.

She turned in a circle.

"Where are you, Father? Oh dear God, help me. Let me find him. Father?"

She felt something touch her elbow, the one shielding her face.

"Ohhhhh," she gasped as she lowered her arm and saw an Indian stand-ing next to her. Her immediate fear passed as she recognized the man from seeing him in the village. Still, this was the closest she had ever been to an Indian. And, certainly, she had never been alone with one.

"Come," he said, pulling at her elbow. "Come."

"I cannot," she cried back, shouting into his ear. "I must find my father."

"Come," he said, nodding. "Come."

Reluctantly, Deborah followed him, the savage, as the natives were called. But this man was a rescuer, not a savage. She had no fear of him. There was so much more to be afraid of at this very moment than a stranger, even if he was all but naked, only a loincloth covering his "inde-cency."

"Father," she cried, the wind swallowing her words, as she saw Stephen through the blowing veil of rain. "Father." She ran and knelt next to him. He was sitting with his bottom on the ground, rocking back and forth, cradling the broken body of Helena in his arms. A heavy limb, snatched from a tree trunk as though it were a splinter, had struck Helena down as she and Stephen searched their way for Theodate's.

Stephen was totally unaware of the storm, the rain that pelted him, the mud he sat in, the wind that had robbed his hat, the sobbing daughter next to him who so feared for him. He was all consumed in holding his young wife, his love. He held her broken head tenderly in his arms, rock-ing back and forth, back and forth, crooning in her ear.

Deborah looked up at her newfound friend, her eyes pleading. He nod-ded his head once. She wrapped her arms around one of Stephen's and forced him to stand as the Indian knelt and scooped up Helena's lifeless body and led the way out of the forest and back to the road. Back to Theodate's.

Chapter 42

Saugus
1637
Deborah

Deborah answered the rap on the door with great expectation.

"Daughter," Stephen said as he stood aside for her to see the woman next to him. A smile crossed Deborah's face when she heard the excitement in her father's voice, something that had been missing since before they laid Helena to rest last summer, once the storm-of-a-lifetime, as it was being called, had abated.

"I have someone I want you to meet." Stephen said. "This is Mistress Anne Hutchinson. Mistress Hutchinson, my daughter, Deborah Wing."

"I am so pleased to meet you," Deborah said, dropping a hint of a curtsey. Anne Hutchinson was a familiar name to most Englishmen—and maybe even more familiar to Englishwomen. Her acclaim as a thinking-woman's Christian reached even beyond the British Isles. Deborah first learned of the energetic, quick-witted, intelligent woman while living in Holland. Word of Mistress Hutchinson's cottage meetings for women traveled far beyond her neighborhood.

"Father has told me much about you." Deborah smiled at her notable guest. "He holds you in very high regard. And, reports of your women's meetings in England and now in Boston have made me most anxious to meet you. It's a great honor. Please, come in."

Deborah looked at the woman who appeared to be her own age and recognized an aura from her own past. Mistress Hutchinson's face was wan and too thin.

When she took her guest's nondescript beige cloak to hang on a knob next to the door, Deborah was mildly surprised to see her visitor's waistcoat was a lovely shade of moss green. Deborah assumed a woman of Mistress Hutchinson's stature would surely wear more somber colors. Men ministers, after all, wore black. The waistcoat was indeed attractive, but its color only heightened the lady's already pasty pallor.

The awe Deborah felt turned into concern.

"Have you eaten?" she asked. "I could fix you a bite in no time at all."

"Thank you, no. A cup of tea however, would make me greathearted. If 'tis not too much trouble."

"Not at all. Please, be seated—here, by the fire."

Deborah's automatic responses took over of heating the water, fetching the pot and the tea in its pewter canister...

"I'll leave you two women alone," Stephen said from the doorway. "I already feel ignored. Remember, Deborah, I brought our guest to your house so she might rest before she speaks this afternoon. I trust you will not weary her with too much talk. I have business in the village, but mehopes, Daughter, that Mistress Hutchinson and I might expect an invitation to share the noon meal with you."

"Of course," Deborah said. "We are quite capable of minding ourselves, Father. Be on your way and we'll see you at the nooning hour." Once the door closed behind him, Deborah turned her attention to the New World's first woman preacher, who, at the moment, needed her ministrations.

"May I be so bold to ask if you are quite yourself? You look a bit piqued."

"You are most kind—and observant. But I am fine. Thank you. A tad nauseous, perhaps. You see, I am with child who should be delivered in another six or seven months. Hence the request for tea."

"I've hard biscuits which might help settle your queasiness," Deborah said, turning toward her larder.

"How many children have you?" Mistress Hutchinson asked.

"Sad to say, I have but five—four sons and a daughter." It had been so long since she'd seen that daughter. Mention of Deborah Junior brought with it a pang of nostalgia. "And you?"

"'Twill be my 15th child—and, I might add, 'tis quite unexpected. Welcomed, but unexpected. I thought I had completed my child-bearing with our youngest two years ago."

"I would have loved more children," Deborah said, "but 'twas not meant to be. I hope speaking today will not tax you too much, being as you are with child. 'Tis good of you to extend your visit to this part of the country just so you could speak to the women of our town. Everyone is looking forward to hearing you—and meeting you."

Deborah placed the steaming pot of tea between them at the table and topped it with a cozy while it steeped. She seated herself on the bench, and for an instant, it seemed as though she were preparing tea in a fine, engraved silver teapot to serve to her Holland friend, Catherina Van Blarcom, in one of their heart-to-heart conversations a world and many years ago. Then, as quickly as the image appeared—in a heartbeat—it was gone. She was back in her rustic house in rustic New England brewing tea in a pewter pot, not silver, and would pour it into thick mugs, not thin china cups.

"Goody Wing," Anne Hutchinson began.

"Please," Deborah interrupted, "call me by my given name. 'Tis much less formal."

"Thank you, then you must call me by my given name, as well. Deborah," Anne began again, a serious expression on her face, "I want to tell you what an exceptional Christian man I think your father is. I have come to know him through our occasional meetings in Boston. He is so very courageous, especially for one his age. His life of serving Christ cannot have been easy for either him or his family."

Deborah smiled softly and nodded. It was pure pleasure to have someone commiserate—and so unexpectedly. But then, from what she had heard of her, Deborah had long thought Mistress Hutchinson might well be a kindred spirit.

"'Tis sad to say, but even his invitation to have me address the townspeople today might cause him grief. I would be sorely dismayed if it did, but," she paused and sighed, "we 'rebels' have come to expect such things."

Deborah looked keenly at Anne. *Bless her heart,* Deborah thought, *she truly does understand the trials Father has been under. She understands because she, too, has experienced them.*

Anne sought Deborah's eyes and continued: "We have much in common, your father and I—and a few select others: my brother-in-law and minister, John Wheelright; the hot-headed, outspoken Roger Williams, bless his heart; and my longtime idealist, Reverend John Cotton. And, of course, my dear husband.

"We are, all of us, of a like mind. However," Anne continued, "we find ourselves, once again, pressed up against an unforgiving stone wall cemented with small-minded objectors."

"It is ironic, isn't it?" Deborah said. "We—all of us—fled our homeland searching religious freedom. And we surrendered all we held dear—family, friends, home, a way of life—for that freedom. There is nothing I want more in this life than to be assured my sons can worship God as they please; worship him in humility, not pomp and circumstance."

Deborah removed the pot's cozy, placed a strainer atop Anne's cup to catch the loose tealeaves, and poured a cup of the hot, fragrant drink that had warmed body and soul for generations.

"Yes," Anne said. "It is for our children that we do this. And our grandchildren."

Her gaze became lost in the steam as it curled from her cup. She added a spoonful of honey and stirred.

"No doubt, we were naive," Anne said thoughtfully, "but we honestly believed we were going to establish a Community of Saints in this New World."

"Yes," Deborah said with the slightest snort, "but we no more than arrived, excited at the prospect of developing our Promised Land, our City on the Hill, than we were faced with yet another set of rules and regulations to be obeyed." She sighed and shook her head, remembering the calamity caused when her father baptized Theodate's baby. "It seems the only difference here from old England is that the restricting sentences are pronounced from different mouths," she said.

"That is so true, my friend," Anne added, grasping one of Deborah's hands in both of hers for a moment before returning to nibble at her hard biscuit.

"I must say," Anne said, "this is the perfect remedy for a squeamish stomach: A cup of tea, a biscuit and a kindred soul." She smiled. "In a way, the 'sentences,' as you so aptly call them, seem even harsher here because they are pronounced by those who also fled the Anglican Church and its Catholic-like doctrines." Anne stopped talking and smiled wryly. "If I, pregnant and queasy as I am this day, were forced to smell a censer filled with incense being swung around by a priest, I believe I would become as dizzy as a goose."

The two women laughed together at the image of stately Anne Hutchinson, mother of fourteen children—soon to be fifteen—being reduced to giddiness, overcome by the sickeningly sweet smell of incense.

Once their laughter tapered to smiles, Anne returned to her previous conversation in all seriousness; the moment of frivolity was gone.

"'Tis sad—it's worse than sad—but we were led to think we thought alike, these new governors of New England and us. Or that it would not matter if we didn't."

The words spit from her mouth as though they tasted of bile.

"Now, however," Anne continued in a softer, more controlled voice, "they—the very leaders we followed in our noble quest—are in charge and, by God, they will conduct our worship—and our very way of life—their way or else. They're not much different than what we left behind. They just don't happen to be Royal."

The two women sat silent a moment before Anne continued: "I mentioned John Cotton as being my ideal. I have known him and listened to him for years. He is—was—my mentor; he is the primary reason my family and I came to this country. I wanted to be near him so I could continue to learn from him. It is from him that I received my inspiration to teach my women followers.

"But, Deborah," Anne said quietly, "Reverend Cotton is not the same man I knew in old England. There, he was open and willing to share his revelations. Here, he wants to secret himself away in a room and study alone, away from those who would learn from him. Her face darkened. She shuddered involuntarily. "There are times when I feel I might very well have reason to fear him one day, rather than adore him. I fear he will one day turn against me and no longer honor our friendship."

"You have heard of my father's travails since we arrived here?" Deborah asked. "How he was punished for baptizing his grandson, his namesake, before another infant who was born only days earlier?"

"Aye, I have heard," Anne said, nodding. "I heard while still in England, before we ever set sail or even booked passage. And, that example illustrates my frustration with the patriarchal, tyrannical rule that is taking hold in this country. We are being denied the very thing we crossed the Atlantic to find. Governor Winthrop and the others in power here, in this new country that was to be free, may speak the words 'Religious Freedom,' but they do not enact them."

Deborah removed the cozy and poured more steaming tea into their mugs.

"Would you tell me of your theology?" Deborah asked a little timidly.

"Of course," Anne said, stirring a spoonful of honey into her tea. She watched the steam curl its way out of her cup. "I have a bit of Puritan in my soul, the same as you. I agree with the Puritan tenets that the elaborate elements of Anglican worship should be eliminated. That they do indeed get in the way of our worship; that they come between God and us."

"Yes," Deborah said, "like you and the censer. How is incense suppose to put us more in tune with God in Heaven?"

"True," Anne said. "Puritans say we Christians need to purify ourselves, then the church. But, Deborah, I also embrace Antinomianism. I suppose 'tis fair to say that I embrace the parts of worshipful principles in a variety of sects that appeal to me, and my way of thinking," Anne said. "But above all, I am not a literalist. I do not believe simply because something is written one way in the Scriptures that it is the only word on the subject."

Deborah was fascinated with what she was hearing.

Anne continued: "I believe with all my heart God hears the prayers that come from my mouth or my heart. I can pray directly to him, without any assistance from a clergyman, thank you very much."

Deborah clapped her hands together a single time: "I could not agree more. In fact, I talk directly to God every day of my life."

"And that's as it should be," Anne agreed. "Do you realize some clergymen actually 'punish' their parishioners by refusing to pray with them? Their poor, unenlightened congregates don't realize they can pray to God by themselves, without the help of a minister. Why, some ministers even refuse to pray with their own wives if they're unhappy about the way she cooked a meal or a cross word she might have spoken in haste. Their own wives! These holier-than-thou men think they can control their wives, or their erring church members, by withholding prayer or grace at meal time."

Anne stood, put her hand high on her hips and leaned backwards to stretch her aching muscles. She walked to the window and gazed out at a strip of lush greenness next to the house which gave way to the muddy pathway as it meandered to town, and beyond into a dark, dense forest.

Deborah basked in the picture of Anne looking out her window. *She's such a small woman,* Deborah mused, *but she's so strong. Right now, though, she looks mighty vulnerable. The first months of pregnancy are so difficult, whether it's your fifth or fifteenth baby. You feel so sick to your stomach; so tired your bones hurt. And soon, Anne will be great-bellied and even more vulnerable. Right now, Anne Hutchinson certainly does not look like a woman strong enough to create such turmoil in Boston and beyond. She doesn't look like she could cause such an uproar over her beliefs that are beginning to catch with women and men alike—just as fire catches to a stack of dried hay.*

"But those ninnies, those foolish women," Anne said to the window-panes, lost in her own forest of thoughts. At last she turned back to Deborah and made her way back to the table, "What women need to realize is that they can give thanks for the food just as well as their husbands."

"No minister or bishop—or husband—can block one's access to God," Deborah added. "Am I not right?"

"You are exactly right," Anne said. "Those are the precepts your father teaches and they are the precepts my father taught me. By the way, did you know my father was also a minister? You and I have may have more in common than we first realized.

"Simply put, Deborah," Anne continued, "I believe we receive God's redemption through faith rather than through deeds. God's word says, 'Your faith has saved you'."

"But," Deborah interjected, "it also says, 'Faith without works is dead.' 'Faith is made complete by works.'"

"Yes," Anne said, smiling, reveling in this discussion with such an astute woman, something she often longed for, something she was trying to instill in her sisters in Christ, her neighbors, living in Boston. "If you have faith, then good works will naturally follow. But when we stand before Him, God and Christ will bless us and judge us on our faith and not our works. John tells us that Jesus said, 'He who believes in Me shall do the works I do.' And, it's written that God saves those who believe. 'Tis God's grace that saves us, not we ourselves."

"Is that what you are going to speak on today?" Deborah asked.

"No," Anne said with a smile. "No, today I'm addressing an even bigger taboo among some of our 'fellow man.' I believe my primary mission on this Earth is to get thinking Christians—women and men alike—to abolish the unthinkable precept of 'Original Sin.' Does that sound heretical to you? Eliminating Original Sin?"

"Oh, no," Deborah said, clapping her hands together again, not once but several times. "I am so happy to hear you say that. I never, not for a moment, ever believed my precious, innocent little babies, or any of those I helped bring into this world, could be guilty of a single thing."

"Deborah," Anne said, "I have been a midwife since my teens when I helped my mother deliver my youngest brothers and sisters into this world. I remember holding those babies in my arms, even as a young girl, and seeing how fragile they were, how angelic they looked...what an absolutely perfect gift they were from God...and I thought, 'Who could possibly accuse these sweet cherubs of any sin?'"

Anne's hand unconsciously found its way to her belly that she hypnotically rubbed around and around. As one, the two women acknowledged Anne's pregnancy and her involuntary action, and shared a knowing smile.

"Is there movement, yet?" Deborah asked quietly.

"A bit. Like a bit of hiccoughing. Would you care to feel?"

Deborah rose and went to her new friend, knelt by her side and gently placed the palm of her hand over the swollen portion of Anne's otherwise too-thin body.

"Yes," Deborah exclaimed. "Yes. There it is. I feel it. Oh, how wonderful, how perfectly wonderful. Babies truly are a miracle, aren't they?"

"They are. And there isn't an ounce of sin in their creation. Original sin is a denunciation not only of Eve, but of all women," Anne said. "'Tis nothing more than a ploy to keep women under the control of their husbands. I am one of the few fortunate women on Earth whose husband does not hold with that."

"As I was before my dear John died."

It was Deborah's turn to be lost in her thoughts: images of John walking in the door of their Holland house; his arms filled with glorious tulips; sitting by the fire reading the Bible to his young family; spreading sweet butter over a slice of bread, hot from the oven. Asking her if she would bake bread for him in heaven.

Bread! The nooning hour!

"I must get our meal started," Deborah said, jumping up. "But we can continue our visit."

As Deborah bustled about, peeling carrots and potatoes to add to the broth already bubbling in the ever-present kettle, she said, "Tell me about the women's meetings you hold in your house. Aren't you afraid of repercussions? Father says Governor Winthrop is determined to stay your preaching—and that he's not alone, that the religious men of Boston consider it unseemly for a woman to preach."

Anne laughed. "I take after my father. He was my tutor, my teacher, my first mentor. He encouraged me to think, to reason and to speak my mind. And speak I do. When I was a child, Queen Elizabeth was my guide. My father taught me to admire her intelligence and how she used that intelligence to rule and gain respect."

Deborah stopped peeling the carrot her held in her hand to search her memory: "Edmund Spencer called her…Glorious." Again, for the briefest instant, her mind filled with the image of John's tulips. "He called her Glorious."

"Exactly," Anne said. "And she was glorious. If it weren't for her, the Pope might well have been returned to the English church. But when Elizabeth beheaded her cousin, 'Bloody Mary,' it ended the Catholics from ever returning. And, too, Good Queen Bess quashed the Spanish Armada. She did things no man thought a woman could ever do. For the first time—ever, maybe—a woman had command of an entire nation and was held in high regard by her countrymen."

"But," Deborah countered, "Queen Elizabeth was dreadfully hard on Puritans. She didn't blink an eye before having a Puritan hauled off to the Tower."

"Ah, don't I know that?" Anne said. "Even though he was not a Puritan, per se, my father spent a good many years behind bars for his non-conventional preaching. The Queen yanked away his license to preach more than once. Still, my father admired Queen Elizabeth for her brains and how she educated herself, learning to speak several languages. Father was impressed how she, a woman, used her education. Queen Elizabeth gained respect from friends and foes alike. The men allowed her intelligence. And that's what I want.

"I want to earn the respect of men as well as women." Anne said. "I want acknowledgment that I, too, am an intelligent being even though I am a woman; acknowledgment that God can speak to me and through me ever bit as much as he can through a man."

Slicing cheese, Deborah said, "I understand you have already accomplished that, at least to some degree. Some husbands are said to regularly attend your 'Ladies Meetings' with their wives."

"They do," Anne said with a laugh. "That's right, they do. My, news does get around, doesn't it? But then, I forget your father is on the Council of Ministers."

The women talked on:

- About the Church's unfair, obstinate insistence that a child's death was punishment brought on by parental sin.

    Deborah: "I can't believe a loving God would take the life of my child because I somehow failed to do my God-given duty. He might punish me, but he would not punish an innocent babe."

- About midwives not being allowed, under any circumstances, to baptize a newborn in danger of imminent death.

   Anne: with a disparaging laugh: "They must be afraid a woman might baptize it into the wrong denomination."

- About the aggravation of women having to sit on one side of the church and men on the other.

   Anne: "Are men so insecure that the presence of their wives next to them would be a distraction?"

- About how young men could vote, but they, the women who taught them, could not.

   Deborah: "I simply cannot understand that reasoning. 'Tis foolish. Who do they think taught these boys what they know? Like as not, 'twas their mothers."

- About the court's edict on their dress.

   Anne: "Why is it these men should ban us from buying a bit of lace or a garment with silk thread, or fine us our husband's hard-earned money if we buy a beaver hat? And, to think men can dictate whether our dresses have short sleeves or that those sleeves cannot be more than half an ell wide. It's enough, to make me want to go out and buy a beaver hat and a dress with very short, very wide sleeves."

As Deborah dropped chunks of cod into the stew, Anne said: "...for instance, Deborah, I believe we mortals receive divine inspiration directly from God. Therefore, we have no need for intercession."

Deborah nodded her agreement. *That was exactly the thinking of her husband and her father. And mine, too,* she thought. *Yes, mine, too.* She had moved on to slice the bread. She laid the knife down and stared at Anne, a quizzical look on her face. "Why is it I see things so clearly with you?" Her words were whispered and Anne did not hear them.

"Here is where we may disagree," Anne warned, smiling at Deborah, surprised to see Deborah was already looking at her. "I also believe God has preordained who shall and shall not be saved."

Deborah's brows knit together. She had heard her father and husband preach on that very subject, still she was not convinced.

"Hmmm, I don't know about that," Deborah said, surprised to hear herself thinking out loud to this learned woman. "I cannot believe that while I was still in my mother's womb God ordained I be here on this day in this foreign country talking with you. I think not. That's beyond my comprehension."

Anne continued: "And, my dear Deborah, I believe that moral conduct—good works—on Earth has nothing to do with ultimate salvation."

Anne smiled as if to ease any shock she might have produced in her hostess. "Deborah, when I speak to my followers, I want you to know I do not speak harshly or in an unwomanly manner."

"Oh, I know you do not," Deborah said, pushing back a strand of hair that had escaped her coif. "You are known for your kindness and Christian ways as much as your..."

"Heretical views?"

The two women laughed.

"I must say, you do not appear to be much of a heretic," Deborah said.

"Maybe it should frighten you just a bit that we seem to think so much alike," Anne said. "My life has been ever bit as controversial as your father's. So I know one heretic per family is quite enough."

"I could never do what you do," Deborah said, "but I also do not believe that's what God has called me to do."

"Pre-destination?" Anne teased.

"Still," Deborah continued without losing a beat but acknowledging the good-natured retort with a smile, "I am proud of you, that you, a 'mere woman,' as some would say, draw bigger crowds with your preaching in Boston than some famous theologians."

"Ah, I may not be famous, but some say I am infamous," Anne said. "'Tis nothing wrong with a woman spreading God's word. I am certainly not the first, and I know I will not be the last."

Deborah walked to the door and pushed it open. Sunlight filled the room. She closed her eyes and felt its warmth on her face. It felt good.

"If only the men in power knew how much power women have—or could have," Anne laughed ruefully. "If only women knew it."

Deborah returned to the table where Anne sat and seated herself beside her. Again they laughed, but before their chortle was complete, the sun, which so recently filled every corner of the room, was all but obliterated as in the doorway stood Deborah's father and sons, every man and boy of them looking ravenous. Could the sun have already traveled half of its never-ending daily path? It didn't seem possible.

"Goodness, what is the hour?" Deborah said, jumping up from where she had just barely sat down. "The meal is all but ready. Mistress Hutchinson, I would like you to meet my sons…"

*   *   *

The two women met again briefly the following morning to say their good-byes.

"Our visit yesterday meant so much to me Deborah," Anne said. "I admit I become discouraged at times. I continually fight Satan, to keep him from making me disheartened, so I can continue to spread God's word. Then, I meet someone like you and I thank God for his sweet messenger of encouragement."

"I, too, am grateful for our yesterday. I shall never forget it, or you, Anne Hutchinson."

"Pray for me, Deborah, and I shall pray for you."

Chapter 43

Saugus
March 1637
Deborah

"Quick, Matthew, run get your brothers. Hurry!"

Panic revealed itself in the tone and volume of Deborah's voice. If only her body could be as sharp.

Nothing about her was working right. Not her mind, not her body. Sluggishness weighed her down. Her arms were too heavy to move, as though a hod of mortar wasted her muscles. Her legs were paralyzed. She couldn't catch her breath.

"Here, now, Reverend," said Marshal Thornbury, "don't give me any trouble. Just put out your hands like a good bloke."

The sight of Marshal Thornbury moving beyond the explanation of his visit into actually trying to truss her father's hands thrust Deborah to launch into action. The laxness that had sapped her energy an instant before fermented into rage. She heard an ugly, high-pitched cry bouncing off the walls in the coldness of the church, but it would be hours before she realized the racket came from her. That was the second time her cries had echoed in a church.

Before her reason could catch up with her reactions, Deborah was at the marshal's back, her fists fiercely pummeling his back and shoulders.

"Please, for the love of God, he is an old man," she cried. "He is a man of God. I pray thee, do not do this to him."

As the marshal attempted to wriggle away from her, Deborah saw him wrestle with her father's hands, making moves to bind them. Deborah sprang into a she lion protecting her cub, her loved one. Her father. That spine-chilling clamor sounded again as she resumed her arms of fists.

She heard the marshal cry out in pain even as she felt a pain in her right fist. Marshal Thornbury rubbed his cheek, glaring at Deborah who stepped back in amazement at what she had done.

"Daughter! Stop it!"

Stephen's bass voice commanded Deborah's being back into its senses.

The three looked at one another in disbelief at what had just happened. They all knew the marshal could now easily place Deborah under arrest, along with her father. No one said a word.

"We will not cower," Stephen finally said.

Deborah covered her face with her hands, drew in a deep breath and unwillingly exhaled it as a halting sob. It shook Stephen's soul. "Daughter, quiet yourself. 'Tis all right, Deborah," he said gently, moving to her as the marshal, still rubbing his cheek, stepped aside. "There's no harm." Stephen put his arms around his daughter and held her tight. "Keep your head high. We've nothing to be ashamed of."

"Come, now, we've a long trek ahead of us," Marshal Thornbury said, anxious to be on his way before more trouble erupted. He had been warned there might be a hassle when he tried to arrest the minister, but he didn't expect an eruption to come from a woman. He was chagrinned that this little bit of a female could give him a shiner—and he knew he would be sporting the remnants of her wrath for days to come.

"Give me your hands," he barked to Stephen.

Deborah sank onto a rough-hewn bench-pew as Stephen stuck out his hands, his fingers folded together as if in prayer. When the marshal grabbed his hands, Stephen stretched his neck to its most-possible height. He was doing as he had bade his daughter: holding his head high.

"'Tis a sorry business, Sir," the marshal said, binding Stephen's wrists with horsehair rope. "But I've me orders."

"What's going on here?"

It was John's voice. Deborah looked up and saw the tall figure of her son poised in the doorway, his flexed arms at his sides, his hands balled into fists. Daniel and Stephen were on his heels, their older brother's fury mirrored in their faces. Matthew, eyes wide, elbowed his way between his brothers' long legs and ran to his mother.

Parishioners and townspeople began to crowd into the church. There hadn't been a spectacle such as this for months.

"I said, what's going on here?" bellowed John. "Who are you and what are you doing to my grandfather?"

"I am Marshal Thornbury, sent from Boston to fetch the good Reverend Bachiler here to appear before the magistrates. Seems he ignored their invitation to explain himself to them, wouldn't come on his own, so I'm here to gather him."

Christopher Hussey joined the Wing boys.

"Out of our way now," the marshal said, authority sounding in his voice, aware of the growing crowd. He fixed a grapnel between Stephen's tied hands to lead him from the church, much as a farmer might lead a helpless, dumb, bull-headed steer to market. "I want no trouble from any of ye. Just mind your own business and let us be on our way."

A deep wall of Wings and Husseys blocked the marshal's way from the aisle. They stood, arms folded across their thrust-out chests, their faces frowning. Intimidating.

"I said, out of our way! Let's not have an ugly scene."

"Move aside, boys," Stephen said, his voice low and faltering, but still surprisingly strong. "Let us maintain our dignity. Remember that we are about the Lord's work. Let us compose ourselves as though he were here among us, as he truly is."

The aisle-way of people slowly backed up, step by step, and out the door into the sharp March air. They formed a passageway of confirmation for their pastor as he passed between them.

"John," Deborah said, reaching out for her son. "Go with him."

Chapter 44

Saugus
April 1637
Deborah

"Mother," John said, drawing deeply on his long-stemmed clay pipe as Deborah cleared the supper dishes, "I went to Edmund Freeman's meeting this afternoon about settling on Cape Cod."

The upcoming removal of Goodman Freeman and others from Saugus had been the subject of an ongoing conversation in the Wing household for more than a fortnight. "Goodman Humphrey and the Plymouth Colony have granted permission for the plantation settlement."

Deborah put aside the trenches and sat down on the bench next to John as he sat at the head of the table.

"Just guess what they are going to call the town," John teased.

"Hmmm. Freemanville?"

John shook his head.

"New Saugus? All the New England towns seemed to be named after the towns the founders came from in old England. So..."

"Nay, but you're close."

Deborah thought.

"Oh! I know—New-Town."

"No, but that's not bad."

"I haven't the foggiest, John. Tell me."

"Sandwich."

"No!"

"Yes!" John smiled broadly. "I knew you'd like that."

"Forever more. How did that name come up?"

"It seems John Humphrey, the magistrate of Saugus and our intrepid assistant governor of Massachusetts Bay Colony, hails from Sandwich, Kent—and he thought it fitting that the plantation he approved should be named after his English home town."

"Sandwich," Deborah mused. "It's been a long time since I've thought of Sandwich. That was a fine town, John. We were very happy there. That's where we lived when we had to leave home the first time."

Her mind spanned back across the decades, and there she was, a young woman, standing with John and their youngsters waiting to board the ship to sail across the Channel to Europe. She recalled John's depression and her own perseverance. She thanked God again for making her capable of helping her husband during that trying time.

She wrapped her hands around the wooden cup still warm from the hot cider she drank at supper. She was talking to herself as much as to her son about Sandwich and the turn of events.

"Our lives changed forever that day."

"I know," John said quietly.

"The entire townspeople, including the mayor came to see us off," Deborah said. "I thought the dock might sink from so many people standing on it. Even the mayor was there."

She smiled at John and patted his hand.

"But that's ancient history," she said, brushing the bittersweet cobwebs from her mind. "Tell me about this new Sandwich."

"Well, for one thing, the countryside of the two Sandwiches seems to be similar: both have flat marshes, shallow harbors and a wide bar that runs northeast, southwest."

A soft smile crossed Deborah's face as she pictured the scene's English counterpart.

"And, in England," John continued, "you remember nearby Buzzer's Belly? Well, here, Buzzards Bay is close to what will be Sandwich, New England."

"Who all is going, John?" Deborah asked. "Has it been finalized?"

"The ten men who began this venture are for certain going and they are enlisting other families, up to six score, to be known as 'undertakers,' who want to remove from here."

Mother and son smiled. They had talked of removing ever since the Boston magistrates mandated her father leave Saugus.

*   *   *

Stephen had asked the Massachusetts church council to dismiss him and his followers from the Saugus church since it was evident there would never be a lasting truce between the dividing factors. The council members were only too happy to grant his wish, especially since they did not believe peace would be possible in Saugus until the good reverend shook the dust of the town from his boots.

They granted his separation from the church on the proviso that he leave Saugus.

Stephen agreed to move on. Who would want to stay now, anyway? But the problem was, he changed his mind. He and seven of his followers renewed their old covenant and made plans to build a new church in Saugus. This time on a hill. Proper like.

Saugus residents, however, disparaged having Stephen, a bit daft as they believed him to be, living amongst them. They complained to the council and the council sided with the townsfolk and told Stephen he must leave.

When it became evident he had no such intention, the magistrates sent the marshal to unceremoniously haul the Rev. Bachiler before them.

Properly chastened, Stephen agreed to leave Saugus within three months. He was offered fifty acres to settle and minister in Ipswich where the community did not think him dottering, where they revered his intellect and Christian faith.

And Stephen had planned to go. He had. But he changed his mind. Again. Nobody knew why. He simply decided not to go. And now the aging minister was scouting for new territory for his flock. The proposed plantation of Yarmouth, near where Sandwich would be, sounded like a good possibility.

Christopher and Theodate had already moved on, living in Newbury—the town where Deborah first thought they would settle.

*　　　　　*　　　　　*

"Tell me the ten men again," Deborah said.

But before John could recite the list, Deborah said, "I assume by ten men, they also mean their wives and children." She smiled at her son.

"Yes, Mother, they mean the wives and children, too." John returned the smile. His mother was unlike any other mother he knew. In fact, he didn't know of a single other mother who would be brave enough to bring her young family to this new land without the support of a husband. There must be others, he just didn't happen to know them.

"Now, then," he said, "the ten men are Edmund Freeman, Henry Feake, Thomas Dexter, Edward Dillingham, William Wood, John Carman, Richard Chadwell, William Almy, Thomas Tupper..."

"That's nine," Deborah said, ticking the names off on her fingers.

"Oh, and George Knott."

"Ten."

Mother and son looked at one another.

"What do you think?" John asked, breaking the silence.

By now, Daniel, Stephen and Matthew had returned to the table and sat silently listening to their mother and elder brother.

Deborah looked around, saw the boys, and patted Daniel's hand as he sat next to her. He was now twenty.

"I think…"

Daniel gently squeezed his mother's hand.

"I think we should do it," she said at last.

"Saugus holds nothing for us. Some of those ten families and some of the undertakers are our closest friends in this country. Theodate and Christopher are gone. Father's going—Heaven only knows where. Maybe he will come with us. At least if we leave Saugus, we can offer him a home."

She looked at her sons, growing so fast. Her eldest was near the age of his father when she first met him.

She could feel her throat tightening. Sentiment. How Deborah hated to be undone by it. She would not be. This was not the time for losing one's senses.

"I want to establish a home for you boys that will be constant. And, I want to build a house and know 'tis the house I will die in.

"I want to wander the world no more. I want to plant myself—and the tulip bulbs I brought from Holland and the herbs from England—and be settled."

A sense of relief flooded over her.

"Yes, John—Daniel, Stephen and Matthew. Yes, I think we should add our names to those removing from Saugus for Sandwich."

The boys cheered. After they quieted down, John said: "There is one factor we haven't discussed yet."

Deborah looked at him. She didn't like the sound of his voice.

"Needs be I am listed as head of the family."

Deborah's forehead became a mass of colliding lines.

New England laws required if a family had a male of legal age, that he head the family. John was now three and twenty.

The image of Catherina Van Blarcom flashed before her eyes and a sharp reminder of the independence she might have had, had she remained in Holland.

"Very well," she sighed.

They never broached the subject again.

Chapter 45

Sandwich, Massachusetts
July 1638
Deborah

"Pardon me, Goody Wing, but would ye have a cup of tea for a poor way-faring stranger?"

Deborah dropped her broom.

Sweeping was a favorite chore in her Sandwich home. It was satisfying to sweep the wide-planked board floor. Keeping house so much easier now that she no longer had to constantly battle a dirt floor.

Even before she completed her twirl to meet the voice that addressed her, Deborah knew it was her father's face she would see framed in the opened, top half of their Dutch door.

"Father! It is you."

Stephen opened the latch of the door's bottom half and let himself in. He stood, legs parted and firmly planted, with opened arms, waiting anxiously to fold them around his daughter.

*   *   *

The family lingered around the table long after they finished their noon dinner of boiled ribs of salt beef topped off with the special horseradish that never failed to bring tears to Stephen's eyes. This time, however, the tears came not only from the bite of the sauce, but from the memories it stirred from so many years past. It was Ann's recipe. A mere whiff of it conjured crystal clear memories of the aroma beckoning him from his studies in the Wherwell stone church to the ivy-covered manse next door. Some of his favorite days were those when Ann would put up enough of the delicacy to last through the winter.

It didn't matter if it was the taste or the memories, either way, the tears that made Stephen's eyes swim were from pure pleasure, not pain.

"So, what are your plans now, Grandfather?" John asked.

"Of course, he will stay here with us," Deborah chimed in. "Please say you will stay with us. Nothing could make me happier."

"I'm sorely tempted to accept your offer, Daughter," he said. "At seven and seventy, my old bones sometimes flat-out hurt."

Last January, inclement weather and all, Stephen and "a company of poor men," as Governor Winthrop would one day characterize them, had limped their way from Saugus to six miles beyond Sandwich to Yarmouth, or Mattakeese, as the Indians called the place. The small band of unorthodox, independent Christians had been granted the status of undertakers to establish a new plantation and a new church. But it proved too much for them as winter had descended, and they surrendered the patent to others.

"Bless thee, Child," Stephen said, "but no. Sandwich is not my calling."

"We have no pastor here," Daniel said. "There is no church being conducted."

"There's not?"

"No," Deborah said, "The Reverend Leverich, a man of great piety and meekness, gave up and has left us. He could not muster enough people to fill the pews, and he grew weary of battling the town's fathers for what he thought was a lack of enthusiasm in supporting the church."

"Surely you were members?" Stephen asked.

"No, Grandfather, we were not members." It was John speaking, sounding so much like his father. "We agreed when we left Saugus to never again attend a church that in any way resembled the church that has caused you so much grief in this country."

"Is that true? Daughter?"

"'Tis true," Deborah answered. She had known this day and this conversation would arise one day and she had dreaded it.

"We worship at home. The five of us. Around the hearth, or around this very table. Daniel and Stephen take turns in reading the Scripture."

"I don't understand," her father said. "Members of my own family not attending church?"

"We keep the Sabbath," said Stephen the younger. "We just choose not to keep it at church."

"Grandfather, we don't feel God can be found in the chaos that seems to be forever stirred up in churches," Daniel said. "The buildings, that is. We feel, as a family, that in God's eye, we are as acceptable a church as any building."

Stephen shook his head as the young man spoke.

"I cannot help but love you all for your stance, but by the same token, I also cannot help but wonder at your wisdom. What happened to cleansing our inner selves and then cleansing the church?"

The Wings were silent. Deborah breathed in deep and let the air out slowly.

"Father," she began, "I do not wish to argue with you…"

Stephen interrupted her. "Well," he said, smiling, mindful again of his mission, "this makes pleading my case easier than I feared it might."

"What's that?" asked John.

Deborah felt the nape of her neck tingle.

"I'm off to Newbury just now, and I want you—all of you—to come with me."

Deborah and her sons looked at him. No one said a word.

"We would all be together again. You, and Theodate and Christopher, their children…We'd be a real family again. I want that more than anything else in this world. Us, a family once more. We could praise God together again. Like we came here to do. They've offered me a goodly land tract in Newbury and I'll seek permission to start up another congregation. 'Twill be as it was when we first arrived. What say you?"

This time, the Wings avoided Stephen and looked at one another.

Who was going to tell him?

Stephen rose to stoke the fire. Daniel reached over to Matthew and pulled him closer as they sat on the bench. John rose to fetch his pipe. He cleared his throat and looked at his mother.

Deborah spoke.

"Father," she said, looking Stephen in the eye, "we have decided to live in Sandwich. This is to be our home. For as long as God grants us breath."

She resisted shuddering at the tension that had infused the room. She worked to keep her breathing even. She so disliked quarreling—especially with her father. But even more, Deborah disliked the notion of following a nomadic life any longer.

When she planted her Holland bulbs beside her house last fall, she vowed to them—herself, really—that they could remain and thrive in this soil. She would not disturb them again. Ever.

Deborah was saddened at what she read in Stephen's eyes. Those eyes, which at one time reflected her own, had lost so much of their snap. The sags and bags beneath them tarnished the luster that once shone from his face. At this moment, her father looked every day of his seven and seventy years.

She reached out and took one of his hands in both of hers. She could feel Stephen pull away. She pulled back, held harder.

"Father, please understand. Do not turn away from us. We love you. We always have and we always will. Please love us—and understand us—as well."

Stephen stood and lifted Deborah with him, she not letting go of his hand.

"Where are you going?"

He raised his chin. "My faithful followers and I are camped in tee-pees on the edge of town," he said. "I just wanted to come by and see you. And ask you to come with me."

Tears filled his eyes again. This time there was no pleasure in them.

"Father, our home is your home. Stay here with us."

"I cannot. I must be on my way."

"When will we see you again?"

"I do not know. I am not the one who caused the problem."

With that, her father turned, rubbed the back of his neck, and walked away from his daughter and her sons.

"May the good Lord cause his eyes to shine upon you," he said quietly as he slowly closed the door behind him.

Chapter 46

Sandwich
November 1638
Deborah

"Tell me again everything you know about Grandfather," Deborah said to John and Daniel who had returned only hours earlier from their trip of a fortnight to Hampton, New Hampshire.

The entire family sat on stools, the bench—or in Matthew's case—squatted on the floor in front of the warm evening fire. Deborah, sitting in her chair, carded with a wire-toothed brush, gently pulling at globs of wool again and again until they became fine fluffs. Once satisfied with the texture, she would drop the transformed sheep's clothing into a basket with other bunches of wool to later spin them into yarn. Still later, she would weave the yarn into fabric to sew each of her boys a suit of clothes and a new dress for herself.

Carding was her favorite part of the process. It required no thinking, freeing her mind to peruse other, more challenging topics.

John said, "As the town's father and minister, Grandfather was granted him three-hundred acres of farmland, as well as a town lot where he's built a most handsome house. He won't admit it, but he's very pleased, that as the town's founder, he was allowed to name it Hampton."

"After his beloved homeland," Deborah said. "Tell me about his home."

"He calls it Hampton House," Daniel said. "Some neighbors have crit-·icized him for building so a large home since he is its only occupant. Too worldly, they say. His library is his prized room. It's goodly-sized with a fireplace and a glassed door. The room's shelves are floor to ceiling to hold all his books."

"Maybe now Father can be at peace," Deborah said. "He's earned it."

"He told us," Stephen said, "that he's not going to let his guard down, that 'life would be too smooth if there were no rubs in it.'"

"The only possible 'rub' I see," John said, "is the Reverend Timothy Dalton, who was sent from England to be a teacher in Grandfather's church. He came with a large congregation, which could prove costly to Grandfather if they lock horns."

"He carries an air of superiority, and," Daniel quoted his grandfather, "'he is still quite youngly and has not yet trod this Earth enough to have earned such airs.'"

"Oh, that sounds like trouble," Deborah said. "I can't help but be surprised he was allowed to start yet a new plantation."

"I asked Uncle Christopher about that," John said, "may be that the magistrates felt that by letting him start a new town, they could kill two birds with one stone—be rid of a troublesome pastor and strengthen their claim to the territory."

"Ooh, those men make me so angry," Deborah seethed, giving an extra tug on the cards.

"Baaaa," Stephen said from across the hearth, sounding as though the sheep could feel Deborah's wrath even though its wool had been shorn long ago.

Deborah looked at him—and smiled. "Well, they do make me angry," she said. "Even when they finally treat your grandfather fairly, it's only because 'twill give them some advantage, too."

"You gave Grandfather my letter?" Deborah asked.

"Of course," John answered. "He said he was heartened to receive it."

"He praised God that the two of you have resolved your conflicts," Daniel said. "Grandfather even confessed that he was the blame for your differences."

"Want to know what I think?" Daniel asked with a smile. "Methinks the two of your are so alike that the friction you naturally create causes a combustion, and a conflagration results."

She frowned at her son, and asked, "How did Father look?"

"Hale and hearty," Daniel said. "Aunt Theodate and Uncle Christopher are well, too. She sends her love, said to tell you that Baby Mary is nearly walking and has yet to see the end of her first year. She also sends gratitude for the blanket you knit for the baby."

Daniel paused and looked at John: "Is that everything?"

"I think so."

"Anything happen here while we were gone?" John asked.

"John Alden and Capt. Miles Standish completed their surveying," Deborah answered. "Now the limits of each man's allotment of land has been defined. That's about all of any import."

Chapter 47

Hampton, New Hampshire
December 1643
Stephen

Hampton

December 1643

My Dearest Daughter:

   I will start my letter to you by telling of my wonderful friends in Casco and Exeter, who have both issued a call for me to be their minister. Goodman Cleeve of Casco has asked I leave my warring parishioners and slandering colleague and take up with them.

   Their invitations have filled my heart with joy and eased the ache in my spirit after such a sorrowful two years.

   My ex-communication of two years past was 'haps the most grievous event of my life. To think that Governor Winthrop would believe the false accusations of Mister Dalton over mine applications of innocence—and there is no doubt of my innocence regarding any improprieties taken with Goody Butterworth.

   By his irregular proceedings and the abuse of power, Reverend Dalton, who is suppose to be the teacher of our church, has been the cause of all my shame. He has dishonored God and brought grief to all God's people in our congregation.

Still, Governor Winthrop wants me to leave Hampton. Again, I am asked to remove myself from my home. How can they ask this? I am as innocent as a lamb of any wrongdoing, Daughter. And at my ancient age, one would think mercy would be shown. But, alas, 'tis not the case.

On this very day, my Dear Deborah, I have writ to the governor and told him I do not see how I can depart hence, not until I—or God—can clear my name and vindicate the wrongs I have suffered of the church I yet serve in.

I wrote that while my cause has been looked into slightly by diverse elders and brethren, it could never come to a judicial searching forth of things and an impartial trial of Mister Dalton's allegations and my defense.

If it would come to trial, I am confident before God I would be redeemed.

I also wrote to Governor Winthrop that the magistrates, elders and brethren sincerely set out to find sin and search into the complaints of the poor, yet they know not father or mother, church or elder. I say, in such a wine cellar to find a cockatrice and not kill him, to have such monstrous proceedings passed over without due justice, stirs my spirit to seek for a writ ad melius inquirendam.

I spoke frankly. I told our governor it is thankworthy—deserving of gratitude—if a man, for conscience sake, endures grief, suffers wrongfully. I ought to endure, without seeking any redress or justice against the offender. I profess it was absolutely necessary to suffer when the Church had no civil power to seek unto than in such a land of righteousness as our New England is.

Daughter, I may, once again, find myself chastened for speaking my mind. But, what have I to lose? I have lost so much already: first, my license to preach in England, and then your dear mother, my devoted Ann, and two other loving wives. I have been hove from one church after another, one town after another, one home after another—the last consumed as though it were in the center of Hell itself. What more have I to lose? My good name? I hardly think so.

In a letter of the year past, you said it be the Devil's fault for these indignities. I, too, believe the Devil has had his hand in these matters.

Although things do indeed look bleak, I will not lose courage, Deborah. And I pray you, too, retain your courage. We are about God's business and he will not fail us.

On another subject, I have heard that your John, Daniel and Stephen are among those in Sandwich who have been enrolled as capable of bearing arms. Let us remember to pray each day for lasting peace in this, our new, God-given home.

Your Loving Father

*   *   *

Hampton
December 1643
My Dearest Daughter Deborah

God be praised! Be certain to give extra thanks tonight, my dear heart. The governor and his magistrates, in their wisdom, have seen fit to reverse their judgment and restore me to my church.

They have not, as yet, repaired me to my office as pastor, but not because of any wrongdoing on my part. The mediators felt our Hampton church is already too divided and did not want to fracture it further by allowing me to be its pastor again just yet.

It is enough for me, for now, to have my excommunication lifted.

Since I wrote you so recently, there is no other news to tell. But I did want to share this wonderful information with you so as to relieve your mind as mine has been relieved.

Your Loving Father

*   *   *

Hampton
May 18, 1644
Governor John Winthrop
Boston, Massachusetts

Dear Governor:

It is with great pleasure that I write to you on this beautiful spring day that God has given us.

I am clearly free of any promise to remove to Casco, and no one mis-likes my inclination to go to Exeter. Everyone in the plantation is thoroughly satisfied and has encouraged me to go forward.

Upon my promise to accept the call to Exeter, the parishioners there have agreed to send forth their letters with requests for help and advice from other churches. I also exhorted them to live in love and peace to help redeem whatever ill opinion the country has conceived of them.

They have met and agreed upon the people and materials of their intended church and set the day of the helpers' meeting, which is the 18th of the next month.

I would be most appreciative if your Worship would communicate with me, this poor relation, and to your Reverend Elders to save me a little pain in writing. I would also be grateful if you would ask Brother Wilson to honor us with his presence, and see me, his old friend, and grant me this last service—save my burial.

For the establishment of a church-estate in Exeter, I freely agreed to the forty-one pounds of the annual wages they paid to Mister Rashleigh to purchase Mister Wheelright's house and accommodations to be mine for my term only, and be left to whoever shall succeed me.

I expect that as soon as I have removed, the people of Hampton will sell what they can of my lot and estate in Hampton.

I ask our government to recompense me for the price I paid them for the plantation—especially since I have never billed them for any maintenance.

As you know, I suffered great losses by that horrific fire (about 200 pounds), along with my entire study of books.

I have been asked to voluntarily remove from this place for peace sake, and while it is not a great distance, the move will be of considerable expense. So, even the amount of three pounds (haply a little more), would be of great comfort and benefit to me. I have, in effect, little or no other means and maintenance to depend upon, but from my lot in Hampton.

Surely you would agree I am legally entitled to such a favor from the state. If not, in your wise and considerable judgement and that of my fellow ministers, I shall not complain. But, if you do agree, then I humbly beseech you as a friend to take my request to the Court—and cast the success upon the Lord above.

I realize I am being bold to trouble you with my letters of complaint and to seek your advice, but I pray you to bear with me.

In conclusion, I promise your Worship—and my ancient friend—my poor service and submit my faithful prayers for you and my reverend brethren. I cease and rest in the Lord, yours to command, his most unprofitable servant,

Stephen Bachiler.

Please bear with my blotted paper—my maid threw down mine ink glass upon it and I had not time to write it over.

*   *   *

Hampton
May 30, 1644
Dearest Deborah

I had thought I would be writing to you from Exeter. But, here I am, still in Hampton.

All arrangements had been made for my removal to Exeter. The Council's magistrates had approved the transfer. I was told in confidence by one who knew full well that the magistrates cared not where I went, just so I removed from Hampton. They evidently feel there can be no peace here as long as I live here. This saddens my heart sorely, but I am ready for a period of peace in my life. If it can not be had in Hampton, then methought, perhaps Exeter.

But, that evidently is not to be, either.

I told the Exeter church members they could not expect to maintain a church and minister long if they did not make provisions for a parsonage for that man. I offered to pay forty pounds towards its building, which would have meant most of my first year's salary. The church leaders agreed with me and we made the settlement.

Then, even as I was about to leave Hampton, I was sent word from Boston that the Council now disapproved of my removal to Exeter and I was forbidden to make the transfer. They mandated I could not gather a church there.

It seems Governor Winthrop, whom I once considered—long ago—to be a friend, has said that all my previous churches have fallen into such divisions that no peace could be restored until I was removed!

The injustice of such a statement makes the hair on my head stand on end.

Thus, several citizens, on my behalf, including our well-loved son, Christopher Hussey, have petitioned the General Court in Boston to look into these matters at Hampton and to, for once and for all, clear my good name.

In the meantime, I continue to make my home with Christopher and Theodate, who sends you their love.

Your Loving Father

Chapter 48

Sandwich
1647
Deborah

Sandwich
April 1647

My Dear Sister, Greetings:

'Tis high time I write and bring you up to date on our family's happenings. We have been so busy, as I know you are.

First, I will tell of the news that makes a grandmother's heart sing: John and his Elizabeth are now parents. Susannah was born a fortnight ago. She is a beautiful child. It is so blessed to have a baby in the house again. Babies, their sweetness and innocence, are what make life bearable at times. You only have to look in their wee cherubic faces to know that God is at work in our lives and that everything will mend itself soon enough.

My other news is that which truly breaks a mother's heart, at least causes disappointment, frustration and embarrassment. And, yes, downright disgust!

If you were not kin, Theodate, I would dare not tell you this. But I need to talk to someone of it, and, next to Father, (whom I durst not speak to about this) you are my nearest relative who is not of me. If I had a daughter of my own here, 'haps I could talk to her, but since I have not, I write to you, confident you will understand my dilemma and keep my shameful secret tucked in the pocket of your mind.

You know, of course, that Stephen married Osheah Dillingham last fall. Methought there was something amiss right from the first, such a rush they were to wed. But I chalked it up to youthful passion. It was passion all right, but, unfortunately, 'twas a passion already spent.

They are dear children, both of them. Either would do anything for family—or for anyone, for that matter.

I do believe they love each other well, but—Heaven help us—they did not love wisely. Stephen was summoned to appear before the Plymouth Court last month and was fined because his and Osheah's child was born "at an unseasonable time" after their marriage.

I am truly embarrassed. If Stephen were of a size, I would turn him over my knee and paddle his behind. But, he is now a man grown bigger than me.

Someone must have informed the Plymouth Court of Stephen and Osheah's misstep. You know how a whole town will talk and how stories grow as they travel from one mouth to another—and it seems, there is always someone with nothing better to do than keep track of time, ticking off each month as it passes after a couple is married. And, if a babe be born before the ninth month arrives, then the gossip shall surely begin.

I do wish people would each tend to their own knitting.

I have the deepest suspicion that it is Marshal George Barlow who informed the Plymouth Court. He is a hateful man with an evil heart and a brittle tongue. 'Twould be just like him to inform upon the young couple.

But the baby is such a dear heart. I can be upset at Stephen and Osheah, but not the babe. I look at that sweet face and I'm reminded again of the sweet faces of my own babies. 'Tis certainly not his fault his parents are such ninnies. But their shame will no doubt shadow him all his life.

Stephen and Osheah do feel poorly about what's happened, but as Stephen said, the fine has been paid and there's nothing more he can do, so therefore, nothing more need be said about it. They seem to go on about their lives as though nothing is amiss.

And, I suppose, that is the best course. I can't help but feel mortified, however. I certainly can't imagine being in their shoes. Just think what Father would have said if any of us ever had a baby out of season.

I'm glad my John did not see this day, and I hope he's not turning in his grave. He would not have looked kindly upon our son displaying such impropriety. Maybe, however, if John had been here, he could have counseled Stephen better than I. I knew not the words to speak to a son about such things. 'Twould be hard enough to tell a daughter what befalls when certain things happen (I cannot even write of them to you, but I know you know what I speak of). So, therefore, 'twould be nigh impossible for a mother to tell a son a solitary thing. 'Tis not done.

It's fallen upon John Junior's shoulders to be both father and brother to Daniel, Stephen and Matthew. And he has done a commendable job. He certainly is not to blame for Stephen's lack of strength, will and common sense.

But, as Stephen said, to fret about it now is as folly as carrying water in a sieve.

Stephen, I must say, however, has done some things right this past while. He bought the old fort on Spring Hill and turned it into a most comfortable home for his little family. He was told it's the first structure to be built in Massachusetts. Since it was built strong for a fort, 'twill probably last forever. True, 'twas built as a fort, but it might just as well be a house. The Indians here are so peaceful and such good neighbors, that no one needs protection from them.

On to other subjects, Sister dear:

I was heartened with your letter telling of Father being well and living in Strawberry Banke. Theodate, what do you know of Father's house-keeper? He wrote that Mary (is that her name?) is a widow and "an honest neighbor." But something sounded amiss in his letter. Mayhap I am overly sensitive and defensive. I hope so.

I hear Susannah crying and Elizabeth has gone to town with John, so I must close.

Write soon. I do miss you and our chats.

Your loving sister, Deborah.

P.S.

I would be most grateful if you would burn this letter once you read it. I would hate to have Stephen's unfortunate news lying around where others might read of it—especially Father.

Chapter 49

Strawberry Banke, New Hampshire
1648
Stephen

"Ohhh, Reverend Mister Bachiler, Sir," Mary cooed as she entered Stephen's study, carrying a tray laden with a teapot and two cups, "such splendid news, you being awarded all that land in your suit against Hampton. You deserve it, you do."

Mary's thigh brushed against Stephen as she sashayed passed him sitting in his brocade-covered, wing-backed chair—a gift from Christopher and Theodate. He was snoozing in the warm sunlight as it streamed through the windowpanes, detailing minute specks of dust lazily floating through the air.

Mary pushed aside Stephen's books and papers on the low table directly in front of him to make room for the tray.

"Methought we should celebrate the occasion," she said cheerily, carrying on the conversation by herself in her bird-pitch voice with its singsong cadence. "I brung me a cup to drink wi' ye." She smiled at him. Seductively. "I hope ye won't think it out of place, me being your 'umble servant and all."

"How did you know anything about this?" Stephen said, straightening up, rubbing his eyes and sounding a bit befuddled. He had dropped off while reading and was slow to rally his wits.

"In town 'as where I heard it," Mary replied. "The whole of town is a-buzz. Just everybody's talking about it. They're talkin' of nuthin' else." Her voice rose and fell with each phrase. "Too bad it ain't cash they give you, but you won't have no trouble sellin' the land for money, do ye think? It'll make a handsome profit, I expect." She leaned over at the waist to fill the cups, strategically placing her backside inches from Stephen's face. "Those rich folks in Hampton can very well afford to pay ye for yer past services, they can. 'Tis a town filled with wealthy folk. Some nerve they have, tryin' to weasel out of what they owes you. Ye was good to them, preachin' to them and tendin' their souls, and them not payin' you a farthing. Shame on 'em. Especially considering ye begun that town, ye did. You're its father, ye are. Double shame on 'em."

Mary swiveled around, still bent at the waist, so that now her front-side was in Stephen's direct view, just where her well-rounded bottom had been. Stephen's eyes were presented with the feast of Mary's buxom bosom, straining beneath her tight bodice. It rose and fell, rose and fell with every breath she took.

She handed her aged employer his cup and waited for him to take a sip.

"Whooooeee," Stephen sputtered.

Mary threw back her head and hooted.

"This is some cup of tea, my fair Mary," Stephen said, once he caught his breath. He was smiling.

"Can't properly celebrate with tea," Mary said, picking up her cup. "Tea's not a fittin' drink to make merry with at a time such as this. Your health, guv'nor." She saluted him with her cup.

*   *   *

As Mary poured Stephen's third cup of "tea," she cozied up to him and wriggled her way onto his lap. She ran her fingers through his hair, a little thinner now and as sparkling white as winter snow covering a barren land.

"What are ye up to, Mary?" Stephen wheezed. "Surely you know I'm a man of more than twice your age. Probably thrice. I'm now seven and eighty—'tis more than four score. Nearly four score and ten."

"But you are still a fit man, Sir," Mary whispered into his ear before nestling her head in his shoulder. Her legs dangled across the far side of the chair holding the unlikely couple. "I've not met a man as fit as ye, I'm sure. Ye'r still a strong man, a vital man, a viral man. I'm sure," she whispered into one ear as she teased his other ear with the tip of her finger. 'Tis an honor to work for thee, Guv'nor." Mary looked at Stephen. His eyes were glassy and drooping. His breathing was slow and regular. Heavy. He'd soon be asleep. "The only honor that would be bigger than workin' for thee, Reverend Sir," she breathed into his ear, "would be if I was to be ye'r wife. Mrs. Stephen Bachiler. I like the sound of that, Sir. I would make thee a good wife. I would make thee feel a young man again."

*　　　　　*　　　　　*

Strawberry Banke
1848
Dear Daughter Deborah:

I cannot stress enough how trying it is for me to write thee of my news. I am so ashamed!

The Devil has been at work in my life again. And he's caused the most dreadful mischief this time. It might very well be my undoing. I am distraught, Daughter. Distraught.

I have committed the greatest folly of my life!

I swear to you, I know not how it happened, but it seems I have wed my housekeeper, the widow Mary Beedle. I remember so little of what happened. Truth be it, Daughter, I remember nothing. The days before our marriage are a swirl of a dark, mirey haze. But Mary shewed me the paper that proves we are wed. Sadly, my signature, although signed distressingly sloppy, does, I fear, look enough like mine to stand up in court.

Without a doubt, the worst of all this is that I was the one to marry us. And, of course, we published no banns.

I know not what else to say to thee, Daughter dear. I pray you will not think too unkindly of your demented Father.

I swallow my pride and muster my courage to write this missive so you hear of this most sorrowful news from me and not a gossipmonger.

I only hope your blessed mother will forgive me when 'tis time for me to join her in Heaven above. And I pray that day will not be far off. I want to go home, Daughter. My soul pants for the eternal rest that has eluded me during my days on Earth. I am so very tired. I am an old man, Deborah, and I am weary of this life. I want nothing more than to go home.

Oh, that this lunacy does not keep us apart, your mother and me. I pray God will not stay me from entering his golden gates because of this most horrid blunder.

Pray for me Daughter, I sorely need it.

Your Humble and Errant Father

Chapter 50

Sandwich
1648
Deborah

"I wouldn't mind staying at home with Ephriam while the rest of you go to market," Deborah said as she swaddled her latest grandchild, John and Elizabeth's first baby born only a few weeks earlier.

"No," Elizabeth said, "you want to go to the village as much as the rest of us. You have Ephriam bundled up snug and tight; he will be just fine. Besides, the sun is shining today."

Winter began harshly in November, and within just a month's time, more snow had fallen longer and deeper than in anyone's memory. Paths had been shoveled from the house to the various out buildings, the root cellar, the road.

"It would do a body good to be out in the sunshine," Deborah agreed. "We've all been cooped up inside for so long that we've nearly forgotten what the blue sky—and our neighbors—look like."

"I'll take Ephriam and see how John's coming with the wagon," Elizabeth said as she scooped up the baby. "We'll meet you at the gate."

"I'm nearly ready," Deborah answered.

Not five minutes had passed before Elizabeth returned to the house on the run. "I forgot the scarf I knit for Goodwife Blanchard," she told Deborah as she headed for her basket of wool balls, needles and various knitting projects under way.

"Where's Ephriam?" Deborah asked.

"He's with John," the young mother answered. "I laid him in the back of the cart while John finishes harnessing the horse and ran back here to get the scarf."

Just then a frightful ruckus sounded from outside; the whinny of a spooked horse instantly chilled the women's blood and took away their breath. They looked at one another, terror in their eyes. Momentary paralysis grabbed them before they could gather their wits and race outside. They saw the horse rearing and heard its frightened whinny as it bolted towards the road, dragging sections of the now-broken wagon behind it, startling the beast even further.

"Ephriam," Elizabeth called, her voice screeching like a crazed robin whose chick had just been stolen from her nest. "Ephriam. Baby, baby," she called as she plowed her way through the snow towards the confusion.

Deborah followed as fast as she could. Tears streamed down her face, even though she knew nothing definitive. The commotion spoke for itself that a tragedy had indeed occurred.

Elizabeth was running around and around, calling, "Ephriam, Ephriam, where are you? I can't find him. I can't find him. Dear God, where is he? Where is he?"

"Darling, try to calm yourself," Deborah said as she pulled her daughter-in-law close. "Don't panic. We'll find him."

The scene was littered of the many things placed in the wagon to take to market: Splintered barrels and crates were everywhere, seed to be milled spilled from its ripped sack of cloth. The women frantically searched the yard where the horse had panicked. But Ephriam was not to be found. "Baby, baby," his mother kept calling. "Baby." Then Deborah spied what had been a pristine snow bank, last night's gentle snowfall having sprinkled a layer of white dust atop it that now sparkled in the sunshine. A splotch marred the otherwise perfect mound; something was there that should not have been there. Deborah ran towards it, calling out Elizabeth's name, then Ephriam's.

The baby's bundled form was all but lost in the snow bank, as though he had been shot into it like a ball exploded from a cannon. The frenzied Elizabeth and Deborah pawed at the snow, trying to retrieve the infant. At last, they had him. Elizabeth couldn't tell the head from the foot of her precious package, not the front from the back. At last, she freed Ephriam from his wrappings—but his tiny broken body was blue. Sitting on the ground, Elizabeth clutched the baby to her breast and rocked her child and herself back and forth, quietly sobbing.

*   *   *

Sandwich
December 1648
My Dear Theodate:

Our darling Ephriam, beloved son of John and Elizabeth, has drowned in the snow. I'll write you more later, but for now, I ask your prayers for the babe's grief-stricken parents.

All my love,
Deborah.

Chapter 51

Sandwich
1649
Deborah

"Mother," called Matthew from the road, picking up his pace as he neared the house. "Mother."

Deborah hurried outside, wooden spoon still in hand, having left dinner's soup to cook on its own while she answered the call. She saw her youngest son, now a strapping man of three and twenty, come striding towards her, waving something in his hand.

"I've just come from town and Farmer Hatch gave me a letter to give to you from Hampton, where he's been this past while."

"Oh, thank the good Lord," Deborah said, anxious to hold news of her sister in her own hands. "I've been that worried."

"See, I told you, no news was good news," Matthew said, reaching her and handing over the long-awaited letter. "There was no need for you to have been so concerned."

"But it's been so long since I've heard from Theodate, I couldn't help but fret.

"I'm going in to brew me a pot of tea and read her message and…" Her voice trailed and her face paled. "This isn't Theodate's hand," she said quietly. "'Tis Christopher's." Deborah turned and slowly walked back to the house. Her enthusiasm daunted; her excitement deflected.

She sat down in son John's chair at the head of the table and held the letter to her breast. She swallowed. Her mouth was tinder dry. Her throat strained against the bit of saliva she forced down it. She put the letter in the pocket of her apron, intending to busy herself with work and read it later, when she felt stronger. Of the sudden, she was queasy, weak.

But she couldn't rise; she couldn't move, think. Her apron weighed her down as though it held pebbles in its pocket. No, a boulder.

"Mother?"

The hushed, inquisitive voice was Matthew's.

"What does the letter say?"

"I know not." Deborah's voice was weary. "I put it away. Unread."

"Let me read it, Mother."

Deborah fished around her apron until she found the pocket opening and, without a word, retrieved the leaden-missive and handed it to Matthew. She folded her hands and rested her arms on the table. Her eyes burned, they were so dry. She closed them.

Matthew carefully broke his Uncle Christopher's seal of red wax and scanned the message, written in a hasty hand on a single page.

Deborah looked at her son.

Matthew blinked hard and returned her gaze. He spoke quietly: "Aunt Theodate has passed, Mother."

A racking sound came from Deborah's throat as she took in a breath. It was as though she had forgotten to breathe the last few moments and the intake of air felt foreign to her. Her body wanted none of it. She gasped again. Pain seared through her heart. Theodate. Her baby sister. Gone.

"On the twenty-fourth of October,' Uncle writes. 'Theodate went to Heaven to be with the Lord, her Earthly mission completed. She had another wretched travail and did not possess the strength to muster this time. The babe was a girl, and in the moments before my dear Theodate died, she and I named the infant after Theodate—her mother, your sister, my wife."

This was the third Theodate that Christopher had lost. The couple's first Theodate, born nine years ago did not survive the rigors of this Earth and passed over as a mere toddler. And now, their last Theodate couldn't survive the distress of the birth, and died twelve days after her mother.

"I am grief-stricken," Christopher wrote. "We meant to have no more children since Theodate always experienced such difficulties—but, alas, our plans were not God's plans and another child was given to us."

"That's enough, Matthew," Deborah whispered. "Thank you. Please give me the letter."

With trembling hands, Deborah returned the missive to her pocket.

"I'll be back in a while. Tell the others what has transpired."

Drained, she stumbled out the door and slowly made her way towards the sea.

I will lift up mine eyes unto the mountains from whence cometh my help, Deborah recited to herself. *Except there are no mountains here, so I gain my strength from the sea, O Lord.*

Reaching the cape's coast, she dropped to her knees on a sand dune and let herself become hypnotized by the waves as they lapped the shore time and again, never ceasing.

The ocean. It always was and it would always be. Here, the ocean came ashore more calmly than up north, near her beloved Pulpit Rock. There, the sea's personality was fierce and angry. It crashed against the rocks. Here, it was steady and mostly predictable.

Deborah found beauty in both settings, but today, the seashore was more to her liking; it was calming. Soothing. Whenever she sat and watched the waves come in and go out—in and out, in and out—she thought, *this is the way God wants me to feel. Quiet. Calm. At peace with the world and with mineself.*

The only sound Deborah heard now, other than the rhythmic pulsation of the ocean, was the occasional plaintive cry of a sea gull. The birds' cries were the sound of her soul.

Her mind was dull. Empty. Like her spirit at that moment. Nothing stirred within her.

She sat and watched nothing.

The sky was the gorgeous azure of fall on a sunshiny day. Too soon now the days would be gray, day after day, with the sun making only rare appearances.

It would have been fitting, had the sun refused to shine on this particular day, Deborah thought, but she was grateful for its strength as it burned off the morning fog. She relished its warmth, both to her body and to her soul.

She lay back on the dune and closed her eyes and listened to the sea and the birds.

Suddenly, her eyes snapped open. *Who was that?* Had someone spoken? She lifted her head and darted her eyes to either side. No, she was quite alone. But she heard the words in her mind as clearly as if John—or Theodate—were sitting beside her, talking to her.

She closed her eyes again and listened:

To every thing there is a season, and a time to every purpose under the heaven:

A time to be born, and a time to die; a time to plant, and a time to pluck up that which is planted.

A time to kill, and a time to heal; a time to break down and a time to build up;

A time to weep and a time to laugh; a time to mourn, and a time to dance.

A time to cast away stones, and a time to gather stones together; a time to embrace, and a time to refrain from embracing;

A time to get, and a time to lose; a time to keep, and a time to cast away;

A time to rend, and a time to sew; a time to keep silence, and a time to speak;

A time to love, and a time to hate; a time of war, and a time of peace.

"A time to be born, and a time to die," she repeated to herself. A time to weep and a time to laugh; a time to mourn, and a time to dance.

We had our time to laugh together, didn't we Theodate? My baby sister. Especially after we grew so close over here, in America.

And, we had times when we wept together.

Deborah reflected on the discussions she'd had with Theodate—some heated, some avoided altogether.

She pressed her lips together softly, remembering how Theodate was astounded at Deborah's outspokenness, especially when their father was the topic of conversation.

We might not have been in tune like bells on every little thing, but we found the peace to love one another in spite of our differences, didn't we?

I do love thee, Sister Dear, and I will miss thee terribly. But one day we will meet together again—you and Mother and John and I. And, I expect by that time, Father will have joined you.

She should return to the house. But not yet. She looked over the endless sea and watched the billows of turbulent clouds as they floated by and out of sight.

'Tis time to mourn.

Chapter 52

Strawberry Banke
1650
Stephen

"What are you doing here?" Stephen barked. "Out of this house at once. Now. Get out, will you?"

"Don't be worrying old man," Mary said, spitting her words out. "I'm getting' out. I can't get out fast enough. I only came ta pick up a few things. You can rattle around in this old 'ouse by yourself. Won't trouble me none."

"Is your man friend waiting for you?" Stephen asked, looking out the window.

"He's just outside and will break down the door to rescue me if I scream for him. At least he's a real gent'man. He will protect my honor even if you won't You are a horrid old man. I can't believe a minister of God would act so. I heard you paid half your fine for not publishing our banns. Now, I have to pay my half, I reckon."

"'Twas either pay up or be hauled off to jail," Stephen said. "How could I publish banns when I didn't even know you and I were marrying? You had me filled with spirits until the spirit of the devil played upon us. You are a Jezebel. A Jezebel."

"Awww, I am, am I?" an indignant Mary cried back. "That's nice, Sir; really nice. And, what does that make you? 'Twas you, after all, who performed the rite,"

"It makes me a miserable fool," Stephen said sadly. "A truly miserable fool. Go on, get your things and be out of here. I want you out of my life."

"You don't even care what's happened to me and me friend, George Rogers, does you? A truly Christian man would care and would help a body out of such a shame."

"What are you talking about?"

"You haven't heard?" Mary asked. "We were tried for 'vehement suspicion of incontinency for living in one house and lying in one room,'" she blurted out. We wasn't doing no such thing. Besides, even if we did, whose business is it any ways? Not those wigged judges."

Stephen laughed.

"You shouldn't laugh," Mary said with a whine. "Me and George are both to be publicly whipped, me after this baby I'm carrying is born, and George on the morrow. 'Taint fair. No sir, 'taint. And, worse yet, I'm to be branded with an 'A'."

"You are with child?" Stephen asked incredulously. "I hope no one will think 'tis my child"

"Don't be so conceited you old fool," Mary said. "Who do you think would possibly believe that?"

"Malicious Mary and Rascal Rogers, you got just what was coming to you," Stephen said. "Taking up that way with our neighbor. For shame."

"What a dreadful thing to do, calling us names like that," Mary splurted. "So, why can't we get a divorce? You and me. If you'd been any kind of minister at all, they would of let us divorce and I could live honestly with my true love, Mister. Rogers."

"As for the divorce, the court will soon rectify our problem and let us go our separate ways. So, live with the scamp, Mary Beedle," Stephen said.

"Live with him. Your soul is already so far sunken that you have not a whisper of a chance to enter Heaven, so go ahead and live with him. Just leave me in peace. Please, leave me in peace."

*　　　　*　　　　*

"Bless my soul, oh dear God," Stephen prayed as he and Christopher made their way from the Boston courthouse. "Bless my soul."

"Come, Father Bachiler," Christopher Hussey said, wrapping an arm around Stephen's shoulder to show both physical and mental support. "Let's be away where we can think rationally."

"Why would the court do this to me, Christopher. Why?" Stephen was whipped; the wind deflated entirely from his sails. "Why would they rule that Mary Beedle and I must live as man and wife? And under the same roof? Why?" He was all but sobbing. "Oh, I am truly living in Hell on Earth." His physical demeanor was as pathetic as his emotional being "No one should have to suffer the injustice that has been placed upon me."

Christopher, who was all that kept Stephen from falling to the ground, said, "Let's go into this pub and revive our spirits."

Once seated, Stephen began to rehash his most-current woes: "First, some of Hampton's 'good Christian folk' petitioned to have the Court see to it that I am not paid for any of my services there. I never received a farthing in cash for all I did for that town. True, they did grant me land, but now they're trying to take that back." Stephen thought a moment, then said, "I am being punished. I should never have petitioned for a divorce from Mary Beedle, or charged her with adultery. I am being sorely punished for my wicked ways. All I wanted was to be free of her. 'Twas all I sought. I seek no vengeance."

Stephen wiped the tears from his face and held his head in his hands. "I am so weary, Christopher. So weary."

"I know, Sir, I know," Christopher said to Stephen with the same love a son by blood would have shown.

"'Tis time for me to go home," Stephen said, suppressing a sob. "Time to go home. I cannot abide this ruling. To live in the same house as that woman would taint the blessed memory of my beloved Ann. The harlot shall not share my table, let alone my bed!"

"She must live under the same roof," Christopher said, "or both of you will be apprehended by the Boston marshal and kept under lock and key until the next quarter's Court session. There's nothing you can do about that."

Stephen looked at Christopher, and said coolly, "Yes. There is something I can do, and by God, I will do it."

Life in England was far different than when Stephen followed his call for religious freedom to the far ends of the Earth. King Charles had been beheaded and Oliver Cromwell was now Protector of England. Episcopacy, as a state religion, had been abolished. No more swinging, smelling sensors. No more elaborate gold cups. No more icons carved of expensive marble. All barriers now gone between those who worship and the one who is worshipped.

"I would be able to worship in peace at home," Stephen said. Christopher knew "home" meant England, not New England. "Not since my childhood has that been the case. I have been at odds with the government and freedom of worship since my earliest days as a pastor." He looked at Christopher and smiled. "But, you know all this don't you, Son? You've lived with me and fought with me during many years of trial. I thank God for you, Christopher. You've been such strength to me in this country. You are the only son I have here.

"But, as disappointed as I have been in my blood sons, I would dearly love to see them once more," Stephen said, as the pattern of a new plan began to unfold in his mind. "I still have friends there. 'Twould be pleasant to sit in the sunshine with them and visit the day away. Oh, Christopher, home to England sounds so tempting."

Chapter 53

On the Road to Boston
1654
Deborah

"Matthew, son, are you certain this is what you want to do? 'Tis not too late to change your mind. We won't be to Boston until tomorrow. You have until then to think it over."

Deborah spoke in hushed tones as she and her boys sat around the popping campfire built for the last night they would all be together.

It seemed impossible she was to lose another child to the great gulf that separated New England from old England.

The five Wings encircled the small fire. It had been years since she had been alone with all her boys, now that they were grown with families of their own.

On this trip, it was just she and John, Daniel, Stephen and Matthew. And, as much as she loved her daughters-in-law, it was meetly to be alone with her sons. She glowed as warmly as the fire before her.

Tonight was special, but, once again, things were evolving.

John, Daniel and Stephen rose and stretched.

"'Tis time to say goodnight," John said, unsuccessfully stifling a yawn. "Morning will be here soon enough."

"Yes," Deborah answered. "In a moment. I want to visit with Matthew a bit longer, yet."

"Mother," John reasoned, "there's nothing more to be said. The decision's been made."

Deborah looked at John, her oldest. He was now forty, about the age of her husband when the family lived in Holland. An eon ago, Deborah thought. Another life. Certainly, another time.

"John, you and Stephen and Daniel go on, if you please. We will turn in shortly."

"Sorry, Matthew," Stephen said with a grin. "We tried."

Deborah frowned at her sons, but turned it into a smile. She would not be goaded nor teased—nor would she lose her temper. This was a special night and nothing would ruin it for her.

"And 'twas a gallant effort, lads, but I'm still his mother and he is still my youngest and … "

She was going to say,…*and he still does as I ask, sweet son that he is.*

But Matthew broke in and said, "'Tis all right. I'd like to sit up and talk a while longer with Mother. I'm not ready to sleep yet, and evidently, neither is she."

After the three other brothers left, Deborah and Matthew sat, leaning against an enormous stump, watching the fire's orange flames flicker, listening to them hiss and crackle as they greedily consumed the new log Matthew added.

"Matthew, there's so much I want to say," Deborah started. But her voice failed.

"Mother," Matthew said patiently, kindly, "we have just about picked this bone clean, don't you think?"

Deborah looked sharply at her youngest son.

"Yes, I suppose we have," she said quietly. She swallowed. "I only want you to be absolutely certain."

"I am sorry. But, yes, 'tis what I want to do. I am not cut out for the rigors of America like the rest of you. I'll be happier back in England. I think city life will be much more to my liking—and what better time to go than now, when Grandfather is returning? And, once he's settled, like we have long discussed, I'll move on to Stroud and oversee our property in Kent County." Matthew wrapped an arm around Deborah's shoulders. The early summer night had a decided nip to it. "And, who knows, Mother, no doubt I'll meet a fair young thing and settle down and give thee lots more grandchildren. Here I am, a man of seven and twenty and still not married. I am sure to meet someone there who is to my liking, and me to hers." He patted his mother's shoulder, cradled in his. "Will you be all right?" he asked gently. "Your baby son leaving and all?"

"Oh, I will miss you, Matthew." Deborah took his left hand, placed it in both of hers, lifted it to her lips and kissed his fingertips. She sighed and started again. "I will miss you. You really have only known America, Matthew. Your memory cannot serve you well about the countries of your youth. You barely even lived in England. You were little more than a babe when we left."

There was more silence. Deborah sighed. Matthew yawned.

"Mother," Matthew said, stirring the fire, "you really should sleep now. Tomorrow will be a difficult day for you, and you need your rest."

"Matthew Wing, are you implying I am elderly?" Deborah huffed good-naturedly and poked him in the ribs. "I am, let me see," she stopped and thought. "Well, goodness, I am two and sixty. Can that be right?" She recalculated. "That's amazing. I expect it's been a while since I've toted my years. Perhaps I better turn in, old lady that I am."

*   *   *

The next morning Deborah, John, Stephen, Daniel and Matthew stirred before first light. Matthew was the first to rise; he coaxed the fire's coals back into life with kindling. Deborah rose haltingly, aching from the cold, hard ground.

I feel every one of the sixty-plus years, she commiserated to herself. *I should never have toted the number.*

"Methinks this might be my last camping trip. The ground seems to get harder as the Earth gets older," Deborah said with a laugh as she retrieved the last of the biscuits she'd baked for their trip and handed them out, all around.

This was the day she had been dreading for such a long time now; it seemed an eternity.

It's so hard. It's so hard. The three-word sentence had repeated itself again and again in her mind all night long. It's so hard.

Breakfast done, their single packhorse loaded (mostly with Matthew's belongings), the Wings walked on.

"I figure we should be at the Boston Harbor well before the sun climbs to mid-day," John said.

"What if Grandfather isn't there?" It was Stephen.

"He will be there," Deborah answered. "He was explicit in his letter about when the William and Francis would be sailing and from where." She smiled as she patted his letter in the pocket of her skirt. "He said we shouldn't bother to come all that way to see him off, but he knew very well that we would."

"And we wouldn't have it any other way," John said. "'Tis the least we can do."

They walked on, watchful of the road's uneven surface and the ever-looming potholes that could as easily break a horse's leg as a human's.

       *   *   *

Deborah stood in a clearing near the pier, shaded her eyes with a bare hand and searched round for her father. The boys had left her with the horse and their belongings while they booked Matthew's passage. She climbed atop a stump for a better view.

My, Boston's grown since we first arrive back in '32, Deborah thought. *So many people now. I would hate to live in a city of this size. Where is Father? I don't see him anywhere.*

"Pardon me, Goody Wing."

Deborah recognized the voice—the booming voice of her childhood that had left its unmistakable sound resonating constantly in her heart and mind.

"Oh, Father," she cried as she turned to greet him.

Stephen wrapped his hands around her waist, lifted her from the stump and took her into his arms. There they stood. Saying nothing. Just hugging one another.

How many years had it been since she felt the comfort of her father? It was wonderful. She'd forgotten the solace of her father's love that she once took for granted—before she grew estranged from him and it.

Finally, Deborah pulled back and retrieved her nose cloth from her waistpocket. Stephen reached into the breast pocket of his coat and took out his own cloth and wiped his eyes and honked his nose into it.

Deborah, again composed, noticed how thin Stephen had become. He was stooped. He had shrunk. And his face was wan. His jacket swam about his shoulders and he continually hitched up his pants, having lost much of the stomach that had once kept them in place.

And how lifeless was his hair, once flying around his head with a mind of its own! Now, his hat removed, it was limp, content to fall in wisps about his ears.

"Are you well?" She could barely get the words out.

"Aye. I am well. Weary, old, but well. And I will be even better once the boat has pulled out and sails me away from this alien land towards my rightful home."

"Matthew sails with you tomorrow, Father," Deborah said. "He and the other boys are making the arrangements."

"Is he now?" Stephen answered a little testily. "Not on my account, I trust." He squared his shoulders, so thin the sight of them made Deborah sad. "I am perfectly able to make my own way across the sea."

Deborah smiled broadly at him.

Softening his tone, he added, "Still, 'twill be good to have him along." He smiled at his daughter. "Remember? Matthew was a mere child when we arrived, and now he's returning home with me as my protector. Although I have never needed anyone to protect me from anything in my entire life, I'll be glad for his company. We will have plenty of time to catch up on one another's news." Stephen reached up and pulled Deborah's bonneted head to his shoulder. "Remember, lass, when we first arrived?"

"Father, do you think I could ever forget?"

"You were a spirited filly back then," Stephen said with a laugh. "Are you still? It's been so long since we've seen one another that I feel I hardly know you any more. I've missed you, Daughter."

"And, I've missed you, Father. Yes," Deborah answered her father's question. "I believe I'm still spirited. Not so much a filly, however. Why, just last night, I toted my age, and while I'm not yet an old nag—in horse terms—I would have to admit I'm quite like an aging mare—but not yet ready for the pasture."

Stephen led Deborah to the shade of an elm tree with a bench beneath it, inviting visitors to rest and drink in the scenery.

They looked out at the harbor with ships anchored a ways out to sea and others tied to the wharves, ready for embarkation and debarkation.

"I've booked us rooms at the inn up the road," he said.

"How did you know we would be here? You said not to come, you know."

"I knew you'd come."

They sat and held hands.

"Do you forgive me for bringing you over here?" Stephen asked, hoarsely.

Deborah looked at him in surprise. "What do you mean?"

"Just what I said. Do you forgive me? I know you wanted not to come, and that you came only because of me."

Deborah closed her eyes and to herself said, *And I thought last night was hard!*

"Things didn't turn out in this New England the way I had imagined at all." Stephen sighed. "There wasn't anything so new here, after all. It seems trouble has followed me all my days, even across the sea."

Stephen reached down and picked a tall blade of grass and ran his fingers along its length. He crumbled it in his hands and tossed it aside. He folded his hands and hung them loosely between his legs. "I guess I expected to experience more of Adam and Eve's Garden of Eden in this new country—not the barrenness of Moses' desert. But, if not the Garden of Eden, then surely the Promised Land." He removed the hat from his head, wiped his brow, and, resting his hands on his knees, worried the hat's brim, edging it slowly around and around. He stared out to sea. "I am indeed sorry to return home feeling a failure. You know what they say, 'He that hath an ill name is half-hanged.' I am half-hanged, Daughter. Half-hanged."

"Father, stop it. You are not half-hanged and you have not an ill name. True, that wicked woman did her best to sully it, but your family and friends know better. Do not return to England feeling as though you failed. You have not failed. Just because your expectations were not met does not mean you failed."

Stephen looked at her. He rubbed the back of his neck. An automatic response. It felt familiar, like an old habit, but he'd nearly forgotten it. He rubbed it again. Funny, there was a comfort in it.

"You came here searching for the peace to worship the way you felt God wanted you to worship. As did I. You did that, Father—and you made it so your grandsons can worship in their manner. And, their children, also—my grandchildren—and they will one day have grandchildren of their own who will have been born into that right. You asked if I was sorry I came with you. I am not sorry, Father. I am proud and humbled to have been a part of your mission. We, all of us who came to America with you, will not let you down. New England, America, will one day be a land where everyone can worship in peace, without fear. And one day this country will attribute part of that freedom to you. They will thank you and others like you. True, 'tis yet far from perfect, Father, but still, 'tis better than what we had. Had you stayed in England, you would no doubt have ended your days in prison. You might have become a martyr, but that would have served no one at all."

Stephen retrieved his nose cloth again. And again he honked.

Deborah thought for a moment while Stephen composed himself. "Father, perhaps 'tis me who owes thee an apology." Her mind instantaneously rolled back the years. "I was not the obedient child you might have wished me to be. Probably not ever. But Father, 'tis you who gave me my will, who taught me that my mind was as sharp as my brothers'. And, because of that, 'tis you who gave me the confidence to teach my own sons when there was no other to instruct them. And, bless their hearts, they more than hold their own with any man in any number of areas. They are sharp, but honest, businessmen. Daniel has proven to be a savvy landowner, as has John and Stephen. They are bountiful farmers and fishermen...And for part of that, we have you to thank."

Deborah pulled Stephen back so he was sitting directly beside her, no longer leaning forward. She wrapped his arm around her waist. "Actually, Father, I don't think either of us owes the other an apology. We are who we are. God made us who we are. I know I hurt you when we removed to Sandwich and stayed there, but I did what I did for the sake of my sons— and me. You taught me that, too. That's why we came here, to America, in the first place, because it was something you needed to do for yourself. You felt it was God's directive And it was," she continued. "I do not quarrel with that. But who's to say that it wasn't God's directive that my boys and I forge our own lives together? Surely not you, Father. And, so, our paths—yours and mine—parted for a time. Still," she hugged herself close to him, "we ended up at the same destination, didn't we? And, still we love one another. That's the most important thing to me, Father. I cannot have you sail out of my life and back to England on the 'morrow without your knowing just how much I do love you. That's why I walked all these miles for all those days—to tell you, face to face, Father, of my love for you." Her chin quivered. She shut her eyes and leaned her head on her father's chest.

*   *   *

Even as the sun rose, the pier was alive with activity. The ship had been loaded the day before and Captain Thomas was anxious to sail while the winds were fair. If only today's "cargo" was as easy to get aboard as yesterday's. It was easier sailing in years past, before passengers outweighed the cargo.

Ah, well, the captain thought, *'tis progress. Nothing ever stays the same. Still 'twas nice when our loads didn't complain and didn't get sick.*

*   *   *

"Look here, would you?" Stephen cried out as they approached the gangplank. "Mister Gimp—Jonah. How in the world are you?" Stephen slapped the old salt on his shoulder which was noticeably more bent than before.

The miserly sailor who had grieved Deborah so on their voyage to America quickly turned around with a snarl on his face, his hands balled into fists.

"Still a grumpy old man, I see," Deborah said in low tones to Stephen.

"Well, I'll be blessed," Mister Gimp said, smiling and shifting his weight to his good leg. "You sailin' back with me, Reverend? Best get aboard. 'Tis time to leave." He grinned at Stephen again. "'Twill be wondrous having ye aboard again, Sir."

The family milled about on the dock, Stephen and Matthew delaying boarding the ship that would return them to their native land. This would be the last time Deborah would ever see her father and youngest son.

With both hands, she grabbed Matthew around his neck and brought his face down to hers, unable to speak, and looked deep into his eyes. When she found her voice again, she said, "Don't forget to tell Deborah Junior everything I told you. Tell her, above all else, that I remember her exactly as she looked the last time I saw her, and that neither that memory nor my love for her has ever diminished."

Stephen put his arms around Deborah and Matthew. "I'll take care of the lad as long as I'm able," her father said.

Deborah nodded and stood back. "May the good Lord cause his eyes to shine upon you, Matthew, Father," she whispered with difficulty.

"And upon thee, my child," Stephen responded. "Upon you and yours."

"'Board." It was Mister Gimp. "Time to get aboard, guv'nor," the ancient sailor told the ancient pastor. He all but pushed Stephen and his traveling companions up the gangplank. He turned painfully on his bad leg to face Deborah. "You comin', Missus?" Mister Gimp asked.

"No. No," she said, "I'm staying here."

Deborah stood at the pier's edge and waved her arm back and forth, back and forth, her brightest-white nose cloth clutched in her hand, flying as a tiny flag. She waved with one arm and then the other until the Francis and William was only a speck on the horizon.

May the good Lord cause his eyes to shine upon you. The thought would not leave her mind.

Then she turned, dry-eyed, to her sons.

"Let's be off," she said. "We can still make plenty of miles towards home this day."

Chapter 54

Sandwich
October 1657
Deborah

"I was sickened at the treatment foisted on the women—on that saintly Mary Austin, an elderly mother of five children, and sweet Mary Fisher, a servant—about the age of my granddaughter, I should think, the budding age of two and twenty."

Nicholas Upsall was speaking to a crush of Sandwich citizens who sat elbow to elbow until every chair, bench and stool was occupied, leaving late arrivals to stand shoulder to shoulder in the great room of William and Lydia Allen.

The Allen house was sweltering from compacted body heat heightened by the continuously roaring fire maintained to ward off fall's nip when there had been more space than people.

At William's nod, Daniel Wing cracked open the door to allow fresh air to whisk its way inside.

"The wardens conducted obscene searches of the women's bodies, looking, it was said, for blemishes by which the Devil's agents might have entered," Nicholas Upsall said. The man's deeply lined face beat a pulsing, fiery red, made all the redder by the whiteness of his hair. He became a grandfather speaking, not merely an orator.

Deborah, sitting next to Hannah, took her daughter-in-law's hand in hers and patted it, comforting her. Most women in the room examined their laced-gloved hands in embarrassment, wincing at the aspect of ever being so humiliated, so shamed. The men were visibly angry at the thought of someone treating any woman in such a dastardly manner—let alone women of God as these two Quaker women certainly were.

"They were taken straight to jail without trial," Upsall said. "Having received word when the women would arrive and where their ship would dock, court officials laid in wait for them—like a stalking tom-cat patiently waits, poised, ready to spring atop a defenseless mouse at the opportune moment. These bullies of men did indeed pounce at the precise moment and at once seized and burned the women's papers and books right there, at the wharf, and then hauled them off to prison. And there they kept them isolated, even to boarding up their windows to keep anyone from the outside from making contact with them. But 'tis well known that thee can't keep secrets long in this country. Ears over here are ever as sharp as on the east side of the Atlantic, don't you know. When I learned of the women's fate, I knew action had to be taken—and quickly," the visitor told his hushed audience.

"Rumors of the harsh treatment being relegated to Quakers these past months had reached Sandwich," Daniel Wing said, "but not one amongst us has heard it spoken first-hand. Until now."

Deborah had blanched. "Our worst fears are being thrust upon us," she said softly. "'Tis disheartening news."

"There can no longer be any denial of the terrible persecution being exacted upon fellow Christians, Quakers notwithstanding, who seek the privilege to worship as God directed them—just as every man and woman in this Sandwich home had sought that privilege," Upsall said.

"Is there no where on Earth that is safe?" Deborah said quietly. "No where that's free?"

"One feels so inadequate in times like this," Upsall was saying. "The situation, 'tis impossible to ignore it, but what can one lone individual do? Most of us certainly have no influence over the governor or court officers—but by God's grace, we figure out what we can do. As for me, I own the Red Lyon Inn of Dorchester, so I know a bit something about the nourishment and goodness of food. I also know about the swill fed to indigent prisoners in that wretched prison. And, I also know most men, especially weak men, have their price—and the price to bribe the jailers amounted to five shillings a week to smuggle in good, hot healthy food to those God-fearing prisoners to help them sustain their strength."

A smattering of gloved-applause filled the room, while some men pounded the floor with their boots or walking sticks in appreciation.

"As I visited with Anne Austin and Mary Fisher over those weeks," Upsall said. "I came to know them quite well and I was impressed by their message about being filled with an Inner Light."

Murmurs sounded. Sandwich residents had heard fragments about this Inner Light and wanted to know more.

"Although the women were most certainly being subjected to just about the worst, most cruel treatment mankind could offer, they maintained an undisturbed peace about them," the inn-keeper-turned orator continued. I not only heard—and witnessed—God's inner-direction with Anne and Mary, but from eight Quaker men who were also unjustly imprisoned and their books seized shortly after the women were arrested. These good folk not only faced imprisonment, but whippings, banishment, enormous sums of fines…Still, they did not waver. Not a one of them. They were not only filled with this Inner Light, but with an inner peace that so many of us long for, but never succeed in finding. And, that's what I want to tell to you good citizens of Sandwich."

There were sounds of agreement, nods of heads, from those gathered in the house of their friend and neighbor.

"We shall have plenty of time since I am here for the remainder of the winter, I fear. A fortnight ago, an 'Anti-Quaker Law' was enacted and I was ejected from my happy home. Timsam Hull, a horse dealer from Barnstable—many here are acquainted with him, I'm sure—offered me a ride to Sandwich, feeling certain this town would be hospitable."

"Here, here," came the words from deep voices.

Upsall fished around the inside pockets of his jacket. "Let me read the exact language of this so-called Anti-Quaker Law." He laughed sardonically as he unfolded the worn paper frayed at the creases from being fetched and folded on a regular basis: "I think the Court thought to chastise me by pointing me out particularly in this 'law,' but they are wrong. 'Tis an honor to be mentioned in the same thought as those two women and the eight Quaker men who are experiencing such grief."

"All right now." He cleared his throat and read:

"The Court having considered of the offenses committed by Nicholas Upsall—that's me,"—he said as an aside, encouraging his listeners to laugh with him. He cleared his throat again: *"The Court having considered of the offenses committed by"* he looked up over the top of his paper at his audience and smiled, nodding his head encouragingly, to which the listeners responded in unison: "Nicholas Upsall" … *"in reproaching* (he stressed the word) *of our honored* (he sounded sarcastic) *magistrate…"* the audience gave out a mock moan *"…and speaking against the law made and published against Quakers, judge meet and have determined that the said Upsall for such his offence shall pay as a fine to the country the sum of twenty pounds…"* an astounded gasp escaped the listeners—an ordinary man earned five pounds a year—*"…of twenty pound, and also that the said fine being paid, he shall depart out of this jurisdiction within one month and not to return under penalty of imprisonment."*

Before the meeting of friends at Neighbor Allen's dismissed that night, it was determined Nicholas Upsall would spend various weeks with various residents throughout the winter months.

Chapter 55

Sandwich
1657
Deborah

"'Tis so good to have you spend some time with us, Mother Wing," Hannah said, as she and Deborah prepared the noon dinner together.

"I miss you—you and John and Elizabeth and their little ones—since your move to Harwich. I know it's but eighteen miles, but it seems much further. There's no chance to pop in for a cup of tea and a chat."

"And I miss everyone here," Deborah said, smiling at Hannah as she began to peel the mess of potatoes with a short, steel-blade knife Daniel had fashioned for use in the house. "But John was determined. He's disgruntled with religion. No, not religion—churches—and he wanted to put some distance between him and the nearest church building.

She circled a blemish in the potato with the tip of her knife and excised it.

"Ever since Father returned to England, John has been more critical than ever of the government and church and—well, the government and church combined, and the foolishness that separates them and yet binds them together.

"Things—worship—certainly hasn't turned out to be what we expected when made our move. To say it's been disappointing is to say not a word at all."

Deborah sliced a piece of potato and popped it into her mouth. She thought as she crunched the vegetable still crisp from its wintering in the cool root cellar:

"For a while," she said, swallowing, "I feared John might never darken a church again, he's so disheartened at what's occurred in his church life. Not his religious life or his association with God, but within the church structure. But," Deborah sighed, "he attends often enough to maintain his freeholder status."

"Has he given any more thought about the Quakers?" Hannah wondered aloud.

"At first, he wanted no part of it, but lately—well, methinks he's mulling it over. We have discussed what we know of it over the dinner table most every noon this past few weeks.

"John is a thoughtful man; he doesn't accept new ways without much questioning and soul-searching—and that's as it should be, I guess. He's a good head on his shoulders and knows how best to use it."

Deborah laughed at herself. "Do I sound like a mother?"

"Aye, and a proud one at that," Hannah answered.

"John does know, doesn't he, that Goodman Upsall is boarding with us this while and will be here for dinner?"

"He knows," Deborah answered, smiling. "In fact, methinks your house guest is part of the reason John found it necessary to do business in Sandwich this particular week. I think he wants to know more about this new religion, and would like to learn about it from one who can answer some direct questions about it."

*   *   *

That evening, after supper dishes had been washed up and the children bedded down, Deborah and Hannah joined John and Daniel who sat with Nicholas Upsall in front of the fire.

Upsall, his white hair standing on end, electrified from the dry air, was speaking directly to John:

"The Inner Light is not a *representation* of God," he said, emphasizing "representation." "It is a *manifestation* of Christ in our lives. 'Tis that direct. That simple."

"It sounds a bit more complicated than that," John said, to which Daniel nodded in agreement. *There would be new obligations,* John thought, *a new depth of empathy and new sympathies to sort out.* "Remember, we are of Puritan stock," John said. "We are here, on this side of the ocean, on this soil, in this house at this moment, because we sought to worship in a 'simple' manner."

"I know that," their elderly visitor said. "We're all here because we sought religious freedom, every man woman and child of us."

"That's true, Goodman Upsall," Deborah said, picking up her knitting needles, "there's not a one of us in this new country who did not have the definite purpose of seeking religious freedom when we left England. No one left our mother country on a whimsy. Our reason was to find a place to worship God in peace—physically and in our hearts. We sought to worship in simplicity."

Upsall nodded and said, "I think it might be said that Quakers have taken Puritanism a step further in distinguishing between what is essential and what is nonessential in our worship of God. Jesus Christ is the one essential ingredient we need."

He reminds me of Father, Deborah mused as her needles struck up their cadence of clicks. *Especially, here, talking to us like this. It's his fervor—and his hair—that most puts Father to mind.*

"You see," said Upsall with the zest of a new convert desperately wanting to share this clear, concise notion of belief with anyone who would listen, "God is real. He is not some imagined theory. He is as much a person as Christ was a person." He waited for his pronouncement to settle. "This means," he continued, "there can truly be an 'I-Thou' relationship between us—us, mere mortal men, and the Living God."

Deborah put down her knitting and turned her attention to what Upsall was saying.

"George Fox," Upsall continued, "said God is not a mere Ground of Being who does not and cannot know each of us as an individual who is valuable in his own right. If God is not fully person, if he cannot be rightly addressed as 'Thou,' then Christ would have been mistaken when he addressed Him as 'Father.'"

The Wings gnawed the meat on Upsall's bone of knowledge.

"How do you define 'Person'?" Daniel wanted to know.

"Not a being with a body, certainly," Upsall said, "but one who knows, who responds, who cares."

Deborah offered, "In the Bible, Jesus says God cares for each single bird on this Earth, and if he cares for even a lowly sparrow, how much more he will care for us."

"You are so right, Daughter," Upsall said. "And that's why God created us in his image. Because he cares for us."

"Christ is the light of the world," Daniel said, quoting another passage of Scripture.

"Amen," Upsall said, excited. "You understand. You see. You are truly the family of intellect I was told you were."

John had been quiet, staring at the flames as they spit and flared, consumed the dried wood to become a whisk of smoke, drawn upward through the chimney and dissipated into the cold night air.

He drew on his clay pipe, noted it was empty and rose to fill it again.

"What think you, John?" Upsall asked

John returned to his seat, tamped the tobacco into the pipe bowl, broke a thin strip of wood from a burning log and lit it, swallowing the smoke he enjoyed.

"I think, as I always have," John said, his words as measured and deliberate as though it were his father speaking, "that God is with us here, in this room, as he was with Jesus in on the day of his birth and in the Garden of Gethsemane. As he was when Christ suffered on the cross. I believe God is as real today as he was then.

"I was taught—we were taught," he nodded at Daniel—"by our father and grandfather—and mother—that God lives in us; that Christ is in us." John looked at Deborah and smiled. "I think, Mother, that Grandfather returned to England too soon. I think he might have found solace among the Quakers."

Deborah nodded.

Chapter 56

Sandwich
June 1658

"Remove your hats this instant!" bellowed the red-faced Jeremiah Huntsman, District Court Judge of Plymouth. "And you are to stand whenever His Honor enters the courtroom." Huntsman's rage caused his head to shake as if stricken with palsy, which, in turn, made his jowls jiggle and his white, curly periwig to shift askew ever so slightly.

None of the fourteen men from Sandwich responded. They sat mute, as a group, on benches before the judge's imposing dais, their black, broad-rimmed hats securely affixed atop their heads—as they would normally have been in their home or anyone's home.

These fourteen men of Sandwich had been summoned to appear before Plymouth County's June Court for refusing to take the Oath of Fidelity.

"By not removing your hats, you are in contempt of this court," Huntsman barked. "What say ye? And, take caution to address the court properly when you speak."

The men looked at one another. Thomas Ewer had been chosen their spokesman. Ewer stood, but only to be clearly heard, not out of deference to the court or the man who reigned over it. He turned at an angle so he could talk to the audience as well as the judge.

"We believe all men are created equal," he said slowly and distinctly in a voice loud enough so no one in the packed courtroom would miss a word. "And, as your equal, judge, we will not remove our hats lest it be considered a sign of subversiveness on our part. And, as our equal, we will not address thee in any manner other than anyone else. God created us all equals, and therefore, we are all esteemed equally by God. Thee and we."

Huntsman banged his gavel. Again and again.

"You will show respect to this court, or you will all be held in contempt and sorely fined," he wheezed. He gazed fiercely around the room. His probing eyes, searching for hecklers, stopped short at the sight of Humphrey Norton and John Rouse, sitting in the very back of the room. The judge squinted at them, dropping his chin to peer over the top of his square-rimmed spectacles.

Norton and Rouse quietly returned his gaze. They were risking more than contempt by appearing this day.

Norton's reputation as a trouble-making Quaker was becoming well established in New England. In England, Norton had offered to exchange places with George Fox, founder of the Quaker society, who was imprisoned for teaching that if mankind has direct access to the Head Teacher, why would they need lesser ones; and that one can know Christ directly, in his own heart or conscience. Christ can be thought of in the present tense because he lives within man.

But, Humphrey Norton was not permitted to exchange places with Fox, and so traveled to New England to right the wrong of a Quaker missionary, an old man, who was nearly flogged to death in a Boston prison. While he was not allowed to assume Fox's lashing pain, he was eventually scourged severely for his troubles.

Norton now rose in the Plymouth Court, fingering the still vivid red "H" burned onto the back of his hand, a forever reminder of the branding he'd received as a "Heretic" for spreading the Quaker teachings.

"Humphrey Norton, you sit down," the judge blared, repeatedly banging his gavel until the head of it was in danger of flying off its handle. "We heard enough out of you and your friend yesterday—and we'll have none of it today."

During yesterday's court session, Norton had vindictively shouted, "Thomas, thou liest!" referring to Gov. Thomas Pence, while Friend Rouse hollered, "Pence, thou are a malicious man."

"The two of you sit down and be quiet, or by God, you will both be whipped into silence," Huntsman threatened on this day.

Norton and Rouse sat, but their demeanor did not change. They elected to support the Sandwich men, not be antagonistic.

The judge wiped the sweat beading on his brow. This was going to be another long, noisy session. *Blast these Quakers to hell*, he muttered to himself as he returned his attention to the Sandwich miscreants.

With even more active red chins and jowls, he said, "You will now rise and take the Oath of Allegiance."

"Nay," said Ewer. "We will not. We owe no allegiance except to God. To do otherwise would be to disobey Christ."

Daniel stood. Ewer sat down.

"'But I say unto you, Swear not at all,'" Daniel quoted from "Matthew." "'Neither by heaven; for it is God's throne. Nor by the Earth, for it is his footstool: neither by Jerusalem, for it is the city of the great King. Neither shalt thou swear by thy head, because thou canst make one hair white or black. But let your communication be, Yea, yea; nay, nay: for whatsoever is more than these cometh of evil.'"

"Yea, yea," the fourteen men chanted. "Nay, nay."

"Order! Order! Order!"

*　　　　　*　　　　　*

At the end of the demonstration, the Quakers' hats still atop their heads, Judge Huntsman assessed each man the punishing sum of five pounds, an amount some would work a full year to earn.

"You can thank God you'll not be locked in jail this day," he yelled, face reddening, jowls jiggling, periwig askew. "That's only because there is no room at this moment and won't be until the new jail is finished.

"Not only are you an affront to the King's religion, but you are an expense," he exploded at the men whose expressions had remained constant during the entire proceeding. "'Tis not cheap to build pens to hold you for your misdoing. But, eventually 'twill be you who will pay for them. You will pay."

"'Tis so good to have you spend some time with us, Mother Wing," Hannah said, as she and Deborah prepared the noon dinner together.

"I miss you—you and John and Elizabeth and their little ones—since your move to Harwich. I know it's but eighteen miles, but it seems much further. There's no chance to pop in for a cup of tea and a chat."

"And I miss everyone here," Deborah said, smiling at Hannah as she began to peel the mess of potatoes with a short, steel-blade knife Daniel had fashioned for use in the house. "But John was determined. He's disgruntled with religion. No, not religion—churches—and he wanted to put some distance between him and the nearest church building.

She circled a blemish in the potato with the tip of her knife and excised it.

"Ever since Father returned to England, John has been more critical than ever of the government and church and—well, the government and church combined, and the foolishness that separates them and yet binds them together.

"Things—worship—certainly hasn't turned out to be what we expected when made our move. To say it's been disappointing is to say not a word at all."

Chapter 57

Sandwich
1659
Deborah

"Baby Beulah is sleeping as peaceful as the meaning of her name," Deborah reported to Hannah who rested in the bed pushed close to the fire.

She smiled at the infant—one more she had helped bring into the world. There had been so many since moving to America, that Deborah no longer kept count. Each baby was a discovery and a blessing, to be sure, but none more so than the offspring of her sons—continuations of herself.

Fed, dry and warm, Beulah slumbered on. She was the center of her infant universe and life was good.

With a much-practiced foot, Deborah rocked Beulah in the cradle Daniel crafted thirteen years and six children earlier for the Daniel Wing offspring.

While Deborah maintained a constant rhythm with her foot, her hands maintained a rhythm of their own as she knit yet another pair of socks. As grandmother many times over, there was never time to merely sit. Besides, to be idle was to be sinful.

Deborah noticed Hannah pulling the blanket closer around her chin, so she rose to feed the fire another log. It was late. The older children had all retired and Deborah and Hannah—and Baby Beulah—waited for Daniel to return from the meeting.

The meeting, for information and friendship this night, not worship, was in Christopher's Hollow, a glen deep in the woods where Christopher Holder preached to the Sandwich Quakers.

It was too costly to meet in one another's homes. Anyone caught concealing or entertaining a Quaker was arrested and could be fined forty shillings—an hour!—until the fine was paid.

"What's the hour?" Hannah asked quietly. Heat from the fire reddened her otherwise too-pale cheeks. Childbirthing was difficult for Hannah. She suffered greatly with each child, and with each child, her health was longer in returning.

Just then, the door swung open and Daniel entered, stomping his feet to be rid of the soggy November leaves that clung to his boots.

As he toasted himself in front of the fire, face first, hands held dangerously close to the flames, he told the women of the latest "crimes" and the exacting punishments against the Quaker converts.

"That George Barlow," Daniel said, shaking his head. "Methinks he feels 'tis his mission in life to make our lives miserable."

"And yet he once preached the word of God," Hannah said weakly but fervently.

Daniel moved to her and planted a kiss on her forehead—then returned to his business by the fire, to warm himself through and through.

Earlier that year the Plymouth Court appointed Barlow as marshal.

Mostly his duty was to keep tabs on the Sandwich Quakers. His predecessor had been paid five pounds for a year's term in office, but the new marshal demanded more.

After all, being Marshal was trying: There were wrongdoers to spy upon (which took considerable time), then he had to arrest them, administer due punishment (including public whippings) and collect all the fines and fees. Certainly, that amount of responsibility was worthy of more than five pounds a year.

So it happened that Barlow was directed by the court to collect the fines—and if the guilty party couldn't pay with money, or refused payment at all, then Barlow was to seize property from that person for the county's use.

Not only was Barlow allowed to determine the property's value, he was allowed to pocket ten percent of all he collected and seized for himself.

"He's done all right for himself by me," Daniel had grumbled more than once, recalling the multiple fines he'd shelled out just for refusing to take the Oath of Fidelity alone. "Why would they think I'd even consider taking such an oath after the court disenfranchised me and the others last month?" he said now. "The county runs short of money and one commissioner says, his voice full of woe, 'How will we ever make ends meet?' And another answers, 'I know, let's order those Sandwich simpletons to take the Oath of Fidelity one more time. That always gets us a few pounds to fatten our coffers.'" The words fairly spat from Daniel's mouth.

Deborah smiled sadly at her son. It hurt to see him so pained again, and to have religion be his source of pain. She thought of how they had crossed the ocean to be free forever of interference in religion. *Will it always be so?* she wondered silently.

It wasn't only money the Wings and others lost, however. Both Daniel and Stephen were among nine Sandwich men to be disenfranchised, losing all privileges of citizenship, including the right to vote.

Daniel turned to warm his backside and held the tails of his coat apart, sending the heat directly to its chilled mission.

"That old Barlow reprobate broke into William Newland's house last night," Daniel said. He looked sadly at Deborah: "'Tis a sad state of affairs, eh, Mother?"

Deborah nodded in agreement.

"Why did he do that?" Hannah asked. "Why would he do that?"

"To collect what he said was rightfully his as payment for William's infractions—nineteen pounds for attending thirty-eight meetings, and another five pounds for entertaining visiting Friends.

"Not only that," Daniel continued, "but he took one of William's horses without notice, and last month, he stole Farmer Winters' corn while the man was on a trip to England." Daniel no longer needed the fire's heat to warm his blood. By now, it was near boiling, coursing around in his veins at an accelerated rate. "He collected seven cows from Farmer Jenkins a while back to make good on a fine, and when one of those cows died a week or so later, he had the gall to return to Jenkins to get another!"

"How do you suppose all of this will end, Daniel?" Deborah asked, her knitting long forgotten. "It can't go on like this for ever."

"Well, there is some good news on that front," Daniel said. "It seems James Cudworth of Situate wrote a letter to a friend in England about the punishment of Quakers, and the letter has been printed and distributed all across the country. "Now at least the folks there will be better aware of what's happening here."

"Did he tell them all of it?" Deborah wondered.

"Aye," Daniel answered. "He wrote about the whippings and the three ear-croppings and the threats of death if English Friends do not stay away from Plymouth County."

"It makes me shudder still," Deborah said, "to think that our friends Christopher Holder, John Copeland and John Rouse were tortured and then had their right ears cut off.

"What kind of despicable men would do such things?"

What Daniel did not tell his wife and mother was that Catherine Scott, Ann Hutchinson's sister, and Mary, Catherine's eight-and-ten-year-old daughter, had both been imprisoned and whipped after they participated in a dramatic protest in Boston. But, maybe the worst of all the punishments meeted out for those who joined that rally was the whipping of a nursing mother.

Is nothing sacred? Daniel thought to himself. He couldn't possibly formulate in his mind the horrors of how he would feel were his mother or wife ever subjected to such treatment. Anyone who tried to harm them would have to deal with him first. They would have to kill him first.

Chapter 58

Sandwich
1659
Deborah

Deborah stood at the make-shift picnic table of boards lain across saw horses, shaded by the great elm tree, and served seconds of the cod cakes to her forever hungry grandsons, or was it thirds? In the distance she saw a cloud of dust moving towards them and began to cover the food.

The entire Wing clan had gathered at the house of Stephen and Sarah, whom he married five years ago, seven months after Osheah died.

This was the Wings' first picnic of the summer, and, because it was Saturday, fish was the fare. Protestant New Englanders routinely ate fish on Saturday because it was so plentiful—especially cod—and because it made practical, economical sense by helping sustain the fishery business.

Stephen's house was a logical meeting place for the family, situated between those of John and Daniel. The adult Wings, including Deborah's older grandchildren, leisurely spread about the lawn, atop quilts, enjoying a quiet visit, while the younger, rambunctious children noisily ran around. On the morrow, the Sabbath, the children would mind their manners, be seen but not heard, but today, they were free to spend excess energy.

As she was about to rejoin the adults, Deborah heard the deep pound of horse hooves along Spring Hill Road in front of the house. Through the fog of dust she saw a horseman crop-whip his sweaty animal, nagging it into an even faster pace. The horse and its rider sped past in a blur.

"Goodness," Deborah said. "Who was that, do you suppose?"

"'Twas neighbor Barlow," Stephen said disgustedly. Her boys had joined her to watch the scene of horse and rider hightailing it towards town. "His unfortunate animals. He treats them so wretchedly."

"What do you suppose he's up to, today?" Deborah asked idly.

"He's probably off to fine someone to cover the cost of a dress his wife is no doubt whining for," Daniel said.

The Wings regrouped to their blankets. Deborah gratefully sank into a chair brought from the house. Her days of sitting on the lawn were over. 'Twas hard enough to get down, but even harder to get back up.

"Mother Deborah," said Hannah, "speaking of George Barlow getting his wife a dress, have you heard about the marshal fining Goodman Ewer, the tailor?"

"No," Deborah answered. "Tell me."

"'Tis a terrible tale," Hannah said. "Thomas Ewer was fined twenty-five pounds for refusing to take the oath and attending Meetings. And, when he couldn't come up with the cash, George Barlow took four yards of Goodman Ewer's kersey and had a coat made up for himself. Well, when Thomas Ewer was called to court to settle his fines, there was George Barlow strutting around in the coat made from the fabric he'd taken from Barlow. I understand Goodman Ewer was angry."

"He was furious," Daniel interjected. "I was there and saw it all. I feared the man might have apoplexy he flushed so red in the face. Finally, when he could contain himself no longer, he asked the court magistrate whether the court would allow that Marshal Barlow was indeed wearing his cloth."

"But, alas, his comment only served to anger the magistrate," Stephen said, picking up the story's thread, "and Tailor Ewer was sentenced to lie neck and heels together 'for his tumultuous and seditious carriages and speeches in court.'"

"Gracious sakes," Deborah said, "and Thomas Ewer, not a well man."

"Because he's not is what saved him," Hannah said, rejoining the conversation she had started. "When the court was told he suffered with a rupture, the sentence was not carried out. At least they showed some humanity.

"That George Barlow is such an evil man," Hannah said sadly. "He's caused so much grief in our little town. But 'haps none more than to Daniel." She smiled at her husband.

"'Tis no secret he's our enemy," Daniel said.

"And, you know what the Bible says about how to treat thy enemies," Stephen said.

"Aye," Daniel said, "but I don't know if I can turn many more cheeks. The man's not broken my spirit, but he has about broken my purse—all those fines for not taking the oath, for attending the Meetings…I'm seriously considering removing to England." He looked at the faces of his family to read their expressions. John rose from his spot on the blanket.

"What the devil are you talking about?" he sputtered. Then quickly added: "Sorry, Mother, ladies." John rephrased the emphasis of his question: "Daniel, what are you talking about?"

"John, you know the sums of my fines levied by that scoundrel. 'Twon't be long until I lose everything I have. At this rate, there will be nothing to show for my life's work here. Nothing. There won't be a farthing or a square inch of property to leave my children.

"If I were to sell what I have—the house, the land, the livestock—and return to England, we could manage nicely," Daniel said. He spoke to the leafless twig he'd picked up and was gently slapping into the palm of his hand, avoiding the family's united pained expression he knew was written on each face.

"Surely, Daniel," Deborah started. She stopped to clear her throat. The words from her mouth sounded as though they belonged to someone else.

"Surely, Daniel," she began again, "things cannot be that bad. If 'tis money you need, I can help. Matthew regularly sends me proceeds from our Rochester property and 'twould please me to be able to help you, Son."

"No, Mother!" Daniel said. Then softening his tone, "I appreciate your offer. But, don't you see? Marshal Barlow would be the only person to benefit. The money would go from your hands to mine to his in a single transaction. Then, the deed would have to be repeated, time and again. I will not give him the money Father provided and left for you. Never."

"There must be another way," Stephen said. "There must be something we can do."

John rose and began pacing, his hands behind his back, his eyebrows knitted into a deep frown.

He's his father's son all right, Deborah thought. *As well as a bit o' his Grandfather Bachiler, with those bushy, knit brows.*

The Wing wives had said nothing, but moved to Hannah's side in silent empathy.

"Exactly how much have you paid in fines to Marshal Barlow?" Deborah asked.

Before Daniel could answer, the sanctuary of Stephen's home was violated. The family had been so lost in conversation that no one had heard the return of Barlow's horse with its resounding hoof-beats until the marshal reigned it to a halt right in their midst.

"What business have you here?" Stephen rose and grabbed the horse's reins in one motion. "Get thee off my land. You are not welcomed at this house."

"I have business here," Barlow sneered down at Stephen from his vantage, high in his saddle. "Official business. Daniel Wing," Barlow barked, "I have papers to serve you. Papers that say you are to pay me five pounds."

"For what?" Daniel replied angrily as he made his way to Barlow, sitting pompously atop his steed. "What could I have possibly done to offend you this time?"

"For what?" Barlow yelled. "For what? I'll tell you for what! Remember a while back when you and two others refused your orders—your direct orders—to assist me in carrying out the execution of punishment to our neighbor? That's for what."

"'Twas an unjust punishment," Daniel said. "A man should not be publicly whipped for remarks made in haste, in the heat of a moment."

"That's not your decision to make," Barlow said. "'Tis the court's decision. And, 'tis your duty to obey the court whatever it says and however you may disagree.

"Here, take this warrant." He thrust it down to Daniel who pointedly folded his arms and refused to accept it. The paper floated to the ground and lay there for the horse to trample when Barlow pulled the reins to make his departure. "I'll be back the first of the week to collect the money," Barlow said. "Have it at the ready."

And with that, he yanked the reins so forcefully that the horse reared on its haunches, pawed the air with its front legs, whinnied loudly, then turned on command and thundered off.

Daniel reached down to retrieve the warrant. "Well, now we know what his mission was when he sped past here earlier," he said, looking at the piece of paper, a copy of what had become so familiar to him these past few years. He dusted it off, smoothed it out and placed it in the breast pocket of his coat.

"Daniel," Deborah said quietly. "I've just remembered. In England, there's a law that allows a man to distribute his ownings to his heirs even though he has not yet died—while he is still living. Know you of it, John?"

"Yes," John said, excitement sounding in his voice. "I know of that law. 'Tis a little-used law, but a law nonetheless."

"What are you saying?" Stephen asked.

"Yes, what?" Daniel asked.

"As I recall," Deborah said, "'tis a disfranchisement of sorts, a form of bankruptcy. You would be declared legally dead by the courts and your property turned over to your heirs."

"That sounds pretty drastic," Daniel said. "Dead in the eyes of the state, but still walking, talking, breathing—while here on Earth? I don't know. I don't know."

"What do you care about what the government thinks of you, if you're dead or alive?" John asked. "If you're legally dead, they cannot fine you for refusing to take the oath."

"Yes," said Stephen, caught up in the excitement—he hadn't been fined as much as his older brother, but enough to understand Daniel's predicament—"because how can a dead man take an oath? How can a dead man assist in a punishment? How can a dead…Mother, this is a brilliant idea. You are brilliant!"

"What would we have to do?" Daniel asked, still sounding wary.

"You would have to write up a will, leaving your property to your children," his mother said.

"There's not much," Daniel said: "the dwelling house, ten acres of upland and three or four improved acres, plus the three acres of meadow."

"And," Hannah added, "the three cows, the steer, the yearlings and calves and…" her voice trailed off.

"And, that's it," Daniel said. "There is no more." He shook his head. "'Twould be strange to be three and forty, healthy as a horse and dead as a doornail, all at the same time."

"Then you'll do it?" John asked. "I'll represent you in court. That is, if you want."

"Of course, I want. Let's see if we can't dust off this old English law and make it work for us," Daniel said.

Smiling, Deborah said, "There would be a great deal of satisfaction to have that all-but forgotten law come to our rescue, after all the laws that have nearly been our undoing time and again. Yes, I like the justice I see in it. Yes, indeed."

Chapter 59

Harwich, Massachusetts
Deborah

My Dear Father

The message came today of your passing over.

I rejoice you are now at peace with God and His Son, and are in heaven with them. Yet, I weep for our physical loss of you—and for the lifetime of struggle that was yours on Earth.

Even though 'tis now years since we hugged goodbye on that Boston dock—the last time we saw one another—just knowing you were alive and walking the cobbled streets of our native England was a comfort. I took solace in closing my eyes, vsioning you holding the children of my darling daughter Deborah and my dear son Matthew. 'Twas nearly as sweet as holding them myself.

But now that I know you are no longer of this Earth, I feel a queer loneliness. A hollowness. An emptiness that cannot be filled. I miss you as I missed my beloved Mother and dearest John when they first departed. The sting is there for thee ever as much as it was for them.

I am alone this day, sitting at son John's desk, as I write you. 'Tis evening and I've just eaten my supper of cold mutton and potato and a pint of cider. The fire is burning splendidly, there is plenty of paper, the well is filled with ink and the quill's nib is finely honed. We can have ourselves a lengthy "chat."

John and his family are in Boston for a week or so. They are combining a bit of pleasure with business. Actually, Father, they are there helping Daniel out of a scrape.

You would be proud of your grandsons—especially just now. They inherited your perseverance and are not going to take injustice lying down.

'Tis quiet here, to be sure, but to tell the truth, I am rather enjoying these few days alone. The solitude allows me to examine the thoughts of my soul as well as my mind. And now, with today's news, I sorely need quiet to reflect on our lives together—yours and mine. We were both a bit loggerheaded, now and again, were we not?

Still we loved one another. Always. Our love was never in doubt, and though there were times when it was strained, it never stretched to nothingness. It could not have.

Oh, Father, I have felt the heaviness of sadness ever since Matthew's black-edged letter arrived, along with a pair of gloves sent as a keepsake of your funeral service. I will give them to Stephen, your namesake.

We repaired our relationship with our letters when you lived in Hampton and we remained in Sandwich. Reading and writing those missives gave me a feeling of being nearer-at-hand to you than some of the times when we looked at one another eye to eye. There were times when our eyes simply could not connect. And other times when blue eyes wanted to slay brown eyes, or vice-versa. Now, remembering those times, I smile. But not then. Then, I would suddenly fill with useless anger that sapped me of energy and good will.

I spent much of this day on the shore, re-reading your letters. 'Twas a wondrous day. I shall treasure those letters for all my days.

I felt a special closeness to you and John, Mother and Theodate, as I sat on the sand and felt the sun warm on my face and watched the ocean waves as they lapped the shore. The waves entrance me, hypnotize me. The sea always brings me comfort.

'Tis a place of grand peace.

Sitting there, leaning against a huge piece of driftwood, the strength of your comforting arms returned to me and I felt the strength of your will as I watched you follow your conscience all of my life.

On this day and with this letter, I will not dwell on the hurtful events that drove a wedge between us, separating us from time to time. I hope never to call the incidents to mind again. As of this day, they are gone and forgotten. Not another soul need know. 'Tis now between you and Mother, and you and God.

As for other times when disagreement arose between us, 'twas because we were so much alike, you and me. My physical being is more that of my mother; but my temperament, dear Father, is that of you. I learned much from you, including self-sufficiency. I also inherited your strong will— along with your sometimes ornery streak of stubbornness, sorry to say. Yes, we two are much alike, I fear.

But today, 'tis a loving pride I feel for that likeness and not frustration or disallowance as many times before. After all, 'tis those traits that have brought me thus far in my life.

"My Father?" I tell people when they ask, "why, he is the good Reverend Stephen Bachiler, a Puritan minister who gave his all to God."

My deepest prayer is that before your final day on Earth, you at last achieved your own sense of peace about following the mission God set forth for you on Earth.

I hope you realized the greatness of your accomplishments, Father. Accomplishments you made in spite of being thwarted at most every juncture.

I pray you saw your life's work was not in vain. I hope you tasted a bit of the sweet fruit of your life's labor.

This new country owes much to you and my beloved John and other ministers like you who insisted on the right to worship freely, as God directed you to worship. You fought for that freedom and you—all of you, us—gave up so much for it.

The importance of your work, and that of John's, is all the clearer and dearer to me now that I am a grandmother and I watch my sons' children grow and develop—just as parents and grandparents have done for generations past, and just as they will continue to do.

Now I fully realize why we remain here in this hard country, this New England, and carve ourselves crude homes in the midst of these wild forests, why we struggle to cultivate these untamed lands, why we place our lives, and the lives of our children, in jeopardy. Why we continue to challenge the government to worship God in the manner we believe he commands us. (I'm beginning to sound more and more like you, Father, am I not?).

The answer has to do with you and me and my children and now their children.

Seeing a continuation of yourself, a second generation and then a third, is truly a remarkable experience. It gives a new, broader definition of life itself. 'Tis this third and fourth generation of ours—plus those yet to be born—that we fought for, and still fight for, you and John, and my sons. And, yes, even me.

'Tis true we came to this land, seeking worshipful freedom for ourselves. But now I recognize that 'twas not just for us. 'Tis also for those of us yet to come.

Father, had God not blessed you with the divine qualities of perseverance, of rightness, devotion, then my grandchildren—and their grandchildren—might never have experienced God's love for them first-hand. We could not have had in England what we have here, trapped as we would have been the triviality you helped erase.

And nothing could be more important in this world than to experience God first-hand.

Father, I know 'twasn't easy for you to follow God's plan at times, but you did it. You did it.

You laid the foundation for our future.

And we—me, my sons and their children—we will keep your faith alive, Father. For generations and generations to come.

I thank God you were mine and I was yours. I am blessed.

Your ever-loving daughter,
Deborah Bachiler Wing

Epilogue

I first pictured Deborah Bachiler Wing as a real person in 1992 at the annual reunion in Sandwich, Massachusetts, of The Wings of America, Inc. We celebrated the 400th anniversary of Deborah's birth on the grounds of Stephen Wing's Fort House, which had been continuously owned by a Wing descendant, until it was sold to The Wings of America. We were told that Deborah and her children walked 100 miles through virgin forests, following animal and Indian trails, from Saugus, Massachusetts, to the land that would become Sandwich. My burning question was: "Who fixed dinner the night they arrived?" That flippant query has led me to an insatiable need to know more about Deborah—and other grandmothers who have lived inconspicuous lives all during America's lifetime. Oh, yes, I finally came to the conclusion that Deborah no doubt fixed her family something to eat that night so long ago.

Afterword

Queen Elizabeth had ruled Britannia twenty-six years when John Wing was born. Religious life became more tolerant after "Good Bess" assumed the throne at the death of her stepsister, Mary—Bloody Mary—who had restored the Catholic faith. Still, even under Elizabeth's reign, it was not safe to indulge in any form of worship other than what pleased The Lady. Any Presbyterian or Puritan who dared to worship as he pleased did so at his peril. Besides religion, Elizabeth dictated most every facet of her subjects' lives, including their dress. It was she who determined the height of their ruffs, a puckered linen ornament worn around the neck, which reminded men and women to hold their heads high.

*   *   *

In 1625, by the time King Charles 1st adjusted the crown to fit his head, Puritan stalwarts John Wing and Stephen Bachiler—and others like them—shared rebellious ideas not tolerated by the Church of England. King Charles warned that Puritanical troublemakers would not be tolerated. It was Charles' father, James 1st, King of England and Scotland, who vowed of the religious rebels, "I will make them conform or harry them out of the kingdom," to which his archbishop added, "They shall pray my way or lose their heads." The already tenuous position of progressive Puritan thinkers took a decided turn for the worse after James' head rolled and Charles mounted the steps to the throne. With other Puritans, John and Deborah Wing and Stephen Bachiler were caught in a historic struggle between authority and sense of duty.

Conclusions

In this is work of fiction, I tried to covey the lives and events of my ancestors and their contemporaries as they might have occurred—but a liberal amount of conjecture was used. The characters' personalities are mine, but based on research. Some events are figments of my imagination, while some true accounts might have occurred in years other than represented. For instance, there's no reason to believe that Deborah and Anne Hutchinson ever met, but wouldn't it have been interesting if they had? William Prynne did have his ears amputated, but the date was jockeyed to fit the needs of the novel. Stephen Bachiler's death occurred in 1656, but was altered for the sake of storytelling.

*   *   *

Deborah Bachiler Wing is to believed to be the woman described in this obituary: "Jan. 31, 1692—The last of January Old Goody Wing Died." Deborah, who would have been 100, is probably buried in the Sandwich Quaker cemetery, beneath an unmarked headstone.

*   *   *

Stephen Bachiler has been portrayed in myriad ways, some more flattering than others. The essence of Stephen portrayed in this fictional account is a compilation of all that I read. Other "scandals" and achievements of his were omitted, or the book would never have ended.

Stephen Frederick Clifton Pierce, a descendent of Reverend Bachiler and author of the 1898 "Batchelder, Batcheller Genealogy, Descendants of Rev. Stephen Bachiler of England, A Leading Non-Conformist Who Settled the Town of New Hampton, N.H. ...," wrote: "Whoever considers that Bachiler's life was wasted because neither riches nor temporal honors were obtained by him, knows little of the manner in which reforms are accomplished. One thing for which he bitterly contended is (now) universally conceded, and people wonder that it was ever disputed. The separation of church and state is recognized as unquestionably right by all his opponents, and his firm stand in behalf of the liberty of New Hampshire loses nothing because it was unsuccessful. Success would have left no doubt of his firmness in standing out when the consequences were certain to be his practical destruction and utter ruin. We know now that he had that firmness which rendered him utterly regardless of consequences to himself when conscious that his motives and judgment were right." In "The Rev. Bachiler—Saint or Sinner," Philip Nason Martson wrote: "Was he a saint or sinner, or more of the first and a bit of the last and therefore essentially human?" Stephen Bachiler died in 1656 at Robert Barbers, now a part of London, and was buried in the new churchyard on Oct. 31, 1656. He paid the church to have the church bells rung at his passing.

*   *   *

According to George Wing, biographer and genealogist, John Wing's sermons "reveal to us a man of strong spirituality, classic learning, masterful characteristics, ready wit, fierce intellect, a facile pen and a ready tongue." Some of John Wing's sermons are housed in the majestic Old Bodleian Library in Oxford. When John Wing returned to England from Holland, his family lived in London's St. Aldermary neighborhood, now known as St. Mary's Le Bow, a few blocks from St. Paul's Cathedral. The church was a gathering place for Puritans who wanted to immigrate to America.

*   *   *

Anne Hutchinson, a controversial religious leader, was banished from Boston to Rhode Island for her beliefs. In 1637, she was killed in an Indian attack at her home in New York, with most of her family.

*   *   *

Mary Beadle Bachiler applied for a divorce once Stephen Bachiler was gone, citing abandonment. In 1674, she married Thomas Turner, who succeeded George Roberts in her affections. Mary Beadle made a remarkable recovery from humiliation to a position of stature and respect in the community, wrote Ross Staples in a newsletter published by The Staples Family History Association.

About the Author

For 25 years, Beverly Smith Vorpahl reported and edited news for the Spokane Daily Chronicle and The Spokesman-Review newspapers in her hometown of Spokane, Washington. She now writes a weekly genealogy column for the newspaper and freelances articles for national magazines, including Family Chronicle, which, in 1998, published "A Probable Personality for Goody Bachiler Wing." It's a well-known fact that it's much more difficult to research grandmothers than grandfathers because so little has been written about our women forebears. Beverly Vorpahl has said: "As a woman who is the product of the 20th (and now 21st) century, enjoying women's rights as well as America's conveniences and conventions, I wonder about my grandmothers. Who were they and how were they influenced by their surroundings and mores, and what jewels of wisdom and common-sense values did they pass on to their children? What thoughts, habits and practices were handed down, generation after generation, and when—and why—did they fall by the wayside? I want to tell the stories of these grandmothers to understand what they and other ordinary but remarkable women like them contributed to the formation of our country."

Appendix

Descendants of Deborah Bachiler Wing

1. Deborah Bachiler—b. 1592 Wherwell, England; d.1692 Mass. (married John Wing)

2. Daniel Wing—b. 1617; d. 1697/98 Sandwich, Mass. (married Anna Ewer)

3. Bachelor Wing—b. 1671 Sandwich, Mass.; d 1740 Plymouth, Mass. (married Joanna Hatch)

4. Thomas Sylvanus Wing—b. 1697 Sandwich, Mass.; d. 1778 Hanover, Mass. (married Hannah…)

5. Thomas Wing—b. 1737 Hanover Mass. d.? Ashford, Conn. Or Dunham, Quebec (married Phoebe Tyler Ward)

6. Ward Wing—b. 1778 Ashford, Conn.; d. 1863 Sutton, Quebec (married Sally Ellis)

7. Hosea Wing—b. 1818 Sutton, Quebec; d. 1881 Sutton, Quebec (married Hulda Beers)

8. David Wing b. 1849 Sutton, Quebec; d. 1904 Ponoka, Alberta (married Julia Elvina Hadlock)

9. Corliss Smith Wing—b. 1874 Sutton, Quebec; d. 1952 Ponoka, Alberta (married Hattie Royce)

10. Genevieve Wing—b. 1895 Madison, SD; d. 1983 Spokane, Wash. (married Lindley Murray Smith Jr.)

11. Beverly Jean Smith—b. 1938- Spokane, Wash. (married David Paul Vorpahl)

Bibliography

1. Apperson, G.L.
   "The Wordsworth Dictionary of Proverbs"
2. Ashton, Robert
   "The Quiet Rebels; Reformation and Revolution 1558-1660"
3. Axelrod, Allen
   "The Colonial Revival in America"
4. Bacon, Margaret Hope
   "The Story of Quakers in America"
5. Besant, Sir Walter
   "London in the Time of the Stuarts"
6. Bouve, Pauline Carrington
   "American Heroes and Heroines"
7. Boxer, C.R.
   "The Dutch Seaborne Empire: 1600-1800"
8. Bradford, William
   "Of Plymouth Plantation—1620-1675
9. Campbell, Douglas
   "Puritan in Holland, England and America, An Introduction to American History"
10. Castleman, Michael
    "The Healing Herbs"

11. Crawford, Mary Caroline
    "Social Life in Old New England"
12. Davis, William Sterns
    "Life in the Elizabethan Days"
13. Dick, Stewart and Helen Allingham
    "Cottage Homes of England"
14. Dickinson, R.J.
    "Ulster Immigration to American Colonies"
15. Dow, Joseph
    "History of the Town of Hampton, New Hampshire From its
    settlement in 1630 to the Autumn of 1892"
16. Doyle, J.A.
    "English in America, the Puritan Colonies"
17. Earle, Alice Morse
    "Customs and Fashions in Old New England"
18. Early, Eleanor
    "A New England Sampler"
19. Fleming, Sandford
    "The Place of Children in Life and Thought of the New
    England Churches"
20. Gruenbaum, Thelma
    "Before 1776 The Massachusetts Bay Colony, from Founding
    to Revolution"
21. Hibbert, Christopher
    "The Story of England"
22. Hawke, David Freeman
    "Everyday Life in Early America"
23. Hill, Christopher
    "The English Bible and 17th Century Revolution"

24. Hillard, Elizabeth
    "Cottages"
25. Holland, Rupert Sargent
    "Historic Ships"
26. Johnson, Samuel, LL.D.
    "A Dictionary of the English Language: In Which The Words are Deduced from Their Originals Explained In Their Different Meanings, and Authorized by the Names of the Writers in Whose Works They are Found"
27. Jones, Rufus M.
    "The Quakers in the American Colonies"
28. Kirby, Ethyn Williams
    "William Pyrnne; A Study in Puritanism"
29. LaMar, Virginia A.
    "Travel and Roads in England"
30. Lewis, Alonzo and Newhall, James
    "History of Lynn, Essex County, Massachusetts"
31. Litoff, Judy Barrett
    "The American Midwife Debate"
32. Lovell, R.A. Jr.
    "Sandwich, A Cape Cod Town"
33. Marshall, Cyril Leek
    "The Mayflower Destiny"
34. Martson, Philip Mason
    "The Reverend Stephen Bachiler—Saint or Sinner"
35. Mitchell, Edwin Valentine
    "It's an Old New England Custom"
36. Morgan, Edmund
    "The Puritan Dilemma; the Story of John Winthrop"

37. Morison, Samuel Eliot
    "Builders of the Bay Colony"
38. Mudie, Rosemary and Colin
    "The Story of the Sailing Ship"
38. McCutchan, Philip
    "The Ships—The Golden Age of Sail"
40. Nylander, Jane C.
    "Our Own Snug Fireside; Images of the New England Home
    1760-1860"
41. Pickles, Sheila
    "The Essence of English Life"
42. Pierce, Frederick Clifton
    "Batchelder Genealogy"
43. Puckle, Bertram
    "Funeral Customs; Their Origin and Development"
44. Reynard, Elizabeth
    "The Narrow Land, the Folk Chronicles of Old Cape Cod"
45. Seaver, Paul S.
    "The Puritan Leadership"
46. Sifakis, Carl
    "American Eccentrics"
47. Trueblood, D. Elton
    "The People Called Quakers
48. Ulrich, Laurel Thatcher
    "A Midwife's Tale; the Life of Martha Ballard"
49. Ulrich, Laurel Thatcher
    "Good Wives"
50. Usher, Roland G.
    "The Puritans and Their Story"

51. Warwick, Edward and Pitz, Henry
     "Early American Costume"
52. Wendall, Barrett
     "Cotton Mather
53. Wheeler, John
     "A Treatise of Commerce (Merchant Adventurers)"
54. Willison, George F.
     "Saints and Sinners"
55. Wing Family of America, Inc.
     "OWL" (Our Wing Lineage)
56. Wright, Richardson
     "Grandfather was Queer; Early American Wags and Eccentrics from Colonial Times to the Civil War"

Printed in the United States
3449

9 780595 201020